Murder
— *and* —
Money

Debo and Mad-c

DENNIS CHARLES JOHNSON

Copyright © 2024 Dennis Charles Johnson.

All rights reserved. No part of this book may be reproduced, stored, or transmitted by any means—whether auditory, graphic, mechanical, or electronic—without written permission of both publisher and author, except in the case of brief excerpts used in critical articles and reviews. Unauthorized reproduction of any part of this work is illegal and is punishable by law.

ISBN: 979-8-89419-388-5 (sc)
ISBN: 979-8-89419-389-2 (hc)
ISBN: 979-8-89419-390-8 (e)

Because of the dynamic nature of the Internet, any web addresses or links contained in this book may have changed since publication and may no longer be valid. The views expressed in this work are solely those of the author and do not necessarily reflect the views of the publisher, and the publisher hereby disclaims any responsibility for them.

One Galleria Blvd., Suite 1900, Metairie, LA 70001
(504) 702-6708

ACKNOWLEDGMENTS

I would like to thank my daughter, Sharita for her encouragement, devotion, patience, and for her help in supporting my dream. I would also like to thank The Ewings Publishing Company for their support and excellent quality of commitment and service in making my dream a reality.

Dennis Charles Johnson May 20th, 2023.

SYNOPSIS

On the streets of Los Angeles, Beverly Hills, and Inglewood. CA. And, in a tainted world of chance, survival, hope, greed, and uncertain success, there are tasks that must be accomplished, and somebody has to be man enough to accept the responsibility of that accomplishment. And, in a world where almost everything you must do is detrimental: Debo, (D-Angelo L Jackson) teams up with Mad-C, (Charles Write) to take on a mission where they must fight to stay alive. But, it's an even harder responsibility to fight to keep the people they love alive, and to hold on to what rightfully belongs to them. Debo and Mad-C use their skills, wisdom, and common sense to deal with the people who are trying to tear their world apart. They're put up against a crooked politician who embezzled one-hundred and fifty-million-dollars from his own political campaign contribution fund, a multi-billionaire, a CEO, chairman of the board of directors of a very prominent yacht club in Malibu, California, and two DEA agents who also have a "little something" up their sleeves. Debo also has the help of his self-adopted sister; Joyvette Hernandez who keeps him in check and watches over him but is also put in harm's way. She's bright, cautious, and very alert. With all this pulling at them, they must keep each other alive. They have until Christmas day to complete their mission. But, will they make it through alive by Christmas Day? Or, will Christmas day find them all dead???

CHAPTER 1

It was just past 6:00 pm on a cold, dark, windy autumn evening. The freeway into Los Angeles was crowded because people were getting off work. The interior of the 2007 Ford Explorer was warm, which helped relieve the stress and the tension of the stop-and-go rush hour traffic. All Debo felt was the grinding of the pavement against the tires of the SUV while traffic was slowly dragging along at six miles per hour. Debo focused his attention on the running board of the Explorer, since that was where he had stashed the fifty kilos of pure cocaine he was delivering to Los Angeles and Inglewood, CA. His boss Charles Write is one of the richest and most feared drug dealers alive. He and Debo met while Debo was recycling cans and bottles. Debo couldn't hold down a nine-to-five job, he was like his dad in a lot of ways. His father, D-Angelo L Jackson, senior sold drugs for a living. He sold everything from weed and pills to cocaine and heroin. He had become so big he was making $1,000 a minute, just selling drugs alone in his hometown of St Louis, Missouri.

When Debo was a kid, his dad put him and his older brother, Omar Jackson out to work selling the local newspaper. D-Angelo L Jackson senior financed the boy's paper route. Debo and Omar grew tired of hustling the newspaper through three feet of snow each day; pushing the heavy, four-by-six-foot, two-wheeled, newspaper cart from house to house because their father wanted them to both be independent when they grew up.

Debo hit his first joint when he was five-years-old, his brother Omar was seven-years-old. Now, neither of them smokes drugs of any kind.

D-Angelo L Jackson, Senior was arrested and indicted in 1965 on several felony counts of drug trafficking, sales of narcotics, and organized crime affiliations. He was sent to Federal Prison for seven years. He was sentenced to serve 125 years for federal crimes and 150 years for state crimes. He spent $250,000 for one of the best lawyers money could buy and was successful in getting his federal sentence reduced to seven years.

Things began to get rough for Ann Jackson; Omar and Debo's mom. They had to move to San Diego, CA, where they were able to start a new life. "Debo" was born D-Angelo L Jackson Junior, on March 28, 1967. He was not a bad looking man for forty-years-old. He has short black hair, fair complexion, six feet tall, and weighed 200 pounds; (all muscle... no fat). When he met Shelly; his beautiful wife of nine years she fell for him head over heels and swore that if he ever left her, she would make sure he would regret it. Debo had everything he could ever want in life; a beautiful wife, money, a lavish estate in San Diego, and Rex, a heavy, mean-looking, ninety-pound German shepherd that loves the ground Debo walks on. Rex even looked crazy at Shelly when her and Debo have their little disagreements.

Debo had lost all track of time and the fact that he was sitting on Mad-C's fifty kilos. His mind was on Shelly and the phone call she received two days ago. The caller wanted to meet with Debo at the Santa Monica Pier in Santa Monica, CA. The fact that the caller did not leave his name was mysterious to Debo. It was only a message for Debo to meet him there at nine o'clock tonight as if the caller knew that he would be in Los Angeles at nine o'clock that particular Wednesday evening. He still had time to get there, rush hour was just about to ease up. After he delivered the fifty kilos to his distributors, gave them their assignments, collected the money he was expecting from each of them, he would head to Santa Monica, then he would return to San Diego to shower and spend time with Shelly.

He bought the estate in San Diego for Shelly's 30th birthday. He took care of all his business in Los Angeles, Inglewood, and Beverly Hills,

California. He knew that while he was gone she would be safe a few hundred miles away with Rex there to protect her.

Debo's Explorer is equipped with radar and a rear surveillance camera to monitor who; if anyone was following him as he headed home. Only a chosen few were to know about the location of the estate in San Diego. He named it *The Shell-Debo,* Shelly wanted it that way; her name first, and it did have a nice ring to it.

Debo managed to make all his deliveries to their five locations.

They each went to separate location; ten went to Crenshaw and Slauson, ten went to sixty-eighth and Normandy, ten to Forty-third and Seventh Avenue, ten to San Marino and Mongolia, and the last ten went to La Brea and Ocean in Inglewood. He never sold or used any of the drugs because of the petty dangers he would be subjecting himself to. He had enough problems delivering and making sure the money was right when it was time to collect.

Debo always worked alone… well, not quite alone; he had his trusty Glock forty-five automatic pistol that he keeps snugged in its shoulder holster. This was just in case something or someone got in his day that wasn't supposed to be there. Debo arrived at the Santa Monica pier at 8:35 pm. He tried to find a parking-space that would accommodate the size of the rather large sports utility vehicle. But, the fact that it was so big wasn't a problem since it was so late and no one was at the beach; no one but people eating, walking from the pier going home, or wherever they go after a full day of fun.

Debo walked to the seafood restaurant where, He and Shelly ate when She, Him, and Rex came from San Diego to Los Angeles, or to Santa Monica. They loved to come here when having a good time was just about the only thing on their minds; especially Rex. It was a nice indoor-outdoor cozy little place, with tables and chairs lined up inside, and wooden park-bench style tables outside, equipped with the usual umbrella centered through a hole in the middle of the table. There were all sorts of condiments; salt, black and white pepper, sugar, soy sauce, and chili powder. The floor is wood-planked with sawdust scattered on it to soak up spilled grease and water, or whatever food happened to wind up on the floor. Debo loved this place... it was his favorite.

After the long drive from San Diego, he was overdue for a hot cup of coffee. He ordered a cup with two sugars and two creams and sat there slowly drinking the hot beverage while waiting for his surprise guest to arrive. He looked up in time to see a five-and-a-half foot tall caucasian man coming through the door wearing blue jeans, a sweatshirt, and black sneakers. His hair was slicked back, and a thick mustache laid neatly trimmed across his upper lip, and his gut was starting to overlap his belt. He wore dress slacks, a pair of penny loafers, a white dress shirt, and a gray tie. The two men spotted Debo sitting at a table near the window with an Oceanside view, drinking his coffee. They walked over to Debo's table and introduced themselves.

"Mr Jackson, I'm Dick Patch," the taller man said, extending his right hand for Debo to shake. Debo looked curiously at the agent, and Dick Patch saw a look that told him he had better say a lot more than just his name.

"I'm, Special Agent Dick Patch, and this is my partner, Monty Rayass. We're with the Drug Enforcement Administration."

Debo's heart nearly leaped out of his chest. He didn't know whether to shake Patch's hand or take his pistol from its holster and shoot him. Debo had a friend down at Parker Center Police Station named Billings; Sergeant Robert (Bob) Billings. Billings is very well acquainted with Debo's occupation and is there for him if the need should arise. Mad-C pays him to keep his business running smoothly. The forty-five that Debo carries is perfectly legal.

"Mr Patch, Mr Rayass... have a seat... now, what can I...?"

At that time Dick Patch cut him off. Patch is the one who seems to be in charge. He told Debo, "Before you say anything, I wanna say this. I know, you, Write, and Sergeant Robert Billings of Parker Center police station. I know where all of your dope houses are and the people who work in them. Let's see; there's Joy, a beautiful woman, Pauline, not bad-looking herself, Tony, Freddy and Jeffery. Did I miss anyone?"

"Doing good so far," Debo replied.

"I have been watching you and your appointed staff members for the past two years, Mr Jackson. Oh.., and don't worry, we're the only ones that know about you and Mr Write. And, by 'we', I mean agent Rayass and myself. No one else in the administration has a clue, and we can keep it that way for as long as you and Mr Write want to. No one knows what we know," Patch said.

"And let me guess… you want…"

Dick patch stopped Debo again before he could get another word out. "We want… NO, I want in on your little empire."

"Or What?" Debo irritatingly asked.

"Or you will be facing a lot of time, and we'll have to put that lovely wife of yours and that mutt out in the streets and confiscate all your cars, that beautiful estate; what is it called… *The Sell-Debo*? All of your accounts will be frozen. And you sir can just about believe that when you go down, Mister Write, all of your distributors, and that pretty little wife of yours go down with you."

"Now hold on…, my wife knows nothing about what I do.

She thinks I'm a cellular communications representative."

"And she'll always think that, Debo… uh…, Mister Jackson, as long as you cooperate with us."

Debo thought; What a blow that would be to Shelly… not only to find out that he lied about his occupation, but he's also involved in drug trafficking and that she could be looking at a considerable amount of time, as well as being an accomplice. It would never stand up in court, but the fact that she would have to go through the entire process. He felt like he was about to regurgitate.

"This is happening too fast, I'll discuss it with Mr Write. Does he know about you two?"

"Not yet…, but I'm sure he will, once you let him know who we are and what we want."

"What does Sgt Billings have to say about it?" Debo asked.

"What can he say? Once all hell breaks loose he'll deny even knowing you or Write; here take this," Patch answered.

Dick Patch handed him a small manila envelope..., and without saying anything, Debo put it in his pocket and continued to listen to agent Patch. Agent Monty Rayass said nothing through-out the entire conversation. He sat and ate some shrimp and French fries he ordered during the conversation.

"Here's my card, Mister Jackson, please let me know what you and Mr Write decide, in say… two days tops. I'll be expecting your call. Oh, by the way, I like this little place, I just didn't know they allowed mutts here," Patch sarcastically said and turned and walked out the door with his little chubby sidekick Rayass wobbling along sucking on a shrimp.

Debo's hands are full and he knows that Mad-C will have a fit. But, no matter, he had to let him know: He couldn't just pay the agents out of his pockets and not tell him. He would find out about it anyway, and that could weaken the trust Mad-C has in him. Besides, not letting him know something so important would only create more problems. Debo couldn't pay all the money anyway, he only clears $200K or $300K a month.

Although Patch didn't disclose any specific amount yet, he will if Mad-C accepts this nightmare. The amount agent Patch would ask for will no doubt exceed Debo's measly $200K a month. He checked his watch, the meeting only lasted an hour. It's 10:15 and Debo hadn't eaten anything. The meeting had spoiled his appetite and it was too late to eat anyway. The restaurant is closing in about ten minutes. If he's hungry when he arrives home, he'll fix himself something to eat. Shelly saved him a plate, she knew he would be late because agent Patch told her when he wanted Debo in Santa Monica that evening.

On the way going home, Debo stopped at a 7-11 Store and got a bottle of water and a bag of chips. He then took the I-5 Freeway to the I-805, and then to the I-905, and was in San Diego in three hours. He put his key in the door and it gave with no problems, except for a squeak in one of the hinges. He made sure Shelly didn't oil it; the noise would alarm them if the door opened, provided someone was awake to hear it. In this case, Shelly didn't hear a thing,. It was 2:00 am and she was sound asleep. The chips would have to suffice because he's too tired to fuss with anything to eat.

He would just shower and go to bed. He took his hot shower and felt the grime of the day roll off his body; the hot water soothed every inch, every muscle. He thought about the meeting with the two DEA agents and dismissed the thought until later. The shower felt too good to ruin. He got out of the shower, put on his blue robe, and went into the master bedroom where Shelly was sleeping soundly as he took off his robe and got into bed.

Shelly stirred and turned over facing him, but didn't wake up. The moonlight coming through the window lit up the room with a very romantic light blue glow that highlighted her face while Debo laid there with his eyes open, looking at her. Her face was a mahogany brown, with small perfect eyes. She has dimples you could see even when she wasn't smiling. Her hair is a long, silky, chocolate, brown. She donned a beautiful bronze complexion at only thirty-seven-years old, just three years younger than Debo. She loved her birthday present; *The Shell-Debo*, with all her heart. It's hers; the house, the land, and all the papers are in her name. It's the best gift she had ever received in her entire life, and she's madly in love with it. But more in love with the man from whom it came, the man she married; D-Angelo L Jackson Junior.

Debo got out of bed and went out on the back deck to see what Rex was up to. He laid beside Shelly but his mind kept racing back to the meeting with DEA agents Dick Patch and Monty Rayass. He sat beside Rex and thought about how very disappointing it would be for Shelly to find out the truth about his occupation. He had been afraid to tell her for fear she would worry and he wanted her to fully enjoy every bit of the life he had built for the both of them. But, for that to come out in the open would probably tear that life apart, it would shred his soul apart and destroy Shelly's trust and belief in him. That's why he bought the estate so far away; so that world would not have to reach her. Now his business is a treat to all he loves most. He sat next to Rex and said,

"Rex, if anything happens to me, I want you to take good care of my baby."

Rex looked up at Debo as if to say,

"Don't worry, I know what you do for a living, you don't fool me." And Debo said,

"Yeah, and that asshole called you a mutt. Remind me to let you take whatever bothers you out on him, I'll handle Monty Rayass."

Rex gave a little whimper and kissed Debo on the hand. Debo turned to go inside and saw that Rex's food dish was still full.

"I guess you must have known what that phone call was about. I wonder if Shelly suspects anything: Dick Patch and Monty Rayass. What a duo; Dick and Ass."

CHAPTER 2

THURSDAY, 9:45 A.M.

It's 9:45, Thursday morning and Debo had slept late because he had arrived home late. Shelly had been up for hours.

She knew he would be hungry when he woke up. She had shaken him earlier to see if he would be down to breakfast. He had stirred and said, "in an hour," and went back to sleep.

Shelly's timing was perfect, because when he got to the breakfast table, the food was piping hot; as was the coffee. Debo took one bite of the hot eggs, toast, sausage, potatoes, and a sip of hot coffee when his cell phone rang to the tune of *It's Our Anniversary*. He always loved that song, it was the song he had made into an anniversary card with a wedding cake and a white heart-shaped balloon with a red light inside. It was their first wedding anniversary.

"Hello," Debo said, into the phone.

"Hey sleepyhead, I tried to call you but your phone was off," Mad-C said.

"Yeah..., I got in about two something this morning. You weren't worried about the deliveries, were you?"

"I already know that to worry about my product when you're in charge is an insult to your integrity."

"Thanks, boss, what's up?"

"I was worried about you, those deliveries make me worry; you'll never know sometimes."

"Yeah, I have crazy with me, he speaks pretty loud and his impact delivers a tremendous message."

When Debo first got the Glock 45 from Mad-C, he test-fired it at Mad-C's estate, and the gun kicked; nearly taking his right arm and shoulder off.

"Damn man, where the hell did you get this crazy-ass cannon?" Debo asked.

"Only the best for my man," Mad-C responded. And ever since then, Debo called the pistol, *"Crazy."*

"I had a meeting last night," Debo informed him.

"Oh yeah, what kind of meeting kept you out all night?"

Debo was used to Mad-C questioning him like that. It reminded him of his mom, Ann Jackson; not really worried but concerned.

"I'll tell you about it when I come over to see you. I'll be there before I go to Los Angeles. What's on your mind?"

"Oh, I nearly forgot: Have you heard about Tony?"

Anthony Brown works for Debo at the Crenshaw drug Distribution Center. "No I haven't. I took him his work and nothing came up, what's cooking?"

"I'm hearing stories that he's trying to leave the team next month," Mad-C said.

"Tony knows too much about our organization to just up and leave, or to even think he can leave," Debo said.

"Well, I'm hearing that he wants to buy his way out, I trust him; I trust everyone you picked for the team. But the thing is, who can I get to replace him? He's put in his share of work for us," Mad-C said.

The only people besides the DEA agents; Patch, and Rayass that knows about *The Shell-Debo were his family*. In fact, Mad-C helped Debo to get the $7.3M estate in a secluded, wonderfully built section of San Diego, CA. He, Shelly, and Rex loves the beach; the weather is great in the summertime because the beach keeps it cool. The zoo is Shelly's favorite, she used to love animals; growing up in Connecticut, Ohio. She moved to Los Angeles, California in search of a better career in the computer field. She troubleshoots, programs, and does just about anything you can do on them. Debo doesn't want her to work because he makes enough money for the both of them to live rich comfortable lifestyles. But, with those two agents nosing around trying to get in on some of the action, he wondered if this financially secure money-making hustle he has is going to soon fall apart.

Well, *The Shell-Debo* is paid for… lock, stock, and barrel. Debo took a moment going through his mind trying to think of how he was going to tell Mad-C, and how he would react. He may understand because he knows the risks involved in the kind of work he does.

Debo went to the post office to get a money order so he could pay the lease on the Explorer. He left his cell phone at home intentionally, in case Mad-C called him before he could get a chance to see him today before he left for Los Angeles. He definitely had to see Mad-C today because the DEA agents want an answer within two days from Wednesday. Maybe Mad-C and Debo will re-consider replacing Tony after tonight. They may even become suspicious of him. Tony, Jeffery Smith, Joy, Pauline, and Freddy Moss runs all the distribution houses, and they all work for Debo. Mad-C has no physical contact with any of them, but he knows them all very well. Debo got the money order and headed back to the house. He was only a couple of blocks from home, but he needed his cell phone. Maybe nothing will come up before he gets back home. He mailed the money order to the leasing agency as he knew the Explorer couldn't be traced back to him, not even by the two DEA agents. Everyone at the leasing agency knows him, and they knew that whatever business he and Mad-C had with them was strictly hush-hush. In return, Mad-C made sure they were very well financially taken care of. It's almost time for him to head to Los Angeles to check on Mad-C's money and to have a talk with Tony. For every fifty kilos of cocaine Debo's people sold, he received ten kilos for himself. Since he didn't sell…, he preferred the money which was much more than generous. Mad-C put Debo's money in an account under the company name, Charles Write, and Associates, which is a multi-billion-dollar enterprise. With it being a cellular cooperation that pulls in billions of dollars annually, Mad-C and Debo can launder all the money they want through the company name. Debo spent about an hour or so before he left; cuddling and kissing Shelly. She, in turn rewarded him with romance way beyond his wildest imagination. He was in a heaven of his own with the most beautiful woman he had ever met. Shelly didn't suspect anything of Debo going out nights; at least as far as other women were concerned. She knew it was business that kept him out. She knew the love he has for her will never fade, falter, or be given to another woman. And by his office being in Beverly Hills, and cellular communications being his job, she knew he would be home late, or not even come home some nights. She knew she could trust him, because what he did was provide her with the lavish lifestyle she had become accustomed to. But when he was home it was heaven for the both of them. Shelly can get the world from her husband, because when she gave herself to him, she gave him the world he has always wanted.

"I should be back by morning baby!!!" Debo yelled to Shelly from the front door as he was leaving. He had given her a big kiss; one that would last her all day.

He arrived at Mad-C's estate at 12:14, Thursday afternoon, which is about a five-minute drive from *The Shell-Debo*. The road to the secured entry gate is decorated with tall, well-manicured, eucalyptus trees. Once you enter the gate, the wonderfully designed "C" shaped driveway is lined with beautiful; red, yellow, pink, and white roses leading to the double nine-foot-tall front doors. Debo rang the doorbell which chimed softly three times. A short well-groomed man wearing a black suit, blue tie and shirt, and a smile that could make anyone feel welcomed, opened the door.

"What's up, Ed?" Debo greeted in a happy tone of voice.

The man standing before him has a balding head, long, low-cut sideburns, dark sunglasses covering his eyes, and the best cologne Debo had ever smelled seemed like it was just poured on the man's body. Debo just had to have some; Shelly would love it.

"Tell the big man I'm here," Debo said, not really authoritatively but in a nice way.

"He's in the back sitting by the pool, he said for you to go on back there." Debo walked through a hallway with very old and expensive paintings on the walls. The floor was the purest of white marble, and the walls were covered with imported snow-white suede. Debo turned a corner of the hall and was at the sliding glass doors to the pool area.

"Hey, big shot," he greeted Mad-C.

Mad-C had the looks that very well described his name; bald head weighed 250 pounds and had solid muscles. He's a health guru, and worked-out eight hours a day, five days a week, and three hours on the weekends. He's 5'8" tall, dark complexion, with bulging arms. His chest is big enough to have played professional football for the San Diego Chargers. He speaks with a lisp; he always did growing up.

"What are you drinking, fella?" he asked Debo.

He knows that Debo drinks brandy-on-the-rocks, he was really asking him if he wanted something to drink.

"Pull up a chair, I won't eat you, where is Rex?"

"He's at home."

"The last time I saw him here, I had to re-marble my hall floor; well not all of it but it did cost a pretty penny. So, what was the meeting about?" Mad-C always felt like and considered himself to be a big brother to Debo ever since he pulled him up out of the ghetto some ten years ago.

"Shell got…"

"Oh.., how is Michelle?" Mad-C cut him off before he could get the words out.

"She's getting along wonderfully, she had received an anonymous phone call yesterday from someone wanting me to meet with them at a restaurant at the Santa Monica Pier," Debo told Mad-C.

"What was the meeting about?"

"The men were from the DEA," Debo told him.

Mad-C's face took a change; the muscles in his neck tightened, his jaw went slack, his mouth hung wide open, and he was lost for words. Ed brought two glasses and a bottle of brandy on a tray for them. He sat the tray down, picked up the bottle of brandy, and poured the two men a drink, then held the bottle and said,

"Is something wrong, Mr Write?"

"Hell yes, something is wrong, can't you see? Leave the bottle."

Ed put the bottle back on the tray and excused himself. Debo waited a minute to let Mad-C regain his composure, and to get his head back together. "Hear me out before you keel over! The one that was doing all the talking: Agent Dick Patch said, 'that he knows about you, me, all our dope houses, and the workers,' and he named them all. He knows about Sergeant Robert Billings of LAPD Parker Center Station."

"This doesn't sound good at all. Hand me the bottle please." Debo handed him the bottle.

"Go ahead… keep talking."

"He said, 'that he and his partner, Agent Rayass; (Monty Rayass) are the only ones that knows about us, and if we want to keep it that way, we will have to let him in the ballgame.'"

"Did he mention a price?" Mad-C asked.

"No, he wanted me to call him with an answer by tomorrow night. He gave me this."

Debo pulled out the envelope Patch had given him at the pier and handed it to Mad-C.

He mentally weighed it and it felt heavy. He opened it and pulled out some pictures; pictures of Mad-C on a loading dock, receiving a shipment of drugs, pictures of Debo loading kilos onto the Explorer, pictures of Mad-C's well protected and secluded driveway, shots of all the trap-houses, and all the workers as well; Tony, Jeffery, Freddy, Pauline, and Joy. Also found in the envelope was a note that read:

"Thanks for welcoming me aboard gentlemen."

"How did they get your phone number at home, isn't it unlisted?" Mad-C asked Debo.

"I doubt that they'll tell me but I'll ask. Oh…, and another thing, he said, 'that they've been watching me for the last two years.'"

"Just the two of them?" "Yes, he said, 'just the two of them.'"

"That could be bad for them," Mad-C said.

"Yeah, and they do have copies of these pictures, and I wouldn't be surprised if they have telephone conversations between me and the workers as well," Debo implied.

"Yeah, I'm sure they have other pictures stashed someplace since they gave these to you," Mad-C said.

"I'll put some people on it at LAPD and see if I can come up with anything that'll tell us where the other pictures are and a tape or two," Debo offered.

"I figured someone would want in on the action sooner or later. But, these are some big boys, and they can play rough. Blackmail goes with the territory," Mad-C said.

"I'll call Agent Patch tomorrow night and see what kind of take he's talking about," Debo said.

"Tell him I'll give him $100K a month… no more, no less, and let me know what he says."

"Okay, Oh, by the way, do you want me to put pressure on Tony to find out why he wants out… or just see what he has to say?"

"No, just see what he has to say for now, at least until I can figure this thing out. After all, it is a very sudden coincidence."

"Okay, is there anything else?"

"Naw, that's it for now, Debo. You can give me a call and let me know what's going on though."

"Sure will," Debo said and left.

He didn't stop by the house on the way to Los Angeles. He'll stop and get lunch or a snack at one of the 7-11 stores once he gets there, and then he will go pay Tony a visit. At least he got the problem of telling Mad-C the bad news over with and is now more at ease with everything. But like Mad-C said, 'It had to be someone to squeeze in on the multi-billion-dollar empire.'"

"Maybe they can be of some help if something goes wrong: The LAPD and the DEA on our side is fair enough. Maybe that's what Mad-C was thinking. But if Patch and Rayass have us, then they very well may have someone else. But, I'll leave that to Mad-C,"

Debo thought to himself.

He arrived in Los Angeles at 3:45 pm and decided to wait until later before he went to see Tony. He stopped by the office to rest awhile; the drive from San Diego made him tired. He sat down on the small twin bed in a specially designed room in his office where he stays when he was in Beverly Hills or Los Angeles for the night.

The office is a two-story brownstone, with a gold plate and the words Charles Write, and associates engraved in a small plaque on the office door. A canopy is attached to the building over the front door to serve as shelter during rainy months. The past few days with Tony, agents Dick Patch, and Monty Rayass, Debo wondered if the Beverly Hills Police were on to them also. The office in Beverly Hills is where Mad-C first started. He was in Venice, California on some business one night, and three guys saw him coming out of a liquor store and decided to mug him. The three guys were gang members and were known to possess firearms. They knew that Mad-C was carrying a large amount of drugs and money. He was on his way to his office in Beverly Hills. One of the men waited for him to come out of the store while the other two stayed back. When he came out he was met with a thirty-eight revolver pressed against the back of his head. The guy that put the gun to his head, demanded he give him his briefcase. In it were three kilos of cocaine and $125K in cash. Mad-C could have struggled with the youngsters and won, but he didn't need the cops; not with that much dope and money on him. He found out later through *some very reliable sources,* who was responsible for the mugging and later got together with a couple of his guys and paid the local gang members a visit. However, little did Mad-C know, they were involved with a big drug operation. He wondered who set him up, but he was confident he would find that out also. He kicked in the door of an abandoned-looking house that was occupied by five young gang members. The first thing he saw was a 200-pound black man aiming a 12-gauge pump shotgun at his head. He already had the 44-Magnum he keeps ready for action. He let off two rounds:

The first one hit the man aiming the gun at him in his chest. The led projectile sent him flying into the wall behind him and to the floor covered in blood and guts.

The man's shotgun landed on the floor across the room while another man came out of the kitchen and caught the second-round in his forehead. The impact snapped his head back while knocking him back into the kitchen. Three more of the gang members were outside in the back talking and drinking beer, rum, and brandy. By the time they were able to figure out what was going on inside, four more of Mad-C's men made it around back and leveled their weapons down on them.

"These are just kids," one of Mad-C's men told the other.

"Yeah, but they are playing with some pretty big toys," the other one said. "Put your hardware over there on that table and step away… way away from them… MOVE!!!" he yelled.

"Do it now!!!" one of the other men yelled. The youngsters stood dead frozen. "Please don't shoot us, mister," one of the gang members standing shivering, cried.

Mad-C came out of the house trying to catch his breath after the useless search failed to turn up any drugs or money.

"I can't find a damn thing," he said.

"Maybe they can help us," one of Mad-C's men said, pointing to the youngsters.

"Okay, little man."

"The name is Big-Boy."

"I said, *'little man'*," Mad-C repeated to the young gang member.

"You've got two minutes to move, let's go," Mad-C ordered.

The one that called himself, *'Big Boy'* went into a tool shed and came out with a shovel and Mad-C immediately raised the barrel of the 44-Magnum to the young man's head.

"You won't stand a chance, ask your friends on the floor inside," he told the youngster.

"No, over there!!!" Big Boy screamed.

He pointed to a pile of junk: old bed-springs and rails on empty propane tanks, a mattress, a rusted swing set, and several Bar-B-Que pit grills scattered in one corner of the yard. Big Boy walked over to the heap of junk and pulled the mattress up, throwing dead leaves, dirt, and old pieces of splintered wood aside.

"Hurry up, or all of these guns my friends and I have are going to start going off."

Big Boy started digging, and without knowing or realizing it, he was throwing dirt everywhere. When he finished he came up with a black duffel bag about the size of a television set. In fact, from the looks of the outside, it appeared to be a TV set inside. The contents gave the bag a square look, and it appeared to be heavy.

"Open it," Mad-C instructed the youngster.

And to his surprise, there were eight kilos of pure cocaine and two kilos of marijuana in the duffel bag.

"Where's the money? When you mothafuckas mugged me you took some money, Where is it?" Mad-C questioned.

"In the house," the teenager answered. "Where in the house?"

"Inside the wall by the door; the front door," the youngster cried. "Well move..., damn-it," Mad-C cursed.

Big Boy went inside and saw his friends lying on the floor, soaked in blood and guts, eyes wide open, and dead as a doorknob. He felt sick, but he managed to step over the two dead bodies, and at the same time he glanced over at the sawed-off 12-gauge shotgun that had fallen out of one of his friend's hands.

"Don't you even think about it," one of Mad-C's men told the youngster before he could turn in the direction of the shotgun.

He managed to step over them and made it to the door and reached over the door frame and released a lever. At that time a drawer slid out from the wall to his right, and in the drawer were thirteen stacks of $100 bills. Mad-C put the money inside the bag and ordered all of the youngsters to the floor next to their dead friends, then backed out the door with his friends following him. Mad-C cursed as he heard sirens in the not too far away distance. He and his men got into a white Ford van and headed down the street. When they reached the corner, four police cars rushed past them. By the time the sirens stopped, Mad-C and his men were long gone.

"Damn, I didn't think we'd ever get the hell out of there,"

Mad-C said. "Yeah, did you see those guys, they were kids?" one of Mad-C's men said.

"Yeah, but they're involved way over their heads with something and someone," Mad-C told the man.

"Well, we got what we came for, and it's a good thing the two I had to take out weren't kids," Mad-C finished.

It's almost 4:00 pm on a Thursday evening, and Debo felt like he hadn't eaten in a couple days. He went to a Starbucks down the street on Robertson Blvd and got himself a cup of coffee and a muffin to hold him. He sat there eating his muffin and drinking his coffee while he read, *The Los Angeles Times.* Nothing much was going on in Los Angeles, except a couple of shootings in South Central, and one in the Valley. He thought about Shelly, and thought about calling her. But, he decided to wait until later. As soon as he finishes his coffee and gets his head cleared from the day's stress and the meeting he had with the DEA agents last night, he would go and see Tony, then call Shelly. He knew that she was alright, Rex wouldn't let anything happen to her. He left Starbucks at 5:30 pm and went to see Tony on 59th and West Blvd. He pulled up in front of a two-story, yellow stucco house, with white trim. A six-foot chain-linked fence was the borderline between the sidewalk and Tony's house.

Debo walked through the gate and up the steps to the front porch: Only to find a rather large Doberman-pincher cuddled comfortably in a corner, unaware that Debo had walked upon him. When they noticed one another they kinda had the same reaction; Debo cursed and the dog barked. "Rusty..., Rusty..., it's okay boy, come on in boss, Rusty won't bother ya." Debo thought 'that if the good Lord was willing, the dog won't bite him regardless of what Tony was saying'. And, if the dog was going to bite him, there was nothing Tony could have done anyway, Debo would have been dead meat.

"Hey, Tee," Debo greeted Tony as he entered the house.

Tony has a pure Persian-rug somehow attached to his ceiling. The furniture is oakwood and wicker, and a staircase wrapped around a corner of the small living-room and disappeared into the ceiling to the second floor. He motioned for Debo to have a seat.

"Good to see ya, boss, what can I do fer ya?"

Debo sat on one of the wicker chairs across from Tony, with a four-foot, antique, oakwood table between them.

"Every time I come here, Rusty creeps up on me."

"Well, it's a good thing he knows ya bi now. He juss barks to let me know dat someone is here; someone he knows dat is."

"So..., what's up, Big-Tee, making too much money, or is someone putting pressure on you? Cause if they are... "

"Naw... I juss wanna go home fer a lil while and git me some ress I'm get'in kinda terd, Debo." Tony can't too much help his mangled dialog, he inherited it from his parents and his country upbringing from Tupelo, Mississippi.

"You really miss home, huh big guy?" Debo asked.

"Yeah..., juss terd uh LA, I wanna bi me a nice home and git me some ress. Maybe take Rusty meet me some fine gal help me spend mi money. I still got the tin you give me. What did the Big Man say?"

"He said, 'that you've put in a lot of loyal and faithful years with us, and he doesn't see a problem with it.' We're just hoping it doesn't affect the rest of the workers. But, seriously, you've earned it, and you deserve it, Tony; God knows you do. Okay, big guy..., I'm starved, I think I'll go eat me something and... b"

Before Debo could finish his statement, Tony said,

"It's about supper time fer me too. Why don't yall stick around and have somethin?"

"I'd better not, Tee, I'll be too full to leave, and I have to stop by Joy's place, then pay Pauline a visit. I want to get home early."

Debo was just getting into the Explorer when Tony yelled behind him from the front door of the house,

"Hey, Debo..., hol-up!!!"

Tony ran out to where Debo was sitting in his car and leaned over into the driver's side window and said,

"Oh yea, I fergot to tell yall I'm given a goin away party fer I leave. I may be able to fine a guy dat can take ma place. He deals in small weight though. I know 'em, he's a real good guy. I met 'em in Nam..., I truss 'em."

"I'll keep it in mind, Tony..., thanks," Debo said and pulled off. On the way over to Joy's house, Debo thought about what Tony said. Mad-C might not go for it; with the DEA agents involved and Tony leaving so soon. And now he wanted to recruit someone else to do his job. No one knows the guy; this could be a set-up. Tony said, 'that he wanted to go back home'. But when he came out here, it was because he claimed to be tired of home. Well, maybe now he's just tired of being out here, or the pressure from the drug dealing and the mess he had to go through behind it.

"I don't know, maybe things are moving too fast," Debo thought to himself.

He took Crenshaw Blvd to Olympic, then to Magnolia Street, and north to San Marino Street. The neighborhood has mostly apartment buildings, but on a few streets there were houses. Joy's house is on the corner: She has the entire corner to herself, and on it is a beautiful two-story stucco house with an attic giving it the appearance of a three-story house. Debo walked up the front steps and was met by two little girls running out the door, apparently late for a school sports practice, or maybe they had come home to eat: After all, the school is right down the street.

"Hi, Tammy..., Hi, Sheila!!!" Debo yelled as the two girls sped past him, nearly knocking him down the stairs.

"Hi, Uncle Debo!!!" the girls yelled back, trying to catch their breath. "Be careful!!!" Debo yelled behind his two nieces.

Joyvette Hernandez is a Hispanic, twenty-seven-year-old, with a beautiful bronze complexion, long blonde hair, smooth skin, 5'6" tall, and weighed 140 pounds; she looked almost Caucasian. She had on a turtle neck sweater, blue jeans, a pair of black boots with fur around the upper part, and was wearing the biggest diamond you've ever seen on her right thumb.

"Hey, Big bro," she said when she saw him standing there.

Joy always have and always will consider Debo her big brother. Debo and Joys' mom were close. If it weren't for Shelly, April Hernandez would have landed Debo, but it never happened.

"Hey, lil sis... how're things here at the home front?"

"Good... real good," Joy answered.

"I was in LA, and I thought I'd stop by and see how you are."

"You were just here the other night."

"Yeah, but every time I bring you your work, I have to check on you to make sure no one is bothering you," Debo said.

"No one has the slightest idea what I do for a living, everyone thinks I do telecommunications from home. So, how are you, you look tired or worried… is everything alright?" Joy asked.

"Yeah, everything's fine."

"Now you know you can't just tell me anything and expect me to believe it, what gives?"

"Can't put anything over on you, huh lil sis? Something came up."

"Not bad, I hope."

"Well, it could turn really bad really quick. You know that Shell doesn't know what I do for a living, right?" Debo asked.

"Yeah, and she shouldn't find out; the way you do things…, how could she?"

"I had a meeting last night that wasn't good at all. In fact, it's the reason I'm here. You're like a sister to me, Joyvette.., and I don't want anything to happen to you!"

"Wait bro, you're frightening me," Joy said, with fear in her eyes. You could see that she was starting to become nervous.

"The meeting I had last night was with two DEA agents."

"Oh, shit," Joy said and grabbed Debo's hand and held it as tight as she could. He held her hand for as long as it took to tell her everything the agent told him.

"So, you see, I'm really worried about her finding out and you going to jail or getting hurt," he confessed. "Bro, I told you when I got into the business, that I knew it was risky, I knew the chances I was taking, and I also know that my Big Brother is not going to let me fall. So, you just worry about Shelly finding out. I know she means the world to you, and I also know that there is nothing you can't work out or handle. D-Angelo Jackson, if you are going to stay in this business, then stop worrying. You will slip and you have too much at stake. What are you doing after you leave here?"

"I was going to go see Pauline and give her some cash, and then I was going home and spend some time with Shell."

"Pauline is not far from here. Give me the money and I'll make sure she gets it when the kids get home. I'm waiting for the man to come and fix my heater, it's freezing in here at night. You go home and get some rest, you look beat. Spend some time with your wife," Joy suggested.

"But, Joy, baby, I… "

"Just do it," Joy said, before he could get the words out to protest. "That's not a bad idea," he thought to himself. That way he could get some rest before he had to be back in Los Angeles to meet with agents Patch and Rayass tomorrow night.

"I can always count on you for moral support, huh, Sis?"

"Don't start that, get out of here and go straight home… I mean it," Joy said. She is very loving and protective of Debo and she always spoke up for him.

D-Angelo L Jackson, (aka Debo) lost contact with his sibling when he went into the drug business. Omar: Debo's only brother and Debo kept in touch through the years. Joy was the only one besides Omar, Mad-C, and Shelly that was close to Debo. Joy was born Joyvette Latrice Hernandez and is from Santa Monica, CA. She met Debo when he and her mom; April Hernandez were working together as security guards at a Thrifty Drug Store some ten years ago; Debo was thirty. He didn't like being a security guard, it was too boring. So, he quit and his life took a turn for the worse and he was IN trouble more than OUT. He started getting worse and turned to recycling cans and bottles, which is when Mad-C found him standing in front of a 7-11 store panhandling for money. After Mad-C took him away from all that, things started to look up for him. He never thought he would be able to afford to buy his wife a twelve-million-dollar estate, or have an office in Beverly Hills, California, or an $80K custom made Navigator Park in his carport; it even accommodates Rex. Debo changed his mind about getting something to eat and decided to wait until he got home to. He turned onto the I-10 Freeway east headed for San Diego. It was still early so he had a little time before rush hour traffic started. He kept going over and over in his mind as to what would happen if Shelly found out about everything. He had managed to keep it from her for this long. Maybe he should come out and deal with the consequences. Just at that moment, his cell phone rang and it was Shelly.

"Hi, baby.., to what do I owe the pleasure of this call?" Debo said when he answered the call.

"Well, since you don't come home some nights, I figured that if you got here early enough, I'll have dinner ready for you."

"Baby, are you a mind reader or what? I was just turning onto the freeway; I should be there by eleven."

"Oh…, good, I'll have dinner ready for you, okay?"

"Okay baby, love you," Debo said.

"Love you too," Shelly said.

Debo hung up feeling like a lucky man to have such a wonderful wife as Shelly. He remembered something that he had forgotten to ask Tony. He dialed Tony's number and he picked up on the first ring.

"Yeah, did yall ferget somethin?" Tony asked. "Yeah, I forgot to ask you something when I was there."

"Yeah…, go head-on… what is it ya wanna ask me, Debo?"

"Mad-C said, 'that you were taking the buy-out plan.'"

"Yeah, I did.., I toll him dat."

"What figure did you have in mind?"

"Well, I was thinkin dat since I won't be wit you guys no mo, and mi money's gonna be a lil light, how's a mill sound?"

"Sounds good to me… I'll tell the big man. I'm sure he won't have a problem with it."

"Okay, thanks," Tony said.

"You're welcome, Tony."

Thursday evening, eleven-o-nine p.m.

Debo arrived home a little after eleven. Shelly heard the Explorer pull up and opened the door. Rex also heard him, although he was in the backyard. They knew when the Ford pulled into the carport, which is located on the side of the house just off the street. It was designed to accommodate six cars. Shelly didn't see him when she went outside; either coming up the walkway, or standing beside the car. He was bent down on the driver's side of the Explorer looking at where someone had keyed it. He cursed under his breath and made a mental note to call and let the car leasing agency know.

"Hey honey, anything wrong?" Shelly asked when she saw him come from around the side of the car.

"Just someone out to have a little fun…, they keyed the car that's all; no big deal."

"Go ahead and get a relaxed baby," Shelly said.

"Oh boy… something smells delicious in here."

"Well it should, It's your favorite; spinach greens, rice, cornbread, potato salad, oxtails, and mac and cheese, with hot buttered yams."

"You have been busy, haven't you little mama?"

"Nothing but the best for my baby."

While she was setting the table, Debo went outside to give Rex a pat on his side; something he does to show Rex that he was well loved by him. Besides, Rex loves the attention.

"How's things boy?" Rex looked up at him and yawned.

"Have you been holding down the fort? I see my favorite girl is still healthy and alive. I'll see what I can do about getting you some good ole cornbread dipped in green juice, rice, and oxtail bones? How does that sound?"

Rex licked his mouth and wagged his tail to let him know that he understood. After dinner, Debo fed Rex, helped Shelly with the kitchen, and sat and watched television. Since he was always in LA, he wanted to see what was going on in San Diego, so he turned to the news. Shelly sat next to him on the sofa, and when he saw that she wasn't interested in the news, he knew that the news could wait.

"Something special you have on your mind, little lady?"

"Yes, but that'll wait until later. I wanted to ask you something."

"Yeah, what is it?"

"Is anything wrong out in Los Angeles?"

"No, why do you ask that?"

"Well, because that phone call that came yesterday afternoon, the guy didn't leave his name."

Debo didn't tell her that the call was as much a surprise to him as it was to her.

"Oh, Shell baby, it was nothing, just one of the guy at the office. He does that all the time; nothing to worry about."

He hated lying to her, but that was the safest thing, especially with everything that's going on. When things get clearer, he'll have to let her know everything. He didn't have anything to do in Los Angeles until the meeting with Patch and Rayass tomorrow night, so tonight he's all Shelly's.

"Baby, I'm beat.., let's turn in for the night?" Shelly suggested. "Yeah, I'm tired too honey, I could use some sleep."

"Who said anything about sleep?" Shelly asked with a twinkle in her eyes.

"Let me shower, and I'll be right with you," Debo told her.

"Can I join you?"

"You sure can."

They both showered and got into bed. After a short while, Debo turned to her and said,

"Baby, you are the most wonderful person I have ever had the pleasure of meeting in my entire life. I would give you the world if I could. You have come into my soul and moved everything around where I can find them. Everything is perfect in my heart because you have moved everything where I can find them there also. In my heart, in my life with you everything is perfect. All my days and nights are full of pleasure because no matter what happens, I have pleasurable thoughts and dreams of you. When God sent you to me, he sent me a miracle: He gave me my own heaven right here on earth in flesh and blood.

You are considerate, loyal, faithful, trustworthy, understanding. And most of all, you are beautiful inside and out."

"Are you sure nothing's wrong?"

"Shell, I don't see you as often as I should or would like to. I don't get a chance to verbally reward you for being my most precious jewel.

I just feel a need to come to you and let you know what I feel about you and how I see you in my heart. There's nothing in the world that can even attempt to live up to you in my life or my world. I try hard each day to find something or to think of something that could be sufficient enough to be rewarding to you. Money is not enough, this house is not enough, just to say I love you is not enough. So, you see… nothing is wrong, everything is perfect." Debo put his hand under the blanket and pulled Shelly closer to him and started kissing her on her cheek, then her neck, then he kissed her forehead.

"Now…, for that something special you had in mind." "Yeah…, you think you're ready for it?" she asked.

"Try me."

Debo looked at her with hungry eyes as she stared into his eyes until their hearts were content.

CHAPTER
3

FRIDAY MORNING, 7:30 A.M.

Debo woke up and eased out of bed, still feeling the wonderful sensation of lovemaking that had put him in a deep sleep last night. He got in the shower and basked in the soothing, relaxing, hot water. He finished his shower, got out, shaved, and decided to surprise Shelly.

"You didn't," she said, with a stunned look on her beautiful face, and excitement in her voice.

Debo had walked into the bedroom while she was still asleep and kissed her on her lips which woke her up. She couldn't believe what she saw: Debo, not being home some mornings, she would never have expected to see what she saw. She woke up to see that in his hands, was a large breakfast tray, garnished with hot pancakes, hot scrambled eggs, hot hash brown potatoes, three multi-vitamins, two slices of wheat toast, and a glass of freshly squeezed orange juice.

"One thing I can say is that you sure know how to wake a woman."

"Yeah…, and you sure know how to put a tired man to sleep."

He left her in bed to finish her breakfast while he went to call agents Patch and Rayass. He searched his wallet for the business card that Dick

Patch had given him. After retrieving the card, he dialed Patch's number and it was his home number. He hung up and dialed his cell number.

"Patch here," a voice said on the third ring. "Agent Patch, this is D-Angelo Jackson."

"Oh, Mister Jackson, talk to me."

"First of all, how did you get my home number? And second, don't ever use it again."

"Well, first of all, Mister Jackson we have our ways; second, if you don't expect me to use it anymore, then that lets me know that we are in business," Patch stated.

"Get something and write this down," Debo told the agent.

Dick Patch told him to hold on and put the phone down. After a short pause, he returned to the phone and said,

"Go ahead, I'm listening."

Debo gave him the location, directions, and the time to meet with him. "I take it you have my cell number now, it should have shown on your caller ID," Debo said.

"That's correct, I do have it now," Patch assured him.

"Okay, then use it, and if I don't answer, wait until I do. I don't want you calling my home number ever again, do you understand me?" Debo stated, then hung up.

He went outside to see what Rex was doing and to let him out for a while to go upfront with him to wipe down the car and a couple of other cars and listen to some oldies on his five-disc compact-disc player while it idled some. It hadn't been driven in a while, and he wanted to give Shelly time to finish eating and taking her shower.

He couldn't hear his cell phone ring over the music; the lights in the car kept blinking. He had activated the built-in cell phone when he turned on the CD player. He climbed into the front seat and turned the music down and began talking as if he was talking to the windshield. He wasn't using his Bluetooth because it was inside the house. He didn't expect any calls this morning, but in-case someone did call he did activate the car phone... you never know.

The receiver was mounted into the ceiling just over the sun visor, and the phone was installed into the dash.

"Hello," he said, irritated. This is His and Shelly's day together and he didn't want to be bothered.

"Good morning, big bro," Joy greeted.

"Hey, Sis.., what's up? Is everything okay? Is somebody giving you trouble? Because if they are, I'll come out there right now and climb in their ass," Debo angrily said.

"No, I'm fine bro, it's just that I called Pauline about the money you gave me to give her and something didn't sound right, it's just... well..., I think you'd better give her a call. She sounded upset and nervous about something."

"Did she tell you what the problem was?"

"No..., she tried, but I couldn't understand what she was talking about; something like 'being shot or shot at.'"

"Okay, thanks baby, I'll call her, are you okay?" Debo asked.

"Just a little worried, but I'm fine. Let me know what happened, okay?"

"I will, Sis.., thanks for calling," Debo said and hung up the phone. Since Joy and Pauline were the only two females on his team, they became very close and have also become the very best of friends. Debo turned off the Explorer and locked it up, then put Rex in the backyard. When he went inside, Shelly was sitting at her computer working on some files.

She didn't know Debo had come back inside the house until he put his arms around her waist and gave her a big kiss. She looked up with her face to the ceiling as he looked down at her. "How was breakfast?" he asked.

"It was lovely, baby, thank you very much," she told him, smiling. "Nothing but the best for my baby," he said, repeating what she had said at dinner last night, with a big grin on his smooth face.

"Now where have I heard that before?" she asked, with a smile still on her face.

Debo had scheduled the meeting with Patch and Rayass for 5:00 this evening. That would put him back in San Diego at roughly 8:00 or 9:00: That way, he can get to rest early. He had work to do in Los Angeles again tomorrow and he wanted to stop by and see what the problem was with

Pauline. He called her to see what the situation was. After all, she is sitting on ten kilos of Mad-C's work.

"Those assholes were running down my fuckin block shooting and yelling and shit!" Pauline told him.

"Did it have anything to do with you?" Debo asked.

"No, but it spooked the shit out of me. I was sitting on my porch outside and this asshole ran into my yard; running from some other asshole shooting at him." "Did you know the guy?" Debo asked.

"I know everybody around here," Pauline told Debo.

"Okay, I'm coming out there in a little bit. I'll have someone come by to sit with you until I get there. I gave Joy something to give you, did she tell you?"

"She called to tell me, but I was so damn pissed…"

"Yeah, she told me she called you" Okay.., hold on, someone will be there shortly," Debo assured her.

"Okay," Pauline said.

Debo ended the call and called Freddy and Jeffery. They work regulations, security, whatever needs to be done. Plus, they work ten keys of cocaine per month. They're two of the best men he has on his team. In fact, they're the only two men on his team now that Tony left. He knew they could handle the job: In fact, they can handle whatever job he gives them. He kissed Shelly goodbye and got dressed. With it being the middle of winter, he dressed in a thick, blue, short-sleeved, pullover shirt, black Levi jeans, Nike tennis shoes, and he took his long black winter coat. He was outside in the Explorer in fifteen minutes headed for the highway. When he arrived in Los Angeles, he exited the I-10 Freeway at Crenshaw Blvd, then went south to 43rd Street and made a left turn on 43rd street to 7th Ave. Pauline lives in a two-story house with white and pink trim. She loves pink, it's been her favorite color ever since she was old enough to know what color was. She thought about taking art as a career, but it wouldn't have worked out. She said, 'that it took up too much of her time and she's not one for just sitting.' That's why she accepted the job working for Debo and Mad-C.

Debo lightly knocked on her door, he didn't like ringing doorbells because they make too much noise. He put a sign on his door; "Do not ring bell, Please Knock!" He thought about disconnecting it but he might be out by the pool one day and wouldn't be able to hear anyone knocking at the front door, so he decided to leave it on.

Pauline's door opened, and a beautiful tall woman was standing in it. "Hey good looking," she said when she saw Debo.

"Hey, love... what's up?"

"Nothing now, it's all over," she answered. "Where are Freddy and Jeffery?"

"I told them to go and get themselves something to eat. They got hungry and I didn't feel like cooking anything. I found out what that was about: A guy from the neighborhood took some drugs from one of my people and thought he could get away. He said, 'that he ran over here because the brothers he took the shit from were some of my people. He didn't think they would do anything to him if he ran over here.' I called my people and I had them just beat the shit out of his ass. First of all, for playing games with my merchandise... second, for running over here knowing what I do for a living, and third, just on general principles. He pushes small rocks and he also smokes; all these curb servers do. I told Jeffery and Freddy when they arrived," she said, then took a deep breath and continued.

"I'm thinking of firing the assholes that were shooting at him so close to my house, they know better. They know I can't be bothered with the police here at my place, but I guess that's what they do." She finished talking and wiped the corners of her mouth with a tissue.

"So, they didn't come over here... the police, I mean?"

"They came in the neighborhood but not over here."

"Okay, as long as everything is alright," Debo told her.

He was relieved and able to relax a little more. At that moment, Freddy and Jeffery pulled back up.

"Hey, Guys!!!" Debo yelled from across the street.

"Hey, Boss!!!" Freddy yelled back from the car he and Jeffery had arrived in. Debo excused himself and walked over to talk to his men.

"Did she tell you what happened?" Freddy asked Debo.

Freddy is bald and muscular, with a diamond-studded earring in his nose and left ear, weighs 180 pounds, 6-ft tall, beefy, dark complexion; about the same height and complexion as Jeffery, only a little heavier. No nose ring, but he does wear an earring in his left ear.

"Yeah, she told me everything," Debo said, and almost laughed. "Man, if we start killing up each other, how are we going to make any money?" Jeffery asked.

"I don't know, but I wanna meet with everyone in about three days. Something's come up," Debo said with a look of concern on his face.

He looked at his watch and it was 3:00 pm. That gives him two hours before he have to meet with Patch and Rayass.

"Thanks for coming on such short notice guys. I knew I could depend on the two of you," Debo told them.

"You can call me any time to come and rescue miss beautiful over there," Jeffery said, referring to Pauline who was still standing in her door. She was indeed a beautiful woman, with jet-black hair, creamy peanut butter complexion, light green eyes, built like a brick shit house, and was the meanest little mama on the block. She wore a pink tank top under her long-sleeved, white button-down dress-shirt, and some pink sweatpants, with pink slip-on open-toed shoes. Her face was as smooth as silk, as was the rest of her skin .

"Debo, you really know how to pick them," Jeffery said with a gleam in his eyes that spelled trouble.

"Jeffery, last time I heard; you had a girl..., what happened?" Debo asked.

"Well, I still have Molly, but don't get me wrong, I'll put it all on the line for that," he said, pointing one of his long fingers at Pauline again. "I'm out of here, guys, I'll see you in three days. How are things going at work?"

"Just work as usual," Freddy said.

"Still hanging in there," Jeffery added.

"Good enough," Debo said and went back to where Pauline was and said,

"You take care, sweetheart, I'm holding a meeting with everyone in three days; I'll see you then."

"OK, you be careful and thank you!!!" Pauline yelled behind him. Debo was back on the I-10 Freeway headed toward downtown Los Angeles. He exited the San Bernardino Freeway at First Street. The downtown Los Angeles Parker Center Police Station, at 150 N Los Angeles Street is a gray marble building with stained-glass sliding doors. Police officers, bail bondsmen, clerks, and maintenance personnel were coming and going. The officer at the front desk; Richard looked like he could use a break. He's thirty-four-years-old, but he looks older for his age.

He's had his share of worry lines around his eyes and forehead, and his voice was rough as he spoke.

"Hello, Mister Jackson," he said as if he was expecting Debo to show up at that particular time.

"Let me ring Sgt Billings for you, sir," Richard said, then picked up a receiver and spoke into it. "Mr Jackson is here to see you, sir."

A moment went by and he hung up, and told Debo to go right up. Sgt. Bob Billings is a heavy-set man, with the tell-tale look of all the years he has put in on the force. There were a few strands of gray hair in his balding head. He had gray sideburns, wrinkles everywhere; all over his face and neck. He wore a blue, long-sleeved shirt with the sleeves rolled up, gray slacks, and a pair of glasses that sat lazily on the bridge of his nose. He had seen his share of crime on the streets and decided to just relax and take it easy. All he wanted was to retire comfortably and put his daughter Becky through college; One of the best money could buy; Stanford, Yale, or UCLA.

"I have a half dozen men on it right now. Okay, get the hostage negotiator over there and tell Lieutenant Grove to handle it, and keep me posted." Sgt Billings was on the phone when Debo walked in.

"Mr Jackson, it's always a pleasure to see you, what's up?"

"There is something I need to tell you, Bob. I had a meeting with two guys from DEA about two days ago," Debo said, expecting the Sgt to hit the ceiling.

MURDER AND MONEY

"Yeah, I knew someone would be wise by now. But, it's a good thing they want in because they know too much to be against us. And, if they were against us, then it's goodbye career and retirement; not to mention college for Becky," Billing softly said.

"Is he asking you for anything?" Debo asked.

"Yeah, $25K a month." Sgt Billings is also on the take for 100K a month from Mad-C.

"Well, that's not too bad."

"What do they want from you?" Billings asked.

"I have to meet with them tonight. In fact, in about forty-five-minutes. But don't worry, because Mister Write agreed to listen to their proposal and see how much they want. But, I'm sure these guys will get greedy, they always do. I'll need for you to find out something for me; there's another $25K in it for you."

"Name it," Billings said.

"I need to know where Patch is keeping the evidence he has on me and Mr Write, and who his lawyers are. Maybe we can get rid of them. If they know, the FBI will probably know soon, and those boys don't play," Debo said.

"I'll do what I can," Billings promised.

"I know you have some pull in the department, Bob…, please, we need that information. When did they talk to you?"

"They came here about a day ago."

"Well, it could be a good thing, at least Mr Write thinks so. But, let's hope it doesn't go bad. I'm having a meeting with my people in a couple of days to let them know," Debo informed him.

"I'll call you when I get something," Billings told him. "Okay, I'll let you get back to your work," Debo said.

"Yeah… which reminds me, I have a hostage situation on the east side. Some crazy husband wants to take his kids from a foster home. Boy, I'll tell you, these nuts never let up," Sgt Billings said.

"Yeah tell me about it," Debo said, and was out the door.

He got to his car and was upset to see a parking citation on his car's windshield.

"I'll give it to Billings next time I'm here," he thought to himself.

Debo pulled away from the curb, not realizing the meter-maid was coming up alongside oh him, and he almost clipped her. "Sorry!!!" he yelled.

She didn't know if he was apologizing for not putting a quarter in the meter, or for almost clipping her.

The chili king is a nice, cozy, chili joint on south Crenshaw Boulevard. Dick Patch and Monty Rayass were seated outside on a bench that was put there to accommodate their customers who wish to dine in an outdoor setting.

"Mister Patch, Mister Rayass," Debo greeted the agents. "Mister Jackson," they both said in unison.

"Glad to see you could make it… let's sit and discuss business, shall we?" Patch said.

"Mister Write somehow expected to hear from someone wanting to blackmail him or us," Debo roughly said.

"Oh, I wouldn't use those terms, Mister Jackson. Think of it as a security investment. You have Billings, and now you have us," Agent Patch said, with a sort of harsh enthusiasm.

"Yeah, Mister Write said something to that effect," Debo growled. "Well, Mr Write knows a good business deal when he sees one," the taller of the two agents told Debo. "Give us a figure," Debo demanded.

Dick Patch went into his pocket and pulled out a slip of paper and handed it to Debo. Debo unfolded it, and read the numbers, One-five-zero-zero-zero-zero. "Per month!!!" Debo yelled, in shock.

"Per month," Dick Patch confirmed.

"What do we get for $150K a month? That's way too fuckin much for hush money."

"Calm down, calm down, Mister Jackson," Patch insisted. "I want a list of the services we get," Debo demanded.

"There will be no list; you get protection from organized crime figures, you get passes; by that I mean, we see something, we turn our heads, we hear something, we close our ears. Any information or tips as to other crime figures will be an extra $25K each, depending on who it is. We interfere with all and any attempts to arrest you, Mr. Write, or your workers.

"Does that sound fair? $150,000 is a lot of money," Agent Patch said. "Yes, that sounds fair enough," Debo confirmed.

"Okay, I want half tomorrow morning and the other half at the end of the month, and after that, once a month," Patch said.

"I'll let Mr Write know," Debo informed him, as agent Rayass was coming out of the Chili King with a big bowl of chili. "Best I've ever had," he said to Debo and Patch.

"Does he ever stop eating? Next time we'll meet at an opera house, maybe he'll sing for us," Debo jokingly said.

Dick Patch stood and extended his right hand for Debo to shake. Debo shook his hand, and said, "Mister Patch," and Dick Patch said, "Mister Jackson."

He handed Debo a note explaining where and how to deliver the money. Debo figured he'll tell Mad-C how much they want and he'll pay the extra fifty grand per month. At that moment the two agents do claim to have evidence that could put them all away for a very long time. Mad-C said, '$100k no more'. But they want $50,000 more, that's $75,000 for Patch and $75,000 for his fat-ass partner.

"FREEZE… !!! LAPD!!! HANDS!!! Show me your hands!!! Show me your hands!!! Who else is in here!!!" one of the officers that kicked in Freddy's front door screamed.

"No one… just me What the hell are you doing here?"

"My job, Mr Moss… doing my job," the officer said.

He was the one who seemed to be in charge. They were all wearing full gear and had automatic weapons aimed at Freddy.

"What in the hell is this all about," Freddy asked, puzzled as hell. "Where are they? … The drugs, where are they?" he repeated.

"I don't know what drugs you are talking about."

Freddy never keeps his product on his person or on his property. He stashes it two houses down in a fictitious name.

"I have a search warrant for you. Are you Frederick C Moss?" the officer asked.

"Yeah, that's me."

While the officers inside the house were searching for drugs and weapons, there were a few more out back in the garage looking. He didn't use drugs and he knew they wouldn't find any there. But they did find a sawed-off shotgun and an Uzi semi-automatic pistol shoved between the mattress and the box springs of the bed. And in a drawer in his bedside table was his 357-magnum.

"I want to see permits for these weapons," the officer ordered.

He only had a permit for the 357, the others were given to him and they weren't registered.

"Put your hands behind your back and stand up?" Freddy put his hands behind his back and the officer cuffed them together.

"Wait... I'll help you up," he told Freddy. He helped Freddy get to his feet and escorted him to one of the police cruisers outside. The other officers came from around different parts of the house and began to huddle around each other talking. They couldn't find any drugs or any more weapons, so they took him to the police station for booking.

Debo was on his way back to *The-Shell-Debo when* his cell phone rang at about 8:30 am.

"Hello," Debo said when he answered the phone. He was confused because he didn't recognize the number on his caller ID.

"Boss this is Freddy, I was just raided," the voice on the other end of the phone said.

"You Just Got What!!!" Debo screamed loud enough to be heard outside the car with the windows up.

"What did you say..., you're where..., you've been what?" Debo was lost for words. He didn't know what to say or think. "Don't panic," he told himself.

"Okay, what happened?" Deb had perspiration rolling down the side of his face, from panic and fear.

"I was at home at about four something watching TV; when this big-ass cop took my door down, yelling; 'Freeze..., LAPD'!!!, looking for drugs and guns," Freddy explained.

"Are you sure it was LAPD?"

"Yep, sure as I'm sitting my black-ass in jail." Freddy was shocked when the door came open and the yelling started.

"What do they have you for?" Debo asked. He was sure that later he would laugh until his side hurts, but for now it's serious.

"A couple of toys I got for Christmas last year." "Oh yeah, I remember, you showed me those. What's your bail?"

"Well, seeing as how I had an automatic weapon, it's $100,000." "Okay, Freddy, I'll take care of it, Can you sit there overnight,

I'm almost home?"

"I guess so if I have to," Freddy cried.

"Okay good, I'll find out who tipped the police off."

"I thought that Sergeant, what's his name, Bill, something?"

Debo cut him off before he could finish his question.

"Never-mind his name, Freddy, you're on a jail phone. I'll get you bailed out, but you will lose the toys, understand?"

"Yeah, boss, thanks."

"Okay just hold tight until morning."

Debo knew that Billings would make sure Freddy never appeared in court, and that the evidence room would somehow lose the guns. They lose things all the time down at Parker Center.

The main thing is to find out who is behind all this.

"What phone are you on?" Debo asked.

"A phone here in the holding tank. I told them I was calling my lawyer."

"Okay, let's not say anymore, you'll be out in the morning.

I'll have Jeffery pick you up," Debo assured him.

"Okay,"

Debo was relieved and able to relax a little more.

He turned off the I-905 and was almost home when Sgt Billings called.

"Hey, fella, I guess you heard, huh?" Debo asked.

"Yeah, I heard, sorry, I'll get right on it," Billings assured Debo.

"I'll bail him out in the morning, or have one of my guys do it. I won't be able to make it out there tonight," Debo said.

"Okay, I'll have someone bring the evidence up; someone I can trust. And you can take the bail money out of my money," Billings told him.

"Are you sure?" Debo asked.

"That shouldn't have happened, yeah, I'm sure. I'll see what judge issued the warrant, and who the Sergeant in charge was. Maybe I can fiddle around and find out where they got the lead. I've got my end, don't worry," Billings told Debo.

"Okay… Champ, good night," Debo said.

"Good night," Billings said and let out a sigh of relief and hung up.

Debo pulled into his carport, parked, and went inside. Shelly was on the sofa watching TV and drinking a cup of coffee. "Coffee this late," Debo said and kissed her on her cheek, then softly on her lips.

"Yeah, I was waiting up for you."

"Are you sure you'll be able to sleep? If not, I'll be happy to assist you, Mrs Jackson," Debo said.

"Rex misses you; I gave him the rest of the leftovers, I hope you don't mind. There's some meatloaf and greens in there. Oh, and I made some more cornbread and fixed the meatloaf the way you like it with cream of mushroom gravy and soy sauce. Go ahead and take your shower while I fix your plate."

Debo took his shower, ate, then went out back to give Rex a pat on his side. "Hey fella, I heard you had the rest of my oxtails, which means you had a great dinner, didn't you?" Rex licked his mouth and gave Debo a kiss.

"Don't thank me, I said, 'oxtail bones'. You should be thanking miss-lady in there. I'm beat, boy…, I'm going to bed, see you later."

Debo let Rex off easy with eating his oxtails.

CHAPTER 4

SATURDAY, 8:30 A.M.

Richard Buringham; the Desk Sergeant at Parker Center Police Station in downtown Los Angeles is standing at the front desk. "Hello, Sergeant."

Richard was busy when he heard the man say, 'Hello Sergeant.' He looked up to see a badge, and behind it was agent Dick Patch of the Drug Enforcement Administration.

"I'm here to see Sgt Billings."

"Have a seat please, he's not in his office at the moment," Richard explained after he checked the chart.

Agent Dick Patch took a seat where there are about four rows of chairs. He wondered how the officers, dressed in their blue uniforms, were able to go out so freely and willingly into the field every day, considering there are people that don't like police officers. Those little blue suits just make them sitting ducks for the first lunatic out there waiting to take target practice. There are literally thousands of them. Agent Patch wasn't one for uniforms, that's why he joined the Administration. DEA is strictly undercover; none of those blue suits with the target over the heart. But they must be proud of their jobs.

"Agent Patch, you can go up now," Richard pleasantly said.

"Thanks," Patch said and went over to the elevators and was on his way to Sergeant Billings' office.

When Gloria opened Billings' door, he was sitting at his desk. "So, we meet again, and to what do I owe the pleasure?"

"We got a copy of an arrest warrant that was issued for the arrest of Fredrick C Moss. Isn't that one of D-Angelo Jackson's boys?" Patch asked, knowing good and well that Freddy works for Debo.

"Yes, I believe so," Billings admitted.

"Okay, I'll do what I can to keep it out of the permanent files. Do you know who phoned in the tip?"

"Not yet, we're working on it," Billings said. "You do know who supplies, Write?" Patch asked.

"No, I don't," Billings lied.

He knew, he just didn't want to give up too much information to these guys. Rayass isn't with Patch all the time but there are two of them involved. "The Colombians are shipping it in from Columbia straight to Write's shipping dock in Long Beach.

The dock once belonged to a very powerful politician named Donald Warwick. I'm sure you've heard of him, Sergeant Billings. Anyway..., Warwick left the country and sold the shipping dock to the Charles Write and Associates Empire. That's how we got his name, although we do have other means of getting what we want," Patch advised. "I'm sure you do... so why haven't you mentioned all this to Write?"

"Well, Sergeant, we can't give up too much."

"What are you into him for?" Billings asked ."I don't understand."

"How much money is he paying you, Patch?" Sergeant Billings made the question easier for him to understand.

"Reasonable; It's not a payment, it's an investment. I'm sure he and yourself have an investment agreement as well..., am I right?" Patch questioned.

"That's true..., yes."

"How well do you know Mr Write and Mr Jackson, Sgt?"

"Why?"

"I'm just asking."

"Well enough to know that you are not playing with kindergarten kids. Those guys are extremely lethal, but at the same time they're fair. Whatever you do, Mr Patch, don't cross them. Mister Write or Mister Jackson has no problem disposing of the day's garbage… if you know what I mean. Mister Jackson has only one request, and that's that his wife never finds out what he does for a living. If she does, all the evidence in the world won't stop him from coming after your ass," Billings said.

"They are both very rich men, and I doubt that they got that way by being naive or stupid. I have no reason or intentions to cross either of them. I'm looking forward to a nice retirement the same as you are. But the only thing is, and it bothers me a great deal. I don't think I'm sure about how long this will last without the guys at the administration finding out. I guess as long as the big guy doesn't find out.

Now, as far as LAPD, I would be very careful if I were you. The locals are doing fine because LAPD is on the take from bigger fish than Charles Write and D-Angelo Jackson. And another thing, keep a tight lid on this, you've been doing good so far. Which is why you haven't been indicted through the years. Just keep your eyes and ears open and your mouth shut and everything will be just fine, Sergeant."

"It's time for me to be getting home; we'll talk again, Agent Patch. But, until then, keep in mind what I said about Write and Jackson: They are not a joke and they won't hesitate to prove it to you," Billings warned.

Debo went over to Mad-C's house to pick up fifty kilos of cocaine. He told him about how the meeting went with Patch and Rayass. Mad-C wouldn't have a problem with Debo paying the extra $50K, as long as the DEA agents know which side their bread is buttered on. He told Debo that he'll have to see how things go. Debo put the fifty kilos of cocaine in the running-board of the Explorer, then headed back to Los Angeles. He would give everyone 12½ kilos; distributing Tony's work between the four of them. Debo knows where to find Tony if need be. He knew that Tony went back to Mississippi: He's out of the business, but he's not out of reach. Debo told the others about Patch and Rayass. He also told them to stay on their toes. The extra $25K each will come in very handy; Christmas is approaching fast and they could use the extra money.

Debo called the car leasing agency about the scratches on the door of the Explorer.

"Hi Mr Jackson, and how are we this fine day?" a voice on the phone said. "I'm doing just fine, and yourself?"

"Good Mr Jackson…, real good."

"Is this Lois?"

"Yes, it is, how may I help you today?" Lois amiably asked.

"I'm calling because someone keyed the Explorer… the driver's side door has a long scratch on it, and I would like to know how to go about…," Lois cut Debo off in mid-sentence.

"The car is fully insured, Mr Jackson, don't worry about it. Are there any other concerns, Sir?"

"No, everything else is fine," Debo assured her.

"Okay, you have a wonderful day, Mr Jackson." "Okay, I sure will, Lois, and thank you for your help."

He arrived at *The Shell-Debo* shortly after leaving Mad-C's estate. He wanted to leave the fifty kilos of cocaine in the running board of the Explorer for travel on his way to LA. Shelly wasn't home but she left a note on the frig, saying 'that she would be back later'. He went outside to check if she had taken one of the Honda motorcycles. He'd hoped she hadn't because it was a little too cold out. He bought them because they like to ride them to Los Angeles because the ride eases a lot of the tension. They usually go to the little spot at the Santa Monica Pier where the shrimp house is located; where he met with the two DEA agents. He saw that she had taken the Nissan, so he went back inside the house and finished reading the note.

"Please forgive me, I didn't have time to fix you anything to eat; I was running late. Last night was wonderful. I love you, see you soon." Debo went outside again, but this time to check the mail.

The mailbox is on the front lawn between the house and the carport. He picked up the newspaper off the lawn; *The San Diego Union-Tribune*. He took the newspaper and the mail back inside the house and sat it on the kitchen table, put some coffee on; a couple of pieces of toast, and a grapefruit. After a while, the coffee pot beeped but he ignored it and finished preparing his toast and grapefruit. After everything was prepared, he went to the table to read the paper and eat.

"All was good and quiet in the city. No one I know is in trouble…, that's good news," he thought to himself. He picked up the mail; bills, Christmas cards, junk mail, and an envelope that read, "Urgent Mr. Jackson." There was no return address nor postage stamp on it. So, that meant that however it arrived in his mailbox, it wasn't mailed. He opened it and read it, and was confused by what it read. He read it again, and it said in two words, "BOW-WOW." The Mister Coffee beeped again to remind him of his coffee and brought him back to the moment. He put the piece of paper to the side and ate his breakfast, but the note wouldn't leave him alone. He cleaned up the mess he had made in the kitchen and went to the bedroom that he had converted into a home office and tried to open the door and forgot he had to use a combination to get in. His mind was still on the note as he entered the calculations for the ten kilos into the worker's worksheets and pay period Plus, the fifty thousand from his account each month for Patch and Rayass. He looked at his watch, and it was nearly one in the afternoon. "Boy, how time flies." He had to make a run and be back later tonight, so he decided to leave Shelly a note before he left. He sat the note on the kitchen table where he knew Shelly would find it.

He went into the bedroom to get dressed and was almost out the door, when he remembered the note from the mail. He didn't want Shelly to run across it, he wouldn't be able to explain it; he didn't understand it himself. No one ever put anything like that in his mailbox before. He was puzzled and worried as he headed towards the door to leave.

He turned on the car ignition, then he remembered he didn't feed Rex. Then it hit him; the note…, 'Bow-Wow'…, "Oh, my God, Rex!" He felt his heart rise to the top of his head. and jumped out of the SUV with the engine still running. The fear of something being wrong with his dog made his knees weak, he felt faint. He was almost to the side gate before he yelled,

"Rex, come here boy, Rex!!!" he yelled louder from the very top of his lungs. He couldn't get the gate open, he had left the keys to the lock and the front door in the ignition on his key ring. He wanted to jump over the gate but his head was too light and his knees were too weak, so he ran to the front of the house and punched in the code to unlock the front door. Once inside, he ran through the living room into the kitchen and out the back door. "Rex!!!" he yelled again, and not a sign of Rex. He got to the dog house and there was a note attached to Rex's house that read, "BANG". Debo looked inside the dog house and Rex was lying there motionless. He saw that there wasn't any blood and Rex was unconscious and still breathing. Debo picked him up and carried him to the Navigator and reached in and opened the rear door of the SUV. He has a piece of linoleum on the floor, in case Rex went with him on some of his runs to LA. He had a custom-made compartment for Rex built into the back of the Navigator for on the road travel. There;s a block of marble about four by four feet on the floor, a food and water dispenser on the sidewall, a pillow, a set of restraining straps across the back window so the window could be let down, a specially equipped air conditioning system for the summer that comes on automatically when the engine is not running and the doors are closed. It cost him a cool $97K hard cash for the custom-made SUV. He called the vet to let him know that he was on his way.

"This is D-Angelo Jackson," Debo said to the vet. "Go ahead, Mr, Jackson," the veterinarian said .

"I have an emergency: My dog... my dog is..."

"Yes, Mr Jackson... what's wrong with it?"

"Rex ..., he's unconscious."

"Is he breathing, Mr Jackson?"

"Yes, but he won't move."

"How far are you?"

"I'm almost there."

"Are you driving?"

"Yes."

"Then please, for God's sake be careful driving."

Debo ran two red lights, a stop sign, caused a car to skip the curb, ran a lady off the road, and was driving eighty miles per hour in the afternoon lunch hour traffic. His head felt as if it was going to blow at any minute.

"Mr Jackson, stay with me, how far are you now?"

Debo had thrown the cell phone in the passenger's seat next to him a block ago and was coming through the door as the veterinarian was talking on the phone. The vet looked up and saw a man carrying a German-Shepherd as big as he was, through the door.

"Mister Jackson, I presume?" the vet asked. He had already alerted staff that Debo was coming in with Rex, and that it was an emergency.

"Put him… it is him, isn't it, Mr Jackson?"

"Yes."

"Okay, put him on the gurney."

When Debo put Rex down, the vet immediately started checking his vitals while rolling the gurney through an open door into another room, with Debo on his heels.

"Mr Jackson, you will have to wait here," one of the assistants said. She noticed the condition he was in, and asked,

"Do you want something to calm your nerves?"

"Please," Debo said .

"Okay, calm down, his vitals are strong, and he is breathing on his own," the lady said.

Debo took the sedative and went to sit down. Whatever they gave him worked fast. He felt like he did in the shower; relaxed… every nerve ending was stress free. He had regained his composure but he was still worried. He wasn't going to stop worrying until Rex was at home safe and sound: Well, sound maybe but not too safe, someone managed to get to him. But how did they get into the yard, and how did they put the note on the doghouse? The only thing that would make any sense, is if whoever it was, drugged him and carried him over to the dog house and laid him in there. No one knew about *The Shell-Debo* but Mad-C, Patch, Rayass, and Joy. They are certainly not suspects. The vet came out from the backroom where he had wheeled Rex to on the gurney, and Debo stood up.

"What's wrong doc, is he going to be alright?" he asked. He was still worried, even though the veterinarian told him not to worry.

"Yes, Mister Jackson, he's going to be just fine."

"What did they do to him?" Debo asked.

"Apparently someone slipped him a sedative; enough to render him unconscious. They wanted him to be unconscious when you found him. What they gave him was similar to what my assistant gave you..., only a much stronger dose, but not enough to do any damage.

"But who?" Debo asked, very confused.

"It's definitely someone experience in that kind of medication; someone that's done it before. They had to be careful not to administer too much, because it could be lethal; causing a stroke or death."

Do you know anyone that deals in dog fights?" the vet asked Debo. "No, I can't say that I do."

"Well, sometimes in order to assure a dog loses a fight, the owner will put the sedative in the dog's food or water. Sometimes the owner will drug his own dog and then bet against him/her. Nobody would know they've been beat; very good method of cheating. I want to keep Rex for another day or tow to be safe. These drugs have certain side effects, but nothing too serious. I just want to keep an eye on him overnight."

"May I see him, Doc?"

"Sure you may, follow me," the vet said, leading him through the same door he and his assistant took Rex through. As they were walking down the long corridor, Debo saw what seemed to be beds like in a regular hospital for people.

"You put dogs in those beds?"

"Of course, we don't put them in cages or on slabs unless they are dead or almost in shock, and sometimes just to check on the animal's condition."

"Oh I see," Debo said. They arrived at a door off in a far corner of the hall.

"This will be us here," the vet said, and turned the knob. The door opened, and there was Rex lying on a table .

"Where is his bed?" Debo asked, as if he had caught the vet in a lie. "We are waiting to see if he is stable enough to be left alone. We don't know what happened prior to them giving him the drug. He may see something that will anger or upset him: Maybe something that could be related to the incident. The drug was somehow fed to him or injected into him."

"Rex wouldn't let anyone get close enough to put a needle in him," Debo informed the vet.

"Well..., there are more ways to inject something. They could have used a tranquilizer gun, or a dart pistol. Does he eat table food?"

"Yes."

"Okay, they could have won his trust by feeding him, and once he trusted them, they could have popped a needle in his rump." Debo was calm and more relaxed, he was also relieved. He would have to ask Shelly if she saw or heard anything last night.

"Do you want cash, or you want to bill me? I have a credit card on me now," Debo offered.

"I'll bill you when everything is all cleared up and you get him back. You can go home and rest assured that Rex is in good hands."

Debo kissed Rex on the top of his head and gave him his usual pat on his side. Rex's right front leg moved just a hair, and so did his tail. Debo thanked the vet, walked back down the corridor and out the front door.

CHAPTER 5

Debo was in the Navigator trying to determine who could have done this.

"Am I bringing trouble to where my wife and I lay our heads? Maybe I'd better let Shelly in on everything. Something is certainly not going right."

He didn't want to wait until something else went wrong, maybe something much worse. He didn't want to call her and ruin the rest of her day with bad news, so he decided to wait until she got home to discuss it with her.

Shelly had grown to love Rex, and that would disturb her. He tried to put this morning's events out of his mind. He couldn't remember whether or not he picked up the note that was attached to the dog house, nor did he remember locking the front door. He drove by the house before he went to Los Angeles and the note was still on the dog house. But he did get the one that was put in the mailbox and took it with him when he went to the vet. He checked the gate and the lock was on it. Nothing was broken or tampered with, but he did leave the front door open. He put the two notes in an envelope, locked the house, and decided he would take the notes to Sgt Billings of Parker Center P.D.

"Maybe he could come up with a clue, a name, something."

Possibly he has something on file about dog fight cases. It's a long-shot, but it was all he has to work with.

Debo was wondering if he should be driving after the sedative that the vet gave him for his nerves. He stopped and got a cup of black coffee and decided to check on the people in the car he nearly ran off the road. He wasn't sure if he ran the car off the road or not. It would probably be gone by the time he got there. Someone may have gotten the license number of his car and reported him as a hit and run. Billings couldn't fix that, this is San Diego. Maybe Mad-C can help him with it, he knows San Diego law enforcement. He called Mad-C at 2:50 pm .

"Ten till three, man the day is going fast," Debo thought, as he picked up the cellphone he had thrown in the passenger seat on the way to the vet and punched in Mad-C's number and nothing happened.

"Oh, come on," he said under his breath, then realized the battery fell out when he threw the phone in the seat next to him.

He replaced it and pressed the power button and it displayed the screen saver allowing him to make the call.

"Speak," a voice came on the phone demanding. "Don't tell me you're having a bad day too," Debo said.

"I'm having a little mix-up down at the dock; nothing I can't make go away. What's on your mind?" Mad-C curiously asked.

Debo knows that Mad-C is usually busy at this time of the day, in the middle of the week.

"Sorry to bother you, but I had a nightmare this morning and… " Mad-C cut him off in mid-sentence.

"We all have those, I'm having one myself," Mad-C roughly said. "I was about to… "

Mad-C stopped him again. "Did I ask you to tell me about it?"

"No," Debo answered.

"Okay, tell me about it."

"Okay, I was about to leave the house and… " Debo told him the whole story, and when he finished, Mad-C responded.

"I'll see what I can find out about what happened as far as the hit and run. I can straighten that out with the locals here. I'll offer to have the car repaired and you're good to go. How are things going out in Los Angeles?" Mad-C asked.

"Like clockwork, thanks, Big Bro, I'll be over there to kick it with you later," Debo promised.

"Okay, don't drink."

"I'd better not, I don't know how much of the sedative is still in my system. I'm driving all the way to LA," Debo said.

"Okay I'm having one myself, my nightmare may not end until I go kick some ass out at the dock. You need to be careful driving," Mad-C said. "Okay…, hey tell Ed not to forget about the cologne: It was some he had on that I love. He's supposed to get me a bottle."

"I'll remind him for you."

"Great, thanks," Debo said, and hung up. He was about to pull off when his cellphone played, "It's our anniversary."

"Yeah, Baby"

He knew it was Shelly because her name and number appeared on the screen. Besides, she made it clear that she didn't want anyone else to have that ringtone.

"D-Angelo, what is this note supposed to be saying?"

"Oh, God no.., not another note! They put another one in the mailbox?" he thought to himself.

"What does it say baby?" he asked, then held his breath because he didn't want to know what it said,

"It says, 'Had to make a ROD, I'll be bank tonight,'" Shelly read. "I wrote that."

"I guess you did; it was on the kitchen table."

Debo replayed what she had just read to him and started to laugh, but Shelly wasn't laughing.

"I was…, I mean I'll explain it to you this evening, sweetheart," Debo said.

"Where is Rex…, is he with you?"

"Yeah, something like that," he answered. "What does that mean?"

"I'll explain everything to you when I get home," Debo promised.

He didn't want to lie to her, he's done enough of that for too long. He'll have to make a decision before he gets home. He didn't want her to worry or know what was going on, but now she has to know. "Stop lying! Stop lying!" kept playing in his head as he pressed his index and middle fingers to his temples in an attempt to suppress the throbbing headache that the thought of continuously lying to her gave him.

"Honey... honey, are you there?" Shelly asked. "Yes baby, I was thinking. What were you saying?"

"I was asking you about what time you will be home?"

"Oh, about ten this evening," Debo said.

"Okay, I'll see you then."

"Okay, bye baby... Hey, Shell, Shell?"

"Yes?"

"I love you."

"I love you too baby," Shelly said, and their call ended.

He stopped at a 7-11 on Broadway and (D) Street and got some coffee. "That was some powerful stuff, poor Rex had to feel good for a while," he thought to himself.

Debo arrived in Los Angeles at 6:45 pm and stopped by Billings' to give him the notes that were left at his house and the citation he got the last time he was there.

"Jackson, I know what you're up against, I deal with it all the time. You need to be very careful, you're getting too big, you weren't as big then as you are now.

Back when I met you, you were small-time and the bigger you get, the more dangerous the game gets. If anything else out of the ordinary happens again, I'm sure you'll let me know."

"Yes, Sergeant, I will..., in fact, you'll be the first to know."

"Okay, it's late, Jackson, get out of here so I can go home,"

Billings demanded. "Oh, and Jackson..."

"Yeah?"

"Don't worry, I'll get to the bottom of this," Billings promised. But, this didn't happen in LA, although there is a chance that someone from Los Angeles found out about *The Shell-Debo* and where it is. Debo made a mental note to check the rear surveillance tapes from the Explorer. He and Billings said goodbye and he left. He was on his way to Beverly Hills to go over some paperwork in his office. He took First Street to Los Angeles Street, and from there to Wilshire and Seventh Streets, then west on to Robertson Blvd. He Was still feeling woozy from the sedative, so he didn't chance taking the freeway. It should have worn off before now, but the vet's assistant gave him a nice dose and he wanted to be safe so he took the streets. He stopped at another 7-11, for more coffee and sat there a minute to give the strong brown liquid a chance to work. He got behind his office and looked in the surveillance monitor that was mounted in the dash. He saw a red light in the front grill of a car that was pulling into the alley behind him. He didn't stop at his usual parking space, he kept going until he came to the end of the alley.

"Oh shit, what's this?" he asked himself.

He saw two men inside the car, but he couldn't make out who it was "Oh no..., not more crooked-ass cops. Damn, is everybody on to us?" he thought.

The two men in the car behind him turned on their siren once, to make sure Debo acknowledged them. He approached Olympic Blvd and pulled over. The two guys got out of their car. One was wearing a sling on his right arm. Debo saw who it was when they got out. It was agents Dick Patch and Monty Rayass who started walking toward the Explorer.

"Jackson, put your hand where I can see them, and I'm not going to say it again..., move it," Patch said.

Debo was confused, mad, and tired. And had already had a bad enough day as it is. He wasn't for any bullshit but he did as he was told.

When they came up to the Explorer, they ordered him out of the car again and told him to put his hands behind his back.

"What the hell is going on here?"

"Look, Mister Jackson, please just follow my lead," Dick Patch authoritatively said.

Debo put his hands behind his back after he took his time getting out of the Explorer. Rayass cuffed his hands together and placed him inside the Maverick. Patch drove their Maverick and Rayass drove Debo's Explorer.

When they got to a side street, Dick Patch said, "As soon as I can, I'll get those things off you." "I would hope so," Debo protested.

They rode in silence for about three or four blocks, when Debo said, "What's going on, Patch?"

"Someone is watching you and this is the only way I could let you know until we can find out who it is and why."

Debo cursed under his breath. "I hope those things aren't too tight or uncomfortable."

"As a matter of fact, they are," Debo cried. "Hold on, big guy… we're almost there."

"Almost where?"

"Here," Patch told him, and turned into an underground parking structure. He saw his explorer sitting next to a brick wall, with Rayass getting out of it. Dick Patch got out of the Maverick and looked over at his partner, then looked at Debo and let him out of the back seat. He looked around, then took the cuffs off him.

"Sorry about that," he told Debo.

Debo was expecting Rayass to emerge from the Explorer eating something.

"Okay, what gives?" Debo asked.

"Someone is watching you and Write," Patch told him. "Who is someone?"

"We don't know who it is yet, but it's not DEA."

"Could it be the FBI?" Debo asked, with concern written all over his face. "I'm not too sure, I don't think so," Patch said.

"'I don't know… I'm not sure… I don't think so' What the hell am I paying you for? That's a lot of money for you not to know shit." Debo wanted to yell, however he said it in a low tone of voice so no one could hear him if someone was close by.

"Has anything strange or unusual happened lately?" Patch asked.

"You know, that's funny, Billings just asked me the same thing. As a matter of fact, yes," Debo answered.

"Wanna tell us about it?" Rayass asked.

"Well it talks," Debo said to himself as if the sky would fall. And from the sling on his arm, it looked like something had fallen and it fell on him. "What happened to you?" he asked Rayass.

"I was injured on a case."

"I guess this is, 'everybody have a bad week,' week…, huh?" Debo asked. He told them about what had happened earlier, and how strange it was. Because no one knew about *The Shell-Debo* but him, Mad-C, Agents Dick Patch, Monty Rayass, and Joy.

"We think it's a drug cartel, but we'll know for sure in a day or so. In the meantime, be extremely careful," Patch advised.

"He is careful, come over here and look at this," Rayass told Patch, as they all walked over to the Explorer.

"Go ahead…, look inside," Rayass told Patch.

Patch put his head through the open window on the driver's side and saw the video monitor with a picture of the back wall. "I could see everything behind me on the way over here," Rayass continued.

"That's good to have, but someone can get around that: They can follow you from any angle of the car, from the sides, the front, or the back. Don't forget about helicopters; you are in a high-stakes game where they use high stakes equipment. They have real fun shit to play with, Mr Jackson," Patch said.

"Yes, I know."

"Okay, don't worry we'll be on it. I'll give you a call soon," Patch told Debo.

"There could be a fat bonus in it for you," Debo told the chubby DEA agent.

"Okay, Mr Jackson…, we're out of here," Patch said.

"Take care of that arm, and stop eating in the shower," Debo said, and laughed.

They all left the underground parking structure and went their own separate way. Once on the road, Debo thought about what Mad-C said about something being wrong down at the dock. He didn't tell Patch or Rayass because he wasn't sure what it was. But it made Mad-C need a drink, and he didn't drink too much during the day. Whatever it is must have been pretty serious. Debo picked up the phone and called Mad-C.

"You must love the hell out of me, don't you, Debo? Okay, lay it on me," Mad-C said, with a smile on his face that Debo couldn't see.

"I have some very important news for you, but I can't discuss it over the phone. I'm in Beverly Hills at the office running through some paperwork. I'll be there as soon as I'm finished. I have to stop by the house first and explain about Rex. So, I'll see you at about... say 10:00-10:30 ... That's not too late is it?"

"If it's that important, no it's not too late. I'm sure that if it could wait until tomorrow, then you would let it wait until then. No, come on by."

"Okay, thanks, see you then," Debo said and ended the call.

He finished at the office, then called Joy, Freddy, Pauline, and Jeffery to see how things were going, while he was still in town.

"Everything is everything," they told him. He thanked them for doing such a good job, then called Joy.

"Hey, Little Sis, what's going on on your end?" He was more at ease than he had been all day.

"Oh, Nothing, Tammy and Sheila are on me about what their Uncle Debo is getting them for Christmas."

"What did you tell them?"

"I told them they would have to ask you or wait until Christmas. They know I can't tell them; they do that to me every year; ask me hoping I'll spill the beans without thinking. They know that every Christmas they get something. They just wanna make sure they are getting something," Joy said. "What do you think would be good for them?" Debo asked.

"I don't know, get them some running shoes. The way they run around here they probably ran the ones they have out by now."

"Yeah, they almost tackled me the other day."

"They had an early day off from school and they were on their way to practice with some friends," Joy explained.

"How is their college fund looking?" "Wonderful."

"Do they have any money in the bank?" "No, not really."

"I'll get them a checking and savings account for Christmas; Put some change in their pockets."

Debo's idea of change is like $50K a piece, $25K checking, and $25K savings each, in care of Joy of course.

"Okay little one, I've got them covered. If you need anything let me know, I'm headed back to the house. I have to take care of some business."

"How is it going with the two new guys?" Joy inquired. She knows not to say too much because Debo warned them about talking freely about business over home phones, cellphones, phone booths, office phones 'ANY' phone. "Everything's okay so far, little one."

"Okay, Big Bro.., see you soon and be careful."

"Will do," Debo assured her.

Debo is her heart, she's always concerned about him. He hung up the phone and headed for home. The effect of the sedative had worn off so he went on and got on the freeway and decided to call the vet.

"Hey, how's my guy?" Debo asked.

"He's fine, he came around just about two hours after you left; no side effects as of yet."

"Okay, keep up the good work," Debo said and hung up.

Now his only thought was whether or not he should tell Shelly about everything. If someone is in fact watching him, then they have to be watching the house. Something didn't feel right Debo's hair started to tingle on the back of his neck. Something was out of place, maybe he was the one having the side effects from the sedative. He dismissed it and headed home. He was about to exit the Freeway when he felt a bump on the right side of the Explorer, but he kept driving. Maybe he ran over something in the road. He exited the off-ramp and felt the car wobbling, and it was low on the right rear side.

"Oh hell, a flat tire, well I'm glad I'm almost home," he thought to himself.

He pulled up into the carport and got out of the car and looked at the right rear tire and it was indeed flat. He looked down at it and saw that there was a hole the size of a quarter in the side of the tire. He looked closer and the rim had a big gash in it. "That's a bullet hole, this is not looking good at all," he thought to himself.

Someone had shot at his car on the freeway and tried to kill him. He changed the tire and went inside the house.

Shelly decided to give him a minute to settle in before she asked about Rex and the note he left. He washed the oil and dirt from the tire off his hands and looked in the mirror and decided against telling Shelly just yet; he has had a bad enough day as it was. "Boy, you sure make a home smell worth coming to, Miss Chef," he told Shelly.

"Why thank you darling," she said and blushed.

"You are very welcome," and to his surprise, he blushed also.

She had fixed boiled lobster-tails, crab-legs shrimp, wild rice, and crackers, with hot melted butter and a homemade nutrition drink. Debo and Shelly never discussed family business during dinner; all that took place in the living room or the bedroom. He helped in the kitchen as usual. He believes that the cook shouldn't have to do the dishes or clean the kitchen, but like a good wife, she insisted on helping.

"Okay, Mister Jackson, let's have it, what's the big mystery?" she asked, with an uncertain look on her face.

"Oh…, Rex must have eaten something last night that didn't agree with him. It scared the living daylights out of me. I must have been nervous when I wrote the note; some spelling, huh?" he amiably said.

"Well, as long as he's alright."

"Yes, he's fine, I took him to the vet and he wanted to keep him overnight to make sure he's okay."

Debo was beginning to feel guilty about all the lies: He kept telling himself that it was for her good. Or was it really for his?

"I have to go see my boss in a few; something's wrong out at the shipping dock," he continued.

"How long will you be gone?"

"Not long, you can wait up for me if you want."

"Okay, I'll hold out for as long as I can until you get back."

"Oh baby…, I'm sorry, how was your day?" he asked.

"That's quite alright, I did some shopping. And do you know I had to go to three different stores to find the crab-legs and lobster-tails? But otherwise, my day was okay…, busy, but okay, thanks for asking."

"You're welcome… at least your day wasn't as crazy as mine was. I'll be back in a little while."

"Alright, see you soon," she said, and Debo was out the door.

How much could happen in a day? Debo's day was an adventure, and there was more to come. He got to Mad-C's house in less than fifteen minutes. He knocked on the door and Ed let him in.

"Working late, Ed?" Debo asked him.

Ed usually turns in early because his days are busy. "Mister Write told me you were coming and requested that I wait up for you, Sir. Mister Write put my rest and my sleep in your hands this evening, Mister Jackson," Ed growled.

"Sorry, I tried to make it as soon as I could."

"I thought I heard voices out here," Mad-C said as he entered the foyer. "Hey fella," Debo greeted him.

"Hey, Mister nightmare, what was so important that it couldn't wait and kept everybody up all night?" Mad-C asked.

"Seems like I am keeping everybody up, Shell is waiting up too. How about that drink? I think I'm ready for it now," Debo said.

"Ed, bring a bottle, and two glasses out here for us. Bring it to the dining room; we'll talk in there. Take the rest of the evening off I'll see Mister Jackson out when he's ready to leave," Mad-C said.

"Thank you, Mister Write," Ed said and left. "Now, what's on your mind?"

"Oh…, just more nightmares," Debo answered.

"This is become the story of your life," Mad-C told him. "I ran into Dick Patch and Monty Rayass on the way to the office this afternoon. He said, 'that someone was watching me and he believes it's a Miami crime figure.' He didn't say Miami but that's all I can figure. I don't know if whoever it is knows about you, or how much they know if they do. I don't even know how much they know about me at this point."

"Debo, what the hell are we paying those idiots for? They get $50K more per month and they don't know who or what's on our asses. Call that dumb son-of-a-bitch tomorrow and tell him I said…," Debo cut him off, to say…

"He's going to call me in the morning with additional information. I'm guessing that they have to dig into their database and see who's pissing us off or who's pissed at us. Someone put a big hole in my tire coming out here. I changed it before I came," Debo told him.

"That's too close, you need a vacation," Mad-C suggested. "I can't, I have people out in LA to think of."

"What about, Michelle?" Mad-C asked.

"I'm still fighting with the thought of telling her."

"I think it's high time you let her in on what's going on."

Ed entered with the drinks and poured each one of the two men their own troubles, set the bottle down, and said…

"Will that be all, Sir?"

"Yes, Ed thanks…, goodnight."

"Goodnight, Sir, Mister Jackson, goodnight to you also; Oh, by the way, I have an early Christmas present for you, Mr Jackson.

Ed extended his right hand and in it was a twelve-ounce bottle of cologne; the cologne Debo wanted and was dying to get some of.

"Merry Christmas, sir," Ed told him.

"Thank you, Ed," Debo said with satisfaction and gratitude in his heart.

"You're very welcome, Sir…, goodnight," Ed said and left the two men by themselves.

"Now where was I?"

Debo rambled through his mind to remember what he was about to say, but his eyes were on the cologne box. He read where it said, 'Shipped from France, imported from Italy'. And under it were the words, *The Cologne Experts* "$250 per ounce. "DAMN!!!"

Debo screamed.

"Yeah, $3,000 isn't bad for a bottle of good cologne," Mad-C said. "Oh yeah…, now I know what it was I was about to say. You told me today that something happened at the dock," Debo remembered.

"I don't know how it could possibly tie into what you are talking about, or even if it does tie into what you are talking about. But I came up ten kilos short on one of my deliveries today…, and that's a lot of damn dope, and money" Mad-C cursed.

"Did you get it back?"

"No, and everything is bolted to that ship. There is no way it could have fallen off."

"Check your cargo from now on for bugs, and check the crew on the ship to see if anyone is new on board. Bad things are starting to happen. I'll see what Dick Patch has for us in the morning: Drugs, drug money, and drug talk moves fast. I'll also check with Billings," Debo said.

"Debo, do you think it could be someone on the outside has gotten to one or more of the people we have working for us?" Mad-C asked.

"I'll look into it, right now anybody is worth looking into."

Debo thought to himself, 'If it is, please don't let it be Joy.'

"My baby is waiting up for me, I'd better get back. I'll call you tomorrow."

"I'll be waiting for your call," Mad-C told him.

"I'll let myself out."

"Alright…, later."

"Oh yeah…, what happened with that hit-and-run?" "Thanks for reminding me."

Mad-C went into his study and came back with an envelope.

"I took care of the legal part of it for you. That's the bill for the lady's car and the light post she pulled out of the ground," Mad-C said. "Should I take a deep breath before I open it? Thanks, Big Bro," Debo said and left.

He sat in the Explorer and opened the envelope. There were two envelopes inside one large envelope. He opened one and pulled out a slip of paper that read, "Crash Auto Repair." It was an invoice for repairs to a 20015 Toyota Corolla estimated at $5,462.38 "Damn, she can buy a whole new car for that. Maybe that's what she had in mind," he thought.

He took the other envelope out and read what was written. It said, "San Diego Maintenance and Fixtures Department, City of San Diego." And that was a bill for another $2,000; not to mention the bill that the vet is sending. It's probably going to cost about $1,000 for Rex. Just waking up this morning cost him close to $10,000… what a life. He also could have been looking at some jail time for the hit and run, plus whatever fines the judge may have imposed upon him.

"Boy, I would have traded the day with Shell in a heartbeat.

Lord let me make it home without anything else going wrong," he prayed. He returned home and Shelly was waiting up for him as she promised. He was only gone an hour and ten minutes. He had taken too much time; actually more time than he realized reading the bills from the accident.

CHAPTER 6

Debo slid the tape cartridge from the console in the dash of the Explorer and took it inside his office in Beverly Hills. Just as he was about to sit down, someone knocked on the door. He sat down, pulled the forty-five from its holster and put it in his lap.

"Come on in, is open."

The door opened, and it was Dick Patch without agent Rayass.

"Hey, Jackson..., how's San Diego this year; and those San Diego Chargers?" Patch teased.

"Just the man I want to see, you got anything for me?"

"Yeah, I've got a lot for you. The people watching you are not a drug cartel. But get this… they used to be gang members way back ten years ago or more. It seems as though they're involved in some way deeper shit now than they were then," Patch reported.

"That was before I got started. How big are they now, and what do they want?" Debo asked Patch.

"I'm gonna lay it on the line for you, Jackson. You see, it seems that Mister Write killed a couple of guys that were associated with some powerful people back then. Those people are the ones watching you and Write. I'm sure he told you that he ran off with $150K in drugs and cash after he killed them. The word is that you work for him, or that you are a big part of his organization and his empire."

"Must be the asshole that shot out my tire yesterday... and I was in the car," Debo stressed.

"You were shot at yesterday?" Patch cried.

"Yeah, just as I got off the freeway going home. They might know where Mister Write live because I went over there and they could have followed me..., sit over there."

Debo pointed to a large office chair and Patch went over and sat in it while Debo sat behind his desk and reached inside the drawer and got the remote to the CD player and pressed play. All they saw was traffic; lots and lots of traffic; all coming up from behind the Explorer. He checks those tapes on a daily basis; everything from yesterday is on this particular tape.

They were about twenty-minutes into the tape, when Patch said, "Stop!!"

"What... did you see something?" "I sure did, the green Maverick I was driving that day in the alley when I pulled you over.

What happened to my light? I only see a red light, where is the blue one!!!" Patch yelled.

"Look, Patch..., help me find out who's following me. We'll deal with the light later, or you can deal with it. Pay attention, Patch."

"Okay, but don't let me forget to fix that light." They watched the tape for a while longer . "Wait!!!" Patch screamed.

"I hope you see something this time."

"How many times did you go to 7-11?" Patch asked.

"Twice, I think; once when I left the vet, and once in LA," Debo told him.

"Rewind back to the one you went to in San Diego when you left the vet; it is in San Diego, isn't it?"

"Yes, Patch, that's where I live." Debo pressed rewind and let the tape move in reverse.

"Okay, stop..., back up about a frame." Debo pressed slow rewind.

"There, you see it?"

"See what?" Debo asked.

Agent: Dick Patch has a trained eye for spotting things out of the ordinary. "The black Mercedes, now go forward to the second 7-11." Debo did as Patch instructed. "There it is again at the second 7- in Los Angeles. This guy followed you to the vet and everywhere else you went"

"I went to see Billings," Debo said.

"Yeah, he probably thinks you went to report him following you."

"Yeah, technically I did. See if you can make out the license plate number," Debo said.

"Yeah, I've got… give me something to write with and a piece of paper."

"Trained eye, I know," Debo growled.

"Well, I'll be damn; he drugged my dog, waited until I found him, followed me to the vet, then to Los Angeles, and probably back here."

"Is that it?" Patch asked when the tape stopped. "As far as today, it is." "Does that camera run while the car is off?" "Yes…, why?"

"Leave it on all night so we can see if someone is parked outside your house. Park it where it can record the street. There was nothing behind you on the freeway upon your return, but that doesn't mean no one was following you. Whoever it was couldn't have hit the side of your tire from behind… no way. There had to be someone off to the side of the freeway. And more than likely, they knew you were going to be on that road at that time. Besides, they do have their ways. Big money does big things," Patch said.

"Yeah…, well get out of here and make my money do big things, I have phone calls to make," Debo told the agent.

"Okay, I'll see what I can get from these plates."

"What did the plate say?"

"They are personalized plates."

Patch looked at the paper he had written the information from the license plate on and said… "PLAYER-5."

"Okay, PLAYER-5… got it." "I'll contact you tomorrow," Patch said.

"And no more of that handcuff bullshit," Debo said. Agent Patch laughed and walked out.

"I'll wait until tomorrow to fill Mad-C in. After all, there's no use going to him with only half of the information. But, on the other hand, if it was the gang members, Mad-C wouldn't know how to contact the other three, that was ten years ago. Maybe Billings can find out something through Culver City Police Department, or Santa Monica. Mad-C told me 'that the day he was robbed, it was in Venice, CA'. But the gang members that did it were staying in a house in Santa Monica where he had gone and shot the two gang members."

Debo has to call Billings to get some names and see if he could match them with the DEA files. Since the gang members are either a drug cartel or are involved with one now, he figured DEA would have something on file. He called Sgt Billings at Parker Center to have him check Venice, Santa Monica, and Los Angeles police departments to see if they can come up with something.

"Hey, Bob, what's up in crime these days?" Debo asked . He called Billings on his cell phone.

"It's hell, as usual, Jackson, what's up?"

"I may have a tip on who drugged Rex and shot at me."

"I'm listening," Billings said.

Debo didn't bring up the ten kilos that *deliberately* walked off Mad-C's ship, it was none of his business anyway.

"I need you to check to see if you can come up with some names for me."

"Shoot," Billings said.

"These guys were gang members ten years ago. They mugged Mr Write in Venice, CA. Their gang headquarters was a house in Santa Monica. I don't know the exact location yet, but I'll check with Mr. Write, he would know, I'm sure he'll remember."

"Okay, anything else?" Billings asked.

"Yeah..., check with Patch; see if he has anything. He's supposed to call me tomorrow with some information. If you haven't spoken with him by then, I'll have him give you a call," Debo assured him.

"No problem," Billings said.

"Okay, have a good one, Bob," Debo told him. "Will do, Debo."

Robert (Bob) Billings, only calls him by his nickname when Debo calls him Bob: Otherwise, they use Sergeant Billings and Mister Jackson, or Billings just calls him, Jackson.

Debo picked Rex up at 10:30 Saturday morning. The vet said that it was okay for him to go home. Debo, Shelly, and Rex always went to Santa Monica on Saturdays and walk along the Promenade and the Santa Monica Pier.

"Is it okay for him to travel?" Debo asked.

"Yeah, in fact, I would recommend it. Take him out for some air and walk him, it'll do him some good; Stretch his legs and let him exercise his lungs."

"Alright, just send me the bill," Debo said.

"Okay, Mister Jackson, if anything comes up give me a call."

"Sure thing," Debo said, and with that, he and Rex left.

It was a warm, sunny day at the beach, and everything was going great, even though it was almost winter. California has funny weather; everyone believes that the people in Washington change the weather, the time, and maybe even the flow of the ocean. They cause floods, hurricanes, and all kinds of natural disasters. Every time Debo thought about it, he became sick in his stomach. But that particular Saturday was warm and sunny... whoever was responsible; Debo, Shelly, and Rex would enjoy it. Debo wanted to go to "Ocean's Finest" to eat. But he thought better of it and said in his mind to forget it; knowing what he knows and not wanting Shelly to know, he probably would never enjoy himself eating there again. "Why did agent Dick Patch pick this particular place that night? He said, 'that he was watching me and concluded that this was my favorite spot.' Well, now it's ruined," Debo thought to himself.

"Let's go to the spot where we eat that wonderful shrimp," Shelly suggested.

"Here goes another lie; even coming out to the beach is no fun anymore. And knowing that the DEA agents know about it, he decided against it. "Honey, we just had seafood for dinner. Why don't we go over by the rides and have some good old-fashioned southern fried chicken, and some coleslaw, biscuits, and French fries," he suggested.

"I just gave Rex some oxtail bones, if he eats chicken bones will they hurt him? You might have to watch what you give him," Shelly advised.

"I don't think they'll hurt him, he's fine now."

"Well…, go see if they'll let him in there, I don't think they will."

"Probably not, I'll just go order and we can go over there on that grassy area," Debo told her, pointing to a picnic-looking area. Rex loves chicken bones, especially fried chicken bones: He loves the grease.

"Okay, that's fine with me… but hurry… I'm starved," Shelly said.
"Okay, but after we finish eating, I need to talk to you."

"While I walk off some of this food, I hope," she wondered out loud.
"Yeah sure, I have to walk Rex anyway… doctor's orders." They got their meals and sat down to eat, and even though it was what Debo suggested, the fried chicken just wouldn't go down. It felt like every time he tried to swallow a bite it would come right back up. The nervousness wouldn't let it stay down.

He thought he'd better go ahead and tell her about everything. He can't keep lying to her, misleading her, and expecting their marriage to work. Somehow, someday it will all come out and it seems as though it is about to come out anyway. They usually don't talk during a meal, but Debo couldn't hold it in any longer. He had to tell her; if he doesn't tell her now he never will. Then it's goodbye marriage because the trust would be gone. He started talking about Christmas since it so close.

"Hey baby, it's always sunny on Christmas Day, huh?"

"Yeah, because we have a Sunny Southern California around this time of year," Shelly said and laughed.

Debo laughed with her, and Rex yawned. "See, even Rex thinks so," she said.

"Baby, what do you want for Christmas?" he asked her.

"Just my man, and his heart, his honesty, his understanding, and all the love in the world from him."

"And I'm gonna make sure you have all of those things because you deserve it all."

He looked at her, with her bright eyes gleaming in the morning sun, her lovely complexion, and her soft voice. He thought he was going to cry; he thought the tears that had built up inside of him were going to spill out and start running down his cheeks, and one did. He didn't know it until she took her thumb, kissed it, and wiped the tear from his cheek.

"WOW!!! Did I do that?" she asked.

'Yes, you did..., when you married me, when you came into my life. Every time I deceive you, every time I lie to you it tears me apart inside. Oh my god if she only knew. So much pain, so many lies, what would she think of me, what would she do? Would she even trust me again, would she ever believe me again, would my word ever be my bond in her eyes again?" he thought to himself.

"Yeah, you did do that. Hey, how about a vacation?" he suggested. "Now, that sounds wonderful, where to?" "Any place you wanna go." "How about Maui."

"Why Maui?"

"I've always wanted to go to Maui."

"Maui it is." 'Maybe I'll wait until after the trip to Maui: NO... I've put it off far too long, and at the rate things are going, it might not wait until the trip to Maui. After I tell her what I have to tell her, there might not be a trip to Maui or anyplace else for that matter.'"

"How's the weather out there this time of year?" he asked.

"Oh, I don't know, but I'm sure we can check with the weather service," Shelly said.

Debo remembered Mad-C suggesting that he take a vacation, that would leave a couple of months to clear this mess up with whoever they were dealing with; whoever it is pushing buttons.

"Baby, I have something I need to tell you," Debo said. When he said it, he swallowed and felt a lump in his throat.

"Yes, sweetheart, what is it, bad or good? If it's bad, save it, I'm having a good day and I don't want it ruined with bad news."

"No, I've saved it for too long." "Then it is bad!"

He took her chin between his thumb and index finger and turned her face toward him.

"Oh, this is serious, give me a chance to hold on," she said, and shifted her body around to face him.

Now he has her full attention.

"Baby, it's all or nothing, I have to get this out now, or I'm sure I'll regret it later if I don't. Okay, here goes: Baby, I've been lying to you for years," he confessed.

"About what, D-Angelo, you never lied to me?"

"Yes…, and I've been doing it for too long. I don't… "

He looked out at the ocean and wished he could just throw himself in, or at least had the nerve to.

"The office in Beverly Hills where I work is owned by a man by the name of, Charles Write, and…,"

"And what," she said, cutting him off. She was growing impatient. "Charles Write is a major drug dealer baby."

When he said that, his heart dropped, and he noticed that his shirt was wet with perspiration from nervousness.

"I don't work in cellular communications, I never have. I run drugs for Charles Write, and I've been doing it for the last ten years." He looked at her to see the expression on her face, and to his surprise, she didn't look surprised at all.

"Now, let me tell you a secret; I know, I've always known."

He felt a bigger lump in his throat. After he swallowed it he said, "But, why didn't you say anything?"

"Because I figured you kept it from me or tried to keep it from me to protect me. D-Angelo, I work with computers, I checked out Write or Charles Write on the computer and found out that the company he own, he uses it to ship drugs and funnel money to and from interstate drug cartels."

"How long have you known?"

"I've known for close to two-years."

"Two years!!!" he screamed, then looked around to see if anyone was watching or listening .

"I'm sure it was hard for you to keep it from me this long. I know that you couldn't stand lying to me…, what made you tell me?

"I got tired of lying, and now there are some difficulties." "Is that why you suggested the vacation?"

"That's part of it."

"What kind of difficulties?"

"Some guys that Write had a confrontation with ten years ago are after him and they are trying to get to him through me."

"So, what now?" She wasn't very happy at all. "Now, I have to get these guys off my tail."

"I'm going to ask you something, D-Angelo, and please don't lie to me."

"Shell, I will never lie to you again, ever."

"Do they know where we live?"

"Yes."

"Have they been to the house?"

"I'm sure they have, but I've never seen them there."

"What happened to Rex the other day, I know my cooking isn't that bad?"

"No, baby it isn't: They somehow managed to get to him and gave him some kind of sedative." He told her everything, even about the car he ran off the road.

"Is that why you really had to go over to see Mr Write the other night; the night I told you that I would wait up for you?"

"Yes, baby, it is."

"That's why I waited up for you, I knew something was wrong. I saw you changing the tire on the car, then I went out there and saw a hole in the tire. It was a bullet hole, wasn't it?"

"Yes, sweetheart, someone shot at me on my way home."

"From now on I'll need you to confide in me, tell me everything and anything…. do you understand me, D-Angelo Jackson?" "Yes, baby, I understand, and thank you for your understanding."

"Is there anything else? If there is anything that I can help you with, I'm here for you."

"But, baby…, I can't and won't involve you in any of this."

"Sweetheart, you already have, I'm your wife remember.

Besides, I have become accustomed to the lifestyle you have provided for me, and you took your life and freedom in your hands to provide that lifestyle, which was a very big chance. I will not turn my back on you, nor walk out on you for making that decision. However; in the very near future, I would consider retiring if I were you."

"I already have, baby.., I already have," he said.

"It's late, I'm getting chilly, let's go home," Shelly said, wrapping her coat around her shoulders.

"You got it, baby..., Rex, you ready to go!!!" he yelled.

Rex jumped up and ran over to where Debo and Shelly were and kissed him on the hand, then kissed Shelly on her arm. Debo gave him a pat on his side and they all left the beach. Rex didn't ride in the back of the Explorer. Debo was in the driver's seat, Shelly was snuggled up against him, and Rex was in the passenger's seat with the window halfway down. Shelly was asleep before they were halfway home. Debo wondered if agents Patch and Rayass were at the beach keeping an eye on them in case someone tried something. He was in the habit of not taking the Glock-45 when Shelly was in the car.

"My baby really loves me; I mean she kept all that inside her for this long; my little secrets. She is a very beautiful woman indeed, the best a man can ask for. If anything; anything at all were to ever happen to her, I will go to no end to get at whoever caused her any amount of harm; mental or physical," he thought to himself.

They arrived home shortly after four that Saturday afternoon. Debo pulled up into the carport and got out, then Rex and Shelly slid out on the same side that Rex had made his exit. She waited for Debo to put Rex in the backyard. After Rex was put up, he picked Shelly up and carried her into the house, kicked the door shut with his foot, and their day ended.

SUNDAY MORNING, 8:00 A.M.

Debo is on the phone with Mad-C.

"Hey, Big Guy, I'm about to call Patch in about an hour or so to see if he has anything for us," Debo said.

As soon he said it, his call waiting alert signaled him that another call was coming in on the other line.

"Hold on a sec," he told Mad-C, and switched over to the other line. After a few minutes, he came back on the line that Mad-C was waiting on and said,

"Yeah, that's him on the other line. I'll get back to you as soon as I see what he has for us." "Where are you?" Patch asked Debo. "At home, why?" "I need to meet with you right away."

"Can it wait, I just got up?"

"Not if you want what I've got for you, I don't think it should wait," Patch told him.

Mad-C wanted answers and he was tired of waiting.

"Okay, give me a few hours; meet me at my office in Beverly Hills in about three hours… say 1:00 pm."

"Okay…, 1:00 pm it is," Patch confirmed.

He thought it would be a good idea to take another road home. He called Mad-C back to let him know that Patch wanted to meet him at the office.

"Hey, it's me, I may have something. That was Patch, he said, 'I should get out there right away.' I told him that I would meet him at the office in Beverly Hills. I'm leaving here in about twenty-five minutes I'll fill you in on what I get."

"Okay, I'll be expecting your call," Mad-C said and they hung up. Debo got in the shower and was only there a minute when Shelly knocked on the shower door.

"Hey, honey, want something to eat?" she asked him.

She couldn't see him because the bathroom was engulfed in steam. The soap he used made her go crazy; it had a fresh, tingly, sweet, masculine smell to it: Shelly loved it.

"No, sweetheart, I don't have time, some coffee would be fine," he told her from somewhere in the steam.

"Okay, I'll bring it to you."

"Put it on the kitchen table for me please, I'll be out there, thanks." He's now able to leave the house and honestly tell his wife what was going on; It felt so good being honest. He went out to the kitchen to get the coffee and Shelly put on a sad face.

"Do you have to go now, baby? You just got up; can't it wait a few hours?" Shelly protested.

"Baby, I want to get this mess over with as soon as possible so I can retire. I have a retirement and a wonderful trip to Maui coming with my gorgeous wife. I'll be right back sweetheart."

"Give me some sugar and be careful," she told him.

Debo loved that sweet, soft, sexy tone in her voice. She was nervous and worried. She always worries about him when he goes out, especially when he doesn't come home some nights. But now, it's okay to let him know that she worries about him. He didn't know that she waited up every night worried and praying that he would come home safe and alive. He didn't know that she couldn't eat for days at a time. He thought she was dieting and that's what she let him think. Women are always watching their weight.

"Give me a call if anything goes wrong."

"Okay, baby..., I will," he said, and kissed her sweet lips on the way out.

He would have taken Rex with him, but he's the only source of protection she had while he was gone. He knew that Rex wouldn't let anything happen to her.

"What you got for me?" Debo asked Patch.

"Well, I've got a few names... Johnny Morris, Randy Carlyle, and a guy by the name of, Robert (Big Boy) Cruse. These guys ran with two other guys by the name of Mack Rodgers, and Laurence Brown. Some construction workers discovered the last two; Rodgers and Brown shot to death in and buried in the backyard of an abandoned house in Santa Monica, California ten years ago while renovating and remodeling the place.

Apparently, someone tried to bury their bodies but the rain washed the dirt away over the years. Whoever buried them used a very large, thick, roofing plastic... the kind used under tar paper. Get this; they were buried with their wallets, money, and jewelry still on them. Information obtained from FBI files stated that one was buried with a sawed-off shotgun, and the other one was buried with an automatic handgun. One was shot through the head, and the other was shot in the chest. Both were shot with a very large caliber weapon. Among the dead are, Mr Mack Rodgers, and Mr Laurence Brown; Ever heard of them?" Patch asked.

"No, I really can't say that I have," Debo answered.

Mad-C told Debo about what happened in Venice ten years ago. But, Debo wasn't going to let agent Patch know that Mad-C was the one who killed those two guys. If the two agents decided to pull out someday, they might decide to get Mad-C for two counts of murder; shit happens.

"What about, Morris, and Carlyle, oh and the other one, Cruse?"

"They are all big boys now into bigger things with a more deadly gang. They got themselves involved with an underground drug cartel here in the States. A guy named Gregory Johnson?"

"Yeah, he's a pretty large fish, I've heard all about him."

"Well, I'd hate to be the one going up against him for any reason whatsoever: Bad news that one, take my word for it. If you or Write are up against him, be careful. No.., be extremely careful," Patch advised.

"You know, that's the same thing Shell said to me this morning, as I was leaving the house. Do I look clumsy or something?"

He decided not to let Patch know that Shelly knew anything. The less he knows, the less he can do.

"Where are the three of them now?" Debo asked.

"Underground, they only come out when there's work to be done."

"Yeah, like damn near killing me and my dog. Is that all?" Debo asked.

"No, what do I get for Mr John, that's extra isn't it?" Patch asked.

"Yeah, it's part of the agreement, I'll throw in the extra $25K Good enough?"

"Good enough..., Oh, and one more thing, Mr Jackson.

These guys are wanted by the DEA and the FBI: I'm saying that to say, if anything happens to either of them; say they get threatened, hurt, or killed even, we look the other way. I'm not saying it's okay to kill or hurt people, or threaten their lives even. All I'm saying is that there is no reward for them: got that?"

"Yeah, got it," Debo said.

"Okay then, anything else?" Patch asked.

"No, not..., hey where is, *Hungry*-ass, Rayass?"

"He went to the doctor for his arm, it's our day off," Patch told him. "Yeah, well, it was mine too. My wife wanted me to stay home with her this morning. I took her to the beach yesterday, that should make up for it," Debo said.

"You mean our beach?"

"Whatever you say, Patch, whatever you say, just keep me posted. Oh…, and, Patch, there may be something in it for you if things go right. Now, out of my office. Go on… get."

Agent Patch got up and left. He was almost down the hall when Debo yelled behind him, "Keep me posted!!!"

"Yeah, I heard you… I will!!!" Patch yelled back and was gone .

Debo locked up his office and left. He took a different route to San Diego; no flat tires, no problems at all. He called Sergeant Billings' cell phone.

"Jackson…, what can I do for you today, Sir?" Billings asked when he answered his phone.

"I just finished talking to Patch and he ran down some names to me; one, in particular, is Gregory Johnson; ring any bells?"

"I'm out on the green, Jackson, give me a call first thing in the morning on my cell, I'll be home. Meantime be careful, I mean be 'VERY' careful. You are in hot shit, those people eat guys like you and Write for lunch. You don't want to know what they do for appetizers."

"Everybody's telling me to be careful today."

"Well, that could be because everybody gives a shit about you," Billings seriously said.

"Okay, first thing tomorrow morning, I'm on my way home, Bob. Hey…, I didn't know you played golf. I'll have to see what you're made of one afternoon."

"Jackson, you won't stand a snowball's chance in hell." When Debo hung up, he called Mad-C .

"I'm coming, I'll fill you in when I get there, or would you rather wait until tomorrow?"

"If it can wait until tomorrow, then okay."

"Yeah, I'm sure it'll hold until then."

"Okay, tomorrow then," Mad-C said and they hung up.

It was close to 9:00 . Debo pulled into the carport, Shelly heard him, and so did Rex. She was on the computer when he entered the foyer.

"You're pretty good on that thing, aren't you?" he asked her.

"Yeah, I would say so, why do you need something?"

"I might before it's all over."

"Okay, if you need anything, just holler."

"Can you pull up police files on that thing?"

"Not without the code to the law enforcement agency," she told him. "If you had the code to say…, the DEA or the FBI or the LAPD, etc."

"All I need is the pass-code," Shelly repeated.

"Okay, no problem," he said.

"If you can get those codes, then you are into some pretty heavy stuff."

"Sweetheart, someone is trying to kill me, now I think that's **pretty heavy stuff**… don't you?"

"Yeah…, I guess it is: Besides, you need crooked cops for that," she continued.

"Yeah, tell me about it." "Hungry? I left something out for you to eat."

"Yeah, I'm starved, I'll run out and say hello to Rex, I know he heard the car pull in."

"Okay, I'll fix you a plate."

Debo went outside and Rex was standing by the door. And within minutes he was kissing Debo and wagging his tail.

"Hey fella," Debo said while patting Rex on his side.

He checked the gate and the pad-lock. He had a floodlight with a motion sensor installed in the backyard so it can come on and go off when someone lurks near the backyard. He also had one installed on the front porch, as well as one on both sides of the house.

"Feeling okay, boy?" he asked Rex.

He looked at the sky and it was beautiful; the air was fresh and crisp. The sun lit-up the backyard and everything was so peaceful and quiet. He sat down on the steps next to Rex and said,

"If all this wasn't going on right now, this would be a wonderful day and a wonderful moment. I have the best dog, a beautiful wife, and a perfect life but it's all being interfered with, and I must stop whoever is interfering with it."

"You can eat now baby if you want!!!" Shelly yelled out the back door, stopping him in the middle of his conversation with Rex.

"Coming, honey; see you later fella," he said to Rex as he went inside. He finished his snack, while Shelly sat with him. She had three cookies and some hot chocolate because she didn't want to ruin her breakfast by eating too much right now. After breakfast they went into the bedroom.

Debo sat there with his eyes closed for a minute, then said, "Thank you, Baby."

Shelly was lying down on the bed facing Debo. She smiled and said, "You're welcome my love."

"Do you know why I'm thanking you?"

"Yes, for the same things I thank you for; for the same reasons we're together, for being there when I need you most."

"I love you, Mrs Jackson."

"And I love you too, Mr Jackson."

It was too early for Debo to leave. He went into his home office to check the tape agent Patch told him to leave in the Explorer recording overnight. He pulled it out before he went back to Beverly Hills and put it in the glove compartment and decided to check the new one after he got back from seeing Mad-C. He watched the tape from the entire day Saturday. He didn't want to take the Explorer to the beach when He, Shelly, and Rex went. That allowed him to see everything he needed. He began viewing the tape from the beginning, but there was nothing for the most part of the day. The postman came to the house, but no one else came to the mailbox. The gardener came… he always comes on Saturday. Something came from UPS… maybe something for Shelly; some kind of package.

A kid handing out flyers came… nothing there. The tape ran until dark and came up with nothing, just regular traffic so far. "Hold it right there," he said aloud.

He stopped the tape, backed it up, and checked it, but he couldn't believe what he saw. He saw a car; a black car, he was sure it was the black

Mercedes Benz that Robert Cruse drives. He froze the frame, backed it up just a hair, and then enlarged the frame. He saw two guys sitting inside the car, then the head-lights came on and went off. He couldn't make out if it was the Mercedes that Patch had shown him on the other tape or not. He enlarged the picture again and the Mercedes emblem came into view, and so did the license plate; PLAYER-5. They sat there for most of the night, left and then came back; maybe to eat something or use the restroom, or both. He finished watching the tape, locked up everything, and sat there thinking to himself.

"Those son-of-a-bitches posted up outside my house and watched it while my wife and I slept inside. That's some scary shit; I'm gonna find out what this shit is all about and then I'll… "

He came out of the office and saw Shelly going toward the kitchen. He went into the kitchen behind her and saw her going on through to the back door and caught up to her and said, "I thought you went to lie down."

"Not without you, did you wanna help me get some vegetables for supper?"

"Sure, sweetheart, I'll give you a hand."

Shelly sat the basket of tomatoes she had picked, on the ground. Rex went over and grabbed a tomato out of the basket and ran around the yard with it dangling from his mouth. Shelly took off behind him; running around the yard after him until she was out of breath.

"Rex, come here and give me that," Shelly commanded.

"Rex come here boy, what are you doing man, huh? What are you going to do with that old thing once you get it out of his mouth, baby?" Debo asked Shelly.

"Beat him with it."

"Rex you're in trouble, here boy!!!" Debo yelled for Rex and he came to him and laid down on his belly. "You just want to play, don't you boy? Give her that old thing."

Rex looked up at him, then at Shelly, then he went over to where Shelly was standing, with the tomato in his mouth. Shelly laughed and said, "keep it, God knows you worked me hard enough trying to catch you."

Shelly laughed, Debo laughed, and for a minute Shelly thought she saw Rex laugh. "I'm going crazy, D-Angelo!!"

"What makes you say that, baby?"

"That dog just laughed at me."

"Come on in here, girl."

Shelly fixed breakfast after they went inside, and she got ready for church while Debo got ready to make his calls and go see Mad-C. He called Sgt Billings first.

"Good morning," Debo greeted. "Hey," Billings responded.

"How did it go with golf, old buddy?"

"Lovely, I didn't expect to hear from you until tomorrow. Golf was lousy, it was too noisy" Billings finally confessed.

"Maybe you'd better stick to catching criminals, you're better at that. Speaking of which, I talked to Patch yesterday and he found something out. I have to go to Los Angeles to check on some things, or I can just run it by you."

"Yeah, run it by me."

He told Billings everything that agent Patch said. Although, he still didn't mention who shot Brown and Rodgers.

"What is Patch doing on his end?" Billing asked.

"Trying to dig the remaining three out from underground," Debo told him.

"Oh, they will surface," Billings assured him. "Yeah, they've been out a few times already," Debo informed him.

"Listen, Jackson, you're playing with dynamite. I don't know how they got with, Johnson, but everybody that goes up against him doesn't usually make it back."

"Yeah, but Sarge, I have to do what I have to do."

"Okay, Jackson, if there's anything I can do, let me know."

"You know, there might be something. Can you get me a code that would release LAPD investigative data to my home computer?"

"What did you say? Never mind, I heard you, please don't repeat it; hold on."

Billings left the phone for about five-minutes and came back.

"Now, Jackson, you didn't get this from me. I have no idea where you got it... got it?"

"Yeah, Bob, I got it."

"Okay, your code will be, *'BEVERLY'*, and don't forget it. I've entered it into the police database. Every law enforcement agency have a separate code, and you have one now. I repeat, Jackson ... I don't know where you got it. I don't even know who you are, got me?"

"Yeah, Bob... gotcha."

"Okay, talk to you later, I'm back on the green in an hour."

"Okay..., good luck, Bob."

"Luck my ass, that's pure skill, Debo."

Debo laughed and ended the call. He called Mad-C and got a recording; 'Your call has been forwarded to an automated answering service, please...' Debo hung up and decided to wait until later. He got in the shower, got out, fixed himself some hot coffee, and ran over some paperwork in his office. He called Mad-C back and got the same recording and decided to call the house phone.

"Write's residence, Ed answered.

"Hey, Ed... this is D-Angelo, is he in?"

"Mister Write is asleep, Sir.., shall I wake him?"

"No, I'll call back, Ed, thanks."

"You're welcome, Sir," Edward said, then hung up.

Debo tried calling again and Mad-C answered on the second ring.

"Answer your phone, Charlie," Debo teased.

"I was trying to go back to sleep the first time it rang, but I might as well go ahead and get up," Mad-C told him.

"Okay, good, I'll be over there in about an hour."

"Make it two, give me time to get up."

When Debo arrived, Ed answered the door.

"Good afternoon, Sir." "Hey, Ed..., working on Sundays now?"

"No, just until six o'clock," the butler said.

"Tell him I'm here."

"He's in his study... go on in."

"Butlers always calls the home office the stud. I guess it's a butler thing," Debo thought to himself.

Mad-C stood when Debo walked into his office. The office has a long oakwood table; the kind you see in corporate meetings with about half dozen chairs around it and a chair at each end of the table. His desk was cluttered with all kinds of junk. Ed didn't bother it because it was off-limits to everyone. He was sitting at his desk watching a football game; *The Washington Red Skins* vs *The Saint Louis Rams*. "Who you got on the Super Bowl?" Mad-C asked Debo. "I have a hundred big ones on Saint Louis, my hometown." He picked up the remote control and muted the sound on the television and the sports commentator's voice disappeared.

"Do you remember telling me about a mess you had gotten into ten years ago in Venice, California?" Debo asked.

"Yeah... and... "

"Well, I talked to agent Patch and he dug up some information for me. Did you know some construction workers that were refurbishing that house and the property out in Vince, dug up two bodies about five or six years ago? One of the guys they dug up had been shot in the forehead, and the other was shot in the chest. The shooter used a large caliber handgun. 'It wasn't a pretty sight' they said. Anyway, one was buried with a sawed-off shotgun next to him, and the other one was buried with an automatic handgun next to him."

"Buried in the yard at the house?" Mad-C questioned. "Yeah in the backyard," Debo answered.

"Okay..., go on."

"Whoever it was that buried them there, buried them with all their personal belongings; wallet, money, jewelry, everything. Agent Patch gave me the names of five guys... ring a bell?"

"Yeah, sounds familiar," Mad-C said.

"The ones that managed to live are now involved with a big-shot drug cartel guy by the name of, Gregory Johnson. Gregory Johnson is the one...,"

"Wait... did you say, Gregory Johnson?" Mad-C cut him off to ask. Debo saw concern streak Mad-C's face, his forehead wrinkled, and his jaw tightened.

"He's a tough puppy," Mad-C warned. "The guys we believe are after us...,"

"What do you mean us, this is my war," Mad-C said with rage in his face. "Try telling them that, because it looks like they have their eyes set on me also."

"Yeah, it does, doesn't it?"

"I would say so," Debo said.

"They wouldn't dare come here because they won't make it within a hundred yards of this place."

"They don't know where you are unless they followed me here."

"They know more than you think they know, don't fool yourself," Mad-C said.

"They shot out my tire and drugged my dog, and I was probably at home when they drugged poor Rex."

"See what I mean?"

"Yeah, and if they can do all that, then they can get to my wife! Oh, by the way..., I told Shelly everything."

"Well, hallelujah, it's about time!!!" Mad-C screamed.

"I had to, things are about to get ugly and I don't want her to be caught off guard on this thing. Now, where was I? Oh yeah... I'm in it, and if they know where to find you or the shipping dock, that could explain the ten kilos you were short. They could have somehow gotten aboard the ship. Those boys have connections and they play rough."

"What names did he give you?" Mad-C asked.

"The dead are Lawrence Brown and Mack Rodgers. The three you let live are, Johnnie Morris, Randy Carlyle, and Robert (Bib Boy) Cruse."

"Wait, Big Boy, one of them did call himself, Big-Boy. So, I guess we are talking about the same guys," Mad-C said.

"Yeah, I guess, I'm having LAPD database information plugged into my home computer, and hopefully Patch will let me do the same with DEA database information. I spoke with Billings and it's a go. I have my code..., I wanna cut down on some of the communication between the boys and us. You never know who is listening. They have satellite that pick up on these phones. So, your conversation is not all your conversation.

"Well, it looks like I... I mean we have a war on our hands," Mad-C repeated.

"Yeah, and it's already started. So, what are we going to do, go to them or let them come to us?" Debo asked.

"Looks like they've already made the first move. Have you already told your workers so they can be on guard?"

"I'm holding a meeting with them tomorrow to let them know."

"Okay, and you know all this goes with the job," Mad-C reminded him.

"If those assholes hadn't tried to jack you, then this wouldn't be happening."

"Other assholes would have come along, there's no way around it."

"Yeah, I guess so," Debo said.

About that time, Ed came in and announced,

"I think I'll retire for the evening, Sir; will that be alright?"

"Sure, Ed, thanks for working on your day off."

"It's 6:00 already, I need to be getting on home too." Debo got up, stretched, shook Mad-C's hand, and said,

"We'll handle it, give me a call or I'll call you," and he was out the door behind Ed.

He was on the phone calling all the workers. He called Joy last, but first he called Pauline, Freddy, and Jeffery to set up the meeting for early in the morning. He considered putting Joy and Shelly someplace. Joy is pretty tough, so he decided to let her watch after Shelly until this is over. He'll cross that bridge when he gets to it. But, right now he has to let everybody know what's going on. This is not their war, and they do have a choice as to whether or not they want to stay or leave. It's time to play dirty, and Mad-C and Debo will have to team up now. He thought 'that if he went to Los Angeles tonight, he wouldn't be home until around ten or eleven tomorrow evening. But he need to spend the night with Shelly'.

He punched in the numbers to Agent Patch's phone. "Patch here," a voice said after the first ring.

"Guess what I've got," Debo said. "What?"

"A black Benz parked down the street from my house Saturday night. I looked at the tape; the one you suggested I leave running in the Explorer, and Bingo.., they're watching the house big-time. I'm thinking about getting Shelly out of there to someplace safe. She and one of my workers; well actually she's like a sister to me."

"Oh, you mean, Joyvette?" Patch asked.

"How did… oh, that's right, you know everything," Debo said. "Can you be in Los Angeles tomorrow?" Patch asked.

"Yeah, as a matter of fact, I have a meeting out there ."

"Meet me at that chili place on Crenshaw boulevard. What is it… *The Chili Place?*"

"*The Chili King,*" Debo corrected.

"Whatever, just meet me there or call me when you're ready. I've got something for you."

"Alright," Debo said. He hung up, pulled into the carport, parked, and went inside the house.

"Hey, sweet thing," he said when he saw Shelly.

She looked stunning, dressed in her silk nightgown and fur house slippers. Debo stood there admiring her with a towel wrapped around her head. "Hungry?" she asked him. "Something light will do."

He opened the door to the backyard and gave Rex his usual pat on his side and said, "Hey, boy," then closed the door and backed into the kitchen. Rex has seen Debo tired plenty of times, so he understood.

"In here!!!" Shelly yelled.

He went into the dining room and Shelly had fixed him a bowl of chili; he loves her chili. No one makes chili like Shelly.

"You look wonderful and sexy… towel and all."

"Thank you baby, how was your day?"

"The usual; no bad news though. Here's the code for the computer, whenever you're ready we can put it in, *or* you can," he told her.

"My baby got juice, huh?" she said, smiling.

"Well…, gotta stay on top of things in this crazy business… Hey Shell?"

"Yes."

"I want to put you someplace where you'll be safe."

"Why, so I can really worry about you, not knowing where or how you are?" She sadly asked.

"If these people know about *The Shell-Debo:* I have something I wanna show you."

He showed her the tape of the two men sitting outside the house in the black Benz. "I don't want you here alone, at least not now. Shell, if something were to happen to you, my existence would end. Do you understand what I'm saying?"

"Yes, Baby, I understand exactly what you're saying; I feel the same about you: That's why I worry so much. That's why I understand why you tried to keep it from me, so I wouldn't worry.

But, I do, I always have after I found out."

She was almost in tears. Debo pulled her to him and put his arms around her, then kissed her forehead and said,

"I know, baby…, I know. I have a lot of places to go and more things to do. But, I guarantee you, I'll be fine. I can't trust leaving you here alone, I love you, lady," he confessed.

"But, D-Angelo… "

"But, D-Angelo nothing. It's not up for debate. I've got someone that will be with you; someone I trust to protect you. This may get rough, and I need someone that can handle the job."

"You mean, Joy?" she asked. "Yeah, baby… Joy."

Shelly knows Joy, she also knew of April; Joy's mom. She knows that Debo adopted Joy as his little sister when she needed someone to help her get out of the rut she was in, Debo was there for her. Joy is very beautiful and she doesn't play. She owns an arsenal of weapons and she knows how to use them all. Nobody Debo employs are wimps, they all handle their business. They have to because they move fifty kilos of pure, uncut, high-grade cocaine per month, and it's very tough work.

"Okay, baby, if you insist."

Shelly also knew that to dispute anything Debo says is a waste of time. He knows everything there is to know about his business.

"When will this take place?" she asked, knowing that there was no use trying to talk him out of it.

"As soon as I can find a safe-place somewhere. I'm thinking about the Bonaventure Hotel in Downtown Los Angeles. I can put Freddy in a room under you or next to you. I'll be in touch with you every night, and if something goes wrong at the hotel they'll both know what to do. I'll need you to take your computer, I'm sure we'll need it."

"You're not going alone are you?" "No, sweetheart, Write and I can handle it. I don't think we'll have to go looking for them; seems like they've already come after us."

"So, what is it exactly you do for Mr Write?"

"I deliver fifty kilos of 100% pure powder cocaine once a month to separate locations in Los Angeles, Inglewood, and sometimes Beverly Hills, California. I make sure all the locations have security and the merchandise is safely delivered."

"How do you do that?"

"I have people who also help me enforce our laws and our rules. I also collect all the money at the end of the month and make sure Write and all the workers get paid."

"That's a lot of responsibility," she said after he finished talking. "I would rather not sell it," he calmly told her.

"I'd rather you didn't sell it either," Shelly said. "What do you say we go out for dinner?" Debo suggested. "You sure it'll be safe?"

"I think they want Mister Write, and they probably want me to lead them to him. I'm not sure if I already have, but I'll know soon."

"Where do you want to go eat?" she asked. "What do you have an appetite for?"

"Chinese, how about some Chinese food," she decided.

"Chinese it is. Go ahead and get dressed and do whatever it is you do to that beautiful face of yours; not that you need to, and I'll go put on something." She went to get dressed, and in about an hour and a half, she came to the foyer looking stunning. She donned her long pearl-blue dinner gown, her white mink coat, sky-blue leather shoes to match her gown, and the broach he bought her for her 36th birthday. It's gold; about the size of a quarter, and there's a circle with a heart in the middle. The arrow piercing the hart spelled her name; It's beautiful. Debo dressed in his all

- 88 -

white three-piece suit, a blue silk shirt, white tie, and he wore his white leather shoes; the ones he had imported from Italy. And last but not least; he splashed on some of the cologne Ed gave him for Christmas.

"Hey, handsome you're looking wonderful, and that cologne you're wearing, what is it?"

"You like it?"

"I love it."

"It's called, *passion*," he told her.

It had a warm, fresh, sweet, (mexi); male-sexy aroma; a debonair aroma to it. "I knew you'd like it."

He opened the door for her to walk out and walked out behind her, closed the door, locked it, and they both left to go and enjoy their evening. He turned on the phone in the Explorer and put his phone on vibrate, then activated the rear surveillance camera. He prayed this would not be the last dinner out together for them. After tonight he's going to make arrangements for her to go to the hotel with Joy until this mess ends. Debo arrived in Los Angeles at nine o'clock sharp, Monday morning Joy, Pauline, Freddy, and Jeffery were all at the office sitting outside in various cars and SUVs awaiting Debo's arrival. When he showed up, Pauline asked him,

"What took you so long, we've been waiting here since 8:30?"

"I took Shell out last night: I get a day off also, you know," he protested. "Okay, let's go…" Freddy suggested.

Debo was wondering if agents Patch and Rayass were watching the entire time.

"You guys go ahead and get your coffee and settle in. I want to make a phone call," Debo told them.

"We already did, in fact, I'm waiting to let some of it out," Freddy cried. "Yeah, we went to Starbucks down the street," Joy added.

"Okay, then have a seat and I'll be right back."

He went into another room in the office and called Patch.

"Agent Patch?"

"You ready, Jackson?"

"No, I'm in a meeting, I was just calling to let you know I'm in town. I was wondering if what you have to say can be said in front of my workers."

"It can, but I would rather not. They may have heard of me, but I don't Personally want to meet them at this time. I personally contact you, and only you… understood?"

"Yeah," Debo said.

"Okay, call me when you're ready, Jackson."

Debo felt as if Patch was paying him and he was taking the orders. "Okay gang, first of all, does anyone have anything to bring to the floor?" No one said anything? "Good, that means that we're running a tight ship. I have a little bad news," he told them and looked around the room at each of them.

They were seated at a table similar to the one in Mad-C's home office; the long oakwood table. This one had to have been assembled in the room because it was too big to have been put there already assembled.

"We have a problem with a drug Cartel that has some kind of vendetta against my boss. There may be, or better yet, there will be some foul play in the very near future. All of you are like family to me, that's why I'm telling you this. You could all be in danger. You all have worked loyally for me for years, and if you feel you're tired, let me know. If you decide to stay, or whoever decides to stay; once this is over and you are left standing, I'll recruit from this group someone to take my place if you guys want to stay in this mess. Not you, Joy, I'm retiring and I want you to retire also. You all will have enough money to live a very satisfying and rewarding lifestyle.

I want to know if I have to call on any of you that I can depend on you." Joy's hand went up, Pauline, Freddy, then Jeffery put their hands up. "Thank you, guys. I know you all might have some questions, and I'll answer them as best I can."

Jeffery stood up: "I know I speak for us all when I say, that boss you didn't really have to ask us, we've been in this with you for a while. You have pulled a lot of us out of a rat hole, and there's one thing I do know… no one else would have done for me what you have done for me. You put your trust in us and let us see what it was like to live like kings and queens. You gave us a life, I personally feel that I owe you, and if something happens to me because I chose this line of work…, then may God be with me. I'm not backing out on you, and you can't throw me out. You've never,

ever backed out on me. So, whatever goes down, it goes with the territory. We are a family, and families don't turn their backs on each other."

"D-Angelo Jackson, have you lost your mind? You are my brother, and that's a fact, I love you, that's also a fact. Whatever happens to you happens to me," Joy announced.

"I love you all…, I mean, you put your live on the line out there for someone else's merchandise: Fifty kilos is a lot of dope. I'll talk to Mad-C about Christmas bonuses sometime this week; Pauline?"

"I'm not going anywhere, and I mean it," Pauline said.

"Freddy," Debo asked.

"Freddy what?" Freddy asked as if to say, 'You'd better not ask me no shit like that, I'm not going anywhere.'

"I appreciate you all… Payday is in about two weeks, does anyone need any cash?" No one answered. "Okay, this meeting is adjourned!" he told them.

They all got into their cars and went their separate ways. Debo asked Joy to stay behind because he wanted to talk to her without all the other workers being present. He sat next to her in her car and sad,

"Sis!"

"I'm listening."

"I'm afraid for, Shell, I don't want her to stay at *The Shell-Debo* while this is going on. I want her in a safe place, but I need someone I can trust with her life."

"And I'm that someone?"

"Yes, you are that someone."

"You mean you love and trust me enough to let me be responsible for someone that means the world to you; your very life?"

"Yes, Joyvette, I do."

"Wow…, I don't know what to say: You're handing me your life to protect. I'll protect her life with every inch of mine, bro," Joy told him.

"Thanks, Sis, it means a lot to me.., she means a lot to me."

"I know Big Bra… I know."

"Thanks," Debo repeated. "You're welcome.

I've already made plans for Tammy and Sheila to go over to their grandma's. I kinda figured I'd be away from them for a while when you told me about the DEA men. She can get them to and from school."

"You'll have everything you need," he assured her.

"I already have everything I need. Have you forgotten who you are talking to, buster?"

"I guess I did there for a moment," he admitted, and went to give her a hug.

"You know I can't stand that," she said, with one hand in the air to ward him off.

"When all this is over, I'm going to tie you down and give you the biggest hug and kiss you've ever had."

"You're gonna have to catch me first," she laughed. "No problem," he advised.

"Just tell me when," she told him. "I will… thanks again, Sis." "Yeah, now get out of my car," she joked.

He got out and waved goodbye as she pulled off down the street. He headed to Crenshaw to the Chili King and dialed Patch's cell phone to let him know he was on his way.

"Yeah, go ahead, Jackson," a husky voice said over the phone.

"I'm on my way to the Chili King now, I'll be there in a half an hour," Debo told him.

"Okay, I'll be there," Patch confirmed, then hung up.

Debo arrived ahead of Patch and was sitting inside watching the news on the television set mounted on the wall for customers to watch as they dined. He smelled the chili cooking, and said to himself, "Rayass may have something here after all. That chili does smell pretty good." The last time Debo ate chili there was years ago, and he loved it then.

"Milton must have pulled another rabbit from under his hat. The chili smells delicious; you can smell the seasonings and the different herbs. It smells like that, down-home *Shelly* tasting chili. But then, no one makes chili like *Shell*."

The bowl Debo ate last night could have won a gold medal. That woman can really cook. He ordered a small bowl just to see what it taste like. He didn't want to just sit there without ordering something. He was sure that Rayass would order a bowl also. He got his order and went over and sat down to eat it. He looked up and saw Patch and Rayass pulling into the parking lot.

When he saw the Maverick come in, he got up and went outside to greet them.

"Patch.., Rayass," he said as he shook the two agents' hands. "Why don't we go in, I have a bowl of chili on the table?"

Patch looked inside the Chili King and saw a few customers seated in various seats and decided against going in.

"This is extremely secret information; I would rather we talk out here for security reasons, you understand." "Yeah, I understand."

It was sixty-five degrees outside as the sun peered through the snow white clouds. When the Chili King door opened, the aroma from the chili mixed with the early afternoon air gave the outside setting a wonderful smell. Not to mention; it was making Debo want to eat his chili right then.

"So, what do you have for me?" Debo asked Patch.

"Do you know a guy by the name of Raymond Anderson?"

Debo thought he had heard the name someplace before, but he couldn't place it.

"The name's familiar I… can't… quite get it. Anderson… Anderson …, I've heard that name, but I can't… Anderson," he thought again.

"Well, maybe this will help; Mister Anderson was working for a fishing boat captain, maybe four or five years ago. He disappeared when boat Captain, Yin: Sue-Lang-Yin was killed: Sue-Lang-Yin was shipping drugs to the United States from China, and Anderson was one of his runners."

"I remember, it was in the news: They never found Anderson.

They had presumed him dead at sea; an accident of some kind," Debo recalled. "Very good, Mister Jackson. Raymond Anderson is Robert (Big Boy) Cruse. We've suspected him of murdering Mr.

Yin, but we found nothing; no body or no sign of him, so everyone figured he drowned at sea and the case was never pursued."

"So, you're saying Robert Cruse is Raymond Anderson?" Debo questioned. "Yes, Anderson hooked up with Gregory Johnson a few years ago. It's Anderson that wants to get even with Mister Write, and they have the money, muscle, and the manpower to do what needs to be done," Debo concluded.

"I need to be able to get into your database," Debo said as if the man that was so into protocol would hit the ceiling, and he did.

"You want what!!!" Patch screamed.

He screamed so loud, other customers heard him and looked over at their table.

"I could get my ass in a very big sling if I gave you access to such data. I'll give you whatever comes up on our database but I can't give you access to the database itself," Patch said.

"Well, it was worth a shot in the dark. But at least we have LAPD's database security code. That'll have to do for now.

Okay, good enough. Thanks for the information on Anderson, or Cruse, or whatever his name is. Agent Rayass, how's the arm?"

"It's coming along," Rayass reported with a mouth full of chili. "You like that chili…, huh, Rayass?" Debo asked.

"Sure do," the agent answered.

"I'll bring you some of my wife's hot chili." "Thanks, Jackson."

"Don't mention it."

Debo's phone rang and it was Sgt Billings. "Hey Bob."

"Where are you?" Billings asked. "On Crenshaw… "

"Meet me at the Crenshaw mall in thirty-minutes," Billing said. "Will do," Debo agreed .

He heard a horn blow and looked over to where the sound had come from and saw agent Patch waving as he drove out of the parking lot of the Chili King. He gave them a wave back and got into the Explorer and headed north on Crenshaw to King Blvd. He got to the Crenshaw mall and parked on the second level and waited for the Sgt. to arrive. He began eating the chili he had ordered earlier, and to his surprise, it was delicious but not quite as good as Shelly's. He was just finishing the last of the chili and thought it would have made more sense to have Milton warm it up before he left. But the aroma coming out of the Chili King made him want to eat it right then. Warming it didn't make too much difference at this point. Billings pulled up in a stall next to where Debo was parked. Debo exited the Explorer and got into the Cruiser next to him where Billings was sitting. "What's up, Big-Golfer?" Debo greeted. "Well, I did well on the green yesterday." "Anything else you do well on?"

"Well let's see, I came up with the name of a guy that fought a case for fighting pit bulls. He was a pro at it, but it got him sixteen months in state prison a while ago; a guy named Johnny Morris…, remember him?"

"You mean our, Johnny Morris?"

Debo wasn't surprised; they were only youngsters when Mad-C ran into them.

"Anything on who tipped off the police about, Freddy?"

"You mean, Frederick C Moss?" Billings asked.

"Yeah.., Freddy," Debo responded.

"Whoever tipped them off didn't leave a name. Just be careful, it could have been someone that didn't like him."

"Yeah, could have been. Okay thanks."

"No problem," Billings said.

"So, you did pretty well on the green?" Debo joked.

He got out of Billings Cruiser and got back into the Explorer and left. He backed out of the parking lot and headed down the ramp to the lower level, then on to Crenshaw Boulevard.

The meetings with Patch, Rayass, the workers, and Billings only took about five hours. He looked at his watch and saw how late it was getting: It's a beautiful quartz with diamonds on every third number. The casing is yellow/white gold on a gold watch band. Shelly bought it for his thirty-seventh birthday. He wears it everywhere and loves the way it matches his gold wedding band. He dialed Joy's cell.

"Joyvette isn't available, please try your call again. Or to leave a message, please press five, or leave your ten-digit phone number and a brief message."

"That woman goes to the extreme. Five minutes it took saying all that," Debo thought out loud.

He didn't want to leave a message so he hung up, put the phone down, and heard it play "It's our anniversary." He picked it up, turned it on, and heard Joy say,

"Hey, you call?" "Yeah, are you busy?"

"No, not really, what's up?"

"I was just thinking if you thought that a room at the Bonaventure Hotel is a good idea?"

"I think it would be a rather expensive idea!"

"Money is not a problem, you know that!"

"Yeah, you're right; you mean Shelly and I?" Joy sounded. like she was either very tired or busy.

"What's wrong, are you feeling alright?"

"Yeah, I'm just sleepy, I went to bed late and got up early for the meeting this morning."

"Oh yea, sorry little mama."

"No problem, bro"

"Yeah, sweetheart, you and Shell."

"Sure, I would love to go, if you think it's best. I would love to live extravagantly."

"Okay, go ahead and get ready and I'll come to pick you guys up Wednesday morning. I don't know how long you'll be there, so pack something that'll last a while and I'll see you Wednesday."

"Hey bro, can I bring my… "

"Bring whatever you want, you'll both be staying in the penthouse suite," he cut her off to say.

"Wow…, a Penthouse Suite at the Bonaventure Hotel; you go Big Bro!!" "Get some rest," he told her and hung up.

He pressed talk and held it for a couple of seconds to redial her number "Yes sir," she answered

"Thanks, Sis."

"You got it," joy said, ending the call.

Debo was just turning onto the I-10 freeway in route to San Diego. His work in LA was finished for today.

CHAPTER 7

TUESDAY, NOVEMBER 6, 9:30 A.M.
(FORTY-NINE DAYS UNTIL CHRISTMAS DAY)

Debo was lying in his bed with his arms folded behind his head staring into the ceiling in deep thought until the ringtone on his cell phone brought him back to the moment. He answered it and it was Mad-C.

"Whatcha got for me this morning?" Mad-C asked Debo. "I got a little something," Debo answered.

"Okay, I don't go to the dock until the middle of the week which is tomorrow. Are you busy? If not, shoot on through here sometime this afternoon."

"I have a few plans, how about I come by there closer to evening?"

"Sounds good to me," Mad-C confirmed.

"Okay, see you then," Debo said, ending the call.

Shelly was showering and Debo decided to take one himself. He loves hot showers: Most women soak in the tub, but the majority of men like to shower. Debo enjoyed the way it massages the body, the way it soothes every nerve, loosens the tight spots.. They both finished their shower and met each other in the breakfast nook.

"Good morning, sweetheart," he said. "Morning, handsome," she responded. "How's my girl?"

"Fresh and ready for the day!"

And fresh she was; this is one woman that is beautiful no matter what; asleep, awake, tired, rested. It doesn't matter; makeup on, makeup off, and she wore a scent that smelled like strawberries and lime; It was indeed a fresh smell.

"I talked to Joy yesterday and you two ladies will be staying at the Bonaventure Hotel in downtown Los Angeles; the penthouse suite. We leave Wednesday morning to pick her up. I won't be able to see you once you're there."

"Oh.., so that's what all the good lovemaking was about last night, I thought I was dreaming. Okay, I'll start getting ready and getting my things together," she said.

"I have to run over and talk to Write in a minute, you can come if you want."

"No.., I'm good he might not be comfortable having me there while he's discussing business. I'll pass, thanks anyway baby," she said.

"Okay, sweetheart.., I'll be back in a bit."

He didn't realize it might bother Mad-C to talk business around her, but he was glad she had thought of it. Like she said, 'it would probably have made him a little uncomfortable,' most people are that way. He picked up his keys off the table and headed for the front door .

"Be careful!!!" she yelled behind him.

It was a gorgeous Tuesday morning and the sun was shining. Debo was listening to one of his Berry White CDs *(Practice What You Preach)*, as he drove down Broadway. It was only a ten-minute drive. He arrived at Mad-C's estate, got out of the Explorer, and walked up to the door and Ed opened it.

"Well that's what I call service," Debo said.

"I was watching the monitors, I saw you coming. How are you today, Mr Jackson? How did Misses Jackson like the cologne?" Ed asked.

"I'm fine and she loved it, thanks again."

"My pleasure, Sir. I'll get Mr Write for you. Please Make yourself at home."

"Whatcha got for me?" Mad-C asked Debo.

He had walked into the room soaking wet, dripping with water, had the AC on, and was dressed in a terry cloth robe and bare feet.

"What are you trying to do catch pneumonia or your death of cold? I don't see much difference in either," Debo preached.

"What's up doc?"

"Yeah.., you keep that up and you're gonna need a doc. I have some more information from Patch. Do you remember we were just talking about Robert (Big Boy) Cruse?"

"Yeah!"

"Do you recall a man by the name of Sue-Lang-Yin?"

"Debo, I run ships," Mad-C reminded him. "Stay with me, okay?"

"Okay, yes I know him he's dead... died in a fishing accident a few years ago, it was all over the news. He ran drugs all over the world, for heaven's sake. Sure, I know him, I've done business with him. What does he have to do with anything?" Mad-C asked.

"For one thing, he wasn't killed by accident, he was murdered by his very own one-man-crew: Raymond Anderson, and get this; *aka* Robert (*Big Boy*) Cruse. Anderson or Cruse, whichever you wish to call him, killed Yin and faked his own death. They both were believed to have drowned at sea, but Anderson's body never turned up. They ruled him "lost at sea". Now he goes by the name, Robert Cruse. FBI and DEA are searching everywhere looking for him and his friends, Jonny Morris and Randy Carlyle. Those are the assholes that's pissing us off. Whatever happened with the ten kilos that were missing? Did you check your crew and dock workers?" Debo asked.

"Yeah, and there was a guy out sick and a replacement was called in by my foreman. I checked the roster and guess who the replacement was!!"

"Who?"

"Jonny Morris; him Robert Cruse, and all the rest of them know good and well I won't be ripped off. They know what happened the last time. Why in the hell would they try it again? Sounds like they're after something," Mad-C assumed.

"If it's a war they're after, they got it. You did off a couple of their boys and took a few dollars, I think it's revenge," Debo told him.

"That was my money," Mad-C said. "Yeah, you're right."

"Whatever... I'm not going to stand for it, Debo: Gregory Johnson or no, Gregory Johnson. Have you talked to the crew yet?"

"Yeah, and they're good to go when we need them. We'll have to hold on for next month's work. This is only the sixth, I can recall the work that's already out if you want me to."

"Yeah, until we can straightened things out," Mad-C told him.

"Okay, I'll get on it," Debo assured him.

"Anything to drink, Sir?" Ed asked Mad-C when he walked into the room.

"Yes, Edward, please!"

"And, how about you, Mister Jackson?" "Sure, Ed, thanks."

"Turn the AC off will you, Edward." "Right away, Sir."

Ed didn't feel the air conditioner because he was wearing a thick, long sleeve, wool sweater, and a thick scarf around his small neck.

"Okay, go ahead and do that and I'll hold up everything coming in until this is taken care of. How is Shelly taking it?"

"She's dealing with it as best she knows how. I'm moving her and Joy out of the way and have Joy guarding her. The rest of the crew will be on-call in case we need them."

"Okay, I have a cabin out in Big Bear Mountains if you need it for a while. You can put them all up there, especially the women," Mad-C offered. "That's not a bad idea," Debo said.

"It's perfectly safe," Mad-C assured him. "This shouldn't last long," Debo estimated. "Yeah, but you never know," Mad-C warned.

"Mister Write, your drinks, Sir," Ed announced as he came into the room with a cart containing a bottle of brandy, two glasses, and some ice. The cart was mahogany with a shining silver tray that stood out against the pure gold wheels, and the black pearl handles.

"Thank you, Edward," Mad-C said.

"You're welcome, Sir," Edward responded, and kindly dismissed himself. Mad-C picked up one of the crystal glasses and Debo picked up the other: They both got some ice and Debo poured them both a drink and raised his glass and said,

"Let's do this."

"It's already done," Mad-C said, raising his glass also.

Their glasses met, and they both drank the strong brown liquid. "Cigar?" Mad-C offered.

"Save mine for the celebration after this is all over."

"Okay... it'll be here," Mad-C promised.

"Let me get going, I have one more night with Shell before She and Joy leave Wednesday morning, and Joy is crazy about being on time."

"You sure you don't want the cabin?" Mad-C asked.

"Hold on to it, I might need it later depending on how things go. I'll be at *the Shell-Debo* for a while. They should be safe there at the Bonaventure Hotel. I'll put Freddy in there with them and keep Jeffery and Pauline standing by in case anyone slips past Joy and Freddy.

"Did agent Patch say where these guys could be found when you spoke with him?" Mad-C asked.

"No, he just gave me the five names I gave you.

The three that made it and the two that didn't. Billings said, 'that they have already surfaced.'"

"We can start by checking on the address Morris left at the dock: I'll get on it. If you want the cabin let me know," Mad-C offered. "Okay, I will, boss, thanks!"

"They've surfaced alright, they drugged my dog, shot out one of my tires, and stole ten kilos from Mad-C. What else do we need to let us know that they drew first blood? I'll have to get my baby to a safe place," Debo thought as he drove home.

He pulled up at *the Shell-Debo*, parked the Explorer in the carport, and got out. Rex heard him and started jumping up and down on the side gate. "Hey, fella," Debo said and reached over the chain-linked gate and rubbed Rex's head. There was something there he must have overlooked; some kind of metal object. He couldn't get it out without breaking it. He went in the house, headed to the backyard and spoke to Shelly without stopping. Then he went to the backyard to the tool shed and got a Phillips screwdriver. Rex ran around his legs almost tripping him but he managed to catch his balance and continued on his mission.

Shelly came out the back door concerned. "What's wrong baby?" she asked Debo. "Someone left us a little present," he told her.

He loosened the hinge and something dropped. "Shell, sweetheart, get me a sandwich bag, please." Debo took the screwdriver and picked up whatever it was by its chain.

He saw that it was a fisherman's club medal from the year 2006.

"A little gift from Anderson; still into fishing I see," he thought to himself.

He put the medal and chain into the sandwich bag and took it in the house to read it under his desk lamp in the office. On the front was inscribed, *10117 Ocean Park Way, Seaman's Fishing and and Boat Club.* Inscribed on the back was a big fish and a fishing rod pictured above a ship.

"Don't tell me that Cruse does his own dirty work," Debo thought to himself.

"Is it important, baby?" Shelly asked.

"It sure is, baby... it sure is." Debo immediately called Billings. "Speak, Jackson," a husky voice said into the receiver.

"Hey, Sarge, I won't be but a minute. Do you remember me telling you about someone drugging, Rex?"

"Yeah."

"Well, they left a little gift."

"I'm about out of here for the night, can it hold until tomorrow?"

"Sure, I'm tired, besides I can't drive I just had a few drinks with Write. I'll bring it by there tomorrow, I have to go downtown anyway," Debo told him."Okay, I'll be here," Billings promised.

Debo realized this could have been the reason the Benz was sitting outside *the Shell-Debo* that Saturday night. Cruse came back to claim the medal he had dropped while climbing over the gate. He probably figured Debo was watching since the Explorer was parked in the carport.

"So, they weren't watching the house after all. It was the medal they wanted," Debo thought to himself.

CHAPTER
8

WEDNESDAY, NOVEMBER 7, 2007, 8:30 A.M.

Debo laid in his soft comfortable bed watching Shelly sleep on a nice Wednesday morning as the sun peeked through the window, lighting up her gorgeous face the way the moonlight does at night. She is the most beautiful creature on this planet to Debo. In his eyes there is no one more beautiful… his love, his life, his world, his soulmate. Lying next to him is his sole purpose for living. And this would be the last time he would wake up lying next to her for the next few days, few weeks, or just maybe he wouldn't come back if the guys that are making things difficult get the upper hand. She looked so sweet, so vulnerable, so easy to harm. He was convinced that he was doing the right thing by sending her to a safe house where she can be spared the consequence of his occupation. He left her lying there and went into the kitchen to put on some coffee. If she woke up and wanted some while he was in the shower, it would be ready.

He came out in his robe and slippers.

"Hi honey, you were sleeping so good I didn't want to wake you."

"Yeah, I had a good night's sleep. Thanks for the coffee, that was sweet of you."

"Anything for my girl. The reservations are made at the hotel. As soon as we are finished eating breakfast, we can head out."

"I'm going to miss this place," Shelly managed to confess.

"I know..., it won't be long, I promise, and this will never have to happen again. I just want you safe and out of harm's way," Debo confessed. Her eyes begin to tear, and she felt a pain in her heart that was put there by the fear she may never see her husband again, or hear his voice, or feel his touch, or smell the scent of him lying next to her, or laughing with her, and enjoying life with her again.

The thought frightened her so terribly her heart sank into her chest. Debo saw that she was about to start crying and said,

"I know it's hard on you baby, but it's going to be just fine. Don't worry about me, I'll be okay."

"But, can you guarantee me that? Can you guarantee I'll get my husband back? D-Angelo Jackson don't you ever do this to me again," she said with tears slowly streaming down her beautiful face.

Debo took his thumb, kissed it, and wiped the tears from her face. "Baby, I promise you will never have to go through this again. Then he kissed each one of her eyes, then the tip of her nose and said,

"Let's go baby, the sooner we get this over with, the sooner we can go back to living our lives."

They got in the car and headed for Joy's place. Debo called her cell and she picked up on the first ring.

"Hey, Big-Bro?"

"Hey, Sis.., we're on our way over to pick you up."

"Have you considered how you're doing this?" Joy asked him. "No, not really."

"Well I have: I got together with the other guys and came up with a plan just in case they are following you."

"Okay, love, I'll be there in a little bit," Debo promised. Joy called Debo back...

"Hey, Bro?"

"Yeah?"

"Let me speak to Shelly."

"Okay, hold on," he said and handed Shelly the phone. A moment went by and Shelly's voice came on the phone.

"Hey, Joy, how are you? It's been a long time since we spoke."

"Oh, I'm fine.., we're about to make up for lost time right now. Do you have a long coat?" Joy asked her.

"Yeah, why?"

"Wear it over here, okay?"

"Okay, but why?"

"I have a plan just in case we're being followed," Joy explained. "Okay, I'll wear it."

"Good, thanks," Joy said and hung up.

They arrived at Joy's house at 1:45 pm Wednesday afternoon.

"Hey fathead, you said in the morning, not afternoon. Next time be on time: Punctuality fathead, we're dealing with crazy asses here.

Hi, Shelly," Joy said as she slid into the seat next to Shelly.

She gave Shelly her long coat and took hers. She also gave her a hat that she wore just for what Joy had planned.

The plan was to meet at a soul-food restaurant around the corner from Joy's house.

"Okay, Shelly.., Freddy is in my place, and you're going to go in the house. Meanwhile, Big Bra and I... we'll go to that soul-food restaurant around the corner. Freddy is going to bring you to the restaurant fifteen minutes after we leave." Everyone did as Joy had instructed and played their parts in her diversion. Shelly and Joy traded coats inside the car and Shelly left the house wearing Joy's coat and hat.

"Now.., they saw me go back into the house, they'll think Shelly is with you but instead she'll be with Freddy."

She called Freddy on his cell phone. "Okay, Freddy.., you guys go on to the hotel. I'll kick back with my brother for a while."

"I don't know what you did but I'm sure if you did it, it'll work."

"Let me show you something... do you see that dark blue VW over there on that far wall?"

"Yeah," Debo answered.

"And the white Toyota parked across the street at the gas station… that's Jeffery, and the blue VW is, Pauline. If anyone would have followed us or Freddy, we would've known it," Joy explained.

"But, if they followed us, I would have seen them in the monitor here," he told her, while pointing to the screen in the dash.

"That can only let you to see behind you, not all around you," Joy pointed out.

"Yeah, that's the same thing, Patch said," Debo thought to himself. "And the black Mercedes SUV parked next to us was Freddy and Shelly. See, even your wife had your back. Those cars were following us because the people driving them could see all the blind spots that the camera or you couldn't."

"Well it's good to know that I'm working with someone with brains," Debo awarded her . "Yeah, you didn't even know they were following you, did you?"

"Honestly speaking, I didn't: I sure pick the best, don't I?"

"Yeah.., here's what's going to happen, you and I are going to kick back tonight, just like I was your wife. So, where to for dinner?"

"Are you sure this is going to work?"

"You said that you made reservations at the hotel, and all the other arrangements were taken care of, right?"

"Right," Debo confirmed.

"Then don't worry, didn't you trust me with your wife's life?"

"Yes I did."

"Okay…, act like it and let's go eat, I'm starved," Joy told him.

* * *

Joy's plan worked; as soon as they left the parking lot with Joy in the Explorer instead of Shelly, Debo checked the monitor and saw white Plymouth following them. He slowed to let it pass and it slowed behind him. We have company," he told Joy.

Joy took the nine-millimeter pistol out of her handbag, and Debo took *Crazy* from its shoulder holster. They drove down Alvarado Street to

Third, then made a right on Figueroa, and another right to Seventh and Figueroa. They went left to Broadway and pulled into an alley and got out in time to see the white Plymouth turned into the alley behind them. Debo leveled *Crazy* (his 45-automatic pistol) at the driver, while Joy leveled the nine millimeter handgun at the passenger.

The driver of the Plymouth put it in reverse and backed out of the alley the way they had come in, doing close to 40 mph. Debo and Joy ran up the alley and looked out onto the street but the white Plymouth was nowhere in sight. They both got in the Explorer and pulled out of the alley and onto the street.

"Well the plan worked, they probably thought they had Shell and I. Did you think *that one* up all on your own?"

"Some of it; actually most of it, Freddy helped put it together."

"You know what?" Debo asked her. "No.., what?"

"The bad guys are going to think you're, Shell," Debo mentioned. "Yeah.., Jeffery mentioned that also during the meeting we had," Joy told him.

"So, now you're in danger."

"I was in danger when I started this. There are some consequences to being rich," she told him.

"I have to stop at police headquarters." "Oh shit," she cursed.

"Just sit and hold your little horses."

"D-Angelo Jackson, you know I don't like police," Joy reminded him. "I won't be but a second."

"Well if they are following us they probably think we're here to report them," Joy jokingly said.

"Yeah probably," Debo said as he took off his shoulder holster with *Crazy* in it, put it in the glove compartment, and took out the medal that he found at the house.

"Be right back," he told Joy.

"You're late," Billings said, looking like he had a hell-of-a-day.

"Wow…, you look beautiful," Debo joked.

"What can I help you with today, Jackson?"

- 107 -

Debo took the medal out if his jacket pocket and laid it on Billings' cluttered desk.

"What do we have here?" Billings asked as he opened the bag and removing the medal and chain. He read the inscription and saw the picture of a fish, a fishing rod, and the ship.

"That's what the *piss-on* that drugged my dog left," Debo angrily said. Billings read the rest of the inscription, and it said..., *Seamen's Fishing and Boat Club, 10117 Ocean Parkway*. "That may be close to Malibu," he said.

"I didn't touch it, you might be able to lift a fingerprint or two off of it," Debo told the Sergeant.

"Yeah, I'll run it by the lab and see what turns up, anything else?"

"No, just some guys tried to hem me up in an alley on the way over here."

"Well, if they followed you, then…"

Debo interrupted what Billings was about say and said,

"Joy put together this fantastic plan to get Shell safely to the hotel. I must say, it worked like a charm."

"What kind of car followed you here?" Billings asked "A white Plymouth."

"Sure, it wasn't one of ours?" Billings asked Debo.

"I don't think so, they saw *Crazy* and headed for the hills. At first I thought it was one of Patch's boys, but it didn't turn out that way," Debo said.

"Yeah, well whoever it was must have left," Billings remarked. "Hold on a sec, Sarge," Debo called Joy's cell. "Yeah, Bro?"

"Is everything alright?"

"Yeah bra, everything is cool… what's up?"

"Turn the key on and look at the monitor in the dash." "Yeah, I see a big picture of a car license plate."

"Yeah, that's the one that followed us into the alley. I blew it up and froze it. Read it to me."

"Okay, Ready?"

"Yeah, shoot"

"Okay, here it is… P-L-A-Y-E-R-2"

"Okay, thanks sis, I'll be down in a minute," he told her, then hung up and repeated the letters back to Billings.

"That's the same plate on the Benz, except the last number on the Benz was a five instead of a two. They seem to be using personalized license plates with the word *PLAYER* on them followed by a number. Do you have Joyvette waiting in the car?"

"Well, yeah… I told her I was only going to be a sec."

"Okay, is that all?"

"For now it is."

"You can't leave her down there like that with people following you."

"Well, after all, this is a police station, and Joy is very heavily armed and knows how to use my weapon and hers."

"Yeah, well the people you're up against don't give a rat's ass about all that. Get your crazy-ass down there and get some protection on her," Billing ordered.

Debo didn't want to take the conversation any further, he just said "Okay," and left.

He was back in the Explorer headed for the car leasing agency. Upon arrival, he walked up to the desk.

"Hello, Mr Jackson, how are you this afternoon?" Lois asked. "I'm fine, Lois, how are you doing?"

"Wonderful, Mister Jackson, just wonderful, and how may I assist you?"

"I would like to rent a car, if it's okay."

"Is something wrong with the Explorer?"

"No, I just want something different."

"Okay, let me pull your file and see what… there we are: What would you like?" Lois asked.

"Something simple…, How about… oh… you pick something for me." "Okay, I'll tell you what… let me see what we have."

Lois knows about Shelly, she didn't want to pry into Debo's social life by asking him who Joy was. So she just mined her business and kept quiet.

"Yes…, here we are, we have a GMC SUV, how's that?"

"Yes, that'll be fine, Lois thanks."

"You're very welcome, I'll just make the necessary changes on the paperwork and you'll be set. Okay all set, see you later."

Debo had a dark-blue, two-door 2008 GMC truck. He also had the people at the leasing agency install the surveillance camera in the truck. He called Shelly on her cell phone to make sure everything went as planned.

"Hi, Baby.., how did everything go?"

"Real good, are you okay?" Shelly asked.

"Yeah, I'm fine, I'll send Joy over there tonight. Is Freddy still there?"

"Yes, honey, he should be in his room."

"Okay, I can call his room and find out. As long as you are there you can have anything you want," he told her.

"Baby?"

"Yeah, sweetheart?"

"I'm afraid!!" she confessed.

"Baby you'll be just fine, I have my best people there with you."

"But, it's you I'm afraid for not myself."

"Baby, I made you a promise and I'm going to keep it. I'll be okay, and all this will be over soon."

Debo tried as hard as he could to convince that nothing was going to happen to him.

"Okay, baby, but you be careful for me, alright?"

"I will, I'll call you tonight, enjoy yourself, go have some fun. Don't worry about me baby, okay," Debo said, then hung up.

He knew how hard it would be for her to enjoy herself, he just said that to try and get her to relax.

"Okay, lil sis where to?"

"I don't know, I haven't kicked it with my bra in a while. Dinner would be wonderful."

"Dinner this early? Oh well, suit yourself, where to?" he repeated . This time he was hoping she could think of someplace to eat but she took too long to answer, and he said,

"You like chili, don't you?"

"Man, I was raised on chili, beans, and bacon." "I know this really good chili joint on Crenshaw," he told her.

"Let's get on over to Crenshaw before I throw you in the back seat and drive this thing myself."

She ate a large bowl of chili with crackers and a large soda herself. Debo had a medium bowl with crackers and lemonade.

"Hey, that was the best chili in town," she said after she had eaten the whole bowl full.

"You haven't tasted anything until you've tried Shell's Chili. You ready to go?" he asked her.

"Yeah, as ready as I'll ever be."

Debo stood up and walked over and stood behind her chair and waited for her to get up. He pulled her chair back for her and helped with the coat she traded with Shelly. They were the same height, Joy, Shelly, and Pauline. So, she didn't have a problem as far as the coat fitting her. He let her lead the way to the door. Once she was outside, he looked back and yelled to Milton that he would see him later and followed Joy to the car. They didn't eat outside because of the weather. They got outside and was hit by the scent of automobile exhaust and wet cement. It had started to drizzle and the pavement was wet under their feet as they got in, bringing with them dirt and mud.

"Thanks for the meal, Big Bro, it was lovely!"

"You're welcome, Sis, anytime, Debo said and they left the Chili King. He was sure he scared the guys off that were following him earlier.

Especially since they saw him go to the police station, so he took Joy to the hotel. They arrived there and Debo pulled the car into an alley to make sure no one was following them this time. No one passed by and no one came into the alley behind them. Joy got out of the truck and entered through a back entrance of the hotel. Debo watched her every step of the way. Besides, she had her trusty nine-millimeter in her handbag, and you could bet she would not hesitate to use it.

She walked up to the front desk which was made of a shiny, very expensive marble similar to the marble on Mad-C's hall floor, only black. The lite-skinned male desk clerk was tall, in fact he could have played pro basketball. His hair was pulled back into a ponytail and he seemed to be wearing make-up of some kind.

He had a fresh look on his face, one that said, 'I haven't a care in the world.'

Joy felt small under the seven-foot giant. Her 5'6" frame was no match for him under any circumstances. He looked down at her and said, "How may I be of service to you, Miss?"

"Hello… I would like room 2200 please."

"Just a moment please," he said, as he dialed a couple of numbers, then asked her name.

"Joy," she told him.

"Thank you, Joy…, Mister Moss will be down in a few minutes."

She decided not to go through the trouble of trying to read the clerk's name-tag, she was just too short. She just thanked him and waited for Freddy. Freddy came down the stairs wearing a T-shirt with a long sleeve blue dress shirt. It looked like he had just thrown it on, only the last three buttons were fastened. You could see that the right side of his waist occupied a rather bulky object. Most likely the 357-magnum he wore when he was on duty as a bodyguard for Debo.

"Hey, love, where is the boss?" he excitedly asked, wrapping his long arms around her waist and leading her toward the elevators.

"He just dropped me off, no one should be wise, we were pretty careful. Some guys did try a little stunt earlier but we took care of it, how's, Shelly?"

"She's doing better than she was a few hours ago. She said, 'she talked to the boss and that made her feel better.'" Freddy told her.

"I'll be staying in the penthouse suite with her," Joy mentioned.

"Well look at you, you go girl," Freddy envied. "Oh, stop it man, I'll go on up and…"

"Here, you'll need this," Freddy said, as he handed her a card with about six small dots and some writing on it and an arrow directing in what position to insert it into the elevator that leads to the penthouse suites.

"This is yours," she said.

"I have another one, that's Shelly's. I'll call her to let her know you're here and that you're on your way up."

"Hey, Shelly, everything okay?"

"Everything is wonderful, when will Joy be here?" she asked him, with a hint of loneliness in her voice.

"She should be coming through the door right about now." At that moment the elevator doors opened and Joy stepped off into the penthouse suite. When the elevator doors closed, they turned into walls inside the penthouse.

"Where are your things?" Shelly asked.

"I'm having them brought up to Freddy's room."

"But, you'll be staying here, won't you?"

"Yeah…, just a security precaution."

"Good enough, let me show you where you'll be sleeping," Shelly told her.

They went through the Penthouse foyer, leading to a living room, dining room, kitchen, and two bedrooms. The kitchen was as big as Joy's living room and dining room put together. Each of the bedrooms has a bathroom, with his and her bathrobes and towels, shower stalls for more privacy during shower, bath slippers, cosmetics, and a flat screen plasma twenty-seven-inch television set on the wall of the bedrooms. The bedrooms were equipped with surround sound stereo systems, a digital clock, a computer with a built-in phone for online communication, and a built-in fax machine.

"This is beautiful," Joy said.

She felt very special and very privileged being in a place like this; and special she is. She just didn't know how special she is in Debo's eyes. And she earned every penny, every bit of luxury he set before her.

"Boy, money does wonders, doesn't it?" she asked Shelly. "Yes, it does…, are you hungry?"

"No, not really, I had a big bowl of chili earlier. But if you're hungry, I'll eat something with you. You know how soup wears off after so long, and chili is nothing but soup."

"You don't have to cook, everything is brought up from the hotel kitchen," Shelly told her.

"Well, what in the world is that great big kitchen in there for?"

"You don't have to cook, but you can."

Shelly handed her a menu and told her to press zero star on the phone to order.

"When did D-Angelo tell you about everything?" Joy asked Shelly. "We were on the beach Saturday in Santa Monica where we usually go, and he just came out and told me."

"You understand why he kept it from you, don't you?"

"To protect me and to keep me from worrying and stressing."

"He told you that?"

"Yeah, I figured that was why he kept it from me. D-Angelo has never lied to me about anything… anything that is, but this. And Joy, I knew for years about what he did for a living."

"So, why did you keep quiet about it? Why let him continue to lie or keep it from you? Or should I say try to keep it from you?"

"I don't know, maybe I figured it would make him feel better if he knew that it was better that I didn't know. So, I didn't let him know I knew."

"Did you tell him that you knew?"

"Yeah…, at the beach."

"Well, apparently you do understand why he lied about it and that's all that matters. He's a very good person, I love him as though he was my blood brother. He has done so much for me, Tammy, and Sheila. But, that's not why I love him so much. I've never had a brother, Shelly. And whatever you do hold on to him, you hear me?"

She looked over at Shelly and saw a twinge of moisture in her eyes. "Yes, Joy I hear you."

They heard the phone on the wall ring, it was the kitchen letting them know that their orders were ready and on their way up. Joy ordered deep-fried fillet of sole, red snapper, hush puppies, chocolate mousse, champagne, and two bottles of cherry water.

"I ordered seafood, I hope you don't mind," Joy said. "Sure, I love fish," Shelly told her.

Shelly hadn't eaten and Joy knew it, that's why she agreed to eat with her; to make sure she ate something. Joy had helped to cheer her up, so did the call from Debo. But she couldn't let go of the thought that something very wrong, deadly wrong could possibly happen to her husband. She was hungry and she knew she should eat but the thought kept stabbing at her.

"Eat, girl, that nutcase is going to be just fine. He has us, and I don't think he's going to leave you for anything on this earth. Eat your food, girl." Shelly felt a little more comfortable hearing those words of encouragement. She fixed herself a plate and began eating with Joy.

Debo headed for the freeway and was off to San Diego. He arrived at Mad-C's estate at 8:45 Wednesday evening. Edward was off sick so Mad-C let Debo in.

"Hey Bro, where's Ed?" Debo asked. "He's out sick."

"Ed is sick? I've never known Ed to be sick. Well, I guess he's human too, huh?"

"Yeah, what's up, is everything okay?"

"Yeah…, I got Shell and Joy settled in at the hotel. What happened with the address of your boy, Morris?" Debo asked.

"I got a 1435 Brooks Street address in Venice, CA," Mad-C told him. "Okay, I'll check on it tomorrow when I go to Los Angeles."

"Are you going alone?"

Debo could tell Mad-C was worried by the look on his face.

"No, I'll take Jeffery with me to make sure no funny stuff goes down. If it does, I'll bring it down. A couple of Cruse's boys tried some funny stuff on me and Joy in an alley downtown while I was in LA. Those guys all use the same kind of license plates. I have seen two of their cars so far, and both have personalized plates with the letters P-L-A-Y-E-R, followed by a number at the end. The Benz is a five and the white Plymouth has a two. There could be others out there. If the medal I found at the house wasn't Cruse's, then it has to belong to Carlyle. I'm having Billings check it and the plates out to see who's driving what, and to see if we can get an address on a business or a residence."

"This shit has gone on for too long. I want this ended, Jackson."

Mad-C found it necessary to call Debo by his surname when something was too out-of-order, or too out-of-reach, right about now, something was too out-of-both.

"Are you ready for some action?" Debo asked. "Try me, Debo."

"Do you want to ride with me and Jeffery tomorrow?"

"Just call me when you're ready."

"We're there first thing in the morning. Tomorrow is Thursday and the fishing and boat club should be open. We'll swing by there when we leave Venice. Billings said, 'that the club is in Malibu.'"

"I'm ready when you are," Mad-C said.

"Talk to me boss," Jeffery said when he answered his phone. Debo had called him to let him know what was going on.

"I'll need you in the morning. I have a job for you to do and I'll need some backup at about 6:00 or 7:00 in the morning. I'll leave here at about three and meet you at your place at 6:00 or 7:00."

"Okay, Debo…, I'll have Leroy open the pool hall, you know where I am."

"Okay, see you then, oh bring a couple of toys; something special," Debo requested.

THURSDAY, NOVEMBER 8TH, 6:45 A.M.

Debo, Mad-C, and Jeffery pulled up in front of an old abandoned, rundown house, with peeling paint, termite-eaten wood, and the steps were about to separate from the front porch. The awning over the front door was barely hanging by a rusty nail and a worn bolt that had also seen tougher weather. The doors and windows were nailed up with beaver-board, the grass was four feet tall in some places, and trash was piled up in the yard around the steps and under a front window.

"Do you think anyone lives here?" Jeffery asked. "It doesn't look like it," Mad-C responded.

"I'll check around back," Debo told them. "What the…?" he heard himself say out loud.

He couldn't believe his eyes: The backyard was well manicured and the back house was gorgeous. The two-car garage and the back house had bars on the windows and a wrought-iron gate at the front door. Debo looked up, and a hair to his right and saw what resembled a camera lens concealed in a tree hole. The tree had seen its share of rain, and had grown tall and was well cared for. Debo pulled *crazy* from its holster and braced himself against the wall next to the door.

"Hey, guys, look what I found!!!" he yelled to Jeffery and Mad-C. "Wow!" Jeffery said.

"That's just what I said," Debo told him. "Is anybody in there?" Mad-C asked.

"I don't know, but there's a camera up there in that tree," Debo said as he pointed to a hole in the tree.

"If there was anyone in the house, we'd have known it by now." Debo told them to get out of sight; not really knowing if there were other cameras around. They took their perspective places. Mad-C was on the other side of the big tree facing Debo and the front door, Jeffery was posted on the side of the house up front where they had all come from to get to the backyard. Debo pushed the button on the door frame and a loud *Ding-Dong* sounded from inside the house. All three men poised themselves just in case someone opened the door looking for trouble.

"Yeah," a voice said, from inside the house.

They were ready for whatever happened, or whoever came upon them with a problem.

"Is Mister Morris home?" Debo asked.

"Who's asking?" the voice inside the house said. "My name is...," At that time, he heard Jeffery.

"Psst..., hey boss, someone's coming," he whispered, pointing to the front of the house.

Jeffery turned and walked slowly toward the front. Debo and Mad-C were still frozen at the front door of the back-house. Mad-C moved around the tree to see what was going on with Jeffery. Debo signaled to Mad-C that he had the door covered.

Mad-C crouched down and worked his way over to where Jeffery had been standing and saw him coming back toward him walking fast.

"Someone was on their way back here. They must have heard the boss talking to whoever it was that answered the door. Because when I got to the front a car was pulling off," Jeffery said.

"Did you see the plates?" Mad-C asked.

"I sure did; *P-L-A-Y-E-R* and the number two at the end. It was a white Plymouth," Jeffery told him.

They were both expecting to hear gunshots at any moment coming from around back. They looked around the corner of the front house and saw Debo standing outside the house talking to someone. He was half listening to the woman who answered the door and listening for gun fire from the front of the house as well.

Debo told Mad-C and Jeffery what the lady said.

"Jonny doesn't stay back here, he used to live in the house up front, but he got himself a job and moved away."

"Yeah, he got a job alright; at my dock and took off with my ten kilos. I can see why his ass moved," Mad-C thought to himself.

"But, something is wrong here; he's tied in with these guys making big bucks, and this is how he lives." Jeffery said, pointing to the mess around the front house and the front house itself.

"Good point, he could live in the back house and the woman in there is lying. That car you saw, Jeffery, was the same car that tried to hem me and Joy up in an alley downtown yesterday. The lady has to know more than she's letting on. I know that if that camera in the tree works, she saw *crazy* in my hand, and she should have seen at least one of you, but she didn't seem to be disturbed by it. I wonder if our boy Cruse was in the house watching. Did any of you notice a black Benz parked out front when we pulled up?" Debo asked.

Neither of them remembered seeing one. Mad-C walked over to the two-car-garage and there were no windows.

"Will that be all, gentlemen?" the lady asked from the same door she was standing in talking to Debo.

The double iron doors were black and they couldn't see inside the house.

"Well, Billings won't have to run this baby, I'm sure I know who it belongs to. Now, all I have to do is put Robert Cruse behind the wheel of the Mercedes…, and wala!" Debo declared.

The address 10117 Ocean Parkway is in Malibu, CA. Debo and Jeffery waited outside in the parking lot in case they spotted the cars with the *PLAYER* plates. Mad-C walked through the turnstile doors. The entrance to the club was the exact image of the architect's mind: The mind of a longtime seaman. The turnstile doors were built into the belly of a fishing boat with a large whale and two fishing rods across the top of the ship's sails. Mad-C stepped up to the shiny wood counter where a man in a sailor's uniform stood with a giant rudder on the wall behind him.

"What can I do for you, Mister… ?"

"Cruse… Chuck Cruse," Mad-C lied. "Mister Cruse, how can I be of service?"

"I am here to see, Bobby… Oh, excuse me… Robert Cruse."

Mad-C figured that if he used a name that a friend or relative of Cruse would use, then the desk clerk would be less likely to suspect anything, nor hesitate about giving him any information.

"Let me check," the man said and got on his computer and started to punch in keys on a keypad. He looked back at Mad-C and said…

"Mr Cruse canceled his membership about a year ago, Mr Cruse."

"Now, why would he do that? I told him I was coming out here from Florida to see him. And after fifteen years my brother still can't do things right. Did he leave an address?"

"I'm sorry, sir, but I can't give you that information."

"But, he's my brother and I haven't seen him in years," Mad-C lied again in protest.

"I'm very sorry, sir," the man repeated.

"Okay, thanks," Mad-C said, then turned and walked away.

"Sorry, Sir," the man repeated, feeling guilty for being unable to assist Mad-C.

"Well, he definitely was a member," Mad-C said when he got back to the car.

"Yeah, or he still is," Debo added.

"Who is or was?" Jeffery asked. "Robert Cruse, and he used that name."

"Did you get an address?" Debo asked.

"He wouldn't give me one; something to do with policy, I guess."

"I'll get Sgt Billings to come down here and get an address out of these assholes," Debo promised.

"What's next?" Jeffery asked either one of the bigger men.

"Don't look like too much we can do here; I'll go back home and tie up some things in San Diego. I'm thinking about moving into the Beverly Hills office.

You can join me if you want Debo, it has two sleeping quarters. I designed it that way because I was there over half the time working anyway," Mad-C offered.

Debo knew because he slept there when he stayed over in Los Angeles. "Yeah, why bring all this crap to our homes? I can be closer to Shell in case something happens and she needs me, I'll be close."

Mad-C and Debo were off to San Diego. "See you tomorrow," he told Debo.

Jeffery went back to Inglewood to await further instructions. "Hey, Sarge, I have a favor I need you to do for me."

"Shoot," Billings said, (Cops always say *'shoot'*, maybe it's some kind of cop thing, or maybe they can't help saying it. It's part of their work anyway.)

"I need an address from the people at the fishing and boat club over on Ocean Parkway and the guy wouldn't give it to Mr Write."

"You've been by there?" Billings asked.

"No, Mister Write went to get some information."

"And you want me to go out there and throw some weight around, am I right?"

"Yeah, just a little."

"And, when do you want me to do you this big favor?"

"As soon as possible."

"Okay, give me a couple of hours, I'm going to a meeting in about thirty-minutes. It's 2:00 pm now, when do they close?" Billings asked Debo. "Around 4:00 or 5:00; I guess. I'll call and check, then call you right back."

"Okay do that, but call me right back," Billings told him. Debo hung up and called Mad-C.

"Yeah, I'm half way home..., I hope nothing has come up!"

"No, nothing else came up yet. Did you happen to see when the fishing and boat club closes?"

"Yeah, I have their business card, let's see..., 8:30 pm. Why, what are you up to?"

"Sgt Billings is going to try and get an address on Cruse for us, and I need to see what time they close because he's on his way to a meeting." Debo copied the time down and called Sgt Billings back with the information. Billings told Debo that he would take care of it for him, and they hung up. Debo decided to give Joy and Freddy a call to see how Shelly was getting along. He would call her once he got to San Diego. He was thinking about Rex. Maybe it's not a good idea to leave him out there alone. Maybe he could see if Omar would keep him for a while until this is over. But, he would have to dig him up from wherever his lifestyle keeps him. Omar didn't want any part of the dope game. Their father brought too much havoc into the house and the family with drugs and drug trafficking. Debo found Omar in Compton on 108th and Imperial where he and his girlfriend Gail lives. Omar moved in with Gail when he met her six-years ago. He does construction work for the Los Angeles Unified School District. Debo always respected his older brother for the decision he made. He has a good-paying job, and a pretty good woman; crazy, but good. Omar used to be close to Rex when he and Debo were around each other about nine years ago when Debo, Omar, and Rex would go places and do things together... until Omar met Gail. When Debo asked his brother to keep Rex until this mess was over with. He agreed but Debo didn't tell Omar what was going on: Just that he and Shelly were going on a vacation for a couple of months.

With that out of the way, he was free to use the office with Mad-C until things blew over. It was starting to cloud up; small patches of dark clouds were moving toward large patches of white clouds, and the weather was cool and sort of damp. He called Joy on his way to the freeway, headed back to San Diego.

"Hey, Bro."

"Hey, Sis.., I'm going to be out at the Beverly Hills office with Mister Write until this blows over. I want to be close to Shell and you guys if you need me or I need you. I just talked to Freddy; you guys are doing a terrific job, thank you."

"Well, Big Bro, you're supposed get what you spend your money for. No, you're very welcome," Joy seriously continued .

"Yeah, I'm getting much more than what I paid for and I appreciate it."

"Oh, stop it, you're my brother, what did you expect?"

"How is Shell doing?"

"She's a little tired I think, we sat up playing rummy for hours. She beat the crap out of me."

"Yeah, she's pretty good at playing rummy, she beats the crap out of me too. Tell her I said I'll call her later. I'm on my way to pick up some things from the house and head back in the morning."

"Don't you have a dog?"

"Yeah, my brother is watching him."

"Yeah…, how is, Omar?"

"He's doing fine."

"That's good, do you want me to tell Shelly you called?"

"Yeah you can if you want, and let her know that I'll call her. It'll give her something good to wake up to. I miss her, Joy!!"

"Just hold on, bra."

She started to call him *boss*, because that's what Freddy calls him, and it's starting to rub off on her.

"I almost called you, *Boss;* hanging around bighead Freddy's butt. I'll let her know you called."

"Okay, Sis.., I've got to pay attention to these nuts on the road, I'll call you back as soon as I get to Diego."

"Alright, I'll tell Shelly."

Thanks," Debo said, and they both hung up.

He looked at the quartz on his wrist and saw that it was 5:30 pm and Billings will be leaving the office going home. Debo dialed the Sgt's cell and heard a raspy voice with a touch of aggravation in it .

"Something wrong, Sarge?"

"You bet something's wrong. Do you remember me telling you a while back about a man that was holding a foster home hostage?"

"About two weeks ago... yeah, I remember, you were on the phone when I came up to see you, what happened?"

"That's what the meeting was about; the man committed suicide right in front of his children and Internal Affairs are coming down on the department because the negotiators screwed up. It's just one big piece of crap after another. I'll be glad when I retire. What's up? Oh ..., the address, I had to go in there and throw more than a little weight around."

With the Sgt's build, he had the weight to throw around. "But I got what you asked for..., ready?"

"Yeah, whatcha got?"

"Robert (Big Boy) Cruse; *aka* Raymond Anderson, 11607 Ocean Street Venice, CA. I also checked the license plate number of both cars *P-L-A-Y-E-R-5* is driven by Robert Cruse, and *P-L-A-Y-E-R-2*, Randy Carlyle drives. Last known address..., you ready? 1435 Brooks Street, Venice, California."

"I was just out there today and *P-L-A-Y-E-R-2* stopped by but decided to keep it moving. So, it's not Jonny Morris that drives *P-L-A-Y-E-R-2*, it's Carlyle."

"As confusing as it may sound, Jackson, I think you've got it."

"Okay thanks,Sgt, go on home and get some sleep, sounds like you could use it."

Debo was at Mad-C's estate at 10:00 Friday morning. He told Mad-C everything the Sergeant had told him, and that Robert Cruse is at 11607 Ocean in Venice, California.

"Okay, that's our next stop, meet me at the office in Beverly Hills." After their meeting, Debo left. He pulled the Explorer out of the carport, and with everything he needed he was on his way to Beverly Hills with an arsenal of weapons. He would stop by the car leasing agency and give them the keys to the GMC truck and have them pick it up for a small fee, plus a handsome gratuity.

FRIDAY, NOVEMBER 9TH, 10:00 A.M.

Debo was at Mad-C's estate at 10:00 Friday morning. He told Mad-C everything that the Sergeant had told him, and that Robert Cruse is at 11607 Ocean in Venice, California.

"Okay, that's our next stop, meet me at the office in Beverly Hills." Debo pulled the Navigator out of the carport, and with everything he needed, he was on his way to Beverly Hills with a large arsenal of weapons. He would stop by the car leasing agency and give them the keys to the GMC truck and have them pick it up for a small fee, plus a handsome gratuity.

CHAPTER 9

SATURDAY, NOVEMBER 10TH, 10:00 A.M.

"Good morning, Mister Cruse," the front desk clerk at the fishing and boat club said when Robert Cruse walked in. The desk clerk wasn't too much taller than Cruse. He wore a white sailor uniform also, only he was much older than the clerk that talked to Mad-C.

"Is Tom in?" Cruse asked.

"Ah… yes he is, hold on a sec and I'll get him," the clerk said. While Cruse was waiting, he took the time to look at the brochures to different fishing resorts. He was contemplating taking a trip after he got the guy that killed his brother-in-law, Mack Rodgers and took off with more than $200,000 in drugs and cash.

"Planning on taking a vacation, or just browsing?" the man asked Cruse, as he stepped behind the long counter.

"Oh, I don't know… maybe.

Listen, some guy came by here asking questions about you. He said he was your brother from Florida," Tom told Cruse.

"Did he give you a name?"

"Yes, he said his name was Chuck Cruse, and later that evening a cop came by and wanted your address."

"Did you give it to him?"

"Yeah, he was an LAPD police Sergeant, and he said that he was investigating a possible murder. He said you killed a man; a *'Yin'* something.., years ago."

"What else did he say?"

"Nothin, just that I can get in a lot of trouble if I didn't give him the address. I also told him that you canceled your membership here at the club about a year ago. Figured maybe they'll spend some time looking elsewhere and stop coming here."

"Was anyone else with the guy that came before the cop?"

"Uh… No, he came in by himself. I'm not sure if anyone was waiting in the parking lot or not."

"Okay, here… you did a wonderful job."

"Thank you Mister Cruse." Tom looked at the folded-up piece of paper and saw that it was a $100 bill. And as Cruse walked through the turnstile doors he heard Tom yell, "Thanks again, Mister Cruse!!!"

Robert Cruse got to the parking lot and was looking around to see if anyone was watching or following him before he got into the black Mercedes Benz. He picked up his cell phone and pressed and held the menu for three seconds and heard a beep and said into the phone, "Dial, Carlyle." The phone automatically dialed Randy Carlyle's number.

"Big boy, holler at me," a voice on the other end said. "Our boy is asking questions," Cruse told him. "Yeah…, what kind of questions?"

"It doesn't matter, the point is he's asking questions about me. He went by the boat club yesterday looking for me."

"Yeah, somebody went over to my mom's house. I couldn't see who it was, I just heard them in the backyard talking."

Jonny Morris' mom is like a mother to Randy Carlyle. Jonny and Randy grew up together as kids, and they consider themselves to be brothers. Randy Carlyle spent a lot of time at Mamma Morris' house.

"Yeah speaking of Morris, where is he hiding these days?" Cruse asked. "Around, I'm sure. I know he did a lousy job at trying to hit Jackson on the freeway. I don't know how the hell he messed that up," Carlyle said.

"Johnnie's on dope, man, you know that. And that's a problem I don't need," Cruse told Randy Carlyle.

"He's supposed to call me tonight," Carlyle said.

"Yeah, well the only way they could have found out about the boat club is through the medal I dropped when I drugged that mutt of Jackson's. Okay, they'll be going by the apartment I used to stay in. Tell Jonny to go by there and wait outside the apartment, but don't give him your car. They probably know your car and mine by now. Give him the gray Tahoe SUV, and tell him not to mess this up. Here, give him this and tell him to get someone to go with him I need you to do something for me," Cruse said.

Carlyle knew what Cruse was up to. Jonny Morris was no good to him on drugs. Cruse figured that it was just a matter of time before Jonny got himself killed or busted. Carlyle looked inside the envelope that Cruse had handed him to give to Johnny, and there were fifty $100 bills in it.

That's $5,000 cash. Robert (Big Boy) Cruse was setting up Johnny Morris to be killed. And who better to do it than the man that wanted them all dead anyway; D-Angelo Jackson. Cruse reconsidered Jonny taking the Tahoe. It was better for him to take the Plymouth, everyone knows that car, especially Debo. And, if he sees it, there's bound to be some trouble.

"Give Morris your car and you take the Tahoe. Your car has been seen too much anyway. The Tahoe can't be traced to any of us."

When he said what he said, it confirmed what Randy Carlyle had suspected. Robert (Big Boy) Cruse was indeed setting Jonny Morris up to be killed. There was nothing Carlyle could do about it unless he wanted the same thing. Maybe Jonny knows someone who could use a little cash. Whoever he gets to do the job with him might get possibly a grand and Jonny keeps the other four grand for himself. But little do they know; the money is a one-way ticket to hell. Debo and Mad-C were at the office in Beverly Hills. They have the address on Cruse which is the one they really wanted. They got in the Explorer and headed for 11607 Ocean Street in Venice, California. It's a narrow street with the cars parked diagonally in front of a row of apartments that were fairly new and favoring condos. Debo parked the Navigator and got out with Mad-C right behind him. They walked up to the newly painted condominiums. The steps were made of acrylic covered wood encased in steel. Mad-C looked through the directory to his left and didn't see the name he was looking for so he pressed the intercom button and no one answered.

"Press the zero it usually calls the manager," Debo suggested.

Mad-C pressed the zero, as Debo suggested, and still there was no answer as he cursed under his breath.

"Let me have a go at it," Debo offered.

Debo was about to try the complicated entry device when a woman walked up, pressed three digits, then pound.

"Who is it?" a woman's voice said.

"It's Me," the lady at the door said into the small speaker. "Hold on."

Debo heard a buzz at the door and the lady walked in.

Mad-C held the door open while Debo pressed the manager's code again; this time using the pound key.

"Manager," a voice said through the same small speaker that yelled at the woman before him.

"I'm looking for Mister Cruse, Robert Cruse."

"Do you live here?" the woman asked.

"Hell no…, If I did, I wouldn't need you to get in," Debo thought to himself, then he said,

"No, I'm a friend of his."

"Then look through the directory and find his name, then press his code. I can't let you in, nor give you his unit number."

"Thank you," Debo said.

What the manager didn't know was that they were already in the building. All they needed was Cruse's unit number. Debo scanned the directory again and no Robert Cruse or Raymond Anderson.

"Now what?" Debo asked Mad-C. "Now we wait, Debo.., now we wait." Mad-C told him.

They went back to the Explorer and Debo put on a compact disc and was enjoying the mellow tunes of Kenny G.

"What do you know about that?" Mad-C asked Debo. "Everything, you should see some of my stuff."

"Oh..., I know you don't play when it comes to good music. I heard some of your masterpieces at *the Shell-Debo*," Mad-C awarded.

"Wanna go get something to eat, or some coffee?"

"No, I don't want to miss this guy, I know what he looks like. You can go grab something and I'll wait here."

"No, I'd better stick around with you in case they show up," Debo told him.

"So, how is Shelly taking all this?"

"She's taking it like a champ. I just hate that I had to lie to her all those years about what I do and she knew all along."

"You mean she knew what you did all these years?"

"Yeah, she said, 'that she checked up on my job; actually my boss and found out that the company was going under years ago.'"

"Well I'll be dipped in shit and set out for the flies."

"She said, 'she kept it to herself because she knew I lied to protect her,'" Debo shared.

Debo was uncomfortable about something. He kept looking in the side view mirror, which gave him a view of the backside of the street. Mad-C noticed the expression on his face and said,

"Is something wrong?"

"Look here in the monitor," Debo said, as he adjusted the rear surveillance camera so it could pick up the white Plymouth parked behind them about six cars down. On that particular street, you had to parallel park, and you could see the tail end of the parked car.

"You mean that white Plymouth standing out like a sore thumb?"

"That's the one."

"You think that's them?"

"I'm positive it's the car that pulled up behind me and Joy in that downtown alley. Do you see the primer on the right rear fender?"

The car was nearly new, but it had seen its run of car chases, hit and runs, shootouts, bangs, and fender-benders.

"Okay, now that we know they can see us, what would you suggest we do?" Mad-C asked.

Debo reached into the jacket he was wearing and pulled *crazy* from its shoulder holster. He slid the slide back on the 45-automatic pistol and checked the chamber. When the slide went forward, he knew the forty-five shell went in the chamber and was now ready.

"I'm going in the building like I'm checking again, then go around the other side," Debo said, as he got out of the Navigator and walked up to the steps.

He waited about two minutes, and a man carrying a bag walked up. He could see the man was either going to a party or giving one. In one hand he had a bag with assorted potato chip bags sticking out of the top, a bag of ice next to the chips, and a case of beer in the other hand. He sat the beer down to get his keys out of his pocket while Debo stood to the side. He was going to offer to help the man but thought better of it. But to expedite things he changed his mind.

"I'm going in, do you need a hand?" Debo offered anyway. Debo didn't look to be the kind of person that would run off with the guy's beer, so the guy accepted his offer. Debo heard jingling, as the man finally came out of his pocket with the keys. He was thinking about how good it would be to have a nice cold beer. The man finally opened the door and they both went in. He wiped the sweat from his forehead that had accumulated from the impatience caused by waiting on the man, and hoped that he would hurry up before the two men in the Plymouth made their move on Mad-C. Debo walked through the door and was met by the smell of fish frying. He heard a baby crying in one of the units down the hall. He could see the kid because the door was ajar. His diaper looked like it was about to fall off. He was probably soaked, which explains why he or she was crying so hard. He walked down a long hallway and heard loud music and smelled cigarette smoke and figured that was where the man at the door was headed. He got to the end of the hall, and to his right was another hall. He walked through the opened fire door with the exit sign displayed over it. "This is taking too long," he thought and started to break into a fast trot. He didn't want to run because he knew that would alarm the tenants in the hall. He came to another exit and the door was closed. He opened the door and there were about eight concrete stairs leading to the sidewalk. He walked down the steps and onto the sidewalk. From there he went around the corner and saw a Sparkles Water truck. On the other side of the truck was the white Plymouth, and still sitting in it was Morris and Jason. Jason was the man that Morris hired to help him off Mad-C and Debo.

Debo motioned to Mad-C that he was in position and ready to act. Mad-C got out of the Explorer with his 44-magnum in his hand, ready to exterminate the obstacles that were in his way. Jonny Morris noticed Mad-C getting out of the Explorer and walked toward the Plymouth. Morris got out of the car on the driver's side, and Jason got out on the passenger's side of the car. Debo saw Morris get out of the car holding a 9-millimeter handgun in his hand. Jason got out with a sawed-off shotgun. Mad-C was already en route toward the two men. He saw the sawed-off shotgun resting at Jason's side. Jason saw Mad-C and leveled the shotgun at him. Mad-C leveled the 44-magnum at Jason, while Morris looked around for Debo.

Before Jones, Morris, or Mad-C could get off a shot, Debo yelled from behind the two men, "Hey, assholes!!!" The two men turned their heads for an instant, just long enough for Mad-C to fire off a round, hitting Jones in the chest and throwing him back toward the Plymouth. At the same time, Debo let *Crazy* wreak havoc on Jonny Morris. The slug from the 45-automatic found its target and drilled a golf ball sized hole straight through the side of Morris' head. Morris stood there for about three seconds already dead and was hit with another round. This time knocking him toward Mad-C. Debo walked back over to the Navigator, and together they both got in and were off down the street.

"Debo, I saw kids out there."

"I did too, and a woman," Debo said.

"Well, thank goodness that they were away from the shooting."

They made it back to Beverly Hills. "That wasn't Cruse," Mad-C said.

"It must have been someone he hired, like Carlyle or Morris."

"I wonder what took them so long to act… to make the hit?" Debo asked.

"I don't know, but I saw women and children out there and I don't like firing my weapon when women and children are around," Mad-C said. Mad-C had taken his wife and daughter; Casey and Tina out for the evening, and was on the way home.

His daughter, Tina, was nine years old at the time. She was moving impatiently in the back seat of the Cadillac SUV.

"What's wrong, sweetheart," Casey asked her.

"I have to use the restroom, Mommy," Tina told her mom. "Honey pull into that gas station so she can go to the restroom."

Mad-C pulled over at Casey's request and was frustrated because a big bobtail truck tried to cut him off; nearly running them off the road and into a parked car. Mad-C honked in frustration while wiping his forehead. Casey reached over and squeezed his right thigh.

"Oh, Charles, what's wrong with these crazy people out here?"

"I don't know, baby."

He didn't have a problem finding out either But, he had his family with him and that saved the guy's ass. So, he thought that maybe he should stay calm and do the right thing. He decided he wouldn't do any teeth smashing tonight: Although the guy did deserve some dental work.

"Here you go, Tina," Mad-C told his daughter, as he pulled about four feet from the two sliding glass-doors that were put there so the customers could gain entrance to the mini-market and restroom area inside the gas station.

"I think I'll grab a cup of coffee, baby you want anything?"

"No, I'm fine, Tina doesn't need anything either."

Casey and Tina had already gone into the restroom in the back of the store.

"Nobody moves!!!" Mad-C heard someone yell. It came from the direction of the sliding doors, not far from the counter.

"You know what this is," the man announced.

Mad-C was in the back of the mini-mart where the coffee machine and restrooms were. There were the usual canned goods lined up neatly on shelves, and two-liter sodas stacked on the floor along with shelves of assorted pastries and doughnuts. The guy that robbed the gas station didn't notice Mad-C when he came in. Mad-C scrunched down behind the coffee machine and pulled his 44-magnum from its holster. He never liked shoulder holsters; he preferred his on his waist. Shoulder holsters made his shoulder feel like something was pulling, pinching, and irritating him. Casey came out of the restroom and startled the man robbing the gas station. The guy turned and fired a single shot, hitting Casey in the chest; sending her to the floor. Mad-C felt pain mixed with rage, fear, anger, and a tightening in his head as he let off three rounds with the 44-magnum and grazed the man's shoulder. When the bullet hit the guy, his gun went off and Mad-C fired another round, hitting him in the stomach, knocking him over the soda case that was displaying Coke, Pepsi, and Seven-Up Sodas. He was dead before he hit the floor. Mad-C rushed over to where Casey was lying, picked her up, and held her in his arms and cried. Then it hit him…, "My Baby…!!!"

"Tina!!!" He looked at the half-opened door to the bathroom and didn't see his daughter.

"Tina… Tina!!!" He ran through the open door and was inside the restroom, when all you heard was Mad-C yelling from the bottom of his soul.

"No, not my baby…, God please not my baby girl, Tina, Tina baby wake up!!!" he cried.

He heard what seemed like sirens, but he couldn't quite tell because his thinking, his ability to reason, his mental capacity had all shut down.

"Mister… Mister… I said, put your hands where I can see them and get on your knees…, do it now!!!" The officer yelled, louder. His voice brought Mad-C back to the moment, back to reality, back to the fact that his wife and daughter are gone forever. The second shot that came from the robber's weapon went through the bathroom door, striking Tina in the head; killing her instantly.

"Stand up, turn around, and put your hands on your head," the officer ordered.

Mad-C did as he was instructed and was arrested and taken into custody at Chula Vista Police Department in San Diego, CA. He was booked for manslaughter and was scheduled to appear in court when he was moved to George Bailey County Jail in San Diego. Mad-C had never had to be in the position to have to be degraded by the pitiful, inhumane, sickening, and unsanitary conditions he was forced to sleep, sit, stand, and even eat. There was urine all over the walls, empty food containers and milk cartons were just thrown all over the floor with inmates sleeping on the urine soaked floor. The local gang members were in a corner sitting on the hard steel benches, lined up against the cold concrete wall. The meals were certainly not enough food to call a decent meal. A long-haired old hippy-looking guy sat scratching his groin unceasingly, with food, stale milk, and saliva dripping from his beard and mustache. Mad-C laid his head in the palms of his hands and cried.

A big 300-pound man sitting next to him said out of sympathy. "Don't cry, my brother, it can't be that bad. How much time are you looking at?"

Mad-C didn't respond so the big man leaned over and repeated his question and added,

"However much it is, it can't be that bad."

Mad-C couldn't understand why the guy was concerned about his time when he had just lost his family on their way home from a family outing.

"I just lost my family," Mad-C told him.

"We all lose our families when we come in here, but she'll come back to you, watch and see. Now, if you lose your mind in here, you ain't gettin that back. But your girl, she'll come running back to you on hands and knees," the man told him.

"No, you don't understand, my wife and nine-year-old daughter were just killed tonight," Mad-C told him.

"I'm sorry, Mister, I didn't realize it."

"Will you please leave me alone?"

He was grieving the loss of his wife and daughter and didn't want to be bothered.

"Bro, did you hear me?" Debo brought him back to the moment. "No, I was thinking, what did you say?"

"I said that they were probably waiting for us to leave so they could make their move on us; seeing as how there were so many people around. But their plans were interrupted when they saw you get out of the Explorer with the forty-four in your hand."

"Yeah, I guess so," Mad-C said.

Debo went to the bar that Mad-C kept in a little portable barroom inside his private office. He knows that no one was allowed in there, but the circumstances had to be an exception. He brought them both a brandy and tonic. They drank the liquid stimulant and was feeling a little better… at least Debo was.

"Is everything alright?" Debo could see that Mad-C was shook-up about something. It's not what just happened, he did that for exercise back in the day.

"I was just thinking, I'm fine," Mad-C assured Debo.

"Okay, I'm going to go shower and lay down and get some rest. I'll be sleeping in my office if you need anything," Debo told him.

MONDAY, NOVEMBER 12TH, 8:30 A.M.

"Good morning, Mr Jackson," greeted Richard Birmingham, the front desk Sgt. at Parker Center Police Station.

"Hey, Sgt Birmingham," Debo spoke, in return.

"Hold on a sec, I'll see if he's in his office," Richard said, as he picked up the single receiver and spoke into it.

He looked at Debo, hung up, and said,

"Well, Mr Jackson, it's your lucky day, go on up."

Debo thanked the officer that was smaller than he was and wore a bright smile with snow white teeth, wide eyed, and had a glow to him, and went over to the banks of elevators that lead to Sgt Billings office. He got to the Sgt's office and was met by Gloria; Sgt. Billings' secretary, who opened the door to the Sgt's office, and waved Debo inside.

"What's up, big guy?" Debo greeted.

"Was that you in Venice yesterday? I've got two dead bodies that came over the wire; a man by the name of, Jonny Morris and another named, Jason Jones. Know anything about that?"

Debo sat there not really wanting to admit to murder Besides, Billings knew who it was that brought all the attention to Venice, California.

"Now, off the record. I kind of figured it would come to this sooner or later. You don't have to say anything that will incriminate you or Write.

I know that Morris is one of the guys that are not on your list of favorite people. However, let me say this; these men are not rookies, they play dirty, and if Anderson knows who Write is, then he also knows that it won't be easy to hit him or you. This sounds and looks like Anderson set Morris up to be killed by you and Write. Robert Cruse, *aka* Raymond Anderson, Randy Carlyle, and Gregory Johnson are very well wanted by us, the FBI, and the DEA. The only thing is, we can't touch Gregory Johnson. We need something heavy on him. And as for Robert Cruse and Randy Carlyle, they are somehow hiding under Gregory Johnson's skirt. Now, if it gets dirty don't hesitate to call me. You and Write might not be able to dance with these guys," Billings reported.

"Okay, Sarge, I'll give you a call if I need you. But, there is one thing I do need from you right now. I need photographs of Cruse, Johnson, and Carlyle so I can pass them out to my people. That way they'll know who they are if and when they see them."

"Okay, no problem, wait here a minute and I'll have them brought up to you." Sergeant Billings looked like he was ready to retire sooner than expected. After a few minutes, Gloria came into his office and handed him an envelope. He knew what was inside the envelope, and so did Debo. Sgt. Billings handed Debo the envelope and asked him,

"How many more dead bodies should I expect before this is over?"

"I don't even want to think about it," Debo replied. The moisture from his top lip was starting to build up into a sweat. He wiped his lip and said, "I just don't want to think about it."

The Sergeant handed him another envelope with the raps-sheets of Raymond Anderson, Randy Carlyle, and Johnny Morris in it. "I don't need this one," Debo told him, as he handed back the photo and rap sheet of Morris.

"Morris is out of action, but the other two I'll pass on to my people. Thanks Sarge…, oh yeah, what ever happened to the prints from the medal I brought you? You know the Fishing Boat Club Medal."

"The prints came out exactly who you thought it would be, Raymond Anderson. And the two player plates belong to a Yacht Club in Malibu. I had Santa Monica PD release the white Plymouth with the P-L-A-Y-E-R-2 plates to us. It should be arriving in a couple of days. I told them it was somehow connected to Anderson, and that it's part of an ongoing investigation. Maybe we can find something of use before they destroy it."

"Good thinking," Debo awarded.

"And that's it," Sgt Billings said. "Okay, Big Guy, since that's it!."

"Yeah, I'm done."

"Then I'll see you later."

"Okay later," Billings said, then Debo left.

TUESDAY, NOVEMBER 13, 6:00 A.M.

The weather was beginning to change. Debo was on his way to San Diego to check on his mail and maybe take a shower. It was a dreary Tuesday morning, the streets and highways were damp from the overnight fog, and the overcast from the morning dew. The tires on the Explorer played a soggy wet tune against the pavement of the long tiring road He loves the early morning fresh air It stimulates him, opening up his brain, and making his body feel fresh like a burst of energy. He rolled down the windows of the Navigator to allow himself the privilege of enjoying the crisp, moist, autumn air while listening to his favorite Kenny Gee compact disk. His mind was on Shelly. He had told Sgt Billings that she was taking this whole thing pretty well, but was she really? The thought was there and it will be there until this is over. He thought of how wonderful it would be to be with her at that moment, holding her next to him, feeling her softness, listening to her voice. He had thought about calling her but it was almost seven in the morning, maybe that would be a little too early. Oh, what the heck, maybe she's sitting up doing something; probably the same thing he was doing; thinking about him, thinking about the man she loves, the man she misses, the man she longs to hold and be comforted by. He turned on his cell phone and heard the message alert beep, which told him that someone had called while his phone was off and left a message, or several messages. He pressed "Okay" on the selection mode and was directed to enter his four-digit pass code to gain access to his messages.

He entered 0-2-6-8, which is February 1968. That was the month and year that the most important and most wonderful being of his life was born, his wife.

"You have two messages; first message sent Monday, November 12th, 11:18 pm.

"Hey, boss, it's Freddy, just checking in. Shelly and Joy sends their love and said to say 'hey'. Give us a call and let us know that you are still among us …, later."

"To save this message press seven, to delete this message press nine." He pressed nine, and the recording took him to the next message.

"Second message sent Tuesday, November 13th, at 6:45 am."

"Hey, baby, I woke up early and couldn't go back to sleep, call me when you get this message Love you, bye."

He pressed nine to delete the message, then he pressed the options button and call appeared. He pressed the call icon and the numbers were automatically dialed. He heard two rings, then Shelly answered.

"Hey, beautiful," Debo greeted, "Hey, what are you up to, handsome?"

"Oh…, nothing much, I'm on my way to the house to check on the mail and take a shower. I thought about calling you but I didn't know if you were up or not. I got your message about a minute ago. How are you holding out?"

"I'm trying to hang in there and missing you and worried stiff about you, otherwise, I'm fine."

"Sweetheart, please don't worry about me, I'll be alright. I have a vacation to Maui, a big fat Havana Cigar, and the most beautiful wife in the world waiting for me. And do you for one second think that I would let anything happen to me and miss all of that?"

She felt special and relieved. She needed continuous inspiration and encouraging. Now she knew that she could have a good day and not have to worry about anything happening to her husband.

"It's a beautiful morning, I wish you were here with me," he said.

"I do too, baby." Debo knew that if he didn't get off the phone, he would wind up saying something to make her want to be with him even more; to be with him right now. He could feel her, sense her starting to cry. He had just made her day, and he didn't want to depress her by saying anything that would make her cry from loneliness.

"I just want you to keep smiling and trust that I'll be okay, okay?"

"Okay."

"Let me get off this phone before water gets into my eyes."

"Is it raining?"

"No, I mean body fluids, the kind that come from being so much in love that each moment away from you seems like an eternity, "Debo explained.

"Oh Yeah, that kind of water. Okay, I love you, D-Angelo!!"

"I love you too, Shell. Talk to you later, sweetheart," he told her, then hung up.

"They got the car; they're calling it a *bloody mess* down in Venice." Carlyle was talking about the incident in Venice that took his friend's life. Jonny Morris and Randy Carlyle were the best of friends before they met Robert Cruse. They grew up together in Culver City, and then Jonny moved to Venice with his mother. He did live in that rundown front house and his mom lived in the back house. Jonny and his mom got along wonderfully together. No matter what, she protected him and spoiled him rotten. He was an only child, a *Mama's boy* until he met Randy Carlyle. Then he started getting into trouble but she never gave up on him, she never let him down. Jonny lost his dad to cancer, now his mom is having her share of health problems; nothing too serious. She's on medication for thyroid and high blood pressure, and she just had a gallstone procedure about six-months ago. And now her baby is gone and he doesn't even know that her only son was set up by his best friend; a man he trusted with his life, a man he looked up to, a man he thought would never defy him, or betray him… let alone set him up to be killed. Randy was considering the possibility that if he got in Cruse's way, or had become a threat or a risk to him, would he set him up too? Or worse, would he just kill himself? This is a dirty game, and no play is fair play, because it's all deadly and foul play.

"What now?" Carlyle asked Cruse.

"Now we put a little pressure on, Jackson. I want to know where that son-of-a-bitch is that blew a hole in my brother-in-law's chest," Cruse said, with vengeance in his heart and killing on his mind.

"I'll stay on, Jackson and see if he leads us to Write. He seems to know exactly when we are onto him. Jonny was about to do him in downtown LA a few days ago, but somehow he figured it out and got the drop on, Jonny," Carlyle said.

He knew good and well Debo and Mad-C had no idea that Johnny Morris would be there. They couldn't have gotten the drop on him if it hadn't been for that damn car. Jonny was just plain and simple set the fuck up, and it pissed Randy Carlyle off to think about it. But they didn't know about the rear surveillance camera in the Navigator, or the one in the Explorer.

"And that bastard had the nerve to go to my place. Good thing the manager didn't give him my unit number when he went by my *place*. But, it won't be long before he figures out that I'm not ever there. I'm sure he's either been back or is going back to see if I'm there. I can't go back there because they're probably already watching the place."

Robert Cruse got up and went to the double glass sliding-doors that lead to the balcony. He had rented a room there for a couple of days since the shooting at his place.

The air was invigorating and energizing to his mind. The scent of bacon, ham, coffee, garlic, and onions traveled from various units surrounding his. It smelled wonderful mixed with the fresh dampness of the morning. It reminded him of when his Mom used to cook breakfast every morning. The smell of bacon, hot cakes, with thick syrup, hot melted butter, and hot coffee.

"You better get in here before the breakfast monster gets your food: Here he comes!!!"

And Robert would run like the devil to beat the food monster to his plate. Then he came back to reality and thought about the mess he would be in if the cops came to arrest him for the murder of Sue-Lang-Yin and he couldn't let that happen, he has too much to do. He must exterminate his brother-in-law's murderer; "Mister Charles Write". Carlyle didn't know what was on Robert Cruses' mind. Was he contemplating setting him up too, or throwing him from the third floor balcony? After all, he knows that Cruse was responsible for the two murders in Venice. It seemed he would dispose of anyone who poses a threat to him.

And now, Randy Carlyle definitely posed a threat to Robert Cruse. Randy's nerves were crawling and biting all over his skin. His armpits and the back of his neck started to dampen with perspiration. He wiped his forehead and neck with his hand and figured that a nice drink…, a real stiff, strong drink of brandy might help to ease the tension and fear, the nervousness in his body, the lump in his throat. He decided to pour both of them a glass, only with more brandy in his glass than ice or soda. God knows he needs it good and strong.

He couldn't help the fear he felt. He walked up behind Cruse and called his name, interrupting his train of thought.

"Big Boy," he called out to Cruse, extending his right hand with the glass of brandy in it. Cruse turned around half startled. He didn't hear his partner in crime come up from behind him.

"I'm sorry, I didn't mean to interrupt you, I just thought that maybe you wouldn't mind having a drink with me."

"Thanks, Randy…, are you alright? You don't look so good." Cruse could see the fear and nervousness in him.

"Is that little thing Sunday still on your mind?"

"No, I'm alright," Carlyle lied.

It really didn't matter what time of the day it was; they drank. They drank heavily as youngsters. As a matter of fact, that's what they were doing in the backyard in Santa Monica ten years ago when Mad-C paid them a visit. Randy Carlyle went inside and poured himself another strong drink. "Don't drink too much, I need you to run over to the boat club," Cruse said.

Carlyle figured it was too far, and he couldn't make it on his nerves and the liquor in his system.

"Who this time?" he thought.

Debo went trough the mail and there were no obscene letters or postcards. He showered, shaved, and called Omar and he picked up on the second ring.

"Hey, bro," he greeted a tired-sounding Omar. "Hey, Debo... how's things going?"

"Pretty good, I'm just calling to see how Rex is doing."

"He's doing real good, eating me out of house and home."

"I forgot to leave you some money. I'll take care of it: I'll be there to rid him of the worry he must be going through. He gets real edgy when I'm gone too long," Debo said.

"Yeah, he just sits by the door you walked out of when you left him here as though you were coming through it at any minute. But, one thing's for sure, his appetite sure isn't suffering."

"Well tell him I'll be there to see him: Put him on the phone."

"Man... I don't want dog spit all over my phone."

"Just put the earpiece to his ear."

Omar put the phone to Rex's ear and watched the dog's head turn from side to side. Rex whined, then barked, then went to the door and started to scratch all the already peeling paint off the frame of the door, then barked again.

"What did you say to him?" Omar asked Debo. "Nothing, just that I'll see him in a few days."

"Yeah.., well he must think you're outside, he's tearing my door down."

"Tell him to heel, If he doesn't, tell him to sit and point your finger to the floor, he'll stop."

Debo had Rex trained by an army buddy of his that trains police dogs and special weapons and tactics team (SWAT) dogs. He also did some work for the FBI and the DEA as a dog trainer.

"Did he obey you?"

"Yeah he's better now, thank God; you should see my door."

"Sorry, bro, I'll pay for it. Imma let you go, thanks a lot bro."

"Don't trip, I still love him too," Omar said, and they hung up. When Omar put the phone down, Rex looked at it, turned his head to one side, then back at the phone, then looked up at Omar, and back at the phone again, barked, then looked at the door. His tail gave the floor a good pounding, and his leg jumped. Omar knew he was about to get up and go beat the door down again. He screamed, "Heel..., sit, Rex!!!" Rex thought better of it and decided to just stay there and stare at the door with his ears standing up and his eyes trained on the door.

Debo thought about Omar and Rex and started to feel sorry for Omar. He knew Rex could eat, but at least he's safe from the people that drugged him at the house. He called Mad-C.

"Hey, Big guy!" Debo said into the receiver. "Hey, Debo..., what's up?"

"Just calling to let you know I made it to *the house*."

"Are you there alone?"

"Yeah."

"I want you to be careful. You want me to come out there and..."

"No, no..., I'm just fine, *Crazy* won't let anybody bother me. I'll be back out there in a couple of hours, I have to pay the workers. Ever since all this started I've gotten behind in paying them. I also advised them that my generous boss will give them a Christmas bonus, after I told them there wouldn't be any more work until this is over."

"Don't worry about the bonuses, I've got them covered."

"How do you wanna deal with Patch and Rayass?" Debo asked.

"This shouldn't last too long; I'll just pay them as I usually have been. Besides, they are still on the payroll, and I'm sure we'll be needing them before this is over."

"Okay, I'll check with Sgt Billings and see if they have anything on the Plymouth. I'm going there anyway; I have to see him."

"Okay, you hurry up and get back here where I can keep my eyes on you. Especially after Sunday... those guys aren't playing around, people are dying!"

Mad-C didn't know that Johnny Morris and Jason Jones were set up to be killed by their own men.

"Okay, I'm on my way back out there. I'm out the door as we speak." Debo walked out of the house, and by force of habit or just plain caution he looked down the street to see if anyone had followed him but the coast was clear. He got into the Navigator and was headed back to Los Angeles. He checked with Shelly to see if she wanted him to get something for her from the house and she didn't need anything. He separated her mail from his before he left the house.

"Hey, big golfer," Debo said when Sgt Billings got up and stood on wobbly legs. The Sergeant knew it was payday and anticipated his just reward.

Billings frowned and said, "How's business?"

"Slow as hell, In fact, that's why I came here to see you instead of calling."

"*Calling*... what the hell do you mean, *'calling'!!!*"

"Well, with all this crap going on all around me and Mr Write, we decided to hold everybody's money until..."

Billings stopped him before he could finish what he was saying. "What the hell do you mean... *hold what money?* You'd better tell me that you're bullshitting me, Jackson!!!" Billings yelled. "Okay, big guy calm down, I'm just pulling your chain."

"Calm down my ass, I'll cuff your ass so fast, It'll take, God a week to get the news. Don't fuck with me, Jackson!!"

Debo pulled out the money and gave it to the Sergeant before the man had an aneurysm or a stroke.

"Don't get so uptight, Bob."

"Uptight hell, man you're trying to kill me."

"No, I wouldn't do that. I guess if you weren't awake, you sure as hell are now," Debo told him.

"Yeah, you damn sure made sure of that."

"Since you're up, do you have anything for me on the Plymouth?"

"Yeah." Billings went over to a filing cabinet that looked like it was bought at a garage sale. The top drawer sagged onto the drawer beneath it. It had a metal bar across the front of it with a hole that looked like a lock once occupied it but is now occupied by a pair of broken handcuffs hanging inside the open hole. Billings removed the cuffs and the bar, then pulled the drawer open and it came to rest on the drawer below it for support.

Billings reached inside and pulled out a file and rustled through the folder until he came up with the one he was looking for. The date on the victim evidence folder read: Sunday, November 11th. The victims were Johnny Morris and Jason Jones. The vehicle was a white 2014 Dodge

Plymouth, license plate number, P-L-A-Y-E-R-2. Contents: One long blue wool winter coat, one long sleeve Pendleton shirt, one box of twelve gauge shotgun shells, 23 grams of powder cocaine, an ounce of rock cocaine, and two free-base pipes. There were three lighters in the ashtray as well. Lying on the front seat was an envelope containing fifty $100 bills: The $5,000 that Randy Carlyle had given Jonny Morris.

"Wow, they were getting loaded. No wonder it took so long for them to act," Debo thought to himself.

"Have you heard from Patch and Rayass?" Debo asked.

"Every time something happens I hear from them. Patch called early this morning, just before you got here."

As Billings was finishing his statement, the intercom buzzed. It was one of those old-fashioned boxes with four buttons and a small hole where the sound of the woman's voice had come from, and wires leading from the box to the floor.

"Yes, Gloria," Billings said into the small hole. "There's an agent Dick Patch to see you, Sir."

Sgt Billings looked at Debo who gave him the go-ahead. Billings didn't know if Debo wanted to be bothered with the DEA agent at that particular time. It didn't matter because he was about to leave anyway. Debo motioned for him to okay the agent's entry.

"Okay, Gloria…, show him in."

When the door opened, a well-built, dark-haired woman stood in it. She brought with her a mild, sweet perfume smell, with Agent Dick Patch standing behind her.

"You may go in now."

"Thank you, Gloria," Billings said. "Good morning, Gentlemen Patch greeted," talking to a tired Billings and an exhausted Debo.

"Good morning, Agent Patch," Billings said. "Hey, Patch," Debo followed.

The three men shook hands, then Billings motioned for Patch to have a seat. The chair was one of those high-backed office chairs. The back was lopsided and the seat looked like it was designed with a hole in it. It looked like someone had set a heavy object in it and set it in a corner for a year.

Sgt. Billings had put the previous chair to rest long ago and this one will soon follow. There was a room down in the basement reserved for junk and dead or dying furniture. Billings had intended to have the chair and filing cabinet put to rest a long time ago.

"What brings you around, and where is your boy, Hungry?" Debo asked, referring to Agent Monty Rayass.

"He's outside getting coffee for everyone," Patch told them. "Yeah and a hamburger for himself. Don't forget that I have something for you, Patch."

"Don't worry, I won't, I stopped by to ask you about what happened in Venice."

Patch knew what happened, he just wanted to know who did it. "Didn't you get a report?" Billings asked him ."Yeah, I got one."

"Whatever the report said happened, is exactly what happened," Billings confirmed.

"I just figured that maybe they left something out."

"No..., no more, no less... everything should be right there in the report," Billings told the DEA agent.

"Was the white Plymouth released to LAPD?"

"It was," Billings confirmed.

"Anything we can use in the Yin murder?

Patch asked.

"Aren't you DEA, you don't do murders?"

"Yes, that's true."

"What are you nosing around in a homicide investigation for?"

"Well, seeing as how Yin was moving a large quantity of drugs from state to state, we have a small interest in the case, Sergeant. And one of the victims, Jonny Morris is associated with Raymond Anderson. The Plymouth; as you know belongs to a yacht club out in Malibu. It's owned by Gregory Johnson; a well-known drug cartel boss. It looks like somebody is cleaning up your little mess for you, Jackson."

Debo nor Sgt Billings wanted Patch to know that Debo and Mad-C were the ones that did the handy work on Morris and Jones.

Gloria opened the office door to announce that Rayass was ready to join them. Sgt Billings waved him in. Monty Rayass was looking bigger than the last time Debo had seen him. He didn't come into the office with anything to eat, so Debo just figured he ate it on the way up. He had only three cups of coffee, he wasn't expecting Debo to be there.

"Sorry, I didn't know you would be here or I would have gotten you a cup, Mister Jackson," Rayass apologized.

"Don't worry about me, I'm leaving anyway You want to walk downstairs with me, Agent Patch, I have something for you. Thanks for everything, Sergeant, talk to you later, Rayass," Debo said, and left the office.

"Hey, Patch… let's take the stairs; work my legs a little." They headed down the steps on their way to the ground level.

"Jackson, this may sound like a stupid question. But, did you have anything to do with Morris and Jones's untimely deaths? They were hit with some pretty heavy hardware," the agent said.

"Yes… that is a stupid question, here's our floor."

They both went through the thick fire door and were in the lobby. They walked out of the building and to the Explorer. When Debo got in, he opened the glove compartment and retrieved a long, thick envelope like the one he had given Sgt Billings earlier.

"Thank you, Mr Jackson, pleasure doing business with you as always. Let me know if you come up with something on that thing in Venice," Patch said.

"Can you get a location on, Johnson? I already have the yacht club address; I need a home address."

"What for?" Patch asked.

"In case something comes up, I'll need to ask him a few questions," Debo said.

"I'm not sure if we have anything on his whereabouts as far as a private home address is concerned, but I'll check. We know he's into heavy drug sales, we haven't been able to catch him with anything, he moves around a lot," Patch informed Debo.

"Okay, thanks!"

"You can check with Billings, he should have more than we do."

"Okay, will do," Debo said.

Patch didn't know that whatever Billings had, Debo had because he had access to Billings database. All he got from the car license plates was the Malibu yacht club. There's no need to phone because nowadays everyone is downsizing to allow the saving of millions of man-hour dollars. Now, all you get is all kinds of unnecessary information. Maybe he can get a private number from Shelly on her computer.... She can run the information he has to hopefully come up with a private number on Johnson and Cruse. Debo was in the Explorer headed toward Beverly Hills. He remembered that Jeffery and Pauline hadn't been paid. When he called them, Pauline answered and said that 'she wasn't feeling well and she would be home all day.' He called Jeffery but he didn't answer. Those automated answering machines don't sit well with Debo. People use them sometimes as a way to monitor and escape being bothered by whoever wished to enter their day. And the agony of it all is that they power off and subject you…, *the caller* to hideous recordings all day for hours at a time. Debo couldn't figure out why most people even bother to buy cell phones. Either they don't use them, or they don't answer them. He decided to call Shelly and have her look for some of the information he wanted from Billings' database. Mad-C had enough on his mind with the problem at the dock and someone trying to kill him. He couldn't move anything until this was over and there is a very large demand for his product. He can't fill that demand because these idiots might try to intercept his deliveries and maybe hurt or kill Debo's workers. In this case, his little sister is one of them. It was Debo's idea to shut down deliveries to LA because of the business at hand.

After this he'll have to pull Joy off the team, she has enough money to last her and the girls a very long time. She can invest in a lucrative business and pass it on to her girls.

He decided to call Mad-C and let him know that he was on his way to the office. He pressed the speed-dial on his cell phone and waited for his phone to ring. "Your call has been." Debo cut to the chase by ending the call and calling the office number. Mad-C picked up on the first ring.

"Hey, are you out here yet?"

"I'm on my way to you now, anything new on your end?"

"No, all is quiet over here."

"Okay, I'll be by there, then I might go over to pay some people later. I'll see you in a minute."

"Okay, later," Mad-C said.

Debo tried Jeffery again and still didn't get an answer. He pressed the end button on his cell and decided to try calling him again after he leaves the office. He pulled up in his usual parking space in the rear of the office, got out of the Explorer and walked up to the back door and punched in the security code to gain entry to the office building and

Mad-C told him to hold on. The door buzzed where the doorknob was located and he walked in and went upstairs. Mad-C was watching CNN Sports. He looked up at Debo with wrinkles in his forehead, and with a deep, raspy voice, he said,

"Is everything cool at the house?"

"So far, so good."

"Well…, sit down, I can't see the TV."

"Oh…, sorry."

Debo walked over to a huge ottoman that was sitting in front of a matching love-seat. The ottoman and love-seat was custom-made from the same company that did Debo's SUV. He has fur on the floor and seats covered under heavy plastic. There was a ten-by ten-foot rug on the office floor in front of the ottoman. Mad-C's office is a burgundy and black decor; the rug matched perfectly. It was burgundy with black trim. Mad-C's office is the only office that no one outside of himself and Debo were allowed to enter, unless he was there to okay others to enter. There's only Mad-C's office, Debo's office, and an office for meetings. There was a state-of-the-art gymnasium; exercise room, a steam room, cardiovascular equipment, punching bags, and pull-up bars. When he or Debo was upset, tensed, or just wanted to work out they would go into the gym and get a good workout. They sat aside time back when they met for working out.

Debo was a little frail for his age, Mad-C had accredited it to drugs and liquor. People have a tendency to judge others when they are down on their luck. Debo didn't use drugs until he became homeless. He saw enough of what it was capable of doing to a person's life, health, finances, lifestyle, and social life. Shelly would never have gone for it; no woman in her right mind would. And he knew that one day in his life he would want and meet a real good woman; one that would love him, care for him, and treat him like the man he knew he could be. Drugs and alcohol didn't play a part. He was always small, especially as a youngster up to the age of about twenty. He was always busy burning calories and not eating balanced meals. He ate when he was hungry, not when others said it was time to eat. He didn't believe in the tradition *eat breakfast at five or six in the morning, lunch at twelve in the afternoon, and dinner at five or six in the evening.* He ate when his belly told him to eat. His gut had its own tradition; It knew what it wanted and when it wanted it. That's when D-Angelo L Jackson, Jr ate.

In other parts of the office was a shower, restroom, closets, small but fully equipped kitchen, living room, and a dining room.

Debo and Mad-C's office has their very own small convenient built-in sleeping quarters. Debo got up to go to the door.

"Where are you off to?" Mad-C asked.

"I'm going down to the car to get something; I didn't want to bring it up without you knowing because I want you to keep an eye on me."

Mad-C reached into a drawer that he had pulled out of a redwood, very well polished end-table and got his 44- magnum and went over to one of the two windows, sat in an office chair, and said,

"Okay, go ahead."

Debo walked down the stairs; they were simple red brick encased in steel and concrete. Each step was two feet long and one foot wide. The downstairs patio was a vision of the architect's mind, he/she must have had a taste for a jungle setting. Everything was wrought-iron, and to make it blend in with a night setting; the decor was all black, and the chairs were woven in black-wicker and wrought-iron. An ashtray sat on the side of each wrought-iron table with marble tabletops. The customary umbrella was placed in the center of the table. A beautiful gray marble water fountain was positioned in front of a three-foot wall. Grass encircled the area surrounding the patio, red brick was placed on the ground of the patio lounging area, and two large palm trees were arranged neatly manicured at each end of the patio itself.

Debo arrived at the row of mailboxes that was midway the front and back doors. There was return mail; some advertisement, a few flyers, and a UPS box on top of the mail boxes. He picked up the box and went to the backdoor.

He put the box between the door and the door jam, to keep the door from closing and locking him out. He had a key, but to save time he just propped the door open with the box. He didn't use the key the first time either because he wanted Mad-C to know he was down there. Mad-C told Debo years ago, after he himself was mugged, to always let him know when he was downstairs, whether he had a key or not. In so doing, Mad-C would know that he was on his way up and was expecting him to walk through the office door at any minute. If he didn't, then something was wrong and he would have to go see what.

He opened the rear hatch of the Explorer and pulled out a duffel bag and slung it over his shoulder. With his free hand, he pulled *Crazy* from its home that was attached to his shoulder and positioned under his coat, and took his left foot and lightly kicked the door shut, then walked in. He bent over to pick up the box that was holding the door ajar, while holding *Crazy* in his other hand ready for whoever and whatever wanted to meet hell. He put the box on top of the mailbox and it leaned to one side, which told him that it probably had been a doorstop many times before he made it one. He walked up the stairs with the duffel bag slung over his shoulder. When he walked up to the door, Mad-C stood and walked over to the door, let Debo in, then shut it and placed the 44-magnum back in the drawer from which he had taken it.

"Here, big guy," he said, handing him the duffel bag containing bundles of money totaling $650,000.00: Mad-C took the bag in his office and put it in a safe.

"Have the workers been paid?"

"Not yet, I'll go take care of them after I leave here, I haven't sorted theirs yet. Or, I might just take it to them tomorrow, I'm tired."

Debo did indeed have a rough month, he decided it would be best to wait until tomorrow. He wanted to be able to think clearly and be alert when he delivered the money. He told Mad-C everything that Sgt Billings had told him and gave him the rap sheets and mugshots of Raymond Anderson, Robert Cruse, and Randy Carlyle.

Neither of them have changed much over the years, especially, Cruse. Mad-C remembered how afraid Carlyle was, and Cruse was the one with the big mouth. He was also the one that put the thirty-eight to his head outside that liquor store in Venice the night he was robbed.

"I'll never forget this one. I really didn't go there to kill anyone... just to get what was mine back and to have a couple of my boys beat the living shit out of every one of 'em. But, that big crazy mothafucka drew a sawed-off shotgun on me.

It's no fun looking down the barrel of one of those. And then his friend came out of the kitchen with another cannon in my face. It was me or them, and I didn't want it to be me. I had no choice but to put them away." When he put the mug shots down, Debo told him that the white Plymouth wasn't going to turn up much unless he checked with Shelly and she found something on her computer. They were tired, so they finished watching the game in silence. Debo was asleep before it ended. Mad-C went to Debo's office and got a blanket to put over him. He sat there looking at him and recalling the day he first met him and how frail and spunky he was. He was thinking about what a man Debo has become. He was looking at him asleep on the office love seat; his self-adopted brother. And nothing had better happen to this man, because whoever causes his death or grief will have hell to pay.

CHAPTER
10

WEDNESDAY, NOVEMBER 14TH, 9:30 A.M.

Debo called Freddy and Joy to let them know that he planned to meet with them and take care of them, he called Joy first. Her cell phone was either busy or off. He hung up and dialed Shelly's cell and she picked up the phone on the first ring. Probably because her caller ID told her it was him calling, by displaying his name and cell number on her screen.

"Hey Hun, how's things your way? I tried to call Joy but she didn't answer her phone."

"She went downstairs to get some exercise and to look around to make sure no one was in the lobby that looked suspicious."

"She needs that phone on and with her at all times!!" He was very upset at the fact that Joy would slip like that.

"It's the small things that cause the major problems," he told her. "She has it with her; it must be off, she grabbed it and left. It might be on by now," Shelly told him, in Joy's defense. "Okay, Baby, I need you to do something for me."

"If I can, you got it."

"See if you can find a private number, a cell phone, or home number on Gregory Johnson. He has an office at a yacht club out in Malibu, and he uses personalized plates with the letters P-L-A-Y-E-R, followed by the numbers two or five. The one with the two at the end is the white Plymouth, we already have it. See if maybe you can get something on the black Mercedes Benz. It's the one with the five at the end of the letters. Check to see if he has a yacht with the same P-L-A-Y-E-R logo or identification number. That's all I have on him so far. I also need a number on a Robert Cruse, *aka Raymond Anderson*. Last known address 11607 Ocean boulevard in Venice, it's a condominium but I don't have his unit number."

"Is that it?"

"Yes, baby, it is for now."

"I'll do what I can, are you alright?"

"Yeah, I'm as well as can be expected under the circumstances. But, I'll be doing really well when this is all over and I'm able to be with my baby. How are you holding out?"

"Just hearing your voice keeps me sane. I just believe in the fact that you promised you'll be alright. And long as I have that promise, I'm okay," Shelly told him.

"That's my girl. Well, little mama, you stay sane and I'll…,"

And before he could finish speaking and hang up, she interrupted him."Hold on, baby, Joy's coming in now."

Joy had been gone for about an hour. She looked dressed for the weather; donning her favorite black sweater, and she smelled like the coolness of winter-green. She also wore her black Levies to match her sweater, a pair of black leather boots, black gloves, and had a sweet aroma about her. Her hair was tied back into a long ponytail which protruded through a hole in the back of her green baseball cap. The cap had no logo on it, just a big (J) for her initial.

"What's up, Bro?"

She sounded like she had been running or climbing a lot of stairs. He gave her a second to catch her breath, then said,

"I have something for you. I'll call Freddy and meet with him this afternoon or this evening. I'm just leaving Beverly Hills. I don't want to come too close to the hotel just encase someone is watching. I'll probably have Freddy and Jeffery meet me at Pauline's. Have you heard from, Jeffery, I can't get in touch with him?"

"No, I haven't."

"Oh, yeah…, I have some pictures of Robert Cruse and Randy Carlyle. I'll have Freddy give them to you so you can recognize them when you see them. You guys don't know what the hell none of these guys look like."

"Yeah, I thought about that when I was downstairs, that's why I came up so fast. I didn't know what dude I was looking for looked like."

"I got you, Sis…, don't trip. Do you want me to give Freddy your envelope or what?"

"No, just put it in my overseas account for me, Bro…, please!!"

"Okay, you got it; I'll wire it over to Switzerland in the morning. It should be safe there. I'll get those pictures to you via, Freddy."

"Okay…, thanks, Bro."

"No problem, tell my baby I said…, no, let me speak to her."

"Okay, hold on," Joy said and gave the phone to Shelly.

"Yes, Mister Jackson, how may I be of service?" Shelly greeted.

"Just keep sounding and looking as lovely as you are, and I'll talk to you soon, baby, okay?"

"Okay," she said, making a kissing sound into the phone. Debo repeated the same gesture back to her.

"Bye, Baby…, and tell Joy I said to keep that phone *on*, and on her."

"Will do," Shelly promised.

It was 4:30, and Pauline wasn't feeling well. This was not her best time of season but, she managed to pull or drag herself to the door. Her hair was a mess, you could see where she had no success putting the plastic rollers in it. For one thing, the color coordination was way off; she had used an *interesting* mix of pink, green, blue, orange, and black rollers lazily in rows in her head. She wore a pink nightgown, with an extra-large white Tee-Shirt, and a pink terry cloth robe. She slipped the robe on when she got up to answer the door. She knew the cold was imminent as soon as she opened the door. She slid on some pink fur; probably rabbit fur house slippers and had a cup of steaming hot, dark brown liquid in her hand with the handle of a spoon dangling around the rim of the cup.

"My goodness woman, what bit you and ran?" Debo asked when she opened the door.

"I don't know, I guess me and this weather don't get along. Your timing is perfect, because I don't think I would have been up to work the way I'm feeling."

"Yeah, you look terrible," Debo said. "Okay, don't push it."

"Well here.., maybe this will cheer you up."

He went in his pocket and pulled out an envelope and handed it to her. She took it over to the sofa where she had been laying, with a coffee table cluttered with cold and flu remedies, balled-up tissue, a coffee cup that was once used for cough syrup or hot flue medication, and a television remote control for the wide-screen plasma TV attached to the wall in front of her. She sat on the sofa and unsuccessfully hit her target which was an end table on the side of the sofa. The envelope landed on the floor instead. She looked in that general direction and didn't see it, then thought,

"What the heck..., leave it there."

Debo started to pick it up, but thought better of it since the area she had designated was full of cold and flu germs and he was not in the mood to get sick. The sofa was a lovely black leather with a pattern of pink cloves stitched through the leather in top quality suede. The throw pillows were a pretty peach-pink.

"Have a seat," she told Debo.

"I called Freddy..., he's supposed to meet me over here."

"I know, he called and said he would be here soon. That was about ten minutes ago."

Debo heard his cell phone play, *"It's our anniversary."*

"That's so sweet, I love that song," Pauline complimented. Debo cut her off so he could answer the phone.

"Hey, it's me, boss, be there in a minute."

"Okay," Debo said and hung up. "It was Freddy."

"Yeah I gathered..., nice ringtone."

He explained to her that he chose that song in dedication to Shelly for their wedding anniversary.

"I love that song, how is Shelly?"

"She's doing fine."

"She's damn lucky too. She'd better be glad that I didn't get to you before she did."

Pauline always had a crush on Debo, not because of his good looks or his fat pockets. But for the kind of person he is; warm, loving, caring, kind, thoughtful, and the sweetest man you could ever wanna meet. The doorbell interrupted her thinking and Debo nearly lost it. He can't stand loud ringing doorbells.

"Can you get that for me please, it's probably, Freddy," Pauline said. "Who is it?"

Debo was in the habit of checking to see who or what was at the door, especially other people's door. It was a precaution, because that extra split second, that extra effort could make the difference between life and death… His. He opened it a little after he heard Freddy's voice.

"It's me," a cold and shivering voice from the other side of the door said. "Me who… ?" Debo asked.

"Oh, stop playing and let him in, it's cold out there," Pauline fussed. "I'm not playing… I need a name. In the business I'm in, you never know what lurks behind a door or wall or window or corner." He thought about his car tire, then added, or freeways."

He opened the door all the way and Freddy looked to be three hundred pounds heavier. Considering how he wrapped himself in his too-big bear coat and thick black gloves.

"Man, you're not fooling around, are you?"

"No, boss, it's freezing out here," Freddy said, squeezing through the door.

"Can you make it by?" Debo asked.

"If I don't, I'll be on my deathbed with pneumonia."

"Yeah, and then you'll look like that," Debo said, and pointed to Pauline stretched-out on the sofa.

"I heard that, I'm sick, not deaf!!"

"I've got something for you."

He handed Freddy an envelope similar to the one he gave Pauline, Billings, and Patch. He also gave him the pictures of the two men with orders to take a set to Joy.

"You have to know who to look for," he told Freddy.

"It did come to mind, I just figured you didn't have to be told."

"There are four including Johnson, one is dead. He got restless and decided to creep up on me and my boss out in Venice the other day." He heard Pauline cough and asked her if she needed anything from the drug store.

"You are the doggone drug store.., Nah, baby I'll be fine, I've got enough junk that's not working as it is. The only thing that works is the coffee."

"Okay, I won't keep you up. You get well; bless your heart. I'll call and see how you're coming along. I put a little Christmas gift in the envelope for you… and yours too, Freddy."

"Thank you, Darling!!!" Pauline yelled, "Thanks, boss,"

Freddy followed.

"You guys earned it."

"Okay you two, get out of here and shut my door; and lock it!!!" Pauline yelled.

"Okay, beautiful …, I'm out of here!!!" Debo yelled back. "Me too!!!" Freddy yelled.

"Hurry up and get well!!!" Debo screamed.

"I'm headed back to the hotel so I can get out of this weather. Plus, I have a post to man," Freddy told Debo.

All the time Freddy was at Pauline's house, he didn't bother to take off his coat or gloves.

"See you later my man, stay warm," Debo told Freddy.

He had asked Freddy if he heard from Jeffery, and he hadn't. He didn't ask Pauline because she wasn't feeling well, and he didn't want to bother her. It could be that he's out with a little honey. While they were at Pauline's house a little while back, Jeffery said he could cheat on Molly. "Okay, get on back there with, Shell and Joy in case there is some foul play. If Jeffery calls you, give me a call."

"Okay," Freddy said. "Don't forget to give Joy the pictures!!!"

"Alright, I won't!!!" Freddy yelled behind Debo as he was walking to the Explorer.

Debo decided to pay Jeffery a visit since he couldn't reach him on the phone. Jeffery owns an apartment building off Eucalyptus and Regent Street in Inglewood, CA. There was an underground parking structure for the tenants, which was well guarded by an electronic gate that opens automatically when the key is inserted and turned. Debo has a key, but he doesn't use the parking structure because it goes down into the lower level of the building and there is a dip where every-time he goes down there, he scrapes the rear end of the Explorer. He decided to park on the street in order to save wear on the hundred-plus thousand-dollar custom-made SUV. He walked up to the security gate, which also required a key. It was the same key as the security carport gate. There were concrete specially placed stepping stones that ran from the gate to each door. The only grassy area was in the middle of the surrounding apartments in an oval-shaped pattern laid out in the courtyard. Debo knocked on Jeffery's door and no one answered. He hated ringing doorbells, but under the circumstances he had no choice.

He rang the bell, and after he pressed the small button that created that loud noise he hated so much, there was still no answer. He tried calling again and got the same hectic voice mail recording. He dialed the home phone number and heard the answering machine. Something didn't sit right in the back of Debo's head. He was starting to sense foul play, either Jeffery got to him or somebody got to Jeffery. He was the only worker that didn't turn in his quota for the month. It wasn't good he couldn't reach him. Debo could always reach his workers... all of them. He went to the pool hall that Jeffery owns. The pool hall is a small building with bars on the outside windows and doors, to keep unwanted visitors out of the small establishment. The door was fire-proof with a black wrought-iron door covering the front entrance. It was bolted on the outside by heavy padlocks to keep intruders from gaining entrance after closing. When the pool hall finally opened, Debo walked through the open doors and was inside. He was met by the strong odor of stale cigar and cigarette smoke, beer, and sweat. He didn't have to wonder why women didn't frequent the pool hall.

Maybe because the men always smell like the pool hall does. He came to the conclusion that that was the reason men kept the place smelling like the men themselves smell; as opposed to getting off from work and going home to the fresh smell of a shower and fresh clothes, dinner and a soft drink, and a sweet smelling-woman instead of other smelly men. The pool hall was kind of a men's sanctuary, a watering hole. He saw a couple of men gathered in a far corner talking and playing dominoes. There was one guy leaned over the faded green felt cushion of a pool table with his opponent quietly standing behind him resting his folded arms on a pool cue watching and waiting for his turn to slam some of the small colored balls into whichever pocket on the green felt-covered table that he wishes to. Debo walked across the shiny, just waxed floor to a bar built to accommodate at least fifteen customers. A dull light hung over the bar, the same kind of light that hung over the pool tables. A light-skinned, dark-haired man with freckles stood behind the bar waiting to drown the troubles away for the husbands who were either losing their money or had lost their wives because they lost their money. The light that was hanging over the bar had two of the four light bulbs lit, giving the place a sort of dark moonlit appearance. Debo couldn't make out too many faces in the light that the overhead lamp provided, but he knew the guy at the bar wasn't Jeffery Smith. The bartender smiled at Debo, exposing a gap where there once was a tooth in the front top of his large mouth.

"Hey, Leroy, have you seen the boss?" Debo asked.

"No, I haven't seen ole, Jeffery in a couple of days. Maybe he's hold up with some girl somewhere," the man with the missing front tooth told Debo.

"Have you heard from or seen, Molly, Leroy?"

"Yeah, she stop by yesterday looking for him." Debo turned around to confront the customers in the pool hall.

"Has anyone seen or heard from Jeffery in the past day or so?"

"I saw him on his way home a couple of days ago," a man at one of the pool tables told him.

"Did he say anything about going anyplace other than home?"

"No, it was closing time and he and I sat and had a few beers and talked a while. But, I haven't seen him since."

"Okay, thanks a lot," Debo said.

He turned around to face the bartender and said,

"Hey, do me a favor; If any of you see Jeffery around or hear from him, tell him to get in touch with me. Or tell Freddy and he'll let me know." Debo was starting to worry: He's known Jeffery Smith long enough to know he wouldn't run off with money or his merchandise.

Well, all he could do was just wait and hope for the best. It's Our Anniversary brought him back to the moment.

"Talk to me," he said without checking to see who it was calling.

If he had, he would have known it was Shelly calling. "Are you okay, Baby?"

"Yeah..., just worried about one of the workers."

"Well the two you left here with me are still here."

"Baby, check with Joy and see if... put her on," he said. "Okay hold on."

He waited a second to let Joy come to the phone. "Yeah, Bro?"

"Have you heard from, Jeffery?"

"No, not since the meeting we had at the office. Why, is something wrong?"

"Yes very, put Shell back on the phone please."

He could hear the sound of a television program and Joy yelling for Shelly to come to the phone.

"Yes, sweetheart?"

"Sounds busy over there, how did it go with the phone numbers?"

"I do have a number on Robert Cruse. I don't know how current it is. It's (310) 555-1490, and it seems to be a private number. I don't know if it's a house or cell. I also have an address only on Gregory Johnson; 909 Pacific Coast Highway. That's in Malibu, CA. I got a number, but it's not private, it belongs to an enterprise. It's (818) 555-0001, ext 4410. That's all I could get from the LAPD database. Now, here's something you may be able to use. I pulled up a name; I was playing with the name on the two license plates, and I messed with it a little and came up with, reyal at Glory Days Boat and Yacht Club. It's registered to a Gilbert Johnson, and the phone number is (818) 555-3095. It turns out it's a private number. And yes it is busy here, gotta do something to keep sane," Shelly added..

"You, my darling are the best, thank you so very much sweetheart, and stay sane."

"You're welcome, Freddy's here, you want to talk to him?"

"Yeah, put him on."

"Hey, boss, what's up?"

"Freddy, have you heard anything from Jeffery yet?"

"No, Boss.., still checking."

"Okay, I checked his place and the pool hall."

"I'll stay on it, Boss."

"Okay, thanks," Debo said, then hung up.

He used the voice tag feature on his cell phone to call Mad-C. "What's up?"

"Hey, Bro?"

"I'm here," Mad-C answered.

"It's me, I'm not too far, I'll be there shortly. I'm in Inglewood just finishing lunch."

"Okay, come on by."

"You want me to pick you up something?"

"No thanks, I ate at Coco's down the street."

"Okay, see you in a little bit."

Robert Cruse dialed Randy Carlyle's number. "Randy here," a voice said, in Robert's ear.

"Hey, Randy…, did you take care of what I asked you to?" Carlyle was just waking up and yawned in Big Boy's ear. "It's all done."

"Everything I asked you to do?"

"Yes…, everything."

"I don't have to check, do I?"

"No, Big Boy you don't have to check."

"Okay, thanks, go back to sleep, Randy."

He had to act, and he knew he didn't have time to play around. The feds could be closing in on him and his brother-in-law's murderer is still out there walking and breathing.

Robert (Big Boy) Cruse had Randy Carlyle go to the fishing and boat club. He knew that Tom would be there because it was planned for him to be at the desk to let Randy Carlyle in the basement.

"Is everything all set?" Carlyle asked Tom. "Yeah, all set."

Randy Carlyle had arrived at the fishing and boat club an hour ago… orders of Robert Cruse.

Cruse was always big for his age, that's why he self-pro-claimed himself, 'Big Boy'. He joined a gang because he wanted to intimidate and bully people, which is what he's doing to Randy Carlyle. Cruse is six-feet, four inches tall, long beard, and a low-cut hair style. His goatee was always kept neatly pointed at the end under his massive chin. He wore no mustache and he weighs 270 pounds, and is very mischievous and ruthless .

Tom had been awaiting Randy Carlyle's arrival, he handed Carlyle a key that was attached to a small board in the shape of a fishing boat, with the words 'Seaman's Fishing and Boat Club' engraved in it. Carlyle followed a long hall decorated with fishing memorabilia and a few trophies on one side. On the other side were pictures of veteran fishermen and women, sea captains, and chairpersons. The carpet had a variety of fish; fish of all shapes and breeds woven into it. At the end of the hall was an elevator. Carlyle pushed the down button and waited. The twin doors slid apart, revealing the inside of the box that Carlyle was to ride to the lower level. He looked at the inside of the elevator and wondered if he should take the stairs. He stepped in and pressed B for basement. The ten by ten-foot box he was enclosed in jerked as Carlyle felt himself being lowered to what he felt was doom. The club had been there for some sixty years, and he didn't know when the last time the moving casket was serviced or checked for repairs. When it jerked, he felt his heart jump and his head felt light.

"Is this a setup too?" he asked himself out loud.

The doors once again slid apart and he knew he had made it safely to the basement. He quickly emerged from the box in which just two minutes ago he felt trapped. The smell of old rotted wood and rope was thick in the air. There were piles of oars and anchors in one corner, and in another corner were the remains of old broken ladders and fishnets. Boxes occupied the wall and floor to his right, and a long table which seemed to be in dire need of immediate care or disposal rested in the middle of the room. The only thing on it was dust. Carlyle walked through a door that stood catercorner to his left.

"Hey, how's my man?" he asked Jeffery Smith.

Jeffery looked terrible; he was stretched out on a bed with his right arm duck-taped to the headboard post. His palms were turned upright, and he was wearing a sheet, a pair of short pants, a torn Tee-Shirt, no shoes, no socks, and the room smelled of urine and vomit. There was a tray with old rotted bread and a molded potato on a plate. His legs were tied to the foot of the bed. He heard Carlyle come in and opened his eyes.

"Hey, how's my man? I'll bet Jackson is breaking his balls looking for you. He probably doesn't give a rat's ass about you, it's the dope and his money he wants."

Carlyle took a strongbox from a drawer that sat inside an oakwood desk that he was sitting on. He opened it and took out a hypodermic syringe. Jeffery knew what was coming and started to beg and plead for the man with the torture device not to administer any more pain and suffering upon him. Carlyle took a spoon from the box and added water and some white powder to the spoon.

He took a cigarette lighter from the strongbox and lit the bottom of the spoon as Jeffery dreaded what came next. Jeffery cried, pleaded, and yelled from the top of his lungs, then cried again and again.

"Where is he, Jeffery?"

"Kiss my ass," Jeffery cried.

"I hate doing this shit, but I have my orders," Randy Carlyle said, and pulled a piece of rope about twelve inches long out of the box and tied it around Jeffery's right arm; the same arm he had duck taped to the bedpost. Then he put the tip of the needle in the spoon, and with a pulling motion, he absorbed the clear liquid from the eating utensil.

"All I want are Charles Write and D-Angelo Jackson. You won't have to go through this anymore. Please, for your own sake. Just look at yourself. You would go through this for a man that doesn't give a damn about you?"

"Oh, he cares about me, and if he knew that you son-of-a-bitches were doing this, he would kill your ass and wouldn't think twice about doing it."

"Are you willing to die down here in this hole for him?"

"I was dead when he found me. It's because of him that I survived all these years with no one else but him to care for me and about me. Yes, I will die down here in this fucking hole looking at your bitch-ass, to make sure he's safe."

"So, what the hell are you crying and begging for?"

"That shit hurts like hell when it comes down. It hurts like you're gonna hurt when he finds me... dead or alive!!"

"I'm tired of hearing your mouth. Here, shut the fuck up and go to sleep," Carlyle said, then he stabbed the needle into Jeffery's arm and pulled some blood from a vain through the needle to mix with the liquid that was already inside the vile, then injected it; blood and all back into his arm.

"You know what, you stupid son-of-a-bitch... you'd better kill me. Because when I get your black ass, you will wish you were never... " Jeffery's words were cut short because he went into a peaceful, dark sleep.

"You're one dumb motherfucker, aren't you?" Carlyle said and left the room.

"Clean up down there and feed him in the morning. Give him some coffee. I hate doing this shit," Carlyle told Tom before he left.

He knew Cruse wasn't going to let Jeffery live. Now he's doing it again; killing again for Robert (Big Boy) Cruse. Cruse wanted Debo because Debo knows where to find the man that killed his sister's husband ten years ago. But he couldn't get to Debo, and that is driving his ass up a wall. It's not fair that Write should live. And, just like Jeffery Smith, whoever protects him can't live either.

* * *

Debo was at the office in forty-five-minutes. He pushed in the code and was granted entry.

"Okay, I've got a number on Cruse and an address on Johnson. It's a Malibu address, it could be the yacht club. We have Morris; the piece of shit that went stupid out in Venice the other day. His mom has a back-house where he stayed; the place we went to."

"He's out of the picture now, so let's go on to the others," Mad-C suggested. "Well, if I can get his mom to talk we might come up with something of use," Debo offered.

Debo was quite sure he could talk her out of Morris' affiliation with Cruse, and how he can be found. But, if not he could always put Joy or Pauline on her. They can get pickle seeds from a watermelon.

"Okay, what do we have so far, on the others?" Mad-C asked.

"I've got a 909 Pacific Coast Highway Malibu, California address. Phone (818) 555-0001, ext 4410. Randy Carlyle drives a 2013.

Tahoe Yukon, license plate number D-C-A-2-9-8, gray in color."

"That's a lot more than we had. I don't know how far it'll get us, but let's get to work on it," Mad-C said.

"Okay, I'll put Pauline on Morris' mom and see what she comes up with. You, myself, and one of the guys can go out to the yacht club. Better yet, after what happened at the boat club, maybe I should give Billings a call and… "

Mad-C stopped Debo before he could finish what he was saying. "Is Malibu within Sgt. Billings' jurisdiction?"

"Hold on, I think not; now that you mentioned it."

Debo took out his cell phone and dialed Billings' cell number.

"Billings here, what can I help you with, Jackson?" the Sergeant said when he answered his cell phone.

"Hey, Bob…, can you go out to Malibu and ask…" Sgt. Billings interrupted Debo, in mid-sentence.

"Malibu is not mine, try Patch… wait I might know someone at the county sheriff's office, give me about twenty-minutes."

"Okay, thanks," Debo said.

He told Mad-C what Billings said and called Pauline. She wasn't feeling very well the last time he saw her. He wondered if she felt any better. He couldn't get Joy to go because he didn't want to move her. She's okay where she is, but he did need a woman to talk to mamma Morris.

"Hey, beautiful, how's everything, feeling any better?"

"Yeah, handsome, I'm doing a little better, what's up?"

"You sure sound a lot better."

"Will you get to the point?"

"Oh yeah… sorry!"

Pauline always had a smart mouth. Some people are just that way; don't mean any harm just speak their mind. Debo wasn't offended, he knows how she is and deals with it.

"I need a really big favor."

"Okay I still work for you, what do you need, handsome?"

"Can you get out of bed?"

"If I have to, what's it worth to you?"

"How about a big hug and a heartfelt, I love you?"

"That's perfect, what is it you need?"

"I need you to go over to a guy's house and…" She stopped him from finishing.

"You know I don't do that!"

"No, sweetheart, I want you to go see his mother and." She cut him off again.

"And I don't want to meet his parents."

"Stop doing that, woman. I need some information from one of the guy's mother that I told you all about at the meeting we had at my office. I need to find out if she knows where any of his friends live. A guy by the name of, Randy Carlyle, or Robert Cruse. I have an address on Cruse, but I don't think he'll be going there anymore, or no time soon anyway. I need an address on Carlyle, and a number where I can reach them both."

"Okay, how soon?"

"Like yesterday."

"I'm on my way," Pauline said and hung up.

Debo finished his call to Pauline and waited for Billings' call. "Okay, here's what I can do. I talked to a sheriff friend of mine, and he'll go to Malibu for me. What do you need exactly?"

"I need some information on Gregory Johnson, I'm sure he owns a private yacht out at the Glory Days Yacht Club. He's supposed to have one harbored there at Dock seventeen slip nine. His yacht is called the "Reyal."

"Okay, I'll let my guy know," Billings assured Debo.

"Thanks, Bob."

"You bet, Debo."

"When can I call you back?"

"I'll call you sometime today."

"Good enough."

Debo hung up and dialed the number he had on Cruse.

"Hello," a tiny voice answered the phone.

"Bingo," Debo thought to himself. He wasn't really expecting an answer. He sat straight up in his seat. Mad-C saw his reaction and focused all of his attention on him and the phone conversation.

"Hello..., may I speak to Mister Cruse?"

"He's not at home, who's calling?"

Debo figured it wouldn't be a good idea to give his name. But at least he knew the number on Cruse was recent and working. He'll call back, or better yet he'll have Joy call him back.

"Can you just tell him that I'm calling from the boat club, please?" He hung up before the woman could ask his name again. He looked like he was in shock.

"What happened?" Mad-C asked, very confused.

"The number on, Cruse is a go, but I'll have to put someone on it. I'll have to get one of the girls to get him to meet with one of them. Pauline is going over to talk to Morris' mother. I'll get Joy to call Cruse," Debo decided. He blocked his number again, in case he was on someone's caller ID and called the number again. The same tiny voice answered that sounded like a teenager, or closer to being a child than a teen.

"I'm sorry, we were cut off before. I just called there a minute ago to speak with Mister Cruse."

"He's still not here," the girl said.

"Who am I speaking with?" Debo asked. "This is his niece."

"Do you know what time he'll be home?"

"He said around 8 or 9 o'clock. Who do I say is calling?"

"I'm calling from the accounting office at the fishing and boat club here in Venice, CA. I'm just checking his credit rating with the club; we do all of our members once a year."

"Okay, I'll let him know you called."

"Alright, thank you so much." Debo couldn't wait to hang up. If Cruse calls the club back they won't know who called him. Anyway, they close at 8:30. All he'll get is a bunch of numbers to dial, then an answering machine and he'll have to push all those buttons they tell you to push . He'll be frustrated before he gets anywhere.

Debo left the block on his phone and dialed the number he had on Johnson. "Sorry, I am not available at this time, please leave your name, number, and a brief message at the tone, or call 555-0001."

After the recording finished, Debo hung up. He didn't dial the number that the recording gave him, because he knew he would only get another voice recording. The number he called before was a private number.

"Okay, boss, what's for dinner?"

"What do they have around here?"

"Well, Coco's around the corner, a 7/11 across the street from there, we could get a couple of chili dogs. There's a KFC, a really good Chinese food place, and a sub-sandwich spot. Oh, and Ben's Cafe, Ben serves breakfast all day, and all the delicious soul food you want; lunch and dinner, and the food is not bad at all."

"I'll go with Ben's," Mad-C decided.

"Okay, I'll call and place our orders.

"Ben's Famous Restaurant..., thank you for calling, may I take your order?" the lady that answered the phone greeted.

"Yes, I would like two black-eyed peas, with smoked neck-bones, cornbread, candy yams, spinach greens, corn-on-the-cob, and a green salad. I would also like two banana puddings to go."

"Okay..., that's... " the woman repeated Debo's order.

"Yes, that's it," he said.

"Okay, Sir.., you can pick up your order in thirty-minutes. We will call you five minutes before it's ready: We want it to be hot when you pick it up."

"Well thank you, I appreciate that."

"You're very welcome, sir.., and we appreciate your business."

Debo hung up the office phone and took the block off his phone and called Joy to let her know to give Cruse a call around 8 or 9 o'clock. She was downstairs again getting some air and checking the parameters. But, at least this time she knew what the men that were involved in this mess looked like. He told Joy that he wanted her to help get Cruse to a location where they can talk man-to-man. Since she was the one that came up with the brilliant plan for the move to the hotel. She had a knack for that sort of thing. She said she would do the best she could, which was all Debo could hope for. And with her doing her best… Debo was more at ease. He knew her best was as good as anything anyone else could do. That meant the job would definitely get done with no problem. Mad-C waited while Debo explained to him that Joy would get Cruse to meet with them someplace. But she told him that it would have to be in an open environment. Because she figured he would become suspicious if it was otherwise in a place where no people would be. She knows that he's not a good person and that no good will come to him. He's already wanted for murder and is paranoid, so she'll have to use her best skills with him.

Debo's phone rang and it was Pauline calling. "Hey there, handsome."

"Hey, sweetheart."

"I have an address on your, Randy Carlyle."

"That's what I want to hear," Debo approvingly said.

"Okay, It's 1531 N Ardmore Ave, Apartment 205."

"Damn, that place is way over on the other side of town, anything on a number?"

"No, Morris' mother said, 'that she didn't have a phone number on, Carlyle. The only reason she had the address is that Randy Carlyle was always there with Johnny Morris.' And she said, 'that they were always together. Carlyle was there one day getting wasted, and he left his wallet on the sofa,' and you know how nosy moms can be. She said, 'she looked in it to see who it belonged to because Jonny had a few people over that day and she wanted to get it to the right owner.' And…"

"How did you get all that out of her?"

"I told her I was an ex of his, and I had some mail that belonged to Carlyle, and since Morris was gone maybe I could get it to him. She had me held up talking for hours. She said, 'that she didn't know that Carlyle had an ex named Joyce.' I told her 'that he probably had a lot of girlfriends that no one knew about; not even his own mom, and I definitely didn't know.' That's why I'm his ex because he played around a lot and I couldn't stand for it, so she felt sorry for me and everything."

The office phone rang and Mad-C wasn't in the office to answer it. Debo told Pauline to hold on while he answers it. He was only gone a few seconds, then came back to the phone.

"Sorry, it was some food I ordered."

"Food sounds good right about now. She offered me some beans and rice, but I was ready to go. What are you eating?"

"Oh, something light," he told her.

He didn't want to run down the whole order, because she had just said she was hungry, and he knew what it was like to be hungry and to hear someone describe a dinner as large as the one he and Mad-C are about to eat.

"Alright, I'll go ahead and let you eat. if you need something else, give me a call."

"Okay, thanks."

"You're welcome..., anytime," Pauline said.

Debo placed a call to Molly on his way to Ben's. Molly is Jeffery Smith's common-law wife. He called to see if she had heard from him.

"No sir, Mister Jackson, I'm scared. He would never do anything like this. If you hear from him will you please have him call me?"

"I sure will," Debo promised.

She sounded like she was a whole lot younger than Jeffery; years younger. He wondered if what Jeffery's bartender, Leroy said about him being out with another woman was true.

Molly said, 'that he never had another woman.' Debo was scared, worried, and mad. He couldn't call missing persons because Jeffery deals in drugs, and there's no telling what he might have on him if the police found him first. Ben's was about six blocks down: Debo was sitting in the car talking to Molly. After their call ended, he started the Explorer, made sure *Crazy* was ready, just in case someone didn't want to mind their own business and went home alive, then he left. He's already had two surprises in an alley, one with Dick Patch and Monty Rayass, and another one in an alley in downtown Los Angeles with Carlyle, so he wasn't taking any chances.

"Well look who's here," Agent Dick Patch said when he saw Debo enter the restaurant.

"What brings the government's most valuable players of the DEA here… especially here? I didn't know you ate soul food."

Debo looked next to Patch who was sitting at a long counter that extended from a few feet from the front door to a back wall; maybe thirty or forty feet, and saw Agent Rayass sitting there eating turkey pork chops, mashed potatoes, and mixed vegetables, with what looked like a Coke or Pepsi.

"How's the arm, Big Man!!!" Debo yelled, from across the diner. "Ready for action!!!" Rayass yelled back, with a bite of meat and potatoes in his mouth.

"So, what brings you here?" Debo asked, again.

"I was just in the neighborhood and went through the alley to see if you were in town. Do you know that a gray Tahoe SUV is watching the office?"

"No, I didn't."

"It's been sitting out in front of the place all day with some guy in it. I just figured he was watching the place."

"Well I'll be damn, are you watching it too?"

"I'm getting paid to watch your back."

"Yeah, or to watch me," Debo thought to himself.

He remembered what agent Patch told him at the beach that night. 'That he was watching him and has been doing it for two years.

"You know you can't be too careful. So, how are things going?" Patch asked him.

"Oh, getting there."

"Meaning?"

"Meaning… getting there," Debo said. "Mister Jackson!!!" the woman yelled, again. "Okay, I have to go."

Debo went up to the counter and got his order. The bill came to $48 plus tip. "Not bad," he thought.

He was on his way out the door and yelled back at Rayass,

"I'll see you later hungry, and keep that arm safe!!!"

Agent Monty Rayass was doing a good job at keeping the arm he sprung a few weeks ago, in real good shape. What better way to do it than with a fork and a spoon, which seems to be his favorite pastime.

Debo got back to the office.

"I hope you don't mind warming that up," he told Mad-C.

"Why would I wanna do that?"

"I ran into Patch and Rayass at the restaurant."

"What..., at a soul-food restaurant!!"

"That's the same thing I said."

"So, what was he up to?"

"He told me 'that a gray Tahoe SUV was watching the office building and that he got rid of him."

"There was only one guy in it?" Mad-C asked.

"Yeah..., I took a couple of back streets coming here. I didn't spot the SUV. I also brought the tape from the console." He put the tape in the DVD player while Mad-C went through the bag with his meal in it. He offered to warm it up and set the table so they could eat, Debo gave him a few minutes to finish. The food wasn't really cold, but it was warm and Mad-C wanted his hot.

Debo played the tape and saw what he usually saw on the tapes... traffic, lots and lots of traffic. He saw a few gray SUVs, but not one that seemed to be following him.

"What do you think?" he asked Mad-C.

"I think we should eat our food, if they're going to try anything let them. That'll save us the trouble of looking for them."

"Yeah, this is taking a while," Debo said.

They have enough weapons to supply a small army, which in fact is what the two of them have. The food was delicious, Debo and Mad-C were as full as they could get or hope to get. Debo called Shelly to see how everything was going.

"Hi, Hun, how's things going?"

"Can you get me a better rummy player? I just beat Joy sixteen games straight."

He heard Joy say something in the background. "How are you, baby?" she asked him.

"I'm fine, just missing you, getting back to my baby is what keeps me sane… keeps me going. I miss your cooking. Write and I just ate."

"Yeah, what did you guys eat?"

Debo ran down the whole order to her.

"Man, you guys ate, didn't you. Do you remember your promise?" Shelly asked him.

"Sweetheart, for me to forget that promise, would be forgetting that I love you, and how much I love you, and why I love you."

"How much do you love me? Not that I have to ask, I just love hearing it."

"The life I thought was mine isn't: You are my life, you hold the key to my very existence. If anything, I mean anything at all were to happen to you, the world I live in, the word love and the meaning of both would be a thing of the past. They would be worthless to me. You are everything I could ever hope for in this lifetime, everything my soul has been searching for, everything my heart bleeds for, everything my eyes open each morning for. Each and every day they open and you are still in my life, I thank God and count my blessings, and that blessing is you. You captivate my soul and stimulate my spirit. That's how much I love you young lady!!"

"WOW!!! Well, you sure left me lost for word. Thank you, baby, and I love you too. Hold on a sec," she said.

There was a short silence, then she came back on the phone. "Joy said, 'that a Sgt Billings is trying to reach you.'"

"I know, I heard the beep from my call waiting alert signal."

"I thought I heard a clicking noise, I thought it was my heart. You know, somehow through all of this that's going on, you always make my day and you are so full of encouragement. That's why every time you ask me how I am handling all this; I say 'that I'm hanging in there.' You keep me hanging in there and I love you with all my heart, Mr Jackson. Go ahead and call your friend, it might be important."

"Okay, sweetheart, you sleep well, I love you."

"Boy…, don't I know it. I love you too."

They both did their traditional kissing ritual through the phone and he hung up and called Sgt Billings back.

"I don't have all day, Jackson I do have a job here, you know. How is, Shelly?"

"She's hanging in there, she's really a very brave person. How did you know I was talking to Shell?"

"Anybody else, you would have answered my call. And besides, Joyvette told me."

"Okay, Sarge… what's up?"

"Gregory Johnson does indeed own a sixty-yard yacht at the Glory Days Yacht Club. The numbers you have are current, so is the address. He screens all of his calls at the yacht club, so you might want to call on the (818) 555-3095 number. But, don't use a cell phone to call the yacht club number. Try to find a company phone, and not Write's company phone if you don't want him to have his office number.

Go to a business and ask to use their phone. But, whatever number you use, make sure he can call back. He's not on his yacht all the time, he travels a lot. He owns a jet which he keeps housed in a private hanger out in San Diego. I've set up clearance for Write to gain access. He has to go to the Chula Vista Police Department in San Diego. I'm sure he can find it., Was that all, Mr Jackson?"

Before Debo could answer, Billings said,

"I found nothing on the white Plymouth, only the shit that was in it."

"What about an address on, Gregory Johnson?"

"I'm still checking."

"Yeah…, maybe Patch can come up with one. Okay, that's it for now, you have a wonderful day. Johnson is a big boy, I'll keep you in mind for something extra," Debo said.

"Please do," the Sgt said, and their call ended.

"Well, Johnson does belong to the yacht club in Malibu, and he does own a private yacht and jet, and we do have clearance to the hanger where he houses the jet."

"Where is it?" Mad-C asked.

"In beautiful San Diego, California."

"Well..., Well... how about that shit."

"All you have to do is go to the Chula Vista Police Department, you're already cleared to gain entrance."

"Boy, what a few dollars can do," Mad-C said.

CHAPTER 11

THURSDAY, NOVEMBER 15TH, 10:00 A.M.

"Talk to me baby sis," Debo said to Joy.

"Well, I did it, I checked with some of my people and put the word out that I'm looking for five kilos. The word is that since we stopped working to let all this blow over, Cruse recruited some workers of his own to work that turf. Everyone knows me, so no one suspects me of being a cop or anything. In fact, they know what I do and they also know that I'm damn good at it. As a matter of fact, your boy Cruse is looking for some good workers. I can go in and…"

"Hold it Missy…, anybody but you, I need you on Shell."

"But, I set up the meet with one of Cruse's top workers."

"One of his top workers, not him?"

"No…, not him, but it's the only way to get to him."

"When do you meet with this guy?"

"Tomorrow, I'm supposed to bring $65,000 cash to 6201 South Gage tomorrow at 8:30 in the evening."

"You did a wonderful job, but…"

"D-Angelo, there is no other way, and if you keep waiting for him to come to you, it might be too late. You, Write, or I for the matter could be hurt or killed; not to mention, Shelly. Now, what are you waiting on? I wanna get this thing over with as soon as possible . I do have two daughters to get home to."

"I know, but have you considered the fact that if something happens to you you'll never see them again, and the same goes for them. Anything can go wrong. What if you are being set-up?"

"I thought about that, and I'm sure you'll be right there watching my back. I know you won't let anything happen to me."

"It's the only way, huh?"

"Yes, it's the only way, and Cruse is funny about who he talks to, especially now that his little secret about the Yin murder is out and the case is being investigated again. He's desperate and he doesn't trust too many people right now."

"Let me sleep on it, Joy. I don't know what I'd do if…"

"Hey, Imma big girl, and I'm capable of doing big girl things."

She was sure right about that. She once beat the shit out of a guy who tried to rip her off for $1,000, putting him in the hospital for two weeks .

"You said 8:30 tomorrow evening?"

"Yeah. "

"I'll call you at five and we'll go over it. What kind of place is it?" Debo asked.

"I don't know, but I told him that it had to be someplace where there's a lot of people. I think it's a nightclub or a bar," Joy told him, and they said bye and hung up.

1581 south Ardmore Avenue, apartment 205 is an old red-brick apartment building. It's only two stories but there were eight units; four downstairs and four more upstairs. It looks like the next earthquake would bring it crashing to the pavement.

"All of these guys seem to live or have lived in shabby apartments or houses; maybe to hide what they do," Debo told Mad-C.

They both got out of the Navigator and walked up the cracked concrete steps. They were afraid that one of them would break apart under their weight and they both would fall ass-first down the two flights of stairs. They reached apartment 205 successfully and saw that the screen door was old and so was the doorbell. Mad-C opened the screen with caution, for fear it would fall apart. If this is a cover it's a damned good one. It looked like crackheads lived there. Debo pulled *Crazy* out of its shoulder holster, and when he did, Mad-C took the 44-magnum from his waistband and knocked on the splintered wooden door. He didn't ring the doorbell because he didn't want to get the shit shocked out of him. Nobody answered the door so he tried knocking harder, and still no answer.

"This looks like a dry run, should I try the doorknob?" Debo asked.

"Why not?"

"Okay, let me over there"

Mad-C moved to let Debo get to the door. He turned the knob and it was loose. He thought it would come off in his hand but instead the door with paint peeling off of it opened. It was time for some military techniques. Debo went in low and to the left, and Mad-C went high and to the right. The apartment was empty, there was no furniture and no sign of it being lived in. They checked the rest of the apartment, then holstered their weapons and looked for some kind of a clue that would tell them something about where Carlyle might be. Mad-C got to the bedroom, which was probably the master bedroom, and called Debo.

"What the hell have we walked into?" Debo cried.

There was a mattress on box-springs supported by empty milk crates. There was an old table-top that looked like it once belonged to a dining room set, only there were no legs; It laid flat on the floor. There was candle wax all over the tabletop, the floor, and the mattress. From the door to the mattress was a trail worn into the floor where carpet used to be. There were old beer and wine bottles and cans everywhere, ashtrays full of burnt-out cigarettes, and cotton balls that were apparently used for torches or shooting up were also on the tabletop. There was also burnt crack-pipe screen lying on the tabletop and floor. In the bathroom were several burnt spoons in the sink and elastic bands hanging over the rod where a shower curtain once hung.

"Man, this looks just like a shooting gallery, a base station, and a whore house all mixed up. These guys are either out of the business, or they moved out of here a long time ago," Debo enlightened.

"That takes us right back to where we started; with Carlyle and not knowing where the hell he is," Mad-C said.

"Let's get out of here," Debo suggested.

They were headed for the door when Mad-C noticed something scratched or etched into the wood by the door frame. It was hard to make out… like it had been there for ages.

"Debo, get this down on something," Mad-C told him.

He took his cell phone and pulled up his memo pad and pressed reminders, then started entering the numbers… (1-4-4-6); 1446: He couldn't make out the street name S… U… P… looks like an O or L and a U or V. He couldn't tell which, and the rest faded out.

"Okay, I've got S-U-P-L, and what looks like a U or a V."

"Try the U," Mad-C told him. "Okay, S-A-P-O-L-U… "

"Sepulveda… Sepulveda!!!" Mad-C screamed. "1446 Sepulveda Blvd."

Debo confirmed it and deleted the remainder of the puzzle and entered the address. "Let's go."

"You ain't gotta tell me twice," Mad-C said. They both exited the apartment and were very careful going down the steps.

"Did you close the door?" Mad-C asked Debo.

"Hell naw, I was afraid it might fall off and make a lot of noise. I pulled it to, though."

Debo started the Navigator and was headed back to the freeway. "Let's take the streets after Western ave. I wanna see what kind of place this is; Sepulveda is a business district. Then we'll head to the yacht club." Jeffery was awake and feeling terribly sick. He had thrown up everything he had eaten the night before. He didn't know what time it was. He didn't even know what day it was, or if it was day or night. All he knew was that someone is going to pay for this shit, and pay dearly. Tom walked into the room with a tray.

"Want something to eat? Damn it smells bad in here."

"Yeah, well if you were locked the fuck up in a hole, pissing all over yourself, pouring bile all over your damn self, and haven't had a bath; not even washed up in God knows how long. How much are they paying you, one, two grand? Who's going to kill me when it's time; you, Randy, or

Robert Cruse? And where the hell are you going to run to when this shit backs up in your fuckin face? Cat got your tongue?"

"I.., I."

"I, my ass, you are way over your head here. Why don't you just...," Jeffery felt a stabbing pain in the middle of his stomach.

"This shit hurts, man I need a fix. I can't... " another pain ripped through his body.

"Please give me a fix."

First, he was pleading and begging his heart out for Carlyle not to give him the drug, and now he's practically begging to get it. "That bastard got me hooked on this shit. Why don't you just... another excruciating pain hit him. "Why don't you just let me go? Do you own this place or just work here? If you just work here, it would be in your best interest to just let me out of here and save your life. Just make it look like I escaped."

"But, how? They have you tied down there pretty good. There is no way you can get loose. They will know I helped you."

"Please..., I'll hide you. The man I work for will look out for you and your family if you have one."

"Yes, I have a wife and three girls, and they know exactly where to find them. I'm sorry... I can't help you."

"Then help yourself and quit your job, because when the man I work for comes looking for me, and it's only a matter of time before he gets here, and everybody involved is going to die." Another pain caught Jeffery off guard.

"We're not talking police or jail. It'll be much worse. And, what's your family going to do when..., Oh, shit I need a fix man... this shit hurts like hell."

Another very sharp pain tore through his whole body. He yelled, then yelled again, and then he screamed.

"Please give me a fix man, this shit hurts too bad..., PLEASE!!!"

Jeffery couldn't talk anymore; he was in too much pain.

Tom sat the tray down, mopped the floor, and sat the pale of water and a rag with soap on the table that Carlyle used as a chair when he tortured Jeffery. He turned to Jeffery and said,

"If you get loose there is no way out of this room unless I give you a key. If I untie one of your hands.., I don't know, Mister Carlyle told me to feed you and clean you up. If I untie one of your hands and let you do it yourself and you manage to get loose… but then there are no windows and no way out of here other than that door. If one of them comes in here and you are loose they might kill you., is that what you want?"

"Do it… Please do it," Jeffery cried.

Tom sat the pale of water, soap, a towel, and a clean sheet on the bed and cut the duck tape from the arm that was used as a pin cushion to feed the drugs through Jeffery's veins.

"That's all I can do,I have to lock the door."

"You did plenty."

Another pain stopped Jeffery in mid-sentence and he grabbed his stomach and moaned.

Tom walked out, came back in, looked at him, and said, "good luck," then turned and went back out the door.

1446 Sepulveda Blvd is indeed a business district, and to Debo's surprise the building was a bank… Bank of America.

"What the… this is confusing me. This guy looks as-though he lives like a bum, a crackhead, and now what, a bank hold-up?"

"I don't think so, I think that if you'd notice, the address was old and fading. That means that it had to have been there for a very long time. I'm thinking ten years at least," Mad-C assumed.

"Oh yeah, and the bank could be where Carlyle kept his money."

"Yeah, and therefore the bank may not have a current address on him."

"I knew that, I was just testing your skills. Can't have anyone on my team that doesn't have kills," Debo joked.

"Yeah.., right!"

"How do you feel about bribing a bank teller?" Debo suggested. "Let's pull some of our resources and see what we come up with. That's federal, and the feds don't play," Mad-C said.

"Patch should be able to help, shouldn't he? I mean, after all, he's practically federal," Debo reminded him.

"Yeah..., practically. Check it out and see what he can come up with. There is nothing too much we can do, they won't give us any information," Mad-C told Debo.

"Okay, where to now?"

"Malibu," Mad-C said.

The parking lot of the yacht club was about a half-mile long and a quarter-mile wide. Debo parked near the front door and they both got out of the SUV and walked up the concrete step to the building. It was a twenty-seven-story, state-of-the-art, gray-stone building.

"Damn, this a big ass place," Debo said. "Well, let's go in," Mad-C suggested.

The double glass doors were about ten feet tall and ten feet wide each. They walked up to the doors and stepped onto a plate that automatically slid both doors apart. The smell of fresh leather and furniture polish rushed through the doors, slamming into Debo's and Mad-C's nose. Debo loves leather; the sofa in his home office is pure leather. He has leather coats, shoes, belts, hats, and gloves; he just plain and simple loves leather. In the lobby of the yacht club, stood twin flower pots, five-feet-tall, and as round as a Volkswagen. There was a waterfall coming from large rocks built into the wall. The water fell into a river with a replica of a yacht afloat in the simulated river, surrounded by trees and a sandy landscapes. The counters were made of thick stained glass, and there were two of them that stood four feet each. There was a digital display board that listed all of the various offices, cruise destinations, and arrival and departure times. Debo stopped at a place in the indexes that was placed in the main lobby on the wall next to the entrance and looked for the Glory Days Yacht Club's executive offices.

"Well, well... what have we here? Mr Johnson is not only a club member, but he's also on the board of directors. The man is CEO (Chief Executive Officer). Well, how do you like those apples?" Debo said.

"Oh yeah, he's very big," Mad-C said.

"Let's see if we can get him on a phone somewhere. We need a business phone to call him on, and what better business phone than the one in his own club," Debo concluded. Mad-C walked over to the guy at the desk who stood five feet tall but was built to let people know that he meant business. And when he said something there was no arguing with him.

"What can I do for you gentlemen?" the clerk asked. "Is there any way you can call or page a Mister Gregory Johnson?"

"No Sir.., we can't call our CEOs on a direct line. But there are phones on the wall to your right. You can use those phones to page, Mr Johnson."

"Thank you," Mad-C said.

"Thank you, Sir.., will there be anything else I can help you with?"

"No, I think we'll be fine," Debo told the short muscular man behind the counter.

They walked over to where the phones were on the wall, with only a cordless receiver and three rows of numbers. Next to it was a copper plaque attached to the wall with instructions on how to use the phone engraved in it.

"To page press three, to call a club representative, press two, to call the operator, please press zero-pound."

Debo picked up the receiver and pressed three to page Gregory Johnson, and a voice in the receiver said,

"To page, enter the four-digit extension into the numeric pad below. "What four-digit extension?" Debo asked Mad-C.

Mad-C went back to the index, then came back and told Debo to hang up, start over, and when they ask for the extension number, enter 4410, which is the 555-0001 number.

Debo did as he was instructed and entered the extension number, and a voice said, "Please stand by, your page has been sent."

"Now what... ?" Debo asked.

"Now we wait."

"Wait for what?" Debo asked.

"Let me see," Mad-C said, and read the plaque that displayed the instructions further. It said, "Note: After you have successfully placed your page, the phone will ring, and your party will acknowledge your page."

They waited five more minutes and the phone rang. "Hello, Mister Johnson," Mad-C said.

"Yes, who's calling?"

"You don't know me, but I'm the owner and CEO of Charles Write and Associates Enterprise in Beverly Hills, California."

"Yes, Mister Write, how can I help you?"

"I have a rather urgent issue to discuss with you, sir. And I was wondering if I could schedule an appointment to see you."

"What kind of issue?"

"I'd rather not discuss it over the phone, sir."

"Okay, tomorrow, my office, 9:00 am sharp!"

"'9:00 am sharp' it is," Mad-C said.

Gregory Johnson knows who Mad-C is and has known for years… fifteen-years in fact. Charles Write was one more step closer to finding out what was really going on.

After they left the yacht club, Debo remembered something. "I'll be right back," he told Mad-C.

He went back into the yacht club and walked up to the desk and the same man that helped them earlier was still standing there.

"Yes, sir, is there something else you need?"

"As a matter of fact, there might be something you can help me with if you don't mind. Can I charter a yacht to Maui? If so, how much would it cost for a weekend? No, make that the full seven days and seven nights."

"Well, I can give you one of our travel brochures and you can browse through it. It would be most helpful to you, I'm sure."

"Thank you," Debo said, and left.

"What was that all about?" Mad-C asked.

"I wanted to see how much it would be to charter a yacht to Maui for Shell and myself."

"I'll tell you what, Debo. If we live through this mess, I'll finance your entire vacation… whatever it cost."

Debo backed out of the parking space and exited the parking lot. "What time is it?" Mad-C asked.

It was more of a thought, but he had asked it out loud, then realized he said it. Mad-C knew the man wore a $120,000.00 Cartier watch, and had a gold clock with platinum minute and hour hands built into the dashboard of the SUV, but he told him anyway. "It's

1:45 in the afternoon, Mister Write. I have to go see Joy and go over the plans to meet with Cruses' people in a couple of hours. I really don't like the fact that she's putting herself out there like that. I'll never live it down if something were to happen to her. I asked her to set up a meeting… not get herself killed, Debo argued."

"Well, you have to think positive; she feels that she knows what she's doing. Look, Debo…, Joy is one of the best you have from what I've heared. If not the best, with, Freddy being second best."

"Yeah, but even the best make mistakes."

"Not with you there, you're her security blanket, you're there to ensure her safety. She knows you don't make mistakes in this business. She feels that with you there, you won't let her make any either. She looks to you for the support she needs."

"Nothing…, I mean nothing had better happen to her, or I'm going after everybody and their families without stopping; and I mean it. I mean it with everything in me," Debo stressed.

"Well, let's just hope nothing happens to her, then it won't have to come down to that, what's next?" Mad-C asked, in order to take the conversation someplace else.

"Uh… let's see," Debo mumbled.

While he searched his brain to find out what the next move would be, his cell phone rang.

"Yeah," he said. "You sound tired."

"I am, I've been running all day."

"I'm just checking to see if you're okay. I haven't heard anything from Jeffery yet, I hope he's alright. Everything is good here; Joy and Shelly went to a movie, I guess they got bored. I'll call you when they get back or have one of them call you to let you know that they made it back okay," Freddy said.

"Okay, thanks Freddy, and keep trying Jeffery for me," Debo said. Freddy assured him that he would.

"Hey, Bob, what's up?"

"Oh nothing, just work as usual. What's on your mind?" Sergeant Billings asked when he answered Debo's call.

"I was wondering how I go about looking for an account number on Cruse or Carlyle at Bank of America?"

"That sounds like a job for the feds."

"That's what I thought."

"Have you talked to, Patch?"

"No, do you think I should? I mean what if the feds get a hold of this whole thing?" Debo asked.

"They shouldn't… agent Patch should know what he's doing."

"Yeah…, Mister Write had the same suggestion. Okay, I'll give him a call, thanks, Bob," Debo said, then hung up and called Agent Dick Patch. "Agent Rayass speaking," a voice said, into the phone.

"Rayass!!! Okay, what did you do to your partner?" Debo jokingly asked.

"He's in a meeting, sir.., is there anything I can do for you, Mr. Jackson?" Debo wasn't used to doing business with Agent Rayass. He figured, 'ole hungry' could probably do the job. After all, Patch did give him his cell phone.

"I need to get hold of an account number on Cruse or Carlyle at Bank of America. All I need is an address, the one I have is too old It's a rundown base station and shouting gallery."

"Hold on," Rayass told him.

Debo heard music playing in the background; very relaxing music. They were just about at the office, when Debo had to swerve to avoid rear-ending a bus.

"Shit," he cursed.

"Was I that long?" Rayass asked, as he came back to the phone and heard Debo.

"No, I almost hit a bus."

"We don't show Cruse as having an account at Bank of America, but there is an old one on Randy Carlyle. The account number is 0022308208. The address he gave the bank was 1435 Brooks Street in Venice, CA."

"Damn, that's Morris' old address or his Mom's. Is that all you have?"

"That's all our database has for now. We'll keep checking on it." Joy took it upon herself to check out the meeting place; knowing Debo would blow his top once she told him or he found out. The place she was meeting with Cruse's people: 6201

South Gage is a rather large place. And there would certainly be enough people around that Cruse wouldn't have to worry about any foul play by Joy, Debo, or anyone else that was supposed to be in on the meeting. Everything and anything was being watched on video camera.

Upon Joy's arrival, she saw the biggest place of business she had ever encountered in one place. The building is so large it took up the entire block. It was a steel-gray, stucco building, with dark navy-blue trim outside. The shatter-proof glass was also a dark blue. Bars were placed around the sides and back of the building. Joy looked up at the two-story building and read the neon sign that brightly displayed; "J's Bar, Grill, and Nightclub." She walked through the front door, knowing that she was going above and beyond the call of duty, but Joy is Joy. She also knew that if Debo found out she had gone in there without him, he would have a fit. He's always concerned about her safety, and this wasn't a very safe place for her to go by herself. She saw what seemed to be a restaurant with tables and a chair at each end of the tables. The floor was carpeted with the usual commercial carpet. She also saw the bar area, which was equipped with tap beer, peanuts, and beer nuts placed in small bowls on the bar. Pictures of various movie stars and celebrities hung on the walls, and gold ceiling fans were mounted over each table.

The smell of spicy chicken, greens, yams, and something prepared with curry seasoning was thick in the air. Her attention was focused on the bar. That was most likely where the meeting would be. There was the usual liquor lined up against the back wall. The bar itself extended about 30 to 45 feet long. Tables were also set in place in front of the bar with white silk table cloths placed neatly on them. Just the aroma from the food alone made her mouth water as she focused her attention on the bar area. Not only were there white table cloths on each table, but there was also a red candle and an ashtray placed on each table for those who like to smoke while they drink or drink while they smoke. Further to the right was a dance floor with flashing different colored lights, to give it a disco or romantic look. Off to the back of the dance floor were more tables and booths for those customers who just wanted to relax and watch the people dance and have their beer or liquor in a sort of off-to-yourself atmosphere. It was a wonder spot; a good place to unwind, relax, eat, dance, and if you want, just have a ball. Joy thought that if Cruse was to walk through the door it might ruin everything, so she decided to leave.

On her way out, she accidentally bumped into a guy that had a few too many drinks. She took a deep breath and held it until she was out the door. Once she was outside, she let go of the breath she had taken and walked to her car. She pulled out into the traffic with the image of the restaurant, bar, and club still fresh in her mind, and the aroma of the food still fresh in her nostrils.

"That place must have cost a pretty penny," she thought to herself. She didn't intentionally take it upon herself to go in there, she was just being safe. At least if she was walking into something or someplace, she would know what the place looks like, every detail. Debo noticed a help wanted sign in the window of the fishing and boat club. He figured that if Jeffery was being held by Cruse and his men, that would be most likely where they have him. He decided to call Pauline, to see if she would mind some 'spy-shit'. He would have Sgt Billings pull some strings to get her in there with no problem.

"Speak to me, handsome," her voice said into the phone.

"Well, I see you are feeling better, or at least you sound better anyway."

"Yeah, I feel a lot better than I did the last time I saw you.

So, to what do I owe the pleasure of this call? I know you want something… what is it?"

"How would you like a job?" Debo asked her.

"I work for you, Big Head, in case you haven't noticed, I have a job."

"I need to put someone at the fishing and boat club.

I know there's some foul play. I'm almost sure that Cruse and his people have Jeffery, and that's the only place I can think of that they would have him. So, I need you to…"

"Yeah, you need me to go in undercover; I'm loving it already, just tell me what to do and how to get in."

"I have all that set up. If they have Jeffery they won't let him live when they're finished with him, he's probably half-dead now."

"Okay, handsome, I'm on it."

"Thanks, Pauline."

"You're welcome, handsome," Pauline said.

Billings came through for Debo, and Pauline got the job.

She hasn't worked a nine-to-five in over half her life. Debo always looked out for Pauline. He met her at the African American museum near downtown Los Angeles about two years before he met Shelly. Pauline had always called Debo handsome, It was in those days the way to successfully flirt. She had a really strong crush on him and was mentally, emotionally, and spiritually in love with him, but it never got serious physically. She gave her respects, blessings, and well wishes to the one woman he did choose to spend the rest of his life with… Mrs Michelle L Jackson. Debo's workers always had an ICOE (In Case Of Emergency) number: Molly was Jeffery's ICOE contact.

Debo called Molly, to see if she had heard from him yet.

"D-Angelo, I thought he was with you. I haven't heard from him in two days, and that's not like Jeffery. I was a little nervous, but now I'm worried, Mr Jackson, I'm very worried," Molly confessed.

"Don't worry, Molly, I'll find out what's going on. In a minute I'll know what this is all about. Hopefully, he's just out someplace letting off steam," Debo assumed.

No matter how much steam any of his workers needed to let off, they must stay in constant contact with Debo. Molly agreed to calm down until he called her back… hopefully with good news. But he'll make sure it's good news, because that's all he's looking for and that's all he'd better get. Daisy's cost, and if Jeffery is somewhere pushing up daisies, then Big Boy, Carlyle, and Johnson will have to pay the cost. Randy went by Mama Morris' to let her know that Jonny Morris, his best friend, and her favorite and only biological son was gone; set up by his best friend. Carlyle had no choice, he had to do what he was told. Even if he was told to take the life of Mama Morris, he would. Morris and Carlyle were the best of friends. He got a little dizzy and everything around him faded out. He was at the point where he had to ask himself what happened to all the years, all the closeness, all the buddy-buddy-bullshit, breaking bread, drinking from the same cup, glass, can, and bottle, doing the same shit day in and day out for years? Even getting to know and develop a relationship with his mom, a relationship worthy enough to call Mama Morris his mother. She became attached to Randy and trusted him with her life, her home, and even her only son's life. Randy Carlyle felt like the piece of shit he had become.

"Hey, Mama Morris!!" Randy Carlyle greeted.

She unlocked the door, the same door that Debo once stood at and talked to Mama Morris.

"Hey, son, what brings you by here?"

She knew that if Jonny wasn't with Randy when he came knocking on her door, or if Jonny wasn't there and Randy was, something was terribly wrong.

"Did you hear about Jonny, Mama Morris?" Randy asked her, knowing she probably hadn't, or hoping she hadn't.

"I heard something about him getting hurt or in trouble. What's that all about? I hope it wasn't anything too serious."

Mama Morris is not a dummy. Jonny Morris is her son, she knows him inside and out. She knew he would end up dead or someone would wind up dead because of him. She's just waiting to hear some bad news about Carlyle, which won't belong either. She'll hear that he's dead, in the hospital, or in jail or prison .

"Randy, you should really consider keeping that thing in your pants, because you are starting to collect way too many ex-girlfriends."

"Yeah, why do you say that?" Carlyle asked.

"Well, because one of your exes came by here looking for you. She said, 'she also knows, Jonny, and that you were out at her place one night, and you left some mail, so she came here to bring it to you, or to try and get it to you.' Boy, you'd better be careful out there before that thing in your pants gets you in deeper than you can pull it out," Mama Morris scolded.

"Did she say what her name was?" Carlyle asked.

"In fact, she did. She said her name was Joyce something; I forgot her last name. She took my heart when she told me where she was from and that she liked beans and rice.' She said, 'that she was raised on beans, rice, pig-ears, pig-feet, pigtails, ham, ribs, yams, greens, oxtails, and cornbread.' She got me when she said, 'hot-water-cornbread.' She just went on and on about how familiar she was with beans and rice. She's a very sweet girl, Randy."

"But Mama Morris listen, I don't know any Joyce," Randy Carlyle confessed. He search his brain to see if by chance he could have met someone named Joyce, or if she possibly came into his life even if for a moment, a day, a one-night-stand. But no, he couldn't remember ever meeting anyone by that name.

"What do you mean you don't know her?"

Randy Carlyle had to think and think fast. Maybe it's the girlfriend of the guy Jonny took with him to do the hit on Write and Jackson. Maybe she's whoever she is, but Randy Carlyle certainly doesn't know or remember a Joyce or why she really came by Mama Morris' house looking for him or Jonny. But maybe he should try to put two and two together. She has to be Debo's or Mad-C's people. Well, whatever the reason and whoever she is, Randy Carlyle would have to go along with whatever game the woman is playing; at lease as far as Mama Morris is concerned. Maybe things had gotten way out of hand and far too out of context.

"What about the funeral, Randy.., are you going with me?"

"Yes, Mama Morris, I wouldn't miss it for the world. I'll call you to see what time and day it is."

"Okay, Randy don't let me down."

"I won't, Mama Morris. What did you say Joyce looked like?"

"Just a beautiful well kept and well-mannered young lady about your height, only a little lighter complexion. She smelled a lot better too. What is that smell on you boy another ex? And why are you sweating so hard, are you alright?"

"Just some work I was doing, I'm fine, Mama Morris," Randy lied. He didn't want her to know that the odor was from nervousness, fear, and regret.

"Well, it's good thing you're off work. Go home and clean yourself up."

"That's my next stop, I just decided to stop by here on my way.

If Joyce calls or comes back by here, tell her I said to give me a call." Which is virtually impossible because she doesn't know his number.

"Randy, have you lost your mind boy? Just a little while ago you told me you didn't know anyone by the name of Joyce. What the hell is going on with you?"

"I usually say that when I don't feel like being bothered," Randy Carlyle lied again.

"There's something really funny about this. Why would a girl I don't even know come by here and pretend to be my ex-girlfriend, and on top of that, try to get information about me?"

Who is this woman? This thing is getting way out of hand. First Jackson and Write comes by here, and now some strange woman pops up a few days later. What the hell does Robert have me involved in? First, he robbed someone ten-years ago, then had me set up my best friend, and now people are coming around here looking for me. Yeah, this is getting way out of hand.., way the fuck out of hand."

"Randy!!... Randy!!!... Boy, do you hear me!!!" Mama Morris yelled, trying to get his attention.

"Ah..., yeah, Mama Morris?"

"Are you alright?"

I'm fine Mama Morris, I'll be here early Sunday morning for the funeral. I'm leaving home about 6:45 in the morning."

"Okay, I'll be here."

"You take care, Mama Morris."

"Okay... and you do the same."

Randy is really worried. These people are getting too close. Jeffery had warned him that his boss would find the people responsible for his kidnapping and torture, and that there would be hell to pay. Now it's starting to sink in. The hunter has become the hunted. Randy Carlyle has to pay Jeffery Smith one more visit, and this visit won't be so nice. Jeffery is going to tell him who Joyce is and how she can be found, or he won't have to worry about withdrawals or anything else anymore.

CHAPTER 12

FRIDAY, NOVEMBER 16TH, 6:30 A.M.

Debo decided to meet Joy early today because he had so much more to do, he didn't want to wait until the last minute. He wanted everything to go smoothly tonight. He didn't want any slip-ups; his little sister's life is at stake and those are very high stakes. Debo, Mad-C, and Joy met at the Beverly Hills Office. Freddy stayed with Shelly while she slept in her room and Freddy slept in Joy's room. Debo didn't want Shelly left alone for any period of time.

"Joy, I want you to meet my boss; Mister Write."

Joy considered it a pleasure to finally meet the man that employed her brother and her. Jeffery Smith was the only member of the team to personally meet Mad-C.

"How are you Mr Write? It's a pleasure to finally meet you in person."

"Thank you, Miss Hernandez. D-Angelo has told me a lot about you, and now I get to meet you; One of the best workers he has, and the little sister of one of the best men I know. Do you drink, Miss Hernandez, coffee, brandy, tea? I also have ginger ale if you'd like."

"Coffee will be fine, and please call me Joy."

"Okay, Joy, coffee it is, and how about you, D-Angelo?"

"I'll have coffee…, black, and stop calling me D-Angelo."

Mad-C went to get their coffees while Joy and Debo sat at the table in the outer office where they had their meeting a little over a week ago.

"I wanna go by that place and check it out, I haven't had a chance to, I've been busy. So, after we leave here we'll go by there."

"I went there yesterday," Joy confessed.

"Are you out of your mind going there alone? And besides, you were supposed to be with Shelly."

"I left Freddy with her, I was just doing research. We have to know what we're walking into. And with such little time before I meet with them, I just thought I'd do it. No one there knew who I was."

"Yeah, you might have a point about us not having a lot of time. What am I going to do with you, Joyvette Hernandez?" Debo asked in a soft tone, after he calmed down.

"What did you find out," he asked, after a long moment of silence. He hated to talk to her in that tone of voice, but then again he didn't want anything to happen to her. As soon as this is over, he's pulling her out of this mess, even if he has to buy her, her own business himself.

"Okay…, first of all, that's Tony's old stomping grounds which could be another reason he's recruiting workers. Tony's gone, and it's wide open. But as for the place itself, it's a restaurant, bar, and nightclub all rolled up into one. When you walk in, you think you're in a little town; it takes up the entire block.

A very large barroom sat off to the left. as you walk in that can seat over forty people easily at the fifty feet long bar. The bar sits between the dance-floor and restaurant, and can easily accommodate eighty people. The restaurant and the nightclub take up two-thirds of the block, while the bar takes up the remaining one-third. The whole place is bigger than two, Mavericks flats."

"What is?" Mad-C asked as he brought a tray with three cups of coffee into the office.

"Joy was telling me about the place where she's meeting Cruse's people tonight. It's going to take me, you, and Freddy to make sure she comes out unharmed."

"So, that makes four of us," Joy said.

"Bro, you and I are going to ride bikes," Debo told Mad-C.

"You don't mean those little scooters you have in your carport, do you?" Mad-C asked.

"Exactly…, you see, if anything goes wrong I want to be able to go where cars can't go if I have to. Joy is going to take the Explorer, it's armor-plated. And besides, it'll look real good, seeing as how she's spending $65,000 cash, she has to look good. I'll show you how to work the surveillance camera in case you need it," Debo told Joy.

"Okay, boss… I mean, Bra… sorry."

"She's been around Freddy too long. He's got her calling me boss," Debo told Mad-C.

"We don't have to sit out here, Joy is family. Why don't we go in your office, Debo?" Mad-C suggested.

They went to Debo's office. Joy has never been in there either.

"Wow you've got it made, this is nice; it's luxurious."

"You should see his," Debo said, pointing to Mad-C. "Hey no one has had breakfast," Mad-C enlightened.

"Well, I thought maybe we can pick up something along the way. Can't work on an empty stomach," Debo offered.

"Okay let's go, I'm starved" Joy agreed.

They left Beverly Hills headed to Crenshaw, then to "M and M's" soul-food restaurant for breakfast.

They arrived at 7:30 am. The front was breathtaking. It was a silver-bluish color, and the front doors were laminated steel, also blue in color; a navy-blue. The window frames were also navy blue with silver window tint to keep the sun from coming through the window into the club. You could tell that they had VIP events because there were barriers assembled at the front of the building to separate the thick red carpet from the rest of the sidewalk, which ran from the curb to the door: Security is a must. The club wasn't open, but the bar and grill were. The restaurant serves delicious meals, while the bar serves hangover remedies.

"These people make money all day and all night," Debo said. "Yeah, tell me about it," Mad-C responded.

The club was shut off from the bar and restaurant, but you could see through the bars that separated them. Debo and Mad-C saw where they would be positioned. Mad-C picked a spot in the back near the back door in case Robert Cruse was there he didn't want him to spot him. He figured it led to the parking lot since the place was too big for it to be an alley that close to the back door. Debo picked a spot just at the end of the bar. Joy was going to be seated away from the restaurant and the dance floor to avoid traffic from the kitchen and noise from the dance floor.

"Perfect," Mad-C told Debo.

"Hello gentlemen?" a short dark-skinned woman said, walking toward them with a pen and pad in her hand ready to take their orders.

"Nothing for us, we're just admiring the place. How long has this place been here?" Mad-C asked.

"Oh, about nine and a half years," the lady told him.

"Maybe Cruse does own the place," Debo told Mad-C. "Yeah…, maybe."

Mad-C wondered if he really did own it. They had a half-hour to be at 909 Pacific Coast Highway, and Malibu is a good distance from Crenshaw and Gage. They made it late… but they made it. Gregory Johnson said 9:00 sharp, and CEOs are known for punctuality.

They arrived there at 9:10 am.

Mad-C walked over to the telephones on the wall; the same ones they used on their previous visit to the Yacht Club. He dialed 555-0001, extension 4410 then hung up and waited for the phone to ring. Debo didn't have time to drop Joy off, so he brought her along. They waited in the Explorer with instructions to check up on Mad-C if he was not back in thirty-minutes. Johnson called the phone back.

"Hello, Mister Write, please take the elevator to your right and come up to the thirteenth floor. There will be a desk about twenty-five feet to the left of the elevators."

Mad-C did as he was instructed. When he got to the desk he was met by a tall, blonde, six-feet one-inch tall woman with long silky blond hair that matched her complexion. She wore a tux, tie, and tail, with a white dress-shirt underneath, and she smelled like roses. Mad-C didn't know if it was from the soap or the perfume she wore.

A very soft, low voice said,

"Good morning, Mister Write, Mr Johnson is expecting you…, you may go on in."

"Thank you, miss…, "

"Mills…, Dorothy Mills," the stunning blonde said. "Thank you, Miss Mills."

She directed him toward a door that stood at least ten feet tall. You could tell the man lived an extravagant lifestyle. The cigar he smoked smelled just like the same Havana brand he smokes. In fact, Mad-C seized the opportunity to take a few. Johnson's office was very state-of-the-art. His desk is clear Plexiglas with two white fiberglass pedestals to support it, instead of legs. The windows didn't have shades nor blinds. They were made into pictures on the wall. They were five feet wide and three feet long. There was a similar waterfall and a yacht in a lake on his wall to Mad-C's left.Two leather sofas were positioned in the middle of the room, with a coffee table similar to his desk between the two sofas. The waterfall was a replica of the one he saw downstairs. Gregory Johnson invited him to come on into the office and immediately stood to shake his hand.

"Mister Write: pleased to meet you. I'm Gregory Johnson, how can I be of service to you?"

Mad-C looked at one of the sofas and back at Johnson and said, "May I?"

Johnson knew Mad-C wanted to sit down and made a mental note to smack himself later for not offering him a seat.

"Of course.., I'm very sorry, please have a seat."

Mad-C figured Johnson wasn't used to having guests in his office, or he had so many that they automatically took a seat, and let it go at that. After all, the man didn't seem to be impolite.

"You have two vehicles registered to this yacht club bearing the license plates P-L-A-Y-E-R-5; a black Mercedes Benz, 2014, I believe. And a white 2013 Dodge Plymouth, License Plate, P-L-A-Y-E-R-2. Those sound like company cars or some kind of organization."

"I don't understand your question.., just a second Mister Write." Johnson got up and walked over to his desk, picked up a remote control then went back and sat on the sofa and pressed two buttons. The two pictures that were mounted on the wall slid apart to reveal two wide windows. He pushed another button and a small bar came out of the wall next to the replica of the waterfall in the lobby.

"Care for a drink, Mr Write?" Johnson asked.

"No, thank you, I don't drink this early, how about a cigar?"

Mad-C went into his coat pocket and pulled out two Havana cigars. "Ah.., Mister Write, I see you smoke the good stuff also."

"I can only stand the best," Mad-C said.

"Now, as for the two cars, Mister Write. Those are company cars, and we sometimes lend them to our customers, associates, employees, and certain corporate staff," Johnson informed him.

"Mr Johnson, the cars in question and Mister Anderson or Cruse, are involved in a police investigation, and your name and this yacht club's name came up. All I need is an address on, Cruse. He has been to my house and one of his associates tried to kill a friend of mine and his sister in a Downtown Los Angeles alley. In both cases, both cars were used. The Plymouth was used in an attempt to kill me in Venice,California. I'm sure you've heard it on the news or have seen it in the papers."

"So, you're the one that killed the two guys in Venice Sunday?"

"That's not what I said. Let me get to the point here."

"Please do."

"Someone is trying to kill me and a friend of mine, and if they're not it sure as hell seems like it. Mister Johnson, if you have anything whatsoever to do with this, you are going down with them. Murder, attempted murder, and drug trafficking."

"Are you implying that I'm in anyway involved in illegal activities and murder, Mister Write?"

"No, I'm not implying anything. I'm letting you know that I know you are involved. And if you don't give me Cruse and his side-kick, Randy Carlyle… yes you will face murder and attempted murder."

"Just what is it you do, Mr Write?"

"I keep people like you and your flunkies off my ass, Mr Johnson."

"Mr Write, I think it's about time for you to be leaving."

"And, Mr Johnson, I think it's about time for you to be waking up. Murder is a rough ride; enjoy the cigar."

Mad-C casually walked out as Dorothy entered Johnson's office and said, "Is anything wrong Mr Johnson?"

"Get me Anderson on the phone."

"What happened?" Debo asked.

"He lied his ass off, that's what happened. I either hit a nerve or embarrassed the hell out of myself. I told him that I know he's involved in drug trafficking. And, do you know what he had the nerve to ask me? That son-of-a-bitch asked what I do for a living."

"What did you tell him?" Debo asked.

"I told him that I slap the shit out of people that lie to me; well not in those words, but he got the message."

"Well let's see what comes up," Debo said.

9:30 A.M.

Debo called Pauline's cell phone, and she picked it up. "Hey handsome, how's my main man?"

"Good…, real good, how's the job coming along?"

"I haven't worked a nine-to-five in so long, I can get used to this. There are a lot of good-looking men here."

"Yeah, but I'm only interested in one in particular…

Jeffery Smith. Do you still have the pictures of Johnson, Cruse, and Carlyle?"

"I still have them, sir."

"Okay, if you see any of those guys, call me or Sgt Billings. The number is on the back of each picture… don't do anything. If you find out where Jeffery is call me first not Billings. I don't want them to get my man killed if he's not already dead."

The windows were rolled down in the Explorer and the air was fresh at about thirty miles per hour. It felt wonderful but Joy was cold. Women always get cold fast anyway.

"Hey, how about some lunch?" She asked. "We just had breakfast," Mad-C reminded her.

"That was 6:30 this morning, it's almost 11:30."

"Girl, you can eat, can't you?" Debo remarked.

"Well, I can use a little something myself," Mad-C said. "What are you guys up for?" Debo asked. "Whatever…, I don't care long as it's food," Joy said. "Reminds me of Rayass," Debo thought to himself. "How about, Ben's?" Mad-C suggested.

"Yeah, they have some dynamite food, huh Big Guy?"

Debo knows the food is the best and didn't mind trying their turkey pork chops.

"Okay, Ben's it is," Debo said.

"You're going to love Ben's food, Joy," Mad-C told her. "I'll love anything right about now, I'm starved."

Debo called Ben's restaurant and ordered for everyone. He didn't want to eat out; he was tired of the streets for now. He just wanted to go to the office, kick back, and enjoy a meal and a good movie from Mad-C's very nice movie library at the office. Then they had to get ready for their rendezvous at Carlyle's club. He had to drive out to San Diego to pick up the motorcycles for Mad-C and himself. He had plenty of time, all he had to do was drive down to San Diego, put the trailer hitch on the back of the Navigator, and pull the bikes back to Los Angeles. Debo decided to use the Navigator instead of thee Explorer for this job.

The phone to the office rang and Mad-C answered it. It was the restaurant with their orders. Debo sent Joy to pick up the food because he was too tired to fuss with the traffic right now.

"Okay, what's the code again?" Joy asked.

"Joy, you can't remember that code to save your life, can you?" Debo scolded. And it just might save her life one day.

"Well, I'm tired too," she protested.

She remembers what she wants to. When she's working, she's the best accountant Debo has. She can divide fifty by five pretty quick, and twelve and a half times five at twelve thousand each. The girl has a knack for numbers. But, give her one simple four-digit code and she's lost.

"Be right back bro," Joy told Debo.

Joy didn't really know what agent Dick Patch or Monty Rayass looked like. She didn't know if they knew what she looked like either. Agent Patch saw Debo's Navigator pull out of the alley.

"I thought I was going to be able to get some rest. Where does she think she is going? Well, I might as well follow her, she's in just as much dang.er as Jackson and Write. What the... ?"

Just as Joy was about to turn on Robertson, Patch saw a gray Tahoe cut her off. She swerved to keep from hitting the SUV and ran up on the curb. The man in the gray SUV sat there for what seemed to be a minute, then Randy Carlyle got out and walked up to the Navigator and said, "Roll your window down."

Joy couldn't hear, nor could she understand what the man was saying, but she knew that he was the man that ran her off the road. Randy Carlyle had a 357-Magnum revolver in the waistband of his pants. Joy rolled the window down and said,

"What the hell were you trying to do, kill me?"

Randy Carlyle thought to himself, "Yeah... that was the general idea."

"Are you alright?" He got a good look inside the car and saw that there were two Havana Cigar tips in the ashtray..

Patch pulled over and sat there watching the whole thing unfold. But, what he didn't see was Randy reaching into his waistband for the weapon he had there.

"Well, you don't have to worry about your husband being upset, the car is in good shape. I don't think I was hurt bad... how about you, Miss?" Carlyle said.

Joy got a good look at the man once her head cleared. She was caught by surprise when the accident happened, but now she was able to focus. She was able to see that the man standing outside the car window was the same man in one of the pictures Debo had given her.

"I'm fine, I just have to call my husband and let him know what happened. You know how men are about their automobiles," she said, trying not to let him know she recognized him.

"I don't think so," Randy Carlyle said to himself.

Joy reached for her cell phone and the nine-millimeter automatic she kept tucked inside her waistband.

"I'm sorry," Randy said, pulling the weapon from his waistband.

Agent Patch saw what he was about to do and jumped out of his car and ran toward the Navigator. About that time, Joy had cleared her weapon and aimed point-blank at Randy Carlyle's forehead, and Patch was aimed at the back of his head.

"Drop your weapon!!! I said drop your weapon!!!" Patch repeated. Joy didn't know whether to drop her gun or what, but not knowing that Randy Carlyle had a weapon on him, she dropped hers and it fell to Randy's feet.

"Oh, shit… not you woman. I said drop your weapon, now!!!" Randy raised the 357 up toward the window where Joy's head was and said, "Good night, Mrs Jackson."

At that time, Patch fired one shot, hitting Carlyle in the back. He didn't want to take a chance shooting him in the head since Carlyle's head and Joy's head were in the same position and lined up perfectly with one another. Carlyle dropped to the pavement. Patch picked up his weapon, then he picked up Joy's.

The phone ranged and Debo answered "Hello," he said. He was hungry and tired by now "Mr Jackson, this is Ben's Restaurant. We are calling to let you know again that your order has been ready for over twenty minutes. Do you want us to deliver it, sir?"

"No thank you, someone should be there shortly to get it."

"Okay, Mister Jackson, we'll hold your order until someone comes for it."

Agent Patch made sure Joy was alright, then identified himself.

"I'm Agent Dick Patch of the Drug Enforcement Administration."

"Oh, You're the cop… sorry, the agent my brother was telling us about."

"Here, take this and step out of the car," he said, as he handed her a napkin to wipe away the moisture he saw forming on her face and forehead. "I'm going to cuff you, Miss Hernandez, but don't panic, I can't let these people see me let you go."

Patch cuffed Joy and walked her over to his car and got on the radio and called agent Rayass. He told Rayass what had happened, and that he wanted him to get there right away. Dick Patch knew that the Beverly Hills Police would be arriving soon.

"Hurry," he told Rayass and dispatched an ambulance.

"You called an ambulance, does that mean that he's still alive?" Joy asked.

"Yes, and I want to have you checked out."

"Can I call my brother?"

"Yes… but tell him not to come here."

"That's not going to be easy."

"Okay, let me speak to him when you get him on the phone."

Patch took her cuffs off, so she could use the phone in his car where no one could see her behind the tinted windows in the Maverick. Patch pulled Debo's Navigator back onto the road so the crime scene investigators wouldn't bother it and walked back over to where Joy was. Debo was already walking down there with Mad-C in tow. Agent Patch turned around and saw the two big men.

"Oh shit," he cursed.

"Call him and tell both of them to go back right now if they don't want to be part of this. It's going to be hard enough getting you out of it." Joy did as she was told. She must have reasoned with Debo and Mad-C, because Patch saw them stop and stand there about a block away on the corner watching what was going on.

Patch gave Joy's cell phone back, he had removed the cuffs but when Rayass arrived he would have to put them back on her until they were gone. The ambulance, Beverly Hills PD, and Rayass arrived.

"Take her and put the cuffs back on her and put her in your car," Patch told Rayass.

"Are you the officer that shot him?" the ambulance driver asked agent Patch.

"Yes, I'm DEA Agent Dick Patch."

He took out his wallet and showed the ambulance driver his badge and ID. A Beverly Hills Police officer walked up to Patch and said,

"Good morning, I'm officer Brandon."

"How are you doing, officer Brandon? I'm Agent Dick Patch of the Drug Enforcement Administration." Patch showed the officer the same badge and ID he showed the ambulance driver.

"Was anyone else involved, Agent Patch?" the officer asked. "No, I'll send your department a full report," Patch offered.

"As long as it's there by 8:00 tomorrow morning," the officer told him.

"What happened!!! Are you alright? I'll kill the son-of-a...,!!!"

"Calm down," Joy told Debo. "What happened?"

"I'm fine please go back. Agent Patch is here and his partner is just getting here. We're about to leave now," Joy told him, and was about to give Patch back the cell phone.

"Just go back, you and Mister Write wait at your office."

He was about to say something but Joy stopped him before he could get it out.

"D-Angelo, I said go back to the office. All you're going to do is mess things up. Now go and let this man earn all that money you are paying him. Go now, D-Angelo Jackson, I'm fine and the car is fine."

Joy always had a way of handling Debo and convincing him to listen to her, especially if it made sense and it made perfect sense.

Patch stayed there and cleaned things up with Beverly Hills Police. He told Rayass to take Joy to the location where they had taken Debo when they cuffed him in Beverly Hills. Dick Patch instructed Joy to call Debo after the police left and have him pick her up, and not in the Navigator, in Mad-C's car or the Explorer.

Mad-C owns a Lincoln Town Car and a wide variety of other very expensive automobiles; the Lexus is just one of his many toys. Debo and Mad-C were wondering why Patch was there. He was at Ben's Restaurant a few nights ago when Debo and Mad-C were there.

"I guess the man is dependable." Debo was satisfied to know that his money wasn't going to waste.

On their way to pick Joy up, Debo said,

"You know, Patch said, 'someone in a gray Tahoe was watching the office the night we ordered the food from Ben's.' And there was a gray

Tahoe down the street just now. I should have known better than to let her go alone," Mad-C said.

"This Patch is good, he's upon it. If it weren't for him my sister would be dead right now. He's after something… or someone," he told Mad-C.

"Well I know one thing he's after, and that's the $150,000 a month, I'll tell you that much," Mad-C said.

"No, I think it's something else… something more important. I just can't put my finger on it. You know, Johnson is a pretty big cookie, it could be him. And I also think he's after Cruse. I don't know, something is just not right. Patch is probably hoping we lead them to Johnson, and I think Johnson owes Patch something; something big. Patch did mention Cruse, Carlyle, and Morris being underground a while back; turn up here."

They were at the spot where Joy had been dropped off. She wasn't worried, she still had her nine.

"Get in here," Debo said from the passenger's side of the 2014.

Lincoln MKX. Now he was able to relax. He was about as relaxed as he was the night they moved Shelly to the hotel downtown.

"Now, I want to know what happened."

"Bro, can it wait until I eat, I'm starved?"

"FOOD!!! You almost got killed and you're thinking about food?"

"I'm used to this, Bro. You seem to be forgetting about the fact that I carry a gun… not because it's pretty, but because I just might have to use it. And if you figure you might have to use a gun wherever you go, then you get pretty used to it. That's the dangers of my job, Big-Bro. Now… can I eat?"

"The woman's hungry, Debo, and so am I," Mad-C complained.

They got to Ben's restaurant and Debo got out and went in to get the food.

"Keep an eye on her, Mad-C."

"I didn't do anything, Bra.., you sent me to get the food."

"Keep and eye on her, Mad-C.

"Mister Jackson, your food is cold and we're not in the habit of warming food. We'll have to cook you another order. Would you like to wait, Sir?"

"Sure, I'll be out in the car, thank you."

"Okay, Sir.., that'll be fine."

"Excuse me… what's your name?" Debo asked before he walked out the door.

"Barbara," the lady answered. "Barbara, I'll pay for it now."

"And under the circumstances that wasn't a bad idea," the woman thought. The order that Debo missed will most likely be given to the homeless and/or the hungry.

"It'll be about fifteen minutes, Mr Jackson."

"Okay, thanks again, Barbara."

Debo got back in the car and told Mad-C and Joy that it shouldn't be but about fifteen minutes before their orders are ready.

"Come here girl," Debo said as he reached over to give Joy a hug. He was glad to see her alive, and if she hadn't needed the money he wouldn't have let her go to work for him. But she's so convinced that she can take care of herself, which she can.

"You know I don't like that, stop it!" she said, in a motherly tone and a, behave yourself kinda approach.

Debo asked about what happened earlier today and Joy explained everything to them. He couldn't scold her because it was him that sent her out to get the food. All he could do was be thankful that she was alive and well.

"Now where was I. Oh yeah, I remember. I was saying that Patch was saying something about Johnson and Cruse being underground. I thought he was talking about all of them. I figured Carlyle and Morris were flunkies. They proved that when they killed, Morris, or set him up to be killed," Debo assumed.

"Yeah, and Johnson had something to do with the Yin killing. Yin moved a lot of merchandise, and when they took him out of the picture his product disappeared also, and was never found. And what was he doing at sea on a ship without product or even fish? This could be bigger than we think," Mad-C said.

"Yeah… well I just want them off our asses," Debo mentioned. The lady that had been so patient with them came out to the car carrying two bags of food and some soft drinks in large cups inside a cardboard container that was designed for that purpose.

"Thank you for waiting, and enjoy your meal," Barbra said as she handed Debo the tray.

"I know I will," Joy exclaimed.

"Thanks again, and sorry for the mix-up, Barbara," Debo said.

They headed back to the office. When they got there they ate, and surprisingly, Debo enjoyed his meal. Joy was stuffed, so was Mad-C. Joy was also tired from being up all day. She went to Debo's office and went to sleep while Mad-C and Debo stayed in Mad-C's office.

FRIDAY, NOVEMBER 16TH, 1:15 P.M.

"Good news.., we can stop looking for Carlyle," Debo pleasantly announced. "You know something… "

Mad-C started to say something, but Debo cut him off. "Give me a second," Debo said and called Agent Patch.

"Jackson, call me back, I'm doing a report on that incident. You got your girl back alright?"

"Yes, thanks."

"Okay, give me about forty-five-minutes and I'll call you back."

"Good enough," Debo said and they hung up. "Now what were you saying?"

"I was saying that Joy is an extremely brave young lady.., and good looking also. Why isn't she married?"

"Well, she had a guy in her life; the same one that gave her Tommy and Sheila. But he ran off with another woman twelve years ago when she already had a two-year-old and was pregnant with the now twelve-year-old. But I'll let her tell you because some people's private lives are better left to be told by them or maybe just not talked about at all."

"I can understand that."

When he said that he understood, he meant it out of respect. There are also some things in his life that are better off not talked about to others. Your privacy must be both respected and understood, and Mad-C did both.

"Hold on, I wanna call Pauline," Debo said, and got his cell.

"Hey love, how's it going?"

"Okay I guess, I'm on my lunch break."

"Well, we got one of the bad guys."

"Good going," Pauline said with a mouth full of salad.

"Well, actually Joy did. He's in the hospital with a gunshot wound to his back. All we know right now is what Joy told us. I'll fill you in on more details when I get them."

"Who is it?"

"Randy Carlyle."

"Well, I don't have to worry about him do I?"

"No you don't sweetheart; nothing on Jeffery yet?"

"No, but, Tom; one of the guys that work here is acting funny."

"Oh yea…, funny how?"

"Funny like jumpy; like he's expecting someone to come through the door at any moment and drag his ass out of here."

"Okay keep an eye on things, and watch him alright?"

"Okay, tell me later about what happened with Carlyle."

"Alright, I will."

"Okay, bye handsome."

"Bye love… be careful, and call me when you get off."

He didn't need to wait for an answer, he just knew she would call him when she got off.

Patch called Debo back and told him everything that happened. Specifically the part about when he told Carlyle to drop his weapon and Joy dropped hers. Patch got a big laugh out of it. In fact, they all laughed about it later. He thanked Patch and Rayass and hung up.

"You know what, Mad-C?"

"Why do you call me Mad-C?"

"Because you're crazy as hell."

"What's up Debo?"

"Patch asked me something before we hung up."

"What did he ask you?"

"He said, 'Jackson you had to see all the police and ambulances down there when you got to that corner.' I told him that I did and he said, 'What were you going to do when you got to the scene... send your sister to jail?' That's what he asked me."

"How the hell can she go to jail? That asshole Carlyle is the one that fucked-up," Mad-C cursed.

"Yeah, but her piece isn't registered, and that much alone would have been enough. Plus the fact that she was involved in a shooting," Debo explained.

"I was going down there to kick some ass," Mad-C said. "Yeah so was I. but who's ass, Carlyle was down?"

"I kick the shit out of 'em when they're down," Mad-C said and laughed.

Debo decided to go and pick up the motorcycles. Mad-C figured he could use the ride and check on his estate. Debo hadn't been home, so he went with him. He stopped at home and Mad-C went to his estate in his car to check on his estate and mail, and to see how Ed was doing. He had left Ed in charge of the estate so the bills could get paid, and to keep the place straight. There wasn't really much for Edward to do since Mad-C was away. There wasn't any house cleaning to be done. He told Ed that Debo and himself almost had this thing wrapped up, and that it shouldn't be too much longer.

He also assured him that he would be able to take his Christmas vacation no matter how long this thing takes.

Debo collected all the mail and decided to sort it later. He called Shelly to see if she needed anything which he always does when he goes home. She wanted some special makeup that she forgot to pack, and her special bikini-set he bought for her to wear to Santa Monica or Vince beach. When this is over, they'll go to their favorite spot at the beach and celebrate, and drink, and eat-up some shit.

It's a beautiful day in San Diego. Debo wished he could stay and enjoy it but he has to get back and take care of the business at hand.

Mad-C returned to *the Shell-Debo* at 4:15 in the evening. They put the bikes on a flatbed that Debo bought for his bikes and jet skis. Time was running out, they had to hurry and get back. They had three-hours and fifteen-minutes to be at the location.

"Why don't we ride the bikes back? It would be a lot easier, and it make more sense that way. Besides, I haven't ridden a motorcycle in a while," Mad-C suggestively confessed.

"Because I'm giving Joy the Navigator, remember?"

"Oh…, yeah, I forgot. But doesn't he know the Navigator when he sees it? You did say that he drugged your dog, so he should have seen it in the carport," Mad-C questioned.

"I had it covered; I keep it covered."

"Debo, did you fall when you were a kid? All the man has to do is pull the cover back and look at the SUV and the license plate number. And how in the hell did he manage to get a note on the dog's house?" Mad-C asked. "He probably put the drug in some meat and gave it to him, or just threw it over the gate. Rex probably ate it, felt dizzy, and went in his house to lay down, and fell out. That gave Cruse the opportunity to jump over the gate, losing the medal, and tacking the note to the dog's house. That's the only thing I can see. The vet did mention a dart gun or a needle. Any other way, he would have had to kill my dog or jump over the gate and got his ass chewed up. But, yeah you might have a point."

"I'm sure I do have a point," Mad-C said, trying to convince Debo that to use the Navigator would be risky for Joy.

"Okay, we're going to go with the assumption that Cruse knows that Navigator."

"Yeah, and if he owns the club and he's there and sees it."

"Okay let's say just for the hell of it that he does own the club and he's there, and he does see the Navigator. I mean, Joy is meeting his people there. What better place to meet where he can keep an eye on what's happening? I'm sure he'll have cameras everywhere, including outside so he can see everything and everybody.

That's why I figured I'd sit in the back in the dark, and you sit with your back to the camera positioned at the end of the bar. If you have her flashing that show-car of yours… I just think it's a bad idea," Mad-C repeated.

"Yeah, I didn't think of that," Debo responded.

"And that's why there are two of us, just in case one of us doesn't think of something that the other one might."

"Okay, change of plans, we'll ride the bikes into LA and rent a car when we get there. I already have an account at a car rental place, and it won't take but a minute, and Joy can take the rental to the Club. No one will know that one but us," Debo finished what he was saying and they left.

It's a nice day for riding. The weatherman said it was 62º. But that was in LA, it's a bit warmer in San Diego. They both were dressed for chilly weather anyway, so it wasn't a problem. The road back to Los Angeles was bumpy but Debo enjoyed it, it saved a lot of time. He was thinking what a shame it would be if whoever shot the tire out on the Explorer did the same to the bikes. Like they say; "there's power in prayer."

They made it back to the office at 6:40 pm: enough time to rent the car and handle their business. Joy was still asleep when they got back. Debo woke her up and told her about his and Mad-C's plan.

"Now, Bro..., I have three cars, why rent a car when you can use one of mine?"

"You know, you guys are always thinking, aren't you," Debo said.

"Yeah.., and you worry about us... oh boy," Joy said.

"Okay, let's go by your place and get the car."

"Uh, brother.., I can go get the car by myself," Joy protested. "And how are you going to get there, on the bus?"

"Yeah.., like I said… 'let's go get the car,'" Joy quoted. "Let's go, crazy woman," Debo said and they all left.

Joy rode on the back of Debo's motorcycle to her house. There was mail coming out of the mailbox. She didn't want any of the neighbors to touch her mail. They are always trying to pry into her business as it is, trying to see if they could find out what she does. She took the mail and put it in the glove compartment of her 2013 Cutlass Supreme. She was always a Chevy girl: She used to hang with the low-riders; not so much the low-rider lifestyle, but the low-rider cars.

"Okay, let me check my house and we're off. Oh my lord!!! D-Angelo, Mister Write, come in here!!!" Joy yelled.

"Damn," Mad-C cursed.

He and Debo had already pulled their weapons when they heard Joy scream. They got there and she had hers drawn as well.

"Shit... how the hell did they find out?" Debo stopped and asked.

"The day we moved, Shelly, they were watching," Joy said.

"Yeah, they followed us into that alley downtown."

Someone had broken into her house and tore it apart. Her bed was just thrown up against the wall, her dresser and bedside table drawers were turned over on the floor, clothes were all over the floor, the stairs, and the dresser. The medicine cabinet had been ransacked, they poured milk and orange juice into her plasma TV, and her stereo system was mangled. They did close to $50,000 to $75,000 worth of damage; Not to mention the back door which was apparently how they got in. It was in splinters and off its hinges. Debo called Sgt Billings to see if he could get someone over there or go himself to check on it. It needed to be boarded up, locked, and determined what happened. Debo and Mad-C moved the refrigerator in front of the back door so no one could get in. They had to have created noise getting in; to say nothing of the sounds of throwing everything around the way they did. They were looking for something... maybe a picture or a name. At any rate, her mail wasn't touched... or maybe it was. They had to leave, time was running out, and if they wanted to meet these guys on time they had to leave now. Joy got in her cutlass, Debo and Mad-C got on their motorcycles and they were off.

Mad-C told Joy he would replace everything that was taken or destroyed; everything except those things that can't be replaced, such as things of sentimental value or family heirlooms.

Debo packed three hand grenades, *Crazy*, and he also brought two desert eagles, a twelve-gauge automatic pump shotgun, and enough ammunition to feed each piece of artillery. Joy brought her set of nine-millimeter automatic pistols. These did not include the one she kept on her that was given to her by Debo. They were especially made in pure gold and fired eighteen rounds each. Each round was cured in a special liquid that automatically poisoned the bloodstream. If the bullet didn't kill you... the poison would.

They arrived at 6201 North Gage at 8:15 pm: fifteen minutes early. She left what she was supposed to bring with her in the car. Debo and Mad-C knew that if she got up to go get it, the deal was going down or a robbery was taking place. Either way, they were ready to move. Debo walked in at about 9:00 and took a seat at the end of the bar.

Joy came in shortly after him. He saw her come in and take a seat at a table across from the bar where she was instructed to sit. Mad-C was out of sight in a corner seated in the dark. No one noticed him because he joined the flow of traffic and blended in with the dancers that were on the dance floor. He was on the side of the dance floor where you could see the bar without looking through the crowd of dancers.

They were all early so they just waited. Joy was beginning to think they weren't coming. They weren't really early; Cruse's people were either late or already there watching. Whoever seated her there or told her to sit there, knew what they were doing. They sat her in plain view of the camera where Cruse, or whoever was in the office could see everything.

Nobody bothered Mad-C or Debo, and they were not recognized or spotted. The plan was working so far. Debo saw a tall, dark-haired, very light-skinned African American man, and a PortaRican looking guy enter the establishment and stand in the door as if looking for someone. Neither one had a suitcase or a briefcase. This indicated that these guys either left the drugs in the car, in the office, or there were no drugs. In which case, somebody lied and there would definitely be trouble. The men spotted Joy and went over to sit at the table where she was seated.

"Where's Cruse?" She asked the taller one.

"I thought I made it clear to you that you are dealing with me or there will be no deal," the man roughly stated.

"Yes, you did say that," Joy remembered.

"Okay, let's make this fast, where is the money?" the man asked. "You don't take me for some damn fool, do you? Now, either you have done this before or you have watched a hell of a lot of television, because I don't see anything either. Like you said, 'let's make this fast'," she quoted.

"I'm going to like you, and I'm sure someone has your back," the man said.

"You sure talk a lot for someone that wants to, 'make this fast,' don't you?" Joy asked.

She saw perspiration coming off his nose and forehead, and he fumbled with his hands. His friend had one of his hands out of sight where she couldn't see what was in it.

Debo couldn't either, but they both knew that the man was most likely armed. The shorter man didn't move, didn't say a word, and didn't blink. "I want you to slowly take your firearm from wherever you have it and pass it under the table to my friend."

"I don't think so," Joy told the guy who seemed to be in charge.

"My friend here has a gun pointed at you as we speak, so please do as I ask."

Joy gave the guy one of the nine-millimeter pistols she had and that satisfied him. He didn't know about the other one.

"Now, quietly get up and follow me outside."

They both got up and walked to the door. He left his friend inside in case Joy had someone watching her back from inside the club that could come up from behind and get the drop on them. Mad-C slipped out the back door, he had already planned to use the back exit if he needed to. He knew he couldn't be seen from the parking lot because there were no camera outback. Only the front and sides had cameras.

"Where are you parked?"

"Over there... the brown Cutlass."

"Is the money in there?"

"Yes... in the trunk."

"Give me the key."

"Where is the stuff?" Joy sternly asked.

She knew now that something was very wrong and that there were no drugs. But little did they know... there was no money either.

"Here," she said, handing him the key. He pushed the button that released the trunk while disarming the alarm.

Joy felt the other nine-millimeter in the small of her back.

Greed makes people do the stupidest things. The man stepped in front of her and went in the trunk of the car. Joy reached behind her and pulled out the pistol she had and pointed it at the man with the bag he had just removed from the trunk in his hand.

Mad-C saw that something was wrong, and that the deal had gone bad. He trained his 44- magnum on the guy's head. The man inside the club was standing near the front door watching. He had come to the conclusion that Joy didn't bring anything inside, so it was obvious to him that everything was going to go down outside. He disregarded the fact that someone was inside the place watching Joy's back. Debo stood right behind him with CRAZY ready. The man at the door saw Joy about to shoot his friend and yelled, "Hey, bitch!!!"

At that time Joy turned around to face the man behind her and saw him pointing his gun at her. She came up with her right hand and leveled her gun back on the man, but it was too little, too late.

The man at the door had gotten off one shot that knocked Joy back against the car. Mad-C looked to see the man who shot Joy; fall to the ground. Debo had drilled two rounds of lead into his body. One of the rounds went through his back and out of his chest. The second one, Debo put in his head while he was dead on the ground. Mad-C fired a shot at the man that was holding the bag, but he missed. The guy dropped the bag and ran between two cars.

He got down low and spat out a round at Mad-C. Debo came out firing at him also. Mad-C was on his way from the side of the building he was shooting from and a bullet tore a chunk of brick out of the wall, changing his mind. The bullet hit next to his eye as he jumped back behind the wall, and when he did, another piece of lead hit the building and this one took another chunk of concrete from the stone structure.

"Shit.., where the hell did that come from? Were there three of them?" He looked to see that there were four other men to the left of the one that was outside with Joy. Debo saw Joy on the ground and ran over to where she was lying. His blood was boiling, and his head felt like it was about to explode, and his heart raced with every step he took. He was more upset than he was when Rex was drugged. A bullet flew past him, crashing into a car door and shattering the window. Another one raced past him and tore the windshield out of another car.

"Damn… they came prepared!" Mad-C thought to himself.

Debo knelt down beside Joy and picked up her firearm and put it in his waistband. He checked her vitals to see if she was alive. Her pulse and heart were beating, but they were both weak.

"Joy… Joy, baby can you hear me?" Debo asked. He looked for blood and didn't see any.

"Joy can you hear me?"

He tried to turn her over without hurting her any more than she already was.

"Don't move me… my chest… it hurts!"

Debo looked at the front of her and still no blood. But what he did find surprised and comforted him: She was wearing a Kevlar vest.

"Well, I'll be damn," he said, and another piece of lead flew past his head, which made him realize he had to move and get her to safety.

"Are you going to be alright?"

"Yeah, I think so," Joy answered.

He moved her along the ground and under a parked pickup truck until he and Mad-C could get some of the shooting to stop.

"Okay, lay here, I'll be back."

He saw that Mad-C was pinned down, and thought he'd give him a little help. Debo ran over to where he had parked his motorcycle and got the saddlebag off of it. He positioned himself between Mad-C and the men that were shooting at him; crouched down between two cars. Debo took two hand-grenades out of the saddlebag and said,

"This shit has gone too far," and pulled the pin out of one of the grenades and tossed it toward the two cars that the men were crouched down between and got down. Mad-C looked toward where the men had been shooting from and saw one of the cars fly about four feet into the air, followed by a thunderous explosion, and breaking into a ball of flames and thick, black smoke.

"Damn," Mad-C cursed.

Debo was about to toss another one when just as he put the attempt in motion, he heard a single gunshot behind him. He turned around to see one of the other four men that had joined in on the action on Cruse's side, standing there with a puzzled look on his face. Debo was going to shoot the guy, but he fell over and Debo saw Joy standing behind the man holding her nine-millimeter handgun slumped to her side. She had shot the man that just seconds ago would have ended Debo's life. She went over to where the man lay dying and shot him again in the side of his head four more times.

Debo heard more gunfire coming from Mad-C's direction and gave Joy an "are you okay" look. She motioned to him that she was okay and he turned around and started shooting at Robert Cruse's men. He saw that Mad-C was into some gun-play with a few more men. At that moment he let "CRAZY"; his 45-automatic cry out at the men. A slug found the shoulder of one of its target, sending him running for cover. He remembered that he still had Joy's car keys, and opened the door of the brown Cutlass with the same hand he held the gun in. Seeing as how Debo had just blown the other one damn near off, he sure as hell couldn't use it. He got in the cutlass dripping blood everywhere, but he couldn't feel any pain in his arm. He couldn't even feel his arm. He didn't know he had a limb on the left side of his upper body.

Joy and Mad-C managed to extinguish the remaining men that were shooting at them. Debo turned to see the man that really didn't have too much time to live if he didn't hurry and get treatment, leaving the parking lot in Joy's car. Debo got on his motorcycle and went after him on Gage driving at ninety miles per hour. It was dark and the wind was beating at Debo's eyes. He could barely see where he was going, let alone the car he was chasing. He fired a shot at Joy's car and missed. He tried to get another round off but a cab got in his view.

"I'm losing this son-of-a-bitch, I can't see his ass," Debo thought to himself. He got on the sidewalk to avoid hitting any of the other motorists that were bobbing in and out of his view. He saw Joy's car make a right and he turned right also. When he did he saw that the man had turned down a dead-end street on the side of a freeway and had no place to go. He turned around and saw Debo coming at him at a high speed and jumped out of the car and ran through some bushes. Debo knew that the man wasn't going to last too long because he was losing blood fast as Debo walked behind him.

He didn't have to run, because as the man was bleeding to death, he was getting weaker and weaker. He ran a few feet and dropped to the dirt and leaves beneath him.

Debo walked up to him and held his gun out to the man's head and said,

"If you go for your gun, I'll have no choice but to kill you."

But he was already dead, it was only a matter of seconds before he closed his eyes. He didn't have the strength to go for his weapon.

"You know, all I want to know is where is Cruse?" The man laid there and said nothing.

"Who owns the club on Gage? You know the club where you tried to kill me and my friends; that club… who owns it?"

The man still kept quiet. After Debo's last question, he never heard anything else because he was dead.

Debo took the license plate off Joy's car and called her.

"I'll called Billings and report your car stolen and take the license plate off of it, it's gone."

"And the guy that took it?"

"Yeah.., him too."

"Take my mail out of the glove compartment for me, will you?"

"Okay, where is Mad-C, is he around?"

"Yeah, he's here, you want to talk to him?"

"No, just tell him that I said I'll meet you guys at the office. Are things all sewed up there?"

"Yeah, but I might have to see a doctor. I think something got shaken up in my chest."

"Okay, do you want me to come up there?"

"Well, if Mister Write doesn't take me, then I'll wait for you. But, don't they report stuff? I mean things like bullet wounds, and… " Debo cut her off to say,

"Well, seeing as how you had on the vest, it's hard to tell what caused the wound. But, I'm sure they've seen a lot of gunshots where the victim wore a vest. If you have to go, okay. But if not I'll be at the office in a few minutes."

"Yeah, I'll wait, because I don't think I can take a bike ride right now. If I go, I'll take a cab," Joy said.

"Okay, Sis, whatever you do, be careful."

"I will," Joy told him, and they hung up.

Debo put the bag that the man took from Joy's car over the dead man's upper body to cover his face and head, then called Sgt Billings.

"Yeah, Jackson I've got someone that saw a gray Tahoe pull up to Joy's house. Two guys got out and went around back. All I could get was a medium-built black man, about 200-250 pounds 5'5" or 6' tall."

"Yeah, that describes Carlyle, alright."

"How is she holding out; Joy, I mean?"

"She's doing okay, Mister Wright offered to replace everything that was destroyed; everything replaceable that is. What about, Carlyle?"

"He lived; I'm holding him out at county hospital. He's not going anyplace," Billings told him.

"Do you have an address on him?"

"I'll have to check his driver's license. I haven't gotten anything on paper yet, or his property. Beverly Hills PD is going to send everything over in a little bit."

"Okay, Sergeant, thanks. Oh, I almost forgot I want to report a car stolen."

"You mean somebody got ahold of that wonderful Navigator I love so much?"

"No, I was talking about Joy's car."

"They took her car too?"

Debo didn't tell Billings what happened, he would call him sooner or later about what just happened on Gage. It's a wonder he hasn't mentioned it yet, but he will. There's no way he's going to not know. LAPD got the shots fired call.

"Any idea who stole the car?" the sergeant asked?"

There's not a lot that gets past Sgt. Billings. He heard about the meeting on Gage tonight with Joy, Write, and Jackson.

"Well, ah… "

Debo was short of words for some reason. He just didn't feel like explaining it right then.

"I'll fill you in later," he told Billings.

"Yeah.., I'm sure you will. I'll be expecting to hear from you.., soon, Jackson."

"You got it, Sergeant," Debo said, then hung up and called the Sergeant back.

"Yeah, Jackson… you forget something?"

"Yeah, I forgot to give you the information on Joy's car."

"You mean the Brown Cutlass?"

"You're good," Debo said.

"Call me," Sergeant Billings said, and hung up. Debo arrived at the office and Joy wasn't there. "Where's my sister?"

"She went to the hospital to have her lungs checked. She took a pretty nice blow to her chest…, even with the vest it was serious," Mad-C told him.

"Yeah, that was good thinking on her part," Debo said. "She's a pretty smart girl, a real survivor," Mad-C awarded.

"Yeah, she scared the living daylights out of me out there. I mean the girl almost got shot once, her house was ram-sacked, and then she goes and gets shot. I would say that's enough for one day."

"I would say that's enough for one month, maybe a year or two," Mad-C said.

"Yeah, maybe I should give her a raise, huh?" Debo joked.

"And you know, you were afraid something would go wrong and she would get hurt."

"Yeah.., and I was there and couldn't stop that bullet," Debo said. with regret.

"Yeah, she was thinking," Mad-C said.

"I'll have to relocate her and the kids when this is over," Debo noted. "For sure, and buy her a car?"

"Yeah, and that too."

Debo is worth over Six-hundred-Million-Dollars. He's hella rich and powerful.

FRIDAY, NOVEMBER 16TH, 11:45 P.M.

Debo called the hospital to check on Joy and the doctor said, 'she had taken a cab home twenty-minutes ago.' He thanked the doctor, hung up, and called Joy's cell phone.

"Where are you off to?" he asked her.

"Back to the hotel..., you guys live a much too exciting life for me," she jokingly said.

"You just left a war; you don't need to be on duty for a while."

"Who said anything about duty? I'm going there to recuperate and get killed in some rummy. At least Shelly has a little more mercy on me than the bad guys."

"I warned you, didn't I?"

"Yeah bra, but it was fun... I'll be okay."

"Thanks, Sis."

"No problem, anytime."

"What would I have done if you hadn't worn that thing?"

"Oh.., bury me, I guess."

"Joyvette stop playin!!"

"I don't know, Bra, let's not think about it. I'm alive and almost well, I'm here, and I'm going to go up and get some rest."

"Okay, call me if you need anything."

"I will..., good night."

"Good night," Debo said, ending their call.

"That woman is going to be the death of me," Debo told Mad-C.

"Yeah, that's what families are for," Mad-C told him.

"Well, welcome aboard."

"Goodnight, Debo, I'm going to get some sleep. That was some pretty good stuff you did out there," Mad-C awarded.

"That was teamwork,..., we did it... not me, we did it as a team. And we're not halfway finished," Debo said, and they both showered and went to bed.

Debo was on his way to sleep when his cell phone rang.

"I've been trying to call you for the longest, Mr Jackson," Pauline said to Debo when she finally got him on the phone.

"I was busy killing people. How are you doing this evening, young lady?"

"Oh.., hanging in there. I think I might have something for you," she said.

"Now, that's what I call progress."

"I'm sure Tom is not working with a full deck, he just sits there in the lounge and stares for long periods of time. If Jeffery is here, I think he got to this guy and rattled his cage."

"Okay, keep your eyes open, Cruse is bound to jump. We just put a dent in his dollhouse; (his army), and I don't know how many more guys he has left so be on alert."

"Okay, I've got my end, I'll keep on Tom, maybe something will give soon. He really seems very nervous."

"Yeah, he's probably scared to damn death. Get some sleep little one, and be careful: Call me if anything goes wrong, if anything looks like it's going to go wrong, no matter where you are."

"Okay, handsome.., good night."

CHAPTER
13

SATURDAY, NOVEMBER 17TH, 8:30 A.M.

Debo and Mad-C made a trip to San Diego to take the motorcycles back. He decided to put them back up following the incident at the club and the car chase.

He put on a pot of coffee, no calls from Billings yet. Although he did want Debo to call him. But, this is Saturday and Robert Billings doesn't work on Saturdays, he's probably out on the green.

Joy called to let him know she was alright… sore, but okay. He talked to Shelly for about two hours and she's still hanging in there. He would really prefer that none of what happened and what was about to happen in the near future was brought up to her or around her. It would only make her worry more. Pauline promised to work Saturday, even though it's her day off. But, she's on a special assignment and it's important that she can be there as many days as they'll let her work. Debo was pretty sure that Jeffery was at the fishing and boat club.

"Tom, are you feeling okay?" Pauline asked him.

"No, not really…, I'm feeling kind of weak; maybe the flu," he lied.

She knows that the flu doesn't make you sit in a chair staring into space.

"You can take the day off, I'll handle things here," she told him. Tom thought leaving Joy there alone may not be such a good idea.

What if she were to stumble upon Jeffery in the basement?

He won't be able to convince her that he didn't know he was down there.

"I've got to pull myself together," Tom thought to himself.

He went into the employees' lounge to think, but that didn't work.

* * *

All he could think about was what Jeffery said. It kept stabbing and stabbing at his brain… beating at his conscience. He thought about his wife and three innocent little girls. Tom is just a hard-working man, trying to support his family, trying to do the right thing. And then Cruse came into his life and brought with him Chaos and destruction. While Jeffery Smith was down in that basement suffering from heroin withdrawals, Tom was suffering from manic depression. He was on the verge of a nervous breakdown. He worried about his freedom, even though Jeffery told him that he wouldn't live long enough to lose his freedom: It was his life he stood to lose. And if he did his daughters would suffer, his wife would suffer, and they would all be left alone. He didn't think it was fair to make his wife raise their three girls on her own. But, there was no way out for him but the way Jeffery Smith had offered him. And if Jeffery and his people didn't get him, then Robert Cruse would.

He looked at Pauline through the window from inside the lounge. She was going about her day, taking and giving information over the phone, processing data on the computer, and didn't have a worry in the world. The same things he used to do, the very same free-from-worry, free-from negativity, carefree life he used to live. It was getting close to lunchtime, and he knew he had to eat but he didn't have an appetite. Maybe if he watched a little TV it might help. Maybe a game show, a comedy, something to take his mind off of the situation he had allowed himself to get into. He reached over and picked up the remote control to the TV, then pressed the power button and the set came to life. He scanned the channels and the news was on all the channel. It was a special bulletin.

Pauline turned around and caught a glimpse of the broadcast. Tom was about to change the station but Pauline stopped him.

"Tom!!!" she yelled from the front desk. "Yes, Joyce?"

"I'm trying to log on to, Seaside Dairy Products account, but something… " She stopped and froze where she was with a look of shock on her face. Tom saw her expression and turned to look at what caused such a bad expression. She was looking behind him at the television set.

"That's… that's… "

Tom saw it too, a picture of Randy Carlyle on the TV screen. "You know him?" she asked Tom, but he couldn't say a word.

She ran into the lounge and turned the TV up, and they both heard the anchorman's voice say,

"A man was shot and seriously wounded yesterday afternoon, in what authorities believe was an apparent attempted murder on a DEA agent in Beverly Hills. His condition is still unknown at this time. That story, and more after this message." The anchorman said, and went to commercial.

"So, that's what D-Angelo meant when he said that he was out killing people. But they said, 'that a DEA agent shot him.'"

Pauline put two and two together. DEA and Beverly Hills PD. She called Debo and told him what she had just seen on TV. While she was on the phone, Tom came out of his shock and was back staring into space… only he wasn't in space… he was in heaven. This could be the answer he needed, the break he was looking for. He had let Jeffery damn near loose, and if he escaped now, who's to say that Carlyle didn't make the mistake. He saw a way out of his misery, but there was still Robert Cruse to deal with. Tom remembered Jeffery also saying, 'that Debo would help him if he helped get him out of there, and that he would kill him if he didn't.'

"Tom…, Tom," Pauline repeated, trying to get his attention. "Oh.., I'm sorry I didn't hear you, what is it?"

"Tom, talk to me, do you know that man?"

Tom sat there thinking and the phone rang.

"Seaman's Fishing, and Boat Club…, Joyce speaking."

"Hi, Joyce, Is Tom in?" a voice on the other end of the phone asked. "Hold on a second, please. Tom, it's for you."

"Thank you. Hello, may I... ?" Tom suddenly stopped.

"Yes... Yes... uh-huh... okay, I got it, before closing tonight. Okay... bye." Tom hung up the phone.

"Tom, does it have anything to do with the news broadcast and the phone call you just got?"

"Yes, now no more questions, please, just listen."

"Okay, I'm listening!"

He confessed everything to Pauline.

"So, the man on the phone was, Robert Cruse. Is that what you're telling me?"

"Yes, that's exactly what I'm saying and he'll be here before we close tonight." Pauline had to think. First of all, she had to call Debo.

"Whatcha got for me, something good I hope."

"It is good, I'm at work and... "

"Work.., Oh, you decided to go in?" Debo interrupted her to ask.

"Never mind that, Jeffery is here in the basement, and they've been shooting him up with drugs. Robert Cruse just called and said he will be here before we close tonight."

"What time is closing?"

"It's Saturday, we close at 4:00 pm."

"Okay, It's 1:30 pm now, I'll be right there," Debo said, then hung up and went to wake Mad-C up.

"This had better be good, Debo," Mad-C said with his head still in his pillow.

Cruse is worried and nervous, now he's really climbing the walls. "This is getting to be a bigger problem than I thought it would be.

Why do I even have to see these people? Now they're coming to my office talking about drugs and murder. What the hell did you use the cars for? You don't take my company cars and try to kill people. What the fuck were you thinking, or were you even thinking at all?" Johnson scolded.

"I've got one of Write's men on ice out here at the fishing and boat club, and he's going to... "

Johnson cut him off... "I don't want to know where the fuck he is, what the hell good is he doing me?"

"I was trying to get him to tell me where Write and Jackson are."

"Hell, I can tell you that. They were right the fuck here in my office. Anderson, fix this shit. Do they know I had anything to do with the Yin murder.., or are they just guessing?" Johnson asked with rage in his voice and eyes.

"Not that I know of."

"What the fuck does that mean? Do they or don't they? Did you open your big ass mouth to anyone?"

"No, Gregory I didn't," Cruse said as he shivered with fear.

"Get the hell out of my office and fix this shit. If you don't, start running motherfucker.

"I need some more men," Cruse cried.

"What the fuck for, so you can get them killed or shot the fuck up too?"

"No, Greg I just… "

"Who do you think you're playing with? Write is no fool, he's a pro at this shit. Take who you need, Robert and fix this shit. Do you understand? Fix it!!!"

Robert Cruse (aka Raymond Anderson) said, "Okay," then left.

Mad-C and Debo are somewhat alike. When they were together, they used a lot of each other's words, styles, and ways of doing things. Maybe it comes from years of hanging around each other.

"This is good," Mad-C said. "Yeah, it's a break," Debo told him.

"Give me a minute and I'll be ready to roll."

"Okay, we can take the Navigator, it'll cut down on our chances of being pumped full of holes."

"What was that you gave me yesterday, a hand grenade?"

"Sure was; US military issue," Debo told him. "Bring a couple."

"What do you want to do, go through the wall?"

"That wouldn't be a bad idea if your girl and Smith weren't in there. But, bring a few anyway, we'll level that piece of shit." Mad-C was furious, he always was around wartime.

Pauline told Tom to show her where Jeffery Smith was being held. He led her down the hall to the elevator and pressed the down button. They got on and heard the motor lowering the steel box from floor to floor. Pauline wondered where that elevator went. She hasn't been on the elevator in all the time she has been there. The twin doors parted and Pauline and Tom got off in the basement and passed all the junk and debris that was stored there. They found the door that led to Jeffery's prison and torture chamber. Tom reached above the door where the key was kept and found it was missing. "Randy Carlyle must have taken it with him when he was there last," Tom assumed.

"Okay, calm down and step aside," Pauline told him.

She continued on up to the door and knocked but it was thick, maybe too thick for Jeffery to hear her.

"Where is he?"

"He's on the other side of the room."

"About how far?"

"I don't know, I let him loose, but the bed he was tied to is about as far as from here to that wall over there."

He pointed to a wall thirty-feet from where they were standing. "Hand me one of those anchors lying on the floor; the smallest one you can find. I wanna bang on the door with it," she impatiently told him. He picked up the one that he figured she must have meant and took it to where she was standing. He started to hand it to her, but thought better of it. After all, he is the man and he should be the one to lift it and pound on the thick door."

Tom pounded on the door but Jeffery didn't say anything. If he did they couldn't hear him, the door was too thick.

"Jeffery... Jeffery Smith!!!" Pauline yelled.

Tom sent another crashing blow to the door. He thought that maybe if he hit it hard enough, it would finally give."

"Jeffery, can you hear me!!!" Pauline yelled, but there was not a sound from the other side of the door.

"Jeffery, can you hear me!!!" she screamed again.

Carlyle must have gone into the room while Tom was off work or at lunch. The key was missing, so apparently Carlyle must have tied Jeffery back up.

"The poor man is probably dead," Tom assumed.

Carlyle probably got him to disclose the whereabouts of Mad-C and Debo.

"So that's what he was doing at the office yesterday," Pauline thought. "Do you think he told Carlyle what he wanted to know and he killed him?" Tom asked.

"If they killed him it's because he didn't say anything," Pauline said in Jeffery's defense.

All she could hope for was that he was alive. Jeffery heard the door and tried to scream but Carlyle had duck-taped his mouth and tied both his arms to the bedpost. All he could do was lay there and hope that his rescuers would be able to free him from the hell hole he's imprisoned in. Tom continued to try to break the door open, knocking on it wasn't doing anyone any good. But at least he knew that someone knew he was down there. And that whoever it was would kill to get him out… or die trying. Tom rammed the door again and it finally opened. The stench that tore through Pauline's nose knocked her aback. She choked and turned from the door with tears in her eyes from the stench. She couldn't go into the room.

"Get him the hell out of there," she ordered Tom.

Tom entered the room and cut the tape that bound Jeffery's hands, then pulled off the gag. Jeffery was weak and nearly unconscious.

"Damn, you stink," Tom complained.

"Get him to some water and some soap now," she told Tom.

Tom drug him to the elevator and pressed the roof access button. When they got to the roof, Tom got off halfway dragging Jeffery toward a room with showers and a workout room; put there to accommodate their customers and club members. He put him in the shower and turned the water on full force. Jeffery was coming around slowly, as he felt the water.

"Cold water," Pauline said and called Debo.

"Talk to me, Pauline… how is he?"

"Fine… where are you?" Pauline asked Debo. "I'm less than ten minutes away."

"Hurry!!!" Pauline screamed. "Okay, I'm almost there."

"I'm calling an ambulance."

"What's his condition?"

"He's out of it, Debo. He has enough tracks down his arm to run Amtrak for a year, and he's weak but alive."

"No, don't call an ambulance, they've been shooting him up. They will only ask a lot of questions. Is there any place where you can put him until I get there?"

"Well..," Pauline had to think; after all, she is brand new there. "Tom..., is there any place we can put him for about ten... no, five-minutes?"

"Here is a better place than any right now If we drag him through the club the smell will draw attention," Tom explained.

"The only place or the best place is here in the shower," she told Debo. "Shower!!! Hold on, I'm here," Debo told her.

"He's here..., go downstairs and let him in, then show him the way up here."

Tom did as Pauline ordered. She looked at her watch and it was almost closing time. Debo went inside the fishing and boat club and was met by Tom.

"I see what Jeffery meant when he said that his boss was no joke," Tom thought to himself.

Mad-C came in behind Debo, after checking the parameter to make sure no one was watching or waiting for Cruse in the parking lot.

"Damn, these are some rough-looking brothers," Tom confessed to himself.

Debo and Mad-C saw the fear in Tom. He was happy to cooperate with the two rather large men that stood before him. And even happier that he cooperated with Pauline to free Jeffery.

"This way, Sir," Tom said.

Debo followed him to the second floor and they were there in less than a minute. He showed Debo where Jeffery and Pauline were at the showers.

"Damn, what's that smell?"

"That's your boy, Jeffery."

"Damn, let's get him out of here," Debo told Pauline,

"Just showering boss. What took you guys so long, did you stop for gas?" Jeffery joked and tried to laugh but found it difficult.

"Let's get you out of here. Pauline take him to my office, here's the key to the front door and the office door. My office has my name on the door."

Pauline washed the smell off Jeffery and was thankful she didn't have to deal with the odor in her car.

They were on their way out the door when Jeffery said,

"Wait, Pauline…, Debo, Tom helped me, and I promised him that if he did you would look out for him and his family."

"What do I look like witness protection? Okay, since he did help get my man Jeffery back, then okay. But, I need him, I don't want Cruse or his men to suspect anything," Debo said.

"Thanks, boss," Jeffery said.

"Yeah… get him out of here," he told Pauline.

Jeffery was dressed in a terry cloth robe with swimming trunks underneath. It was all Tom had to give him to put on after the shower.

"Damn, it's freezing out here," Jeffery said, shivering.

"Yeah, but it smells better." Pauline smiled and took a deep breath of fresh air.

"I'm going to go through hell to kick this shit, Pauline."

"Yeah,.. but you have us, it's going to be okay," she told him and they left. It was nearing closing time and Debo had to figure a way to trap Cruse.

"Tom, show me where they kept him."

Tom took Debo to the basement, while Mad-C stood guard at the front door with the 44-magnum tucked securely inside his waistband. Tom and Debo got to the basement and the odor took Debo aback.

"Damn, they took my man through some shit. Tom, clean up this shit, flip the mattress, and change the sheets on the bed, and hurry up," Debo ordered.

Tom finished cleaning up in ten minutes. Debo laid in the same bed that Jeffery was tied to and put the sheet over himself, then turned in a fetal position facing the door.

"Close the door, and when Cruse gets here tell him you couldn't find the key to the door and had to break in to clean up and feed him. Damn it stinks in here," Debo said.

He wished they would hurry up and get down there so he wouldn't have to smell the stench anymore.

Tom went upstairs and told Mad-C Debo's plan. Mad-C went down to the basement and hid beside the stack of boxes that were lined up against the wall and turned the long table on its side in front of him for cover.

He was now positioned between the boxes and the table. He put a couple of fishing boat anchors in front of the table and got down on the floor and waited. They were hoping that Tom wouldn't screw up and get them both. killed. Debo saw that it was five-minutes to closing.

"Five minutes to go," he thought to himself.

When Tom returned to the basement, Mad-C looked up and was about to let him have one in the head.

"Don't shoot, don't shoot, it's me, Tom!!!" he screamed. "What is it, Tom?" Mad-C asked.

"Mr Cruse just called and said they were on their way. He said, 'we are on our way.'"

"Okay, go in there and tell him," Mad-C aggressively said.

Robert Cruse came through the door and was followed by three other men: real serious-looking men wearing long black French coats and black gloves.

"Take them to the basement and get that son-of-a-bitch Smith out of there," Cruse ordered Tom.

Tom led the way to the elevator, and while he and the three men were on the elevator, he tried to come up with something; some way to let Debo and Mad-C know that he was with the men that Cruse sent down there.

Robert Cruse stayed upstairs, just in case. He sat at the desk and watched the turnstile door and was wondering how he was going to kill Jeffery Smith. He decided to leave that up to the men he brought with him. "Why can't he just come down here himself? He send me down here with three grown-ass men like you guys can't find your way to a basement. Well, here we are, gentlemen. That's the door you want over there. I'm going back upstairs, I don't want to see nothing, hear nothing, or know nothing... bye," Tom said as he turned around and got back inside the elevator.

He closed the doors and pushed the stop button to hold it on the basement floor, which is what Debo had ordered him to do. Debo had planned for him and Mad-C to come out of the basement alive, and needed quick way to the top floor. If Debo and Mad-C didn't make it, Tom was out of there. The men walked toward the door and Mad-C rose up. Debo heard the door open and put his hand tighter on the grip of the forty-five, with the sheet still covering him, and aimed toward the door where the men would come through.

"Okay, let's go," one of the men said and started to pull the sheet back off of Debo. He saw Debo look at him, and he looked at Debo.

Then he looked at the forty-five automatic and saw it looking at him and said, "Oh, shit!!!"

He tried to get to his weapon but it was too late. Debo let *Crazy* spit trouble in the man's face; drilling a hole through his right eye. Mad-C came up from behind the other two and hammered a forty-four slug into the back of one of the other men. By that time, the third man had pulled his weapon and got off a shot at Mad-C. Mad-C threw himself to the floor behind the boxes and the table where he was when they came in. Debo rolled across the wet floor of the small room he was in and fired two shots. One hitting the man in the leg, ripping meat and tissue away as the bullet passed through his leg, tearing a hole in the table that Mad-C was behind, just missing his head by a fourth of an inch.

Mad-C came up from behind the table and pointed the 44-magnum at the man that was bleeding from his leg on the floor.

"He can't do anything, he's down. What are you going to do shoot him?" Debo asked Mad-C.

"Like I told you..., I kick 'em when they're down," Mad-C said, and put two rounds in the man's head.

He walked into the room and aimed the gun at the man that Debo shot in the eye and pulled the trigger, sending another round from the 44-magnum smashing through the man's head. Mad-C looked at the red-lighted arrow at the top of the elevator and saw that it was still on the basement floor.

"Tom, open the door!!!... Tom, I said open the door!!!... Tom!!!" Mad-C yelled, and the double doors came open.

Mad-C got on the elevator and Debo took the stairs. They both got to the top floor around the same time and looked to see that the lobby was empty.

Robert Cruse must have heard the shooting and decided to leave. When Debo got outside he saw the black Mercedes Benz bearing the license plate P-L-A-Y-E-R 5. Cruse looked at Debo as he pulled the 45 up to try and get a shot off at him but a car got between them. When the car moved out of the way he saw the Mercedes turning out of the parking lot, going down the street. Ocean Park Way was not the street for Debo to have a car chase or a shoot-out on.

He went to the Navigator and pulled out the saddlebag that he used on the motorcycle and took it inside the Fishing and Boat Club. He reached in the bag and pulled out four grenades and handed Mad-C two. Debo went down to the basement and pushed the button to hold the elevator, on his way off, and went into the room where Jeffery had been held hostage. He pulled the pin from one of the two grenades, then said,

"So long, hell hole," and tossed the grenade across the room and it landed under the bed that Jeffery was tied to. Debo ran back to the elevator and jumped in; closing the doors and felt it shake.

He heard the noise from the explosion, then he knew that part of his business was done at Seaman's Fishing and Boat Club. He got to the main floor lobby and stepped off the elevator and heard another explosion upstairs... and another one.

"'Mad-C isn't fooling around up there," he said to himself. Mad-C came down the stairs and said,

"All done on my end."

"Okay... let's get out of here," Debo suggested.

Debo and Mad-C were satisfied with the damage they had done with the grenades and to Cruses' men. Once they were outside, Debo turned, pulled the pin from the grenade he had left and threw it through the turnstile doors. All you could see was fire, thick black smoke, glass, splintered wood, and concrete blowing out of the front of the building.

They were in the Navigator and gone down the street before the authorities could arrive.

"Okay, it's time to pay Carlyle a visit," Mad-C said.

He was on the warpath and there was no stopping him once he got started.

"Debo you damn near shot my head off in that basement?" Mad-C cried.

"Yeah, that was a close one wasn't it?"

"That was a little too damn close if you ask me."

"Sorry… next time I'll aim higher," Debo said, and they laughed.

Debo took good care of Tom and made sure he and his family were safe. He and Mad-C made it to the office at just under 5:30 pm.

"Where is he?" Debo asked Pauline.

"He's in your office sleeping. He ate ten dollars worth of Snicker bars and threw up almost every five minutes, but he's better now. I finally got him to sleep."

"Okay, good, I'll call Molly and tell her so she can stop worrying." Debo picked up the office phone, he had left his cell in the Navigator. He dialed Molly's number and she answered. She sounded terrible; as though she had been worrying since Jeffery's kidnapping.

"Hi, Molly, this is D-Angelo Jackson."

"Oh hi, Mister Jackson, how are you? You're not calling with bad news, are you?"

"No, Molly.., in fact, I have some good news and some bad news. Which do you want first?"

"The good news…, tell me the good news. That's what I've been waiting on for, God knows how long," she impatiently said.

"Okay, Molly, the good news is that we found him."

"Oh my God, yes thank you, is he okay? Is he hurt? Where is he? How can…"

"Hold on, Molly…, he's okay, he's safe, and no he's not hurt. He's here with me but he won't be able to come home for at least three or four weeks."

"What happened to him?"

"The people that kidnapped him…,"

"Kidnapped!!!" she cut him off to say.

He had to tell her what happened, that way she wouldn't think he was out there on drugs all that time, and that is exactly what it would look like. Anyone that didn't know any better would have assumed that to be the case.

"Yes, Molly… kidnapped, maybe he can tell you all the details better than I can. But, when he was kidnapped, the people that took him tortured him. They shot drugs in him on a regular basis, for pretty much as long as he's been gone, but he's doing fine now."

"When can I see him?"

"As soon as he's feeling better, okay?"

"Can I speak to him?"

"He's asleep now, we'll see after he wakes up."

"Thank you, Mister Jackson."

"You're welcome, don't worry he's going to be just fine, alright?"

"Okay, I feel a lot better knowing that."

"I feel a lot better having him back too."

"Please let me know when I can talk to him, Mr Jackson!"

"Okay, Molly.., I will. I have to go now, I'll talk with you later."

"Soon… ?"

"Yes, soon," Debo assured her.

They wanted to get Jeffery out of the way. Those looked like some pretty big boys, and white men don't do black men's dirty work, unless the black man is rich and powerful.

"Somebody's behind Robert Cruse, and it's somebody big," Debo assumed. "Are you thinking what I'm thinking?" Mad-C asked.

"Only if you're thinking, Gregory Gilbert Johnson."

Debo thought about what Sgt. Billing said about Gregory Johnson when he said, 'that most people that went up against Johnson never make it back alive.'

"But who cares about his reputation?. If those were Johnson's men in that basement, it doesn't look like they'll be making it back either. How's that for your reputation, Mister Johnson?"

"I'm starved," Pauline said.

"Oh.., no you don't, I took the liberty of ordering barbeque. No one is going anywhere; everyone stays where you are, it should be here shortly."

"I heard that," Debo said, in agreement. "I'm for that too," Pauline pitched in.

"I ordered enough for Jeffery in case he wakes up hungry. You know something, Debo.., this is the first time I've met your crew I must say you have a very loyal bunch here. I mean they can be trusted, they take orders and take them very well, and the teamwork is out of this world. They made a commitment and stuck to it. They carry out their duties with diligence, prestige, and without fear or concern for their own well-being or safety. I must say you have put together a pretty damn awesome crew. After this is over, everyone is invited out to my estate as special guests; spouses and children included. I really admire our little team, D-Angelo."

"Yeah, I'm pretty proud of them myself. After all, I picked the very best. Well, actually they picked me," Debo proudly bragged.

The office phone rang and Mad-C picked it up on the first ring. "Write and Associates; Charles Write speaking," he said to the caller. "Mister Write?"

"Yes?"

"I'm downstairs with your order sir," the delivery man announced.

Mad-C put the 44-magnum in his waistband and went downstairs to get the food. Debo stood by the steps with CRAZY ready in case it was a setup. But everything was normal and the delivery man was legit. They ate and everyone got stuffed and just sat and talked.

"I wanna go by the hospital tomorrow and give Carlyle a good going over. I don't know when visiting hours are, but he's gonna need to answer a few questions for me. I don't wanna bother, Billings, he's probably playing golf tomorrow, and he gets messy when you disturb his golf game. That's probably why he hasn't called me yet. I know he knows by now. He knows about everything that goes on because he gets it first hand," Debo said.

"I'll call the hospital and see when visiting hours are tomorrow," Pauline offered.

"Thanks, Pauline."

"You're welcome handsome."

"Hey, stranger," Joy greeted. She was happy to hear from him.

Everybody was worried about each other.

"So, how did everything go?" Joy asked. "We got him back alive."

"Back… back from where?"

"Back from the assholes that took him, Robert Cruse and his band of bitches. They had him locked in a basement at the fishing and boat club out in Venice. They shot him up pretty bad with heroin, but it's okay we got him out of there in time."

"Boy, you've had a busy week, huh?"

"Yeah, and I'm beat, how are you?"

"I'm fine…, ready for action!"

"We'd better hold off on the action for you for a while."

"Spoilsport!!"

"I just want you alive."

"Yeah, the last time I argued with you I got shot. So, I'm good with whatever you decide, Big Bra,"

"What's Freddy up to, is he okay?"

"Yeah, he's here playing Rummy with Shelly and I."

"When did you become so proper? 'Shelly and I,' woman please. Put, my baby on the phone."

"Okay, ole country bumpkin.., hold on."

"Hey, Honey.., how's your day going?"

"Busy…, very busy, are you okay?"

"Yeah, I'm good."

"I have some mail for you, and the makeup and bikini you asked for. I'll give it to Joy or Freddy to give to you."

"When can I see you, D-Angelo?"

"Soon, baby… real soon."

"I miss you and I love you."

"I miss and love you too, baby."

"Okay, just don't stop."

"Never, sweetheart. Put Freddy on for me. I'll call you before I go to bed, okay baby?"

"Okay… here's a kiss," she said. She threw him a kiss over the phone and handed Freddy the phone."

"Hey, boss, I thought I was in on the thing out on Gage."

"I needed someone to sit with Shell and I need Joy with me," Debo explained.

"I still can't come up with anything on Jeffery. I think they've got him, boss," Freddy reported.

"No, I have him, they did have him but I went in and got him out of there. They had him at the fishing and boat club out in Venice. Mad-C and I went there and pulled him out. Randy Carlyle is down, he's in the hospital. I'm sure, Joy told you."

"Yes, she did.., you and Joy have been having all the fun."

"Hold on, I might need you shortly and put Joy back over there where you are."

"Okay, boss.., just holler, I'm overdue for some action," Freddy said. He was beginning to sound like Joy. Debo wondered if the two of them were rubbing off on each other.

"Okay, just checking on you guys," Debo told Freddy. "Okay, talk to you later.

"Okay, later." Debo turned to Pauline and said, "Whatcha got for me?"

"I've got Monday through Saturday at 8:30 am-5:30 pm, and, 6:00 pm-9:00 pm, and 9:00 am, until 2:30 pm on Sundays."

"Thank you darlin; you know you really amaze me sometimes. Did you write all that down?"

"No, I memorized it."

"That's very good," Debo commended. "Thank you, Handsome."

9:30 PM

"Since nobody is leaving here tonight, I'll bed down in Debo's office. Pauline, you can either use my sleeping quarters or find a spot on the floor someplace. There are some covers and blankets in the workout room closet," Mad-C said.

"Jeffery is knocked-out in my bed," Debo added..

Debo and Mad-C put some blankets on the main meeting room floor and laid down. Pauline decided to join them on the floor and engage in the conversation they were having. Debo called Shelly and they talked for a while.

"D-Angelo, besides having to kill people and hide your wife, do you have any regrets about getting into the business?" Mad-C asked.

"You know… I knew there would be dangers, even the danger of being caught or killed. I got into the business because I had no place else to go, no place else to turn. You didn't pull me into a hellhole.

In fact, you pulled me out of one. I would have probably sold my soul to have been able to get out of the rut I was in," Debo confessed.

The blinds were open and the moon gave the office a glow. They could see each other even with the lights off. The moonlight allowed them to see a clear silhouette of each other's faces; no color… just that certain moon-blue. Debo was facing the ceiling, he turned his head to face Mad-C and thought about how amazing it was that the moon could shade the color of things and put its own special glow to it.

"I was spared from having to do that. Regrets.., no, because you never know what bends and turns your life is going to take. So, you remain flexible so you can bend and turn with it. But the funny thing is you have to go wherever it takes you, wherever it leads you, and be able to deal with it on its terms. And in order to reap the benefits, you must accept the consequences if there are any. No…, I don't have any regrets as far as my lifestyle or my financial status is concerned, or even the people I've met along the way up. But, I do however, understand that killing people is a major sin and one of the worst. And there are consequences to that which I'll have to deal with once I'm gone. But, as far as now, I have no regrets. How about you… ?"

"The only thing I regret is not having my Cassy and little Tina to share it all with anymore," Mad-C admitted.

"What I regret is the same thing Mr Write regrets; 'Not being able to share it all with anyone'," Pauline pitched-in.

"You, Pauline, are young and beautiful, and you have tons of money. You'll find the right guy soon enough," Debo told her.

"Yeah, I guess when I sit down and sit still, I'll be able to enjoy and appreciate a relationship. I'm too busy now, besides I don't want to bring my future husband into the kind of work I do… even if it is a prosperous occupation. And like you said, handsome, 'It has its consequences.' It plays an important role in the longevity and outcome of a healthy relationship. I don't want to start a relationship where there are consequences at the beginning."

"Yeah…, I heard that; at least you're honest, Pauline," Mad-C said.

CHAPTER
14

SUNDAY, NOVEMBER 18TH, 8:30 A.M.

Pauline woke up and Debo and Mad-C were gone. She found a note on the restroom door. Somehow they knew that that would be the first place she would go: "Going to the hospital to see Randy Carlyle, keep an eye on my man Jeffery for me. When he wakes up, make sure he gets whatever he needs. There may be some Bar-B-Q left. If not, go get him something and be careful. I left my key on my desk for you: Be back soon…, Handsome."

They arrived at the hospital at 10:00 am. Since they knew that Cruse knew Carlyle was there, Mad-C stayed back just in case Cruse decides to pay his friend a surprise visit. Debo walked through the double sliding doors onto a cheap carpet; new but cheap. He checked with the receptionist to see where Randy Carlyle was. She directed him to a bank of elevators and told him to go to the third floor and ask the nurse at the nurses' station. Debo did as he was directed. When he walked up to the nurses' station, he encountered a short, middle-aged woman of African American descent. She looked as though she had been up all night working. She probably worked a double shift. Nowadays you have to work double shifts or have two jobs, especially with Christmas being right around the corner. Debo understood why she was so willing to lose sleep in order to make the extra money.

"Hi, I'm D-Angelo Jackson, and I'm here to see Randy Carlyle."

"Room 305," the lady told him, pointing down a long hallway that bent after a few feet.

"Thank you," Debo said, and walked down the hall.

You could see the door once you rounded the bend. The door to Randy Carlyle's room was made of a heavy metallic material. This is the kind that is used for fire doors to avoid fires from spreading from one room to the other. (305) was displayed on the door just above Debo's head. He got on his cell phone and called Mad-C.

"Mad-C, can you come up here and keep an eye out for me? I don't want any surprises while I'm in Carlyle's room."

"Okay, I'm on my way."

"Okay, thanks; it's room (305)."

"No problem."

.Debo walked into the room and the curtains were closed. Carlyle's back was turned at an angle because he was wearing a full-body cast with the upper part of his body in traction as he slept. Debo opened the curtain and let the sunlight beam into Carlyle's face.

"Hey, mothafucka…, what's up? Now you can make this easy on both of us by telling me where Cruse is Or, you can just lay there while I pour this hot-ass coffee down that cast you have on."

Debo took the coffee cup and put it to Carlyle's feet so he could feel the heat. Where is Cruse, Carlyle?"

Randy Carlyle didn't say anything.

"I know you can talk, you got shot in your back, not your fuckin mouth. Now, where is Robert Cruse, Carlyle?"

There was still no answer.

"Okay, suit yourself," Debo said, and tilted the cup and let the hot coffee run down the cast. Carlyle let out a loud scream.

"Where is Cruse, Carlyle?"

"Fuck you," Carlyle said and spat on Debo.

"Okay, mothafucka, you want to play fuckin games?"

Debo cursed. He was mad, impatient, and tired of Carlyle's bullshit games. He went into the bathroom across from Randy Carlyle's bed and poured the coffee in the sink. He came out, stood next to Carlyle, and pissed in the cup.

"Where is Cruse, Carlyle?"

"I said fuck you, I'm not telling you shit."

Debo walked up to the bed and leaned over Randy Carlyle and poured some of the urine in his mouth. He tried to spit it on Debo, but Debo put his hand over his mouth. At that moment, Mad-C came into the room.

"Is there a problem here, Debo?" Mad-C asked. "Yeah, I can't get this son-of-a-bitch to answer me." Debo turned back around to face Carlyle and said,

"Look, we have your cell phone, your address, your identification, all your shit. I'm just asking you to save us some time and tell us what we want to know."

Randy Carlyle still said nothing.

"Fuck this shit," Mad-C said, and pulled out the 44-Magnum, then pulled the hammer back and put the barrel in Randy's mouth where Debo had recently poured urine.

"Okay, you stupid mathafucka, open yo mouth, or I'll open the back of your fucking head. And I don't give a shit who hears the shot. I want to know where that son-of-a-bitch is, RIGHT

NOW!!!" Mad-C yelled.

Randy Carlyle's eyes opened wide and he couldn't swallow. He shook his head frantically up and down.

"Okay..., okay I'll talk."

"Let me tell you one thing... whatever comes out of your mouth had better be the truth, because if I have to come back here, I won't be asking questions, I'll be coming back here to blow yo ass back into yesterday. DO YOU UNDERSTAND ME?" Mad-C angrily said.

"Yes, I understand."

Mad-C pulled the 44-Magnum about an inch from his mouth and said... "TALK!!"

"Okay... alright... I'll tell you. He's at 4515 Colt Brilliant Drive, Venice, California."

"Is it a house or an apartment?" Debo asked.

"A house," Carlyle answered.

"Let's get the hell out of here," Mad-C said. "Hold on," Debo said.

He went back over to Carlyle's bed and poured some more of the piss on Carlyle, and said,

"You left my man smelling like piss, so I'll leave your breath smelling like piss," then poured the rest of it down Randy's throat. With that, he and Mad-C left the room.

Randy pushed the emergency button to summon the nurse.

The same tired middle-aged woman that was at the nurse's station when Debo came up, was the one that answered the emergency call.

"Yes sir, Mister Carlyle, how are we, and how was your visit?"

If she could only read Randy's mind, she would know that his visit just fucked up his day, and possibly his life.

"I need my sheets changed and some mouthwash. And, can you bring me a phone or roll this bed out in the hall and I can use one? I need the phone first," he told her.

She looked at the cables holding his leg in traction and said, "Well, I'm not supposed to unhook those things, but just this once.

I'll need to change your sheets anyway. I'll get the sheets while you're on the phone. Oh, and I'll get your mouth washed also."

"Thank you," Randy said.

He gave her a number to dial for him and she dialed it, then put the phone to his ear and went to get the mouthwash and sheets.

Due to the seriousness of the gunshot wound, Carlyle had limited use of his arms and hands. The gunshot wound to his back would have killed him or paralyzed him permanently from his neck down, had it been two more inches to the right. Robert Cruse came to the phone...

"Yeah, hello... what's up?"

"Listen to me carefully, Jackson and Write were by here. They got your address and everything out of my cell phone," he lied.

"Say WHAT!!!" Robert Cruse yelled.

"They might be on their way to your place. I'm sorry, they got hold of my wallet, my phone, everything... there was nothing I could do," Carlyle lied again.

"I'll call you later, thanks," Cruse said and slammed the phone down. "Shit, that idiot we had over at the boat club was more faithful than this asshole, he just gave my ass up. I'll take care of him later," Cruse thought.

He was pissed…, now he had to get out of that house. The room he moved into after Debo and Mad-C hit his apartment in Venice was too small, so he moved back to his house on Colt Brilliant. Now he has to move again.

"If I have to move one more damn time; the hell with that, I'm not moving. Let him bring his ass on," Cruse said aloud.

Debo knew that Carlyle would probably call Cruse and warn him, but Debo had other plans. Carlyle is worried stiff, knowing that Cruse would have him killed for sure; Probably tonight. He has to get the nurse to change his room. She changed his bed and helped him wash his mouth out.

"One more thing, please," he said,. "What's that, young man?"

"Can you change my room? My life is in danger and I need you to change my room and don't tell a soul where I am."

"Mr Carlyle, I'm not authorized to do that. Only the head nurse or your doctor can do that, sir."

"Did you hear what I said? I said that my life is in danger."

"Yes, I understand Mr Carlyle, but… Hold on a minute," she said and left the room and went to her station to call the emergency number to his doctor.

"Hello, Dr Brock, this is Nurse Brown at county."

"Yes, Nurse Brown, what can I do for you?"

"We have an emergency here, doctor. A patient has requested to be moved to another room. He says, 'his life is in danger.' He's the gentleman that came in Friday; the gunshot wound patient."

"Yes, I recall, tell him I'll be there in about an hour."

"Okay doctor, thank you," the nurse said and hung up. She went to give the message to Carlyle, and to explain that she couldn't move him.

The law requires that his doctor is present during movement of any patient. Carlyle waited until his doctor came. If Cruse came before the doctor did… oh well, just another bad day.

Debo called Freddy and made an appointment for them to meet at the office as soon as possible. Freddy said he would be there in forty-five-minutes. When he said it, he remembered something and called him back.

"Hey, Freddy!"

"Yeah, boss?"

"Don't come now, I'm sending Pauline over there to be with Shell and Joy."

"Okay... got it, boss," Freddy said and was off the line.

"Hey, Love.., I need you to go and take Freddy's place at the hotel, I need him here for a couple of days."

"Okay, Handsome, I'll go kick it with the girls for a while and bask in the luxuries of life. Sure, why not," Pauline accepted.

"I have some things that I want you to take to Shell for me."

He gave Pauline the makeup, mail, and bikini Shelly wanted and sent her on her way. Freddy arrived at the office at 2:30 pm. When he got there, Mad-C and Debo were already in a meeting. Freddy pushed in the code and the door buzzed to allow him entry. He walked up the stairs and was formally introduced to Mad-C. He had heard a lot about him, but this was the first time they met in person.

"Freddy... this is the guy that signs everyone's paychecks; Mister Write." Debo looked at Mad-C, then back at Freddy and said,

"Mister Write, meet Freddy, one of my best worker. Freddy, Mister Write and I were discussing how we're going to move on, Cruse. We have a location on him and we've decided to move in on him at four o'clock tomorrow morning. That's why I'm pulling you in tonight," Debo told him. "Well, I'm ready boss, I told you that on the phone."

Freddy pulled out the 357-Magnum he kept and gave the cylinder a spin to demonstrate how ready he was.

"That's very impressive, but Debo has some toys of his own; some real special shit... some 4th of July shit," Mad-C told Freddy .

"Now you're talking," Freddy said. Dr Melvin Brooks arrived at the hospital an hour later and walked up to the nurses' station where Nurse Brown was seated and said.

"Hi, Nurse Brown, where is the patient?"

She escorted him down the hall to Carlyle's room and stood there while the doctor and Carlyle discussed his problem.

"Okay, Mr Carlyle, under the circumstances we can move you to another room but you'll need to sign a release form just in case your condition worsens during movement. You do understand, don't you?"

"OK, anything… just please move me fast," Carlyle cried.

The doctor called in a special technician to dismantle the cables, and move Carlyle to the fifth floor and reconnect the cables.

"How are you feeling, Mister Carlyle?"

"Not good at all."

"I'm sorry to hear that Mister Carlyle. Now you must understand that by law I can't disclose your whereabouts to anyone except law enforcement. Is that clear? I must tell any and all law enforcement agencies where you can be located."

"Yes, doctor, I understand."

"I knew it… I fucking knew it; I knew you were going to get my men blown to hell. You are starting to become a liability, Robert, and I don't like it at all," Gregory Johnson told Robert Cruse.

"Randy told Jackson and Write where I live. They could be going by there looking for me."

"Good…, get you the fuck out of my hair. Okay, what do you want me to do, keep giving you men to get killed?" Johnson asked Cruse.

"No, I've got a few guys that can use some money."

"So, what the hell did you do get my men killed so you could save some money? Write and Jackson knows who those men belong to. They know who they are up against; they're not idiots like you. They know that you don't employ the kind of men you've been giving them to kill. Just lay low for a couple of days; give me time to think. The more you move, the fucking worse shit gets. I'll take care of Carlyle myself. He's no good to anyone anymore," Johnson said.

"Thanks, Greg."

"Yeah, thanks my ass I just don't want you running your mouth about anything you know."

"I would never do that, Greg."

"Yeah, that's bullshit, because if those two got hold of your ass, you'd give your mother up to get the fuck away."

Gregory Johnson is a hard man; his dad worked in a steel-mill in Kentucky and didn't take crap off of anyone. He worked hard for his money and worked extra hard to keep it. Gregory Johnson was the only boy out of six children, and being around a house full of sisters, he always had to be the protector. And being that he was the oldest of the six, he didn't want to work the mill all his life like his father did. He went out on his own at just a teen and sold his first joint and was considered the businessman of his neighborhood." He called all the shots and made all the rules, and he was the only one who could break them.

(5:00 pm)

It's the weekend, and Debo decided to go over to Omar's house to see how Rex was getting along. He arrived at 5:00 pm.

"Sorry Bra, I didn't know you were eating dinner," Debo said.

He knew it was five in the evening and most people do eat dinner at 5:00 or 6:00 in the evening. Omar had a "well-to-do" house in Compton, CA; nothing fancy…, just your regular two-story stucco, three-bedroom house. They both wanted kids, but Gail wasn't sure because the money wasn't right. And Omar didn't want to ask Debo for the money to put in the bank to support a child. He figured that if he was man enough to father a child, then he's man enough to work and support one, no matter how rich his younger brother is. So, in case they decide to have a child they would convert the spare room into a nursery. All of Gail's friends have children or a child, and in every case the father up and left. But, Gail's worry was the money to support a child, or children.

Debo walked out back where Gail was hanging her laundry. Rex was out there with her, and as soon as Rex saw Debo, he leaped up from the ground, and in his haste to get up, he kicked Gail's laundry basket over. Her clean clothes went flying everywhere. She mumbled something that Debo couldn't hear and continued hanging clothes.

"Hey, there big boy," Debo said. As soon as he said, "big boy," he remembered what he had to do in the morning and decided to hurry up because he didn't have much time. He wanted to get some sleep because he didn't want to be tired when he went to Cruse's house. Rex jumped all over him tracking muddy, dirty little dog prints all over his freshly laundered pants and shirt while kissing him all over his arms and chin. When Rex stood on his hind legs, he was five feet tall.

"Okay, okay boy…, calm down," Debo commanded.

Rex got down off of him and sat beside him, and swept dirt and mud with his tail as he wagged it from side to side. Debo played with him for about fifteen or twenty-minutes, then walked over to Gail and said, "Hey, Sis,.. how's everything going?

I see you're still doing laundry the old-fashioned way."

"I like my clothes to smell fresh, and there's nothing fresher than the outdoor freshness. Dryers burn and fade your clothes."

"So, how have you been?" Debo asked.

"I'm doing well, how about yourself, how have you been? How was your vacation, or are you still on it?"

"Yeah, I'm still on it. I just came by to give Omar some money for my boy, Rex…, and to pay for the door he scratched up."

"Yeah, he almost tore my door off. You don't have to worry about anybody bothering you with him around. Some gang members came in my backyard the other night, not knowing that Rex was there. I guess they were running from some rival gang members or the police; I don't know which, but Rex took a plug out of one of them. And you know me, D-Angelo; 'you leave me alone and I'll leave you alone', that's how I am. Mess with me and you're messing with trouble.., no ifs, ands, or buts about it."

Gail was an honor student in school, and was raised around a quiet family. She has four years of college at USC, majoring in culinary arts, and can cook up a storm.

"Omar said, you give him table food, but I use a lot of seasoning, so I don't give it to him. How's, Michelle?" Gail asked.

"She's doing okay… hanging in there," Debo said, which was not far from the truth.

"Is she enjoying her vacation?"

"Yeah, she's basking in the lap of luxury. I'm going to go holler at Omar. Here, get yourself something for Christmas, okay?"

He handed her ten $100 bills. He didn't really know whether or not he would be around for Christmas. But, if he made it through this, he would also invite his brother and sister-in-law out to *the Shell-Debo* for Christmas. He wanted to send them on a cruise for the holidays, but we'll see.

"Big Bra…, tell me something good," Debo said when he entered the house.

Omar was watching the news. He always watched the 6:00 news after dinner, then a movie, and off to bed early to get ready for work the next day.

"Everything's everything. How's the vacation going?"

"It's going as well as can be expected," Debo lied.

He knew that Omar was no fool. Omar knew that something was up with Debo, but he respected Debo for not involving him. Anything Debo needs, Omar would do it and Debo knew that. D-Angelo L Jackson Junior chose his lifestyle. He didn't want to see his brother hurt, killed, or in jail or prison behind helping him out in situations that he knew was inevitable as a risk in his occupation. Respect goes a long way with Omar and D-Angelo Jackson.

"Omar, I know you're not feeding into this vacation bullshit, and I thank you for not saying anything to Gail. I appreciate you watching Rex for me. I had to get away from the house for a while to take care of some business. There are some people out to get the man I work for, and they are trying to get to him through me and some people that work for me. I don't know exactly when they are following me. That's why I haven't been over here because I don't want to bring any of this to your home either. I love you for your understanding and I appreciate everything that you stand for. Keep living your life the way you are big bra. Here, take this."

He gave Omar $5,000 and said, "Merry Christmas", then handed him another $500 and said,

"Get the door replaced and get some food for my boy, Rex. I don't know how long this will take, but I'm sure it won't be too long. I will be going on vacation to Maui with Shell after this is over. I have to be going. I love you, big bra, and keep me in your prayers. I gave Gail a little something for Christmas also."

Debo went to the door and thought about Rex. He turned around and went to the back door, opened it, and Rex ran and jumped up on the screen that he had also shredded. Debo opened it and gave Rex a pat on his side, and said,

"See you soon boy…, be good."

He didn't see Gail, she had already gone inside the house and was probably in one of the back bedrooms.

"See you later, Sis!!!" Debo yelled.

He heard her yell back, "Okay… you take care, and tell Michelle I said hey!!!"

"Okay!!!" Debo yelled back and walked back into the living room and put his hand on Omar's shoulder and said,

"See you later, big bra."

Omar had a slight tear in the corner of his eye. He was afraid for his brother. He started thinking back to St Louis when they were kids pushing the newspaper cart and clowning around, and how they used to ring people's doorbells and run. And how they played GI Joe and set on old car tires and pretended they were riding motorcycles with the little girls on the back. Now his little brother is all grown up and living a very dangerous life just like their father when he was alive. His heart cried out for his little brother.

"Please, D-Angelo be careful, I love you, and I want to see you at Christmas… ALIVE!!"

"You will, Omar…, you will. I love you too, Bra," Debo said and left.

He didn't see the tears in his brother's eyes, and Omar didn't see the ones in Debo's eyes either. He got back to the office at 7:45 pm and Jeffery was doing a lot better.

"Hey, stranger," Debo greeted.

He was happy to have Jeffery back. Jeffery was opening the pool hall alone the morning he was kidnapped. Leroy usually opened but he called in sick and Jeffery went instead. He didn't know the black Mercedes Benz or what Cruse looked like. Cruse was sitting in the Benz outside the pool hall with the black tinted windows rolled up talking on the phone with Randy Carlyle.

"Are you sure he's coming in?" Cruse asked Carlyle. "Yeah..., He's supposed to, he should be there any minute."

Carlyle was supposed to kidnap Jeffery but he was busy collecting drug money for Robert Cruse.

"I think I see him."

Robert Cruse was parked between two cars on the street in front of the pool hall. His was the second car of the three. Jeffery didn't notice him sitting there.

"Yeah, that's him," Cruse said and hung up.

Jeffery put the key in the black wrought-iron door and opened it, then he opened the wooden door behind it. He didn't see Cruse come up from behind him. As he turned to close the door a hand held it open. Jeffery saw the man with the weird goatee and said,

"What the fuck do you think you're doing... robbing me?"

He reached in his pocket for the 38-revolver he kept there and felt a fist pound into his stomach. He bent over in pain, and the impact from the blow to the back of his head took him to the ground. It wasn't hard enough to knock him out... just knock him off balance and to the ground. In doing so, he could gain control of the situation. He took the 38-handgun from Jeffery Smith's pocket and held it up to his head. He could have used his own gun, but if he had to shoot him he would rather shoot him with his own weapon. That way he wouldn't have to get rid of his.

"Get up and open the door," he ordered Jeffery, and Jeffery did as Cruse ordered him to do .

"Where's the safe? I know you keep everything in there"

"The safe is empty."

"Don't fuck with me, get in there and open it, or they'll find your ass in here with a hole in your fucking head."

Jeffery gave Robert $150,000,00 from the safe.

"Where's the dope? I know there is some, where is it, Jeffery?"

"I sold it all, that's why there's so much money here," Jeffery told him. "Come on, let's go," Cruse ordered.

"Go where…" and before Jeffery could say another word, Cruse had rammed another fist into his midsection.

"I said don't fuck with me, didn't I? Now, let's go, dammit."

After Jeffery caught his breath, he led the way to the door with Cruse following close behind him. Cruse locked both doors so that no one would suspect anything, and told Jeffery to go to his car.

"I don't drive my car here, I live too close."

"I know where the fuck you live."

Cruse decided he would have Carlyle go and move Jeffery's car later. It wouldn't make a whole lot of sense for his car to be at his house and he wasn't, especially for as long a period of time as he'll be gone. Everyone thought that Jeffery had just gone someplace and was having fun with the ladies.

"Molly wants to talk to you. I told her that you'll be able to talk to her after you wake up. How are you feeling?" Debo asked Jeffery.

"A lot better… thanks, boss."

"You're welcome. I told Molly everything. She's just glad to have you back and she wants to see you. I told her that it would be a while before she could see you. I want you to get your strength back."

Jeffery called Molly and told her again what had happened, but she had already heard it all. All she was interested in was when her man was coming home. He told her in a little while and she started crying. He didn't like it when she cried, especially when it's because of him.

"It's for the best, baby. The junk those guys were shooting in me is going to take time… at least a few more days. I won't be able to even go outside for a while because all I'm going to want to do now is get more. And I don't want you to see me go through that, I'll be in a lot of pain."

"So, you're not alright?"

"I'm a little better than I was before my boss found me. But, if I leave here now I won't be for too long. I'm alright, just give it another week or so."

Debo interrupted their phone conversation "Let me talk to her." He handed Debo the phone.

"Hello, Molly, this is D-Angelo Jackson again."

"Oh, hi Mister Jackson. I want to thank you for taking care of him. I don't know what I would have done, thank you for getting him back for me. I just want to s… " Debo cut her off.

"Molly, listen to me, I'm going to have a friend of mine take him there tomorrow, but he can't stay overnight… okay?"

"Will you please, thank you so much!!"

"You're welcome, Molly; here's, Jeffery."

He gave Jeffery back the phone and he told her that he would see her tomorrow and hung up.

"Jeffery, are you up for it? I mean, do you think you can handle it? Because if not, we'll wait," Debo said.

"I'm sure I can, Debo. Who's going with me, Pauline?"

"Yeah… she seems to be able to handle it."

"Yeah, if that guy at the fishing and boat club hadn't done what she said, all hell was going to break loose… and she didn't even have a gun!"

"She didn't need one," Debo said.

CHAPTER 15

Debo, Mad-C, and Freddy were at the office. They all got up at 3:00 Monday morning.

"It's time to make plans and figure out how we're going to do this. I'm sure there are houses next door to the targeted house. And there are going to be neighbors, and there is going to be noise, lots of noise. I'll take the front, and you guys can take the sides and back," Mad-C announced.

He remembered ten years ago when he went in through the front door. Robert Cruse would remember that also, or he might not even be there. Debo believes that Cruse and Johnson were somehow together in this, and it's deeper than it looks. He's sure that Cruse and Johnson did the Yin murder but he needs something concrete. But, either way, Cruse is a threat to him and he has to take care of that problem then go after Johnson.

Johnson is probably who set Mad-C up to lose the ten kilos off his ship. And he could've been involved in the mugging ten years ago by the gang members. Johnson had mentioned a long time ago that he thought whoever operates in Los Angeles County, should be charged regardless of who it was. But, when he found out that it was Charles Write, he decided he would fry the bigger fish he had to fry with him.

Johnson knows who Charles Write is. He also knows who Carlyle, Cruse, and Morris are. And, he knows a hell of a lot more than he's letting on. The muscle at the fishing and boat club were Johnson's men. They might have a few men at Cruse's house waiting for them because Cruse knew that Mad-C and Debo were going to show up at his house. However, this was going to be in and out, hit and run.

"I don't want to lose my Navigator. The only reason I'm taking it is because it's armor-plated. It'll stop anything short of a missile, a Rocket Launcher, or cannon, and if we need to we can use it for cover," Debo said. "Don't forget to bring some of those fire-crackers with you," Mad-C said.

"Okay, are you ready?"

"Yeah."

"Freddy?"

"Ready when you are."

"Okay, let's do it," Mad-C said.

MONDAY MORNING, NOVEMBER 19TH, 4:00 AM

The house at 4515 Colt Brilliant is a beautiful three-story home. It's beige and white and has a long walkway from the sidewalk to the front porch. Debo could see lights on upstairs but no movement. Downstairs was dark with the exception of one room, and it seemed to be the kitchen... or maybe a den. They all checked their weapons: Debo pulled the magazine from the bottom of the forty-five-pistol grip, then slid it back in and pulled the slide back at the top of the weapon and released it to put a round in the chamber. Mad-C and Freddy checked the cylinders of their weapons and they were ready for action.

The three men got out of the Navigator all dressed in black coats and gloves. They wore all black as to make a positive ID virtually impossible. The three of them dressed exactly the same. It was still dark at 4:15 in the morning. Mad-C went up to the front door, Freddy went to the side where the light was on in the window downstairs, and Debo went around back. They gave each other fifteen seconds to get into position. Mad-C tried the front door and it was locked. Debo tried the back door and it was also locked. Then he saw a sliding glass door but he couldn't get to it, the screen was locked but the glass door was ajar. He took his pocket knife out and cut just to the left of the lock and put his index finger through the small cut and lifted the lever that secured the lock. He then eased the screen door open and checked to see if there was anyone inside. If there was an alarm it would have sounded, but none did, so he slowly pulled the door open and stepped inside the warm dark room and heard a television on in one of the rooms but he couldn't tell which one. It seemed to be coming from down the hall. He saw a king-size bed to his right and a plasma TV on the wall in front of him.

The room was moonlit but Debo could see that he was in a rather large bedroom. He was in the master bedroom but the bed hadn't been slept in. He eased his way to the door and the sound of the TV set got louder. It was coming from the room with the lights on down the hall. Someone had to be in there but he didn't know if they were sleeping or not. He eased further down the hall and came to the room with the lights on and the television playing. The door was open and Debo had already pulled the forty-five from the holster beneath his shoulder and held it in both hands with his finger on the trigger. He heard a loud bang come from behind him and turned around and one of Cruse's men was behind him lying on the floor. Mad-C had gone around to the back door because he couldn't get in through the front. Debo turned back around in time to see the man coming to the door of the room he was standing next to. He let him get halfway out the door and fired one shot that knocked the man back into the room and over the sofa he had been sitting on. They heard running upstairs and followed the sound of the men's feet stampeding against the floor, ending up at the top of the steps. There were three men running down the stairs. Debo and Mad-C let off several rounds, hitting two of them, bringing them down to the bottom floor. Freddy heard some movement in the backyard and went to see if it was Debo or Mad-C. It was neither, it was two more of Cruse's men on their way into the house.

Freddy came from the side of the house and yelled, "HEY!!!" The men immediately aimed at Freddy and fired. Freddy ducked around the corner just in time to see splinters of wood break away from the house where his head was. He stuck the 357 around the corner of the house and fired three shots at the men that were shooting at him: hitting one of them. He didn't know how bad the man was hit, he just heard him yell, "I'm hit!!"

Freddy stuck his head around the corner again and saw one of them on the ground. He wasn't moving and Freddy didn't know whether he was dead. The other man that Freddy couldn't see had positioned himself behind a tree. He shot at the man on the ground and saw him move.

"If you weren't dead, you are now. Where the hell is your friend?" Freddy said to himself.

He looked around the corner and the man fired another round from behind the tree. Freddy backed back around the corner and didn't see the man that was shooting at him, it was too dark and he was too far away. Freddy fired two more shots blindly into the dark. The third man on the staircase ran back up the steps after seeing his two accomplices go down. He ran into a bedroom and stood in the doorway out of sight while firing at Debo and Mad-C. They couldn't see the man behind the door, so Debo took out a grenade and pulled the pin. He motioned for Mad-C to take cover and Mad-C dove to the floor and under a large coffee table. He threw the grenade through the door and the explosion blew the man out of the room and over the railing, landed right next to Mad-C with his eyes open. Freddy went around the front of the house and on to the other side. He saw the tree and the man standing behind it. It was hard for him to see to get a good shot at him. He had to chance hitting the man and taking him down or missing him and giving up his position. It was cold and the wind was blowing cold air into Freddy's eyes, making them water. He wiped the tears from his eyes with his gloved hand and tried to focus again on the man that was hiding behind the tree. He moved just enough so the moonlight could pick up a glimpse of him. Freddy pulled the trigger and the hammer found the head of the 357 round and sent it drilling into the tree. The man behind the tree moved again facing Freddy. Freddy saw him completely and let go of another round, and that one hit its target. The man dropped, saturating the dirt beneath him with blood and brains.

"You okay?" Debo asked Mad-C. "Yeah, I'm good."

"Freddy!!!" Debo yelled.

"Yeah, Boss, I'm here!!!"

"Get everyone and let's get the hell out of here, this took too long, the law will be here in a minute."

"They're here!!!," Freddy yelled as he heard sirens coming from a close distance.

They all headed for the Navigator, got in, and left. "Guess what," Debo said.

"What?" Mad-C responded.

"Robert Cruse was not in that house. I guess he knew we would be there."

"Yeah I guess he did, we're having a bad time catching this piece uh shit," Mad-C angrily stated.

"We'll get him, and when we do…," Freddy added.

"Yeah, when we do, it'll be all over for his ass," Debo threatened. Jeffery and Molly had a ball; they sat and discussed how difficult it would be without him being home. He told her, 'that no matter what, if there ever comes a time when I can't be found, no matter what people might say. I'll never cheat on you and I'll never just up and leave you for nobody; EVER!!' Molly is a gorgeous, five-foot five-inch tall, with hip-length brunette hair, and the most beautifully tanned completion he's ever seen on a woman.

"It may not take as long as a month, but I'm fighting an addiction right now, and I can't really trust the fact that I can do it out here alone. That's why Pauline came with me, because Mr Jackson knew that you wouldn't be able to control me once the withdrawals started. It's like I've got to have it. It's not a mental illness… it's physical and it hurts like the devil coming off of it. So, just hold on, sweetheart and I'll be coming home soon. I can't go to a doctor or a hospital because they'll ask questions. So, I need you to make sure Leroy takes good care of my pool-hall. I'll call him and let him know that you are the boss and no one better give you any lip as far as that pool hall. Any problems, you let me know," Jeffery said.

Pauline's phone rang, it was Debo calling. "Hey, handsome, what's up?"

"How's my man coming along?"

"He's a real gentleman," Pauline assured him.

"Okay, whenever you leave you can take him back to the office or wait for me to get there: Tell you what, you can take him to Freddy's room at the hotel if you want, and I'll have him keep an eye on him. If I need Freddy again, I'll have you go over there and keep an eye on, Jeffery, okay?"

"Sounds like a winner to me, I know that when that stuff calls, you answer."

"Yeah, you got that right," Debo told Pauline.

"Let me speak to him."

"Yeah, Debo?"

He told Jeffery everything that he had just told Pauline, and he had no problem with it. Debo told him to enjoy his visit with Molly, and they both hung up.

9:30 AM

"Good morning, Mr Carlyle," the man with the chart in his hand greeted. "And, how are we this morning, sir?"

"You're not Dr Brock," Randy Carlyle noticed.

"No, I'm not, I'm the day nurse. Do you need anything; water, something to eat?"

The day nurse took Randy's water pitcher off the small table that swiveled over him for easier reach. He went into the small restroom, and upon his returned he was holding a nine-millimeter handgun in his hand. Randy Carlyle closed his eyes while the man attached a silencer to the barrel of the weapon. He picked up a pillow from the bed and Randy knew that there was nothing he could do. Either Robert Cruse or Gregory Johnson had sent someone there to kill him. Just like Cruse sent Randy Carlyle to set up Johnny Morris. Randy feared this moment, he knew that it was inevitable. "Can I have a cigarette first?" Randy Carlyle asked his would-be assassin.

"I guess so."

"Thanks, they're over there in that drawer. They don't allow me to smoke in here, but I managed to smuggle some smokes in to smoke when no one's around."

"Smoke your brains out, because you're not going to be around long enough for them to kill you," the man told Carlyle while he was searching in the drawer for the cigarettes.

"Well, I guess you're just doing your job."

"Yeah, and I hate doing this shit, but it's a living. I don't see any cigarettes," the man reported. And, as he turned back around to face Carlyle, he was surprised to see that cigarettes weren't the only thing Randy had smuggled into his room. Randy Carlyle saw a look on the man's face that told him the obvious. He knew he was gone because he was looking down the barrel of a 38-caliber revolver handgun. And before the man could get off a round, Carlyle had ended his life with a single shot to his head. He knew that once Cruse or Johnson found out the hit-man didn't successfully complete his mission, someone else would be there to do it. He had to get out of there and the doctor wasn't going to help him do that. He couldn't bend the rules even a little for anyone. The only thing Randy Carlyle could do was to make a deal with the feds or the DEA agent that shot him. He knew that if he went to prison he would be dead in no time.

Richard Beringhm was at the front desk at Parker Center PD when Debo walked in.

"Hey, Rich," Debo said, walking up to the desk. Officer Richard Buringham was still looking tired. He was always at the desk earning his paycheck. He must have seen millions of people going and coming over the years. And, probably answered about the same amount of questions and phone calls, and gave pretty much the same amount of directions to concerned visitors, lawyers, bail bondsmen, and a whole slew of other people in other job positions that came through that door each day.

"I'm still here, up every day, I have to get my money: Bills to pay, you know. What… you want the sergeant, or did you come to see my handsome mug?"

"I guess I may as well go on ahead and get this over with," Debo said. "Mr Jackson, what exactly do you do for a living?"

"Well, Rich I'm trying to be like, Bob," Debo lied.

"Oh, you're into law enforcement?" the nosy officer asked.

He had no idea how much he wasn't into law, but they were into him for about $200,000.00 a month.

"Yeah, something like that," Debo told the officer.

"I'll check to see if he's in his office, hold on."

"Yeah, this guy must be getting tired, he's never this nosy," Debo thought to himself.

Okay, Mister Jackson, he said, 'for me to send you the hell on up', in those words.

"In those words?"

"Yes, Mr Jackson, in those words."

"Thanks, Rich," Debo said and went to the bank of elevators, and up to Billings' office.

"What's new, Bob?"

He was trying to see if Billings had heard about all the commotion in town lately. But, hell… he's the police sergeant at the main police station right in the heart of the city. Why and how wouldn't he know?

"Jackson, I'm not going to chew your ass out because I knew this was going to happen. Do you remember me asking you how many dead bodies I would have to hear of during this mess and you said, 'that you didn't want to think about it?'"

"Yeah, I do recall something to that effect," Debo said. "Something to my ass… "

"Yes, Sergeant, I remember." Debo was being serious this time. He saw that Billing was in no mood for jokes.

"They kidnapped a friend of mine and they were going to kill him. They shot him up with heroin for about a week straight. I couldn't just sit around and let them kill him. And I couldn't tell you because you guys would have spooked them and I wouldn't have gotten him back, or if I did he would have been dead," Debo explained.

"And, what about the house on Colt-Brilliant? Were we going to screw that up for you too?"

"That was personal, Bob."

"Personal hell, It's all personal, Jackson!!"

"Bob, can you check on something for me?"

"No, you have access to the whole damn database, do your own checking, hell you do your own killing."

"Oh…, that was really low, Bob."

"Yeah, you're right, I know who you're up against and you have no choice, but I'm busy, Jackson."

"Yeah, I just figured since I was here you wouldn't mind. Besides, I've been so busy I haven't had a chance to check."

"Yeah you've been busy alright, start cleaning up your own trash," Billings fussed.

"Doesn't LA city do trash? *I'm a tax-paying citizen.*"

"Jackson, do you know that the day you pay any taxes will be the day I run for president," Billing told him.

"Do you have Randy's cell phone?"

"No, property does… why?"

"I need a phone number out of it."

"Don't tell me, Cruse's, right?"

"Right… he was supposed to be at the house on Colt Brilliant this morning, but… "

Sgt Billings cut him off to say, "I don't want to hear about it."

"But a minute ago you asked me about a body count."

"That was a month ago, do you want to wait for Randy Carlyle's property or what?"

"Yeah sure, I'll wait."

"It'll probably take some time, they're probably at lunch."

"No, I'll come back, call me when you get it," Debo said.

"I want to try some of that chili, I'll meet you at the chili place and bring it to you."

"Okay, good then I won't eat anything."

"Okay, Jackson, is that all?"

"Yeah, I guess for now."

"Okay, out of my office, I've got work to get done, I do work for a living you know."

"Yeah, but you don't have to," Debo told him. "Out, Jackson, get out now!!"

"See you later, Bob," Debo said and left.

It was almost lunchtime for Billings but Debo wanted to eat now. He eats when he gets hungry. There's no telling what time the officer in charge of property would be back from lunch, but he decided to wait.

"Hi, Sweetheart," Shelly said when she answered Debo's phone call. "Hey baby, how are things with you?"

"I'm alright, just lonely as hell."

"Tell me about it," Shelly said. "Honey, I need you to go into the LAPD database and see if you can find a connection between Robert Cruse and Gregory Johnson or Raymond Anderson and Gregory Johnson. I think there is something up with them, something very serious. And look for a connection between Gregory and Sue-Lang-Yin…, the boat captain that came up dead about six or seven years ago. And, if you get too lonely give me a call."

"Okay, baby…, I will. I've been beating the dust out of Joy and I got a hold of Pauline last night. Jeffery is doing better."

"Is Joy there?"

"Yeah…"

"Let me speak to her."

"Okay, hold on a minute." Shelly put the phone down and went to get Joy. When Joy came to the phone she said,

"Hey, bra, what's up?"

"Who told Shell about Jeffery?"

"Oh that, Pauline was telling me and Shelly overheard her. I told her that some guy got stupid at his pool hall and he's taking some time off."

It's not like Debo is lying to Shelly again, he just doesn't want to upset her with details. She's going through enough as it is.

"Okay, that was quick thinking."

"Hey, bra, Shelly and I were talking and I didn't know you rode horses."

"I'm a regular, John Wayne on a horse."

"Yeah, right," Joy teased.

"You think it's funny; I'll take you and Shell out and I'll show you how to handle one of those babies."

"Yeah, I've got to see this."

"Don't trip, I'll show you."

"Here, Man.., here's your wife back," Joy said and put Shelly back on the phone.

"Okay, baby don't forget to check on that for me."

"Okay."

"Put, Joy back on for a minute, I love you, sweetheart."

"Love you too," Shelly said and handed Joy the phone. "Yeah, Bra?"

"Joy, how is Jeffery, is he healing alright?"

"Well, his arm looks bad. I don't think they cared about how they shot him up. I've seen tracks and these are sloppy."

"You're not still in front of Shell are you?"

"No, she went in her room after she handed me the phone.

But, it looks like they missed about a hundred times. He has some big ass sores and dark spots on his arm. He needs a doctor, but otherwise he's okay."

"He can't see a doctor unless I can call someone that I know I can trust to keep quiet. I'll check on it," Debo said.

"Okay, anything else, Bra?"

"No, that's it for now, tell Shell I'll call her later, I have a meeting in about forty-five-minutes. I'll talk to you later," Debo said, then hung up.

1:30 PM

"So you want to eat some good chili, huh?"

"Yeah.., I smelled it cooking the day I met you at the Crenshaw Mall," Billings said.

"Have you heard from Patch lately?" Debo asked Billings.

"Not since the shooting out in Beverly Hills. where is the chili I'm starved?" Billings asked Debo.

Debo arrived before Billings and had already ordered the food. "It should be ready anytime now."

The short, middle-aged black man who owned the Chili King got to know Debo. He always fixed him an extra special bowl with hot chili peppers. He loves his chili hot; the hotter the better. Shelly couldn't understand how he could ruin his meal by eating it too hot to enjoy.

"I got yours mild, you might be a wimp," Debo told him. "Yeah, spicy food gives me heartburn," Billings confessed. "DEBO!!! Your order is ready… just the way you like it," Milton yelled from behind the counter.

"Good, thanks, Milton." Debo took his food and walked back over to where Sgt Billings was seated.

"Hey, Debo..., if you need anything else... "

Milton was pointing to the counter stacked with cakes, cookies, pies, bottles of hot sauce, crackers, and coffee cups.

"Just let me know," he said.

"I'll get something before I leave. As a matter of fact, put a can of jalapeno peppers and some crackers on my bill, Milt."

"Okay, thanks, Debo."

"This is delicious," Billing told Debo. "Everybody I bring here says that, even Shell and she can fix some jamming chili."

Debo reached over and got the hot sauce that was sitting on the marble-top table and added some more to his chili.

"How in the hell can you eat that stuff so hot?" Billings asked and reached for a glass of water and handed it to Debo.

"Here, I know you're dying for this. Come on take it, I won't tell a soul. I really feel for you, you don't have to impress me, Jackson."

Debo accepted the glass of ice water and put the glass to his mouth like he was going to drink some, then took it away and said,

"No, I'm good..., I don't need it."

"You'll need it when you go to the bathroom, and I'd hate to be there for that one."

They finished eating and got up to leave. Debo got the bag with the jalapenos and crackers in it.

"Thanks, Milton," Debo said and he and Billings walked out the door. It was a cool and windy afternoon and the wind had blown all the pollution out of the air and was sweeping trash and leaves into the gutter. It saves the merchants the chore of sweeping. It sprinkled a bit and the ground was wet; not much, but still wet.

"Please don't track that mud in my car, Jackson," Sgt Billings said. Debo found some grass in a flowerbed to wipe his shoes on. He looked back to see if Milton was watching him tear up his flower bed but he was busy taking orders. Debo got in the on the passenger's side of Billings car, and Billings got in on the driver's side. Billings sat there for a minute to give his stomach a chance to settle.

He asked Debo to get the bag he put in the glove compartment. Debo pushed the button that released the latch holding the glove compartment closed. He felt around inside until he found the bag, then grabbed it and handed it to Sgt Billings and said, "here...,"

"I don't want it, Jackson, you do."

"Okay, thanks, soldier. How was the green yesterday?"

"It was wonderful, the only problem was I kept being interrupted by my cell phone. And you can guess what that was all about, I'm sure."

"Yeah, I'm sure I can," Debo said, feeling a bit guilty.

"Okay, Jackson, take this stuff and have it back to me by morning, I have to put it back in property."

"Will do," Debo said and opened the car door to get out. "O-uh-oh..., what was that?" Debo said.

"If you don't know, you will because you'll feel the next one." Debo had passed gas while getting out of the car.

"One of the luxuries of eating good chili," he said, and closed the door.

Billings started the car, backed out of the parking space, waved at Debo, and was headed north on Crenshaw Blvd.

Debo went to get into the Navigator and looked down at his feet. He went over to the same flower bed where he had wiped his shoes earlier before getting into Sgt Billing's car. He looked back to see if Milton was watching him and Milton was standing behind the counter rubbing his index and middle fingers against his thumb beckoning... "Pay me." Debo laughed waved at Milton, then got in the Navigator, and left.

3:00 PM

Maureen Morris arrived home and listened to her messages. "You have two messages," the machine announced.

Maureen didn't like using cell phones since they are said to cause cancer. She sticks to the conventional phones. (First message):

"Hey, Mama Morris, this is Mabel Washington at the Bingo Hall. Are you coming this Wednesday? If not, there is a member that would like your seat. Call back and let us know as soon as you get this message." (Next message): Hello, Mama Morris, this is Randy, I need a favor. I'm in the hospital and I just wanted to ask you if you could call a number for me and ask to speak to Roy. I can't get to a phone."

Randy Carlyle didn't want to chance anybody seeing him out in the hall so he didn't ask the nurse to roll him out there to use the phone. Now he's facing murder charges. There are round-the-clock police guarding his room. And, since he's cooperating with the feds as a material witness for the FBI, he's pretty sure that Cruse and his men will get to him. All the police in the world couldn't save him now. Maureen Morris knew what Jonny and Randy were into, and wasn't surprised that he was in the hospital. Nor was she surprised to learn that Johnny was dead. All she could do was pray for them.

"Call who?" she asked, aloud; really talking to no one.

She pressed rewind to listen to the message again and heard the caller say…,

"Call, Roy and have him call some friend of his to come get him out of this hospital. They're trying to kill me Please, Mama Morris. Do it right away, I'm at County Hospital!!"

The phone beeped to let the caller or the listener know that the maximum time allotted for the message had expired.

Nurse Brown walked into Carlyle's room and told him that he had to give her back her cell phone, and that she might have an important call from her daughter or someone. She really wasn't comfortable with Randy Carlyle using her phone, but he begged her and she knew he was in some sort of trouble. After he had asked to call his mother, she couldn't refuse him because she has children of her own. They're grown but to her they are still her babies, and whatever they need she's there to help or listen to their problems. Nurse Margret Brown is a devout Christian and believes in helping people that either can't or won't help themselves. She sees lots of cancer patients every day, and she gives her tithe in church regularly which she believes also helps dying patients. Her blessings comes from God and she blesses others with what God gives, or whatever she can do to help someone she does it. She felt bad because the man that was shot in Carlyle's room stopped at the desk while she was checking charts and asked about him. She told him she couldn't give out the kind of information he was asking for. Then he asked for visitation information. She turned around to get a hospital visitation schedule which had information on visiting hours, dropping off and picking up patients, and certain items that visitors can or cannot bring to patients while visiting. That split second was all it took for him to get one of the charts. The particular chart he took just happened to belong to Randy Carlyle. Nurse Brown turned around to hand the man the information, and was surprised to find him gone. A few minutes later she heard a gunshot coming from Randy's room. The police were called and Randy was moved again. This time not at his own request. It was at the request of the Los Angeles County Sheriff's Department. Randy Carlyle is being held for voluntary manslaughter and was moved to a room in the hospital jail ward. Now he's in trouble with the police, Mad-C and Debo, Cruse, and Johnson. The police want him for the crimes he's committed, Gregory Johnson or Robert Cruse want to kill him, Debo and Mad-C just want to talk to him… maybe kill him.

MONDAY, NOVEMBER 19TH, 5:00 PM

Debo got to his office and took Randy Carlyle's cell phone out of the bag and turned it on and it came to life. He pressed the button and "Please enter Your Pin" was displayed.

"This dumb mothafucka got a damn lock on his phone and I can't get in it. I know Billings' people checked the damn thing.

He could have told me this shit. I guess he couldn't give me the phone book without the phone. Well, I'll check the wallet; see what we get," he thought to himself.

He took the wallet out of the clear plastic bag and checked it.

"The fact that he has a lock on his phone means he wasn't such a dumb mothafucka after all, huh?" Mad-C concluded.

He searched every nook and cranny and still came up bone dry; no phone number on Cruse. A picture attracted Debo's attention. It was a picture of a woman; a short dark-skinned woman with dark hair. She looked to be about 50-55. He knew her face from someplace. He turned the picture over to see if there was a name or date on it, and there was a date… 6/04…

June 2004, the summer of 2004. He looked at the background and the scenery was unfamiliar so he didn't see anything recognizable. He had to put the picture back in the wallet because everything in the wallet and the wallet itself is recorded as evidence. He stared at the picture for the longest time to lock the image of the woman's face in his mind. He knew the person, there was no doubt about it. He showed the picture to Mad-C.

"Hey, Mad-C… Does the person in this picture look familiar to you, like you've seen her someplace before… I mean recently?"

Mad-C took the picture from Debo and looked at it, then gave it back and said,

"No, why.., do you think you know her from somewhere?"

"Yeah, I'm sure I do."

Debo was wondering who the lady in the picture could be when his cell phone rang. His caller ID told him that the caller was Dick Patch. He answered his phone as if he was glad or surprised to hear from him.

"Hey, where have you been hiding?"

"Jackson, I do work for a living, you know."

"Patch…, why does everybody keep telling me that?"

"Well, maybe because everybody works for a living but you. Try it some time, then you can say it to the next man you meet that doesn't work for a living," Patch answered.

"Oh…, that's funny, Patch, what do you need?"

"I need to talk to you soon."

"How soon?"

"Like the day before yesterday."

"Okay, meet me on Robertson and Olympic, southwest corner."

"Okay, I'll be there in forty-five minutes," Patch promised.

The southwest corner of Robertson and Olympic was an empty lot. Debo's office is right down the street so he decided to walk. He didn't really care who saw him at this point. He had CRAZY with him and had the 45-automatic ready to go into action if need be. There was a bus stop in front of the lot. Debo sat down on the fiber-glass bench that was put there for the convenience of the commuters who wished to wait on public transportation.

It was a nice crisp day; Debo was wearing a light-blue turtleneck sweater, baby blue jeans, and a pair of Nike tennis shoes, with his usual black leather jacket. He was thinking about the picture..., and then it hit him. The woman in the picture was Maureen Morris; Jonny Morris' mother.

"But, what the hell was Randy Carlyle doing with a picture of Johnny Morris' mother in his wallet? I'll have to look into it later," Debo thought aloud.

Dick Patch broke Debo's concentration when he walked up and sat down beside him on the bench. Patch is DEA, but he dressed in dark brown pants and a sweater with a long winter coat to match.

"Kinda stylish," Debo thought. You couldn't tell he was wearing his service weapon. "Nice weather we're having today," Debo said starting the conversation.

"It's not the way I like it, I'm freezing, where are you parked?"

"Patch you know where..., at my office. Why should I drive down here?"

"Oh yeah, I forgot you work. Let's go to my car," Patch suggested. Debo knew that Mad-C was at the office and didn't want to see anyone at this time. He knows that when certain people get into a bind, they tend to run their mouths. Joy's meeting him was accidental, but for some reason Patch trusted her. Maybe it's because she and Debo are so close. The car that Patch drove was parked at a gas station about fifty feet from where they were sitting. They both got up and walked across the lot behind them. They felt the crunch of rocks under their feet, which made a noise with every step they took. They arrived at Patch's car and they both got in.

"Jackson, do me a favor."

"Yeah, Patch…, what is it?"

"Get out and look at the front of my car."

Debo breathed a sigh of irritation and got out, walked to the front of the car and looked at it.

"Okay, now what!!!" he yelled.

Patch flipped a switch and Debo saw a red light on the left side of the front grill of the car, and a blue light on the right side.

"What are you showing me, Christmas?" Debo asked. "No, do you remember my blue light was out and I… "

"Yeah, Patch, what was so important? You didn't get me out here for this, did you?"

"No, that's not what was important."

"I hope not."

"What I got you out here to tell you is that there are some pretty big guys asking questions about you and Write. They say 'you know who they are'."

"When did they get in town?"

"About three days ago."

"Yeah, that's about the time Mr Write paid Johnson a visit. And he wasn't very happy when he left.

"Yeah, what did he say to him?"

"He told him he knows he's selling drugs, and that he and Carlyle are also involved in murder and organized crime."

"Yeah, he said a mouthful, didn't he? That gives him a pretty good reason to wanna shut you and Write up. If it got to our ears, it's pretty deep shit."

"Yeah, I guess it's all pretty deep shit, Patch."

"He's big, Jackson…, very big. You be extremely careful. I'll keep an eye out, and I'll also keep my informant's eyes and ears sharp. How did Carlyle make out?"

"He's alive, but if he works for Johnson or Cruse he won't be for long, because he gave us Cruse's whereabouts and I know he called and warned him that we would be paying him a visit."

MURDER AND MONEY

"I was told that some guy was killed in his hospital room, it wasn't Carlyle was it?"

Debo just told the man that Carlyle was still alive.

"No, Patch…, it was someone that went there to hit Carlyle, and it wasn't, Cruse."

"Okay, Jackson, be careful, we'll do what we can to find out more about these guys."

"Okay, Patch…, thanks."

"No problem."

"Talk to you later," Debo said, ending their meeting.

"Was there an ID or driver's license in the wallet?" Mad-C asked Debo. "Yeah, but the only address on it is the one on Ardmore."

"Okay, we'll have to pull Cruse to us."

"WAIT!!" We still have the realty agency We can check with them as soon as they open tomorrow. If we can get an address on Carlyle, then we can search his place and see if we can find something else on, him."

"We already hit both of his places."

"Yeah, but he's going to need someplace to run to and hide," Debo said ."Yeah, I guess you're right," Mad-C admitted.

"I know what wouldn't be a bad idea," Debo offered.

"What's that?"

"Have Freddy watch place for a couple of days… say maybe a week or so to see if Cruse shows up. Carlyle is out of action and Cruse will have to handle the business himself. So, he's bound to show up if it's his place," Debo suggested.

"That sounds like a good idea, it could work," Mad-C said. "It will work," Debo assured him.

They went to the house on Colt Brilliant to see if they could get in, but the police had boarded it up since it was considered a crime scene. The FBI and the DEA, (Patch's boys) had confiscated the house because it was believed to have been bought with money from the sales of drugs and organized crime. After they finish with it, the house and everything in it, it will be auctioned off by the landowner. Debo and Mad-C couldn't go inside the house it was too risky. Five people were killed on that property, so they sealed it up tighter than a drum. To be found looking around a crime scene investigation where five murders took place would probably mean looking at some extensive jail time. Agent Dick Patch couldn't even get them in there, and DEA is one of the law enforcement agencies investigating the crime. Dick Patch already feels he knows who is responsible for the murders. Better yet, he knows. He purposely didn't tell this to Debo earlier when they met on Olympic and Robertson. But he figures Debo and his people had a lot to do with it. That's one of the reasons he warned Debo and told him to be careful.

Freddy said, 'that he didn't mind going over and watching the club on Gage for a few days to see if he can catch Cruse going in and out.'

9:30 PM

It was cold outside to Freddy, but then Freddy is always cold. He can't stand the winter because it gets too cold and he hates the summer because it gets too hot.

That's one of the reasons he never really worked a 9-5 job. He liked working for Debo because it allowed him the opportunity to sit at home and stay warm in the winter, and sit under his air conditioner in the summer. All he had to do was check his money and leave.

He was doing fine now because it was warm in the car. He parked across the street on the side of a trailer park so he doesn't look too obvious. Even in the cold winter weather women dress in shorts, short skirts, or dresses with stockings; not only to go to the club but every day. You'd think their legs would be freezing. Maybe they are, but you can't be cute and sexy unless you look cute and sexy. And as far as clubbing, CUTE is the norm.

The Happy Hour Nightclub, Bar, and Grill was busy and packed. There were some beautiful ladies and handsome men coming and going. Some were drunk, and some were on their way to being drunk. One man was arguing with a woman who seemed to be his date or his wife. The argument suddenly turned real ugly real fast and a customer or a bouncer at the club stepped in and resolved the issue by smashing the guy in the mouth. Freddy had come to the conclusion that the bouncer was obviously security. He made the man leave and let the woman stay.

There were no further incidents from the man at that point. This is usually the case when someone is doing something wrong, either the woman or the man. In this case it looked like the woman.

There was no sign of Cruse. Freddy wasn't with Debo, Mad-C, and Joy the night they visited the place. He was thinking about going into the club and mingling to see if he could hear anything in the air. Debo told him to watch the place he didn't say for him not to go in. He thought about it and figured, "What the hell, they wouldn't know him from Adam.

He stepped out of the car wearing the same big winter coat and gloves he wore to Pauline's house the night he met Debo there. He looked so big that the bouncer would have a hard time bouncing him out of the place. It's a good place to relax and unwind. He ate, danced, and drank plenty of ginger-ale. He didn't drink any liquor because he was on duty. Eleven o'clock at night and the club was just starting to jump. People were partying like mad and no one seemed to be tired. Maybe this is how they spend their life or their evenings. If they had jobs they'd be at home on a Monday night trying to get ready to get up and go to work the next day. Maybe some of them leave work early and party at night. Whatever the case, Freddy was having a ball.

His fun came to an end, and work kicked in when he saw what seemed to be a large transaction of some kind going down. Two men had walked into the place and sat at a table across from the bar where two other men were already sitting.

Freddy saw one of the men that came in, hand the other man that was already sitting at the table an envelope. The man accepted it and handed the other guy a briefcase. The man that had walked in stood up, shook hands with the other man, and both men walked back out the door they came in. One of the men left sitting at the table got up and went to the back., no doubt watching his friend's back. Freddy couldn't follow him to see where he was going, but he made a mental note to check it out later, or the next time he visits the place.

"Hi, honey," Shelly said when she answered Debo's call. "Hey… how's my girl?"

"I'm good, baby, I have something for you, I had to dig deep. These people have other law enforcement agencies databases that you can tap into on this thing if you know how."

"Okay, sweetheart, whatcha got for me?"

"Well, I found out that Gregory and Raymond are brothers, and…"

"Well, I'll be damn," Debo interrupted.

"Hold on that's not all, there's more. They don't have the same father but they do have the same mother. Both mother and father are deceased, and Johnson's father. He owned a steel mill and Anderson's father was an entertainer. He used to sing and play drums for some band years ago: A band called the MOB (Men Of The Brotherhood), until Anderson (aka) Robert Cruse started selling drugs and hanging out with known gang members."

"Yeah, that has been his whole life. I figured there was something between them. I'm willing to bet anything that Anderson and Johnson pulled the Yin job together, also."

"Hold it… there's more: He got a job on a fishing boat at the age of seventeen, and just like you said, 'Sue-Lang-Yin was the captain who employed him.' They shipped exotic fish from country to country all year round. Anderson's mom and dad died in 1995. Cancer killed his mother; I don't know what killed his father. But when their mother passed, Johnson and Anderson aka Cruse got together and hooked up their little scheme to rip Yin off," Shelly finished.

"You did a wonderful job, baby… Just wonderful. Thank you my darling. How are things going? I mean, are you going places, doing anything?"

"There's not many places to go, I'll be fine baby, and I love you," Shelly said.

"I love you too, we're getting close baby, it'll all be over soon and we can go back to our lives," Debo promised.

"I can't wait," Shelly said. They talked for a while longer, blew kisses over the phone, and hung up.

"I knew that Mad-C and I would have to go see Johnson again. He might not want to see us, but he'll have no choice. We are with some pretty powerful people, and we could bluff our way in if we have to. There must be a way to get a hold of Johnson's address," Debo thought and called Shelly back.

"Wow, you are lonely, aren't you?" she said.

"Baby, Johnson owns some stock, probably in the yacht club. Can you check with the IRS and see what comes up. Check the Department of Business Owners or any franchise or someplace, any place. I need an address on, Johnson."

"That sounds federal, but I'll see what I can get," Shelly said. "Okay, baby, and I'll check with Patch maybe he can get one of his FBI friends to help. The man lives somewhere, and somebody has an address on him."

"Okay, I'll do what I can," Shelly assured him.

Debo call Patch to see if he could help find an address on Johnson. He opened his cell phone and dialed agent Patch's number.

"How are you, Mister Jackson?"

"Hey, Patch…, I need another favor."

"Sure, I'm full of favors. What can I do for you, Jackson?"

"Is there any way you can get your federal friends or IRS, or somebody to find an address on, Johnson; either Gregory Johnson or Gilbert Johnson? I need a home address."

"You know, Jackson, I was looking into that just before you called, because of the guys I told you about. They're the ones that are asking questions about you and Write. The agency's brass believes Johnson sent for those guys. So, if we find anything, I'll let you know."

"Thanks, Patch, how is hungry doing?"

"Agent Rayass is doing well, in fact it was him that suggested we check on Johnson. We never could come up with a permanent place of residence on him, but that was some time ago. We're checking now for updated data from our state of the art Source Of Information bank."

"Well speak English man, you sound like a fed or something."

"I am a fed or something, and I'll also check or have agent Rayass look into it also. Good enough English for a 'Fed', Mister Jackson?"

"Call me when you get something, Patch," Debo said.

CHAPTER 16

TUESDAY, NOVEMBER 20TH, 8:00 A.M.

Randy Carlyle is desperate; he has to try whatever he can to get out of the hospital jail-ward. He would have been able to depend on Johnny Morris; his best friend to get him out. Jonny would have done just about anything Carlyle asked of him. The funeral was quiet Sunday; not many people attended. Randy Carlyle helped Maureen Morris pay for the whole thing. Maureen Morris had taken out life insurance on Johnny Morris when he joined a gang. She instinctively knew that gang life would take him away from her. And, now the man that has Randy Carlyle, is the same one that put Jonny in his grave and is out to put Randy in his grave as well.

8:30 AM

Mr Carlyle you have a visitor," the Sergeant told Randy.

Randy's bed was wheeled to a room where only he his visitors are allowed to visit, but there were County Sheriff Deputies monitoring his visits through acrylic glass. Roy was searched for weapons and illegal contraband before he was admitted into the visiting room that Carlyle was in.

"What the hell did you do now?" Roy asked Carlyle. "You have to get me out of here," Randy Carlyle urged.

"How.., this is a jail ward and there are police out there with guns, and they are real guns."

"Roy, I'll make it worth your while."

"It won't be worth a damn thing if I'm dead or in here with you. I don't know, Randy man!"

"How does a hundred grand sound to you?"

"A hundred grand sounds like you can keep your ass in here."

"I'll give you a quarter of a million dollars... just please get me the hell out of here tonight," Randy Carlyle pleaded.

"Damn... now you're talking, but can I trust you?"

"Roy, I've got the money, what are you worried about?"

"No, Randy..., that's not what I'm worried about. Getting mine is what I'm worried about."

"You'll get your money," Randy Carlyle assured him.

He called Roy because Randy and Roy pulled off an armored car job a long time ago; around the time Randy Carlyle met Jonny Morris. Jonny and Roy were good friends, but Roy started spending too much money too fast and too often, then goes and brag about his success as an armored car stick-up artist. The feds got wind of it from someone that didn't care much for Roy. He did eleven years in federal prison, but no one was hurt or killed so they went easy on him.

"Okay, I'll do what I can, you won't hear from me, just be ready to go tonight," Roy told him.

Randy Carlyle is scheduled to appear in federal court on December eighteenth; one week before Christmas, for voluntary manslaughter and attempted murder of a federal officer. If convicted on both counts, he could be looking at twenty-five years to life in prison. He could get a lighter sentence, because the hit-man entered his room with the intent to kill him. Randy documented the fact that his life was threatened and someone was trying to kill him. He'll most likely end up with twenty-five years in state prison if he doesn't end up dead first.

9:45 AM

Freddy called Debo at almost 10:00 am to tell him how everything went last night at the Club. He didn't leave until 4:00 this morning, but he had a ball. He met a woman that was cute, single, lonely, and horny. She had been going to the Happy Hour Nightclub, Bar, and Grill for many years. He needed Misty because she could tell him a lot about what goes on at the club and possibly who owns it.

"Hi.., I'm Freddy, and your name; miss beautiful?"

"They call me Chocolate," the woman said.

"Oh, I see... Sweet Chocolate, the name certainly matches the face and the body. You are one beautiful lady."

Beautiful she is..., she's a deep dark chocolate with dark-black eyes and jet-black hair down to her waist. She's as soft as silk and not a mark on her. Her teeth were pearly white, and she smelled of course, like chocolate.

"What is that you're wearing, soap or body-oil?" Freddy asked. "It's scented oil, I had it made special. It's called 'Chocolate.'"

"How long have you been coming here, Chocolate?"

He looked at her glass and noticed that it was empty. He looked around for the cocktail waitress and spotted her two tables down with a tray in her arms taking people's orders. Freddy waved at the lady.

"May I help you?" she asked. She was stunning, with long pretty legs, and a lovely smile.

"I'll have a Coke and whatever the lady is drinking."

The cocktail waitress knows Chocolate and what she drinks. She was used to Chocolate having different men buy her drinks, but only for conversation..., nothing else, just talk.

"I've been coming here for about five-years now."

"Good, then she should know who the owner of the place might be. Freddy thought to himself.

"Do you use cocaine?" Freddy asked.

"I snort from time to time but I drink mostly. Let's talk about you," she suggested.

"Well, I'm single, rich, and as you can see; handsome."

"That's a mouth full," Misty aka Chocolate said.

"Do you know something, this is a beautiful place I would buy it in a heartbeat if it was for sale," Freddy said, trying to get her to open up about who owns the place.

"Well you can forget about that," Misty told him.

"Why do you say that?"

"Because, RC just bought the place three years ago, and I doubt that he'll sell it."

"Yeah.., well I still like it," Freddy said.

At that time the cocktail waitress came over with their drinks and whispered something in Chocolate's ear and sat the drinks down.

"Excuse me for a minute, I have to use the lady's room," Chocolate said, as she got out of her seat.

Freddy stood up and went around to her chair and pulled it back for her. "Thank you, Freddy..., be right back," Chocolate said.

Freddy saw her go through the same door that the man with the envelope went through, and just like him she just disappeared into the darkness. There was a long drape or curtain hanging there that Freddy couldn't see past. Just a light that came from under the curtain after she walked behind it, witch told Freddy that there was a door behind the curtain. The light he saw the first time he went there under the curtain when Chocolate walked back there was gone. He waited for about twenty-minutes and Chocolate didn't return.

"Excuse me, Miss," he said, grabbing the cocktail waitress lightly by her arm.

"Yes, what is it, Sir?"

"Can you tell me where Chocolate went?"

"She went out the back," the waitress told Freddy.

He had a good mind to take the 357-Magnum and go back there to see what was really going on, but that's not what he's there for. He could be blowing his cover for nothing; it could be just a jealous lover.

"Thank you," he said, and put a $20 bill on the table for the drinks and her tip and walked out.

"So, you think that RC stands for, Robert Cruse?" Freddy asked Debo.

"Well, we have Carlyle, and we can damn sure ask him."

"But, that doesn't mean he's going to tell us anything," Freddy said. "I'll bet you $100 to your $1 that Robert Cruse owns that place. And I'm also willing to bet that Johnson bought it for him so he could move drugs easily," Debo assumed.

He thanked Freddy and told him what a good job he was doing and hung up. He called Shelly to see what she had and Joy answered the phone.

"What's up, Bra?"

"Hey, Sis.., put Shell on, please."

"She's in the shower, is there anything I can tell her?"

"Yeah, have her check to see who owns the Happy Hours Night Club on Gage, the one we went to. You know the address don't you?"

"The one I damned near got killed at?"

"Yeah, that's the one."

"Okay, Big Bra, is there anything else? How are you holding out, D-Angelo?" Joy sounded worried about Debo.

"No, that's it for now, and I'm doing fine, sweetheart. Just keep an eye on my girl for me, okay?"

"You know I will."

"How is Jeffery coming along?"

"He was doing a lot better last night when I saw him at Freddy's room. I went to check on him because Freddy told me that he had to go over on Gage to the Club. Pauline and I got you, Bra."

"I was just on the phone with Freddy. If something was wrong, he would have told me. Pauline is still there?"

"Yeah, she said, 'that she's going home tomorrow.'"

"Okay, have Shell check on that and call me back."

"Okay, Bra," Joy said, and they hung up.

Debo called Freddy back. "Sorry, were you done?" Debo asked. "That's okay boss, as a matter of fact, no that's not all. I saw a drug transaction go down.., a pretty big one. And the girl I was telling you about; Chocolate… they went through the same door she did."

"Yeah, it's probably the office," Debo assumed.

"Something else seemed odd. When the cocktail waitress brought our drinks, she whispered something in, Chocolate's ear and…"

"Yeah, you told me. They have cameras in that place. I don't know if I should send you back there alone, they could be on to you. That's probably the reason they pulled the girl away from you. Just hold on for a couple of days. I'll see what Shell comes up with and call you, okay?"

"Okay, boss, let me know if you need anything else."

"Okay, Freddy, I will, you did a good job. At least we know that someone at that club whether they own it or just work there, is on our shit list. Good night, Freddy."

"Good night, Boss."

* * *

Randy Carlyle was wondering if Roy could pull this off. He was in a special room because of his condition. It might be hard for Roy to pull this off. Debo and Mad-C had to talk to Randy Carlyle, only this time without their guns. That was the whole idea of having him put in a special room before, because they could get their weapons in. Now, by him being held in the jail-ward, they couldn't take in any weapons of any kind.

"I'm here to see, Randy Carlyle," Mad-C told Nurse Brown.

"I'm sorry, but I'm not allowed to let anyone in the jail-ward. I'll have to summon an officer to assist you, Mr…"

"Write…, Charles Write," Mad-C said. "Hold on for a minute, will you please, Mister Write?"

The woman picked up a phone and softly spoke into it, and about two minutes later a sheriff's department sergeant came walking down the hall toward Mad-C, Debo, and Nurse Brown.

"Good afternoon everyone, I'm Sergeant Ansell, Can I help you, gentlemen?"

"Sergeant Ansell, my name is Mr Write and this is my associate, Mr Jackson. We are here to visit with Mister Carlyle. I believe he's in the county jail-ward."

"Yes he is, but you'll have to fill out some forms and leave your driver's license at the front desk. Visiting is only twenty minutes."

"That will be just fine, Sergeant, thank you," Mad-C said.

After they both completed the forms and left their drivers' licenses, they were admitted in to see Carlyle.

"Hey, stranger… remember me?" Mad-C asked.

"Yeah, I remember you, you don't have that piece of shit gun with you now," Randy Carlyle told him.

"Are you sure?" Mad-C asked. "They don't allow them in here."

"Well, I can still piss," Debo said.

"Let me make you a deal you can't and better not refuse. All I want are Cruse and Johnson. They're after your black-ass anyway. And the longer you bullshit the closer your buddies get to killing you, which personally I don't give a shit. But I need them out of my way so I can continue with my life. If we eliminate those two all you have to worry about is what the police will do to you, I don't need you, you're just a piece of shit patsy, you're no good to me, and I'm sure that after you get out of prison you'll be glad we moved Johnson and Cruse out of your way. Now, how does that sound? Look at it as us being on your side. We need him, we want him, and if we don't get him before he gets to you, then tough shit. But, however…, if you tell us how we can get hold of an address on Cruse and Johnson, then bam!!! Your worries are over. They've already sent one of their messengers here for you once and you got lucky. They're trying to kill you… plain and simple. You had better get them before they get you; where are they?" Mad-C finished.

"Yeah, luck runs out, Randy. Where does Gregory Johnson live?" Debo asked.

"I don't know exactly," Carlyle said out of fear and damned good sense. "What the hell does that mean?"

"It means that I've only been out there once and I wasn't paying any attention to the road. I was busy talking to Robert."

"Yeah… and probably drunk as hell too," Debo commented.

"Are we talking, town, city, or valley?" Mad-C asked.

"It was hot as hell; The valley, San Gabriel Valley somewhere."

"Was it a house?"

"Yes."

"What about a phone number?" Mad-C asked. "I don't know his phone number," Carlyle said.

"Who owns that Club on Gage in Los Angeles?" Debo asked.

"Gregory Johnson owns it, but he put it in Robert's name," Carlyle said, thinking that he has nothing to lose.

Mad-C was right, they are trying to kill Randy. And if Debo and Mad-C could stop them, he has a chance to live .He was also thinking that Roy might not be able to get him out of there tonight or any other night. And, if he did, he would have to hide. And if he breaks out Johnson and Cruse will hear about it and that'll make him an easy target. Randy Carlyle was sure he was doing the right thing confessing to Mad-C and Debo. Their visit was interrupted by Sgt. Ansell.

"Your visit is over fellas, times up!"

Mad-C heard a buzzer, which confirmed that their twenty-minutes were up.

11:30 AM

Debo and Mad-C are at the office discussing the events of the day. "Well, well… So, Mr Johnson does own the Happy Hours Night Club?" Debo confirmed.

He wasn't surprised, just satisfied to have that information.

"Now we're getting someplace, we can really rattle his cage. Freddy said, 'that he saw a big drug deal go down in the club', and they tried to rob Joy at the same club. And that girl, Chocolate… the one that Freddy met told him that someone with the initials 'RC,' either wouldn't or couldn't sell the place because it was just bought," Mad-C said. "Things are beginning to add up," Debo added.

"Do you think we should pay our boy Johnson a visit?" Mad-C asked. "No, not now, I've got Shell checking on something for me. Let me see what she comes up with, it might just prove that Carlyle's story is true, or show he was lying his ass off."

"The man's damn near dead, lying to us won't do him any good. Telling us the truth is about the only way for him to stay alive."

Mad-C had a very good point. If they got to Cruse and Johnson before Cruse and Johnson got to Randy, the least of Randy's problems are solved.

Debo called Shelly to see if she had anything for him.

"Hi, Sweetheart.., how's your morning going? Not as busy as mine I hope."

"Well, as a matter of fact, it was kinda busy. I've been on the computer half the morning checking on the information you wanted. The club on Gage is owned by Gregory Johnson; Could be your guy. He also owns a yacht, a jet, a helicopter, and a ranch in San Gabriel Valley… 45,000 acres, and five horses. This man is filthy rich," Shelly concluded.

"Yeah, tell me about it."

Debo already knew that Gregory Johnson is a rich and powerful man. Otherwise, he wouldn't have any cause to get in Mad-C's way. After all, Mad-C is also a very rich and powerful man.

"I have an address to the ranch, it's 11001 Oak-pine Lane, and it's in San Gabriel, California."

"Thank you, sweetheart, you're better than the best!!"

"Well, because I married the best, do you think it could be rubbing off?"

"Flattery will get you everywhere."

"So, you're flattered?"

"Very…, stay beautiful, and I'll keep you up all night tonight, okay?" He keeps her up until 3:00 in the morning, and sometimes until daybreak. But, at least she knows that he's alright, especially when she's on the phone with him all night.

"I'll be looking forward to it. So, aren't you going to reward me for the information?"

"Whatever your heart desires my love."

"A kiss would be wonderful, Mr Jackson."

"Then, a kiss it is." He threw her a kiss and his love and she did the same and they hung up.

3:15 PM

The day is nearly over and there has been good news so far. Debo's cell phone rang and he let it ring; hoping it was more good news. He answered it on the fifth ring.

"I was afraid you weren't going to answer," Agent Dick Patch said when Debo answered the phone.

Patch had called to give Debo the information he had on Gregory Johnson. He told him the same things Shelly did, except for one small thing; Gregory Johnson is after a lot of money.

"Is that it?"

"That's it."

"Hell, a lot of mothafuckas are after a lot of money, what the hell good is that going to do me?"

"I just thought maybe it would help."

"Yeah.., you've been a real big help, Patch, thanks a lot."

Shelly told Debo, 'that these people have other law enforcement agencies that you can tap into.' She must have managed to get into the DEA database, because she gave him the same information that Dick Patch just did.

WEDNESDAY, NOVEMBER 21ST, 1:00 AM

Roy had walked into the county hospital with twenty-four sticks of dynamite strapped to his chest. He was waving what appeared to be a television remote control in one hand, and an automatic handgun in the other. Nurse Brown immediately called for Sergeant Ansell.

"I want Randy Carlyle out of here right now… and I'm not going to keep saying it… and I'm not going to wait all day for negotiators and all that bullshit. So, 'DON'T' waste my time."

"What's your name, sir?" Nurse Margaret Brown asked.

"I said I don't have time for bullshit. Let me show you that I mean business," Roy said.

He was about to press one of the buttons on the device in his hand, when Nurse Brown spoke up and said,

"Okay-okay..., please don't. Sergeant Ansell is here now, he's the only one you need to speak with."

Roy turned around to see a muscular man with graying sideburns, wearing a gray two-piece suit, with black leather shoes and no tie. He had already pulled his service weapon from its holster and saw that Roy had a weapon also.

"Now take it easy: What seems to be the problem? I remember you, you, weren't you just here yesterday? Sure..., you came to visit Mister Carlyle. What is it you want?" the sergeant asked.

Nurse Brown had faded into the background. She went to her desk to look for the sign-in sheet from yesterday's visits and saw where Roy had come to visit Randy: It was 8:30 am, Tuesday morning.

"The problem is you're not hearing me. I said DON'T FUCKIN PLAY WITH ME or I'll blow this mothafucka up right now."

"Sir, we have patients in this hospital, and if you... "Roy cut the sergeant off in mid-sentence...,

"Well, say goodbye to all those mothafuckas, because you've wasted too much time already. You're gonna be patients right the fuck now. Say good night, assholes!" Roy said as he put his thumb on the red button of the remote device.

"Alright... Alright!!!"

"Go get the patient and move him to the roof," Roy ordered. The only patient he was interested in was Randy Carlyle.

"But we don't have elevator access to the roof," the sergeant told him. "Look, sergeant... whatever the fuck your name is... you have two minutes," Roy told him, then pushed a button on the device.

Everyone got down on the floor thinking Roy had detonated the dynamite. But instead, he sent a signal to a friend of his.

"What in the hell is that?" Sergeant Ansell asked, looking toward the ceiling "That's telling you that your time is up. Get him to the roof, now," Roy ordered.

The sergeant had his men roll Randy Carlyle's bed down the hall to the freight elevator. Roy had long ago taken Sergeant Ansell's firearm. "Okay, Sergeant, let's go, I need some security," Roy told him.

"Roy, Sergeant Ansell, and Randy Carlyle were the only ones on the elevator headed for the roof. Roy knew about freight elevators. He made a special point to make sure Randy's bed could be moved to the roof with no problems. The three got to the roof and the elevator doors opened Sgt. Ansell realized what he had heard downstairs. There was a helicopter on the roof of the hospital: When Roy pushed the red button on the remote device he signaled the pilot to get in position. When the Sergeant got the call from Nurse Brown that Roy was there waving a gun and wired with explosives, he called for back-up. But the deputies on the ground didn't know about the helicopter.

They assumed it belonged to the hospital to be used for air-lifting patients. Once they were aboard the helicopter, Roy told the sergeant to get on his radio and order the ground units to stand down and let the helicopter go. If he didn't comply it would be blown up with everyone aboard; especially him. No one knew that Gregory Johnson had men watching Carlyle and they saw everything that was going on from the roof across the street a few yards away. The sergeant did as Roy ordered him to and told his men to stand down, but to hold their positions. The helicopter lifted off the roof and was airborne.

"We did it!!" Roy told Randy.

Roy had also used dynamite on some of the armored car robberies, so this was nothing new to him. He does this kind of thing for the thrill of it and brags about it. But, this one wasn't for thrills, Roy was broke and needed the money.

"Yeah we did it, Roy..., I knew you could. What do you wanna do with the cop?" Randy asked.

"Let him go, I'm not going to kill a man unless I have to, and I don't see anything telling me that I have to," Roy told Randy.

At that moment they felt a jolt, then they felt the helicopter doing a nosedive. It started whirling around in circles, soaring further to the ground.

Sgt Ansell looked at the pilot sitting there dead, and yelled, "I told those idiots not to shoot!!!"

"SHOOT!!! Who the hell shot at us!!!" Roy screamed.

No one aboard the aircraft knew how to fly except the pilot."Oh, shit!!!" Roy screamed.

"Shit!!!" Randy yelled, and before they knew what happened the helicopter crashed into the side of the hospital and bounced off, losing its propeller. It came out of the nosedive and crashed into the ground. The helicopter fuel ignited and the aircraft burst into flames and black smoke. The dynamite that Roy was wearing was not live. Everyone aboard the helicopter died in the crash, including Los Angeles County Sheriff's Sergeant Mark Ansell.

"Stand back everybody: Okay, you guys, get a few hoses in there and get those people back!!!" the lieutenant in charge ordered.

Marlin Gravel is kind of chubby, with a full head of blonde hair He wore bifocals and walked with a walking cane after suffering an old war injury. He always chewed gum. Smoking was never his thing and he didn't care that much for being around people who smoked cigarettes, cigars, pipes, anything.

"Lieutenant!!! Lieutenant!!!" a news reporter yelled over the noise and commotion at the scene.

"Not now, wait in line with everybody else," the lieutenant said.

"Didn't Sergeant Ansell tell his men not to shoot at the helicopter? Why did they shoot at it, knowing that he was on board? Can you explain that, lieutenant?" the news reporter asked.

"I said to wait until I can answer your questions. If you can't do that, I'll have to arrest you for obstruction of justice. Now move and let me do my job!!! Get me some more hoses in here someone. And..,"

Before he could get the words out, the helicopter exploded again, sending pieces of hot metal and charred body parts flying into the air and falling to the ground.

"Cord off a parameter and get everyone behind it."

Gregory Johnson's men hit their target and kept Randy Carlyle from testifying about what he knows of Gregory Johnson's operation, including

Robert Cruse, the Morris and Jones killings, also organized crime, and drugs sells that he, Cruse, and Johnson were involved in. They made it look like one of the deputies shot the pilot and brought the helicopter down.

Nurse Margret Brown had decided to go to work at a convalescent hospital, at least the dangers were considerably minimal. This way she had a better chance of seeing her retirement. She had already put in enough years to have retired, but she didn't want to just sit around the house and get older. So, she took her credentials, resume, and her job references to one of the local nursing homes where she eventually became head nurse. Her daughter and son convinced her to make the job change. No more long hours, just something to keep her busy. She loved working with and helping the patients; people in general.

WEDNESDAY, NOVEMBER 21ST, 7:30 AM

Mad-C was up early in the workout room of the office while Debo was still asleep. Mad-C went into his sleeping quarters and shook him awake.

"Yeah... what is it? What time is it?"

"Seven-thirty."

"In the morning: What... you've got a lead on something?"

"No, the phone is for you, is your cell off?"

"Yeah, Mad-C, thank you," Debo said, and took the call. "Hello? Oh, hey, Sis.., what's up this early in the morning? Is Shell okay, are you okay, Jeffery? Give me something good, it's too early in the morning for everything to be okay and you're waking me up."

"Turn on the news; the morning news," Joy instructed.

He grabbed the remote off his desk and pressed the power button and the flat screen TV came to life. It was already on the news station. He heard the voice of the news anchorman say,

"Early this morning, a private helicopter was shot down at county hospital.

The victims included Sheriff's Department Sergeant Mark Ansell, an unknown man by the name of, Roy Davis; forty-five years of age, a patient by the name of, Randy Carlyle; thirty-seven years of age, and the pilot, whose family wishes his name not be revealed. It started out to be what Sheriff's deputies believed to have been an attempted escape from the hospital's jail-ward. Roy Davis was said to have been wearing close to two dozen sticks of pure dynamite while holding the sheriff's deputy at bay with an automatic handgun. The pilot of the aircraft suffered a single gunshot wound to his head. Everyone else aboard was killed on impact of the crash."

"Sis, let me call you back, is, Shell up?"

"No, not yet."

"Okay, Baby, thanks."

When Debo hung up, he called Mad-C to give him the news, or to see if he had heard it on TV. But, Mad-C couldn't hear him because he had gone back into the workout room to finish working out. Debo walked in while he was lying on a black leather bench, pressing 450-pounds of iron weights.

"Hey, big guy, you've gotta hear this," Debo anxiously told Mad-C. "45, 46, 47, 48, 49-50. What is it, Debo? You and your phone call at 7:30 in the morning is interfering with my workout. And, Debo nothing and no one interferes with my workout. If this isn't important, I'm gonna shoot your ass in both those legs you just walked in here on. Now... what is it?"

"Carlyle tried to escape at about one-thirty or two this morning. He had some guy try to get him out of the hospital's jail-ward by helicopter. But, someone shot the helicopter pilot and it went down along with a county sheriff's deputy that was aboard. I guess they kidnapped the sergeant. Somebody was sent there to shut Carlyle up."

"Yeah... well, if they shot the helicopter out from under his ass... I would pretty much say they did indeed shut his ass up."

"Okay, all we have now is the club. Freddy said, 'that the girl he met there called herself, Chocolate, and that she's been going there for a few years now.' Maybe she can give us something on Cruse. And, you know he's not alone. It could be his brother who put those men on us at the house over on Colt Brilliant: Not to mention the ones that came to kill Jeffery in that basement at the fishing and boat club."

"Yeah, well now it's about time to pay Mr Johnson another visit."

"Where, at his house?" Debo asked.

"No, not yet.., we'll save that one. We'll go to the yacht club, I'm almost finished here. I'll just finish up, take a shower, and I'll be ready to roll shortly. We can grab something to eat on the way."

"Sounds good to me," Debo confirmed.

Jeffery called Debo, to let him know that he was doing better, and to also let him know something else.

"Good morning, boss," Jeffery said when Debo answered. "Hey, sport, you must be feeling better. I've already had some good news today, and I know you have some for me too, right?"

"Yeah, Joy told me 'that she called you about, Randy Carlyle.' It was good news for me too. He's the one that did this to me. But anyway, I am doing a lot better, and thanks for the visit with Molly. Now I have some good news. When Cruse kidnapped and robbed me, he took some money out of my safe; $150,000.00. What I did was..." Debo cut him off.

"You know, Jeffery..., you went through some really tough shit, so don't worry about the money. I'm not worried about it and neither is my boss; we'll get it back. All that concerns us right now is that you get better so you can get back to work when this is over, if you want to. We're just glad to have you back alive, that's all."

"Thanks, boss..., but I was about to say that they didn't get your money. I had your money taken out of the safe and put in the bank. Your money is still safe," Jeffery explained.

"I'll tell you what, you keep it, you've earned it. Mister Write and I will get ours back from Johnson, plus the ten keys they took."

12:00 PM

Cruse called his sister, Misty Rodgers, Misty Rodgers was the late Mack Rodgers wife; the gang member Mad-C killed on the couch in that house ten years ago. Misty decided to keep her last name and use Anderson as her middle name when she got married to Mack Rodgers. Raymond Anderson (aka) Robert Cruse's little sister was just having lunch with some people from the club at a very expensive restaurant in Beverly Hills, CA, and she had to get back to the club soon. She and her friends were in a discussion about what happened at county hospital, when her brother called. "Hey, Bobby, can you call me back? I'm in the middle of having lunch with some friends."

She calls Robert Cruse Bobby because it's short for Robert. She doesn't call him Raymond or Ray now that he has changed his name to Robert. She didn't know anything about the Yin incident. He told her that he changed his name because he didn't like being called Ray or Raymond.

"This is very important and I need to talk to you now," Robert told her, sounding upset.

"What's it about?"

"It's about the guy you met at the club the other night."

"I meet guys there all the time. Is there a certain guy you have in mind?"

"The one you were talking to when Donna brought you to the back office. Monday night," Robert reminded her.

"Okay, I'll meet you at the club after I get off," she told Robert. "No, I'll meet you at the hotel."

"Okay, after work at the hotel it is. Hey, Bobby, don't you know a guy by the name of Randy Carlyle?"

"Yeah, he's a friend of mine, why?"

"You mean he was a friend of yours."

"What do you mean, 'he was a friend of mine?'"

"I mean he was killed in a helicopter crash this morning trying to escape from the jail-ward at the hospital. It's been all over the news," Misty told him.

"I just woke up, thanks for telling me. I'll see you this evening."

"Okay, Bobby."

Robert Cruse didn't want to meet his sister at the club because Mad-C and Debo knows about the club. He didn't want her involved in anything just in case they showed up unexpectedly. When he sees them he wants to be ready for them, and not with his little sister around. She didn't know that the guy Robert was talking about could be mixed up with or is working for the man that killed her husband. Chocolate got off work at 6:00 pm Wednesday evening and called Robert.

6:15 PM:

"Okay, Bobby, I'm off work now. I have to make one quick stop, then I'll be at the hotel. What room is it?"

"Room 3021, I'll leave word for them to just let you come up."

"Okay, I'll see you in about an hour," she told him.

After the house on Colt Brilliant was shot up and five people were left dead, Robert had to relocate. He rented a room at the Bonaventure Hotel until he could find another place to live.

Misty arrived at the hotel at 7:20 pm. She walked through the large glass door and up to the counter. The same counter that Freddy, Shelly, Pauline, and Joy had walked up to.

"Hello, my name is Misty Rogers, and I'm a guest of a tenant in Room 3021. I believe he told you that he was expecting me.

"Oh yes, Miss Rodgers, Mister Cruse is expecting you. Should I have someone show you up, or do you know the way?"

"Please do, I haven't been here before, thank you."

"You're very welcome, Miss Rodgers," the clerk said, then pushed a button on the console in front of him on the desk. Seconds later a bellhop came to assist Misty.

"Room 3021," the desk clerk told the bellhop.

The bellhop could see there was no luggage, so he didn't feel it necessary for him to ask. They got on the elevator and stepped onto the thick, plush, beige carpet. There were candles along the walls in gold candle holders, and a golden chandelier in the ceiling, and candles where lights would normally be.

Misty loved the walls; they were a beautiful dark coffee brown. She was very impressed with the decorators because she loves dark brown, especially chocolate.

"Here we are Miss Rodgers," the bellhop announced.

Misty thanked him and gave him a $20 tip. He accepted it, smiled, then said,

"Thank you," and walked toward the elevators. Misty knocked on Robert's door. He didn't have to ask who it was. He could see that it was Misty when he looked through the rather small peephole. "Hey, Sis.., make yourself at home, are you hungry? Want something to drink?"

"No, thank you, I ate lunch. I'll have something to drink," she told him.

He pointed to a portable bar on the wall across from them and said, "Make yourself at home."

She went over to the small bar and took a glass from a shelf on the wall, got some ice from a portable refrigerator, and found the drink of her choice.

"Misty I'm gonna need you to think back, this is very important. A guy came into the club the other night. He had soda and he bought you a drink; he was a tall, black guy, 200-250 pounds, good looking. Do you remember him?"

"Wait a minute… you mean the… "

Cruse stopped her before she could complete what she was saying. "The guy you were talking to when Donna sent you to the office. Do you remember who I'm talking about?"

She knew exactly who it was when Cruse said that the man was good-looking. He introduced himself as single, handsome, and rich. She sip her drink and wiped her lips with the tip of her index finger, and said,

"Yeah, I remember him.., what about him?"

"Do you remember what he said his name was?"

"Let's see… Fred, Frederick, Freddy. I think he said, Freddy. Yeah, that's it… Freddy."

"Are you sure it wasn't Jackson or Write?"

"No, it was, Freddy."

"What did he want?"

He realized after he asked her that question, that it could have been a stupid question. Looking at her would tell you what any man would want with her.

"You could have asked Blue that question. I told him that when he called me into the office."

"But, I'm asking you, what did he want? What did he say to you?"

"All he said was 'that he was single, handsome and rich.'

He asked me if the place was for sale, and if it was, who is selling it."

"What did you tell him?"

"I said the place was not for sale. That you had just bought it three years ago."

"You told him I bought it?"

"Yes I did, why?"

"You gave him my name?"

"No, I called you, RC. I'll never give your name to a stranger," Misty told Robert.

"Okay, Look, I'm almost sure he'll be back. When you talk to him again, don't give him my name or Gregory's name, just see what he wants."

"What..., is something wrong? Do you know him or something?"

"Well..., if he's who I think he is, he's working for the man that killed Mack ten years ago," Robert told his sister.

"You mean my Mack.., my husband?" she asked, confused.

"Yes, your Mack... Mack Rodgers. I didn't say that he is the one that killed him. I said he's working for the man that did. Don't do or say anything that will make him suspicious," Robert told his sister.

"Don't worry, I can sit there and make him think he scored."

"He's not trying to score; he's trying to get information about me and Gregory."

"Okay, then he won't know that I know anything," Misty assured her brother.

"Chocolate, be careful, these people are serious and they're very rich and very dangerous."

"Okay, Bobby..., I'll only play with him a little bit."

"Yeah don't get yourself hurt, and don't tell him who you are either. Just let him go with, Chocolate. You don't have a police record so they can't trace you or run you through their database. If they do, nothing will come up because you're not in the system."

"Alright..., very protective and loving brother. I'll be careful," she said in a sassy tone.

8:00 PM

Debo and Mad-C were in San Diego checking up on *the Shell-Debo* and Mad-C's estate. The weather was starting to get a bit cooler, but they both were used to it, as a matter of fact, they love the weather. It was close to 8:15 pm, and they were sitting on Mad-C's patio. It was built like a back house with a long front porch and a swing sofa. The porch was made of wood with a special finish that was weather and water-resistant. On the other side of the porch was a futon sofa-bed. They sat on the futon having themselves a drink and talking while they watched-out over Mad-C's massive acres and acres of land.

"Mad-C, what are you going to do with all this land by yourself?"

"Well, I'll eventually find the right lady to help me grow older on it."

"Oh yeah, you have your eyes on Pauline… that's right."

"I don't know, Debo.., she seems to be a pretty bright and wise young lady, she meets all the requirements. She's beautiful, smart, trustworthy, down to earth. I like a woman who's down to earth; not afraid to speak her mind. I've noticed that about Joy also. Pauline is a sweet person; always willing to help, from what I've seen."

"Yeah, and I've noticed you seeing, too."

"She's also enthusiastic, she has her own money. I'm sure it won't be the money she's after. She knows what I do and she doesn't have a problem with it so far… she's perfect," Mad-C awarded.

"Well, I wish you two the best. Are you dating each other?"

"Well, yeah, kinda."

"Well, kinda is a start," Debo said, hoping that Mad-C and Pauline would hit it off.

If Pauline does get with someone it may as well be someone that wouldn't want her for just money and her looks. She needs someone that appreciates her for who she is, and Mad-C just described who she was in his eyes. The television was on in a room across from the patio and Debo would glance at it every once in a while.

"Mad-C, who's going to do the work when I retire?"

"I don't know, I have more than enough money, Debo.., I'm tired, you're retiring, your friend at police headquarters in Los Angeles is retiring. I've got enough on those two DEA agents to let them go now. The only thing keeping them around is that we might need them before this is over with. They don't seem to be trustworthy to me, something smells with them."

Debo knows that when Mad-C smells something.., then something definitely stinks.

"Maybe we should…" Debo ended his conversation and stared at the television set.

The evening news was on and they were playing a rebroadcast of the morning news; The incident at the hospital where Randy Carlyle and the other men died. He saw something odd.

"What is it? You look like you've seen a ghost," Mad-C said. "That lady," Debo pointed out.

"What lady?"

"The lady they're interviewing, she's the lady in the picture. That's Jonny Morris' mother. Mad-C, If you turn it up some can we hear it out here?" Debo asked.

Mad-C got the remote control out of a drawer that was built into the armrest of a futon.

"This is an estate, I have surround sound out here."

Mad-C turned the volume up and Debo heard the woman say, 'that Carlyle was like a son to her, and that she had just talked to him.'

"They took my Jonny… just killed him in cold blood, and now Randy. Those two were all I had, and now I have no one."

Maureen Morris had tears rolling down her face as she talked to the anchorman and the world.

"That's the lady in the picture that was in Carlyle's wallet; the same lady that came to the door when we went over to her house out on Brooks in Venice. Pauline hit it off with her pretty well. I wonder if… "

"I know what you're thinking, Debo, and it doesn't look like she's up to answering any questions any time soon. She's going to have her hands full with the law and burring that asshole."

"But, what if we tell her that we're after the men who killed Johnny and Randy?"

"I don't know if it would work."

"Yeah, it could."

"How's your man doing, is he getting any better?"

Mad-C was trying to calm Debo down so he could enjoy the rest of the evening on the patio.

"Yeah, he's doing a lot better, he called me to tell me the money Cruse took wasn't your money. He said, 'that it was some money he was saving, and that he still has the money from the work.' I told him to keep it, he earned it. We'll get it back from Cruse and Johnson… plus, your ten keys he stole. Okay, now back to you and Pauline. I want to see you both happy, Mad-C. And I know that she can make you happy, and she needs a good, loving, and caring man. So, what do you say? Can I ask you something?"

"Sure, what is it?"

"Why do you spell your name W-R-I-T-E?"

"I didn't, my father did, it took him years to learn how to spell Wright. The first thing he learned to spell before he could write was the word 'write'. He was kinda slow."

"But, Write is your last name Didn't your father have that name as a child?"

"My father's name was Bradford E Wright until he changed the spelling of his last name to the one he was used to spelling, which is Write."

"Yeah, well all you need is a good woman, Mister Wright."

"Yeah, you're right," Mad-C said .

They both heard the humor in Mad-C's last statement and laughed.

9:30 PM

Joy and Shelly had just finished their tenth game of Rummy; eight-to two in favor of Shelly.

"Oh, girl, I just can't beat you, but I learned a lot. I could probably pound poor D-Angelo to death."

"I'm sure you could probably beat the socks off a lot of people…, hey, Joy?"

"Yeah?"

"You are a really good person, what happened? I mean you are very beautiful, you have a lot of money, and two wonderful girls. I just can't understand why you chose to do this, other than the money is good. I mean…, I'm just saying."

"I know what you mean, Shelly. My daughters' father ran off and left me for someone else. Well, actually, he didn't want to do anything, he didn't want to work, go to school, set any kind of goals for himself; not to mention his family. And when he did do something, he never finished it. I couldn't support two girls and a husband, he's supposed to be the breadwinner. But in today's society the husband and the wife are supposed to pull together, compromise, and do everything together. I never expected him to do it all, but just do something. So, he found someone that was willing to support him, or that's what I was led to believe; someone to cater to him, to take his abuse, and just let him lay-up on her flat broke. So, he left me and the kids, I already had Sheila, she was two and Tammy was on the way, she's twelve now. He left right after Tammy was born and we haven't heard anything from him since. He hasn't seen his daughters in ten years. I was left alone to support them and to take care of them and myself. My mom was a security guard right around the time Debo… I mean D-Angelo was. My mom had a crush on him at the time, but when he quit the security guard job they lost touch with each other.

That's when D-Angelo went to work doing what he does, that's when he met Mr Write. He went by the store where my Mom worked one day and I was there. I knew him pretty well because he used to come over to our house a lot. He saw that my mom wasn't doing too well on her check alone and I was thinking of becoming a security guard. That's why I was at my mom's job. D-Angelo knew about Sheila and Tammy, and he knew that I couldn't afford to support them on what a security guard made. See…, after their father left, I was forced to quit one of my jobs because. I had the kids by myself. They were two and four years old at the time. D-Angelo saw that I needed help and offered to help me; no strings attached," Joy explained.

"Well, Joy you're now the sister I never had and I always wanted."

"Awe…, thank you, Sis, and I feel the same way. That's why I love D-Angelo so much, he's just an all-out good person. I do what I do because then I needed the money. And now it's to keep a close eye on my brother and to watch his back.

He even started taking care of the girls. He made sure they had everything and didn't want for anything, and to this day they call him Uncle Debo. I tell them he is my brother because in my heart and soul he is my brother. That's why I told you, Shelly.., you have a damn good man and one of the best persons in the whole entire world. Now as to your question; I started working for D-Angelo because of what he started doing for Mister Write. I knew how dangerous it was, and by him always being by me and the girl's side all those years, I just felt compelled to help protect him. If he was out there, I was out there making sure he came back. I will go to the end of the world with D-Angelo L, Jackson. I will do anything for him and my two girls. So, I didn't really choose to do this, it chose me. Anything else you want to know while I'm running my mouth?"

"Well, you've… "

"If there is, just let me know, Sis."

Shelly never really looked at Joy as a family member, or even as a sister in-law until now. And if by chance she had known about Mad-C killing Mack Rodgers; Robert Cruse's brother-in-law, then she would understand how important it is to Joy not to lose her brother. She could really learn to love Joy being her sister-in-law. She already feels a strong bond between the two of them.

"I think you about said it all. What time is it?" Shelly asked. Joy looked at her watch and was surprised to see how time had passed. "Girl it's 9:30."

"Boy, time flies when you're having a good conversation," Shelly said.

"So, what are you doing the rest of the evening, wanna watch some TV?"

"No, I guess I'll turn in early tonight. D-Angelo kept me up all night last night on the phone, I love it though. I really enjoy our little talks at night, and it's a comfort to him also," Shelly said.

"Yeah, and I'm glad we had a chance to talk, I enjoyed it," Joy told her. "So did I, and I learned a lot. We have to talk more often."

"Well, that's what sisters do. Can I ask you something?"

"Ask."

"Do you have any regrets about marrying him?" Joy asked.

"Girl, heck no, I would marry him again and again, and over and over. I know your girls are glad to have each other. I'm an only child and it gets lonesome," Shelly said.

"Well, not anymore you're not: Now you have a sister that loves you, because I can love anyone that loves my brother as much as you do," Joy proudly told Shelly.

"Thanks, Sis…, love you too.., see you in the morning."

"Good night, Sis," Shelly said, and they both went to their room. Joy showered, dressed for bed, and went out to the kitchen to get some warm milk and two cookies. She ate the cookies, drank the warm milk, and went back to her room. She had no sooner laid down when her phone rang. She looked at her caller ID and it was Pauline.

"Hey, girl, Is anything wrong?"

"Nah…, I just can't sleep, I've been up all night thinking."

"Thinking about what?"

"The boss," Pauline said.

"Look, girl, that nutcase know exactly what he's doing, he'll make it out of this, don't worry."

"I'm not talking about your brother, I'm talking about ..,"

"You mean Mister Write?" Joy asked, confused and excited.

"Yeah."

"Joy… you okay!!!" Shelly yelled.

"Yeah, Sis, I'm on the telephone with Pauline…, I'm fine!!!"

"Hey…, what's going on Miss Lady?"

"I don't know, I think I'm falling for Charles," Pauline confessed. "Oh boy, that's a juicy one, talk to me girl."

"Calm down, Missy…, nothing is said or done, but I am interested in him though, and I think he likes me too."

"So, what's there to think about? What are you going to do wait till you're an old ass hag before you get yourself a good man? And believe me... good men are not easy to come by. So, when you find one you like... JUMP on it, I mean him, I mean... you know what I mean!"

"Do you think I'm ready, Joy?"

"Look, Lady.., you're the only one who knows when you are ready. But, if you're asking me... "

"I'm asking you."

"Yea, I think it's about time, all the good men are being snatched up fast. If you two do get together I wish you the best. I think he's a really cool guy. I was just telling Shelly 'that if you are cool with my brother, then I'm cool with you,' and Charles is cool with my brother," Joy told Pauline.

"Thank you, Joy, I really needed those words of encouragement."

"So, do you think you'll be able to get some sleep tonight?" Joy asked. Pauline.

"Thanks to you I will. I knew I was calling the, right person.

"Did you?"

"Did I what?"

"Call the, 'Write' person. Get it... The 'Write' person."

"Aw, go to sleep, crazy lady. Goodnight Joy, and Thanks."

"Goodnight, Pauline..., I mean Misses Write." And that ended their conversation and their call.

10:00 PM

"Well, I'm going to call it a night, Mister Jackson."

"Yeah..., me too Mister Write. I'm going to go by the house and make sure everything is alright and bed down for the night," Debo said.

"You know I don't have to tell you that you're more than welcome to sleep anywhere you want in this place," Mad-C said.

"Yeah, thanks, but I wanna go check on the place and get in the bed and just think about my baby. I can pretend she's there lying beside me."

"Debo, you done flipped.., out of here," Mad-C jokingly said.

"Okay, see you in the morning, or afternoon, or whenever you're ready to head back."

Debo made it to the Shell Debo after 10:00 pm. He showered, got ready for bed, set all the alarms, then got into bed. He turned off the lights and reached for his phone and called Shelly's cell. She was just getting to sleep when the phone woke her up. "High, Baby," she greeted.

"Hey, Baby..,guess what I'm doing."

"What are you doing?"

"Baby, I'm sorry, is it too late?"

"It's never too late when you call me. Besides, I'm awake now. So, what are you up doing this late?"

"Guess… it's no fun if you don't guess."

"Okay, you're thinking of me."

"Yeah, I was, but I'm talking to you now. Take another guess."

"I don't know, I already guessed, now be fair and tell me."

"Okay, I'm lying in our bed with the lights off, on the phone with my baby. It's actually beautiful when the room is moonlit."

"I'm gonna get you for this, that's not fair," Shelly cried.

"Baby it's a beautiful moment, it's as though you were lying right here with me talking to me."

"Okay, you got out of that one."

"So, how was your day, sweetheart?" Debo asked.

"It was educational after Joy and I finished playing Rummy."

"Did you let her win?"

"Yeah, and after we finished playing, she also won my heart."

"And how did she manage that?"

"Well, she told me the most interesting things; after I asked her of course."

"And, what did you ask her?"

"I asked her why she chose to do what she does for a living."

"And what did she tell you?"

"She told me for one thing, 'that you are a very important person in a lot of people's lives, especially mine and most definitely in hers."

"She told you everything, didn't she?"

"Yes she did, and it brought tears to my eyes. You keep being as wonderful as you are, Mr Jackson, and you could have the world."

"I already have my world, I have you, my little sister, and my two nieces."

"D-Angelo, do you know what she said to me?"

"Oh… now you want me to guess. Be fair, tell me what she said to you."

"She told me 'that she loves me because I love you so much.'"

"Yeah she's sweet," Debo said.

"And she's beautiful with a wonderful heart," Shelly told him. "Yeah, she's the best, and she really looks out for me. When I asked her to guard your life with her own, she had no problem at all with it."

"She's jeopardizing her life for me, D-Angelo!?"

"Yeah… something like that: She's just looking after her sister-in-law," Debo said.

"Being responsible for someone else's life is a big responsibility," Shelly told him.

"Yeah… a very big responsibility," Debo added. "What time will you be back out here?" Shelly asked. "In the morning, do you need anything?"

"No, I'm okay…, just the mail if I have any."

"Okay, sweetheart, Joy really got to you didn't she?"

"Yes, she did."

"Yeah.., she gets to me too. Goodnight, baby," Debo said, ending the call.

CHAPTER 17

THURSDAY, NOVEMBER 22ND, 10:00 A.M.

Debo and Mad-C arrived at 909 Pacific Coast Highway at 10:10 am and walked through the tall glass doors of the Glory Days Yacht Club and waved at the desk clerk then signed the sign-in sheet that was on the front desk. They couldn't go directly to Gregory Johnson's office because they needed clearance or a passkey. They walked over to the phone and Mad-C entered the numbers including the extension number to paged Gregory Johnson. After Mad-C hung up, they both crossed their index and middle fingers and waited for the phone to ring. After a few seconds…

"Thank you for calling, Glory Days Yacht Club. You have reached Gregory Johnson's Office: My name is Dorothy, how may I help you?" the secretary greeted.

"Hi, Dorothy…, I'm Mister Write, is Mister Johnson in?"

"What did you say your name was, sir?"

"Write…, Charles Write, and I request to see Mr Johnson if I may."

"Mr Write, can you hold for just a second?"

Dorothy left the phone. After a moment she returned and said, "Mr Johnson is not in at the moment. He won't be in until later, would you like to leave a message, Mr Write?"

"Yes.., tell him I'm here to speak with him concerning his brother, Raymond Anderson, and a Mr Sue-Ling-Yin."

"I will be sure to let him know the minute he comes in. Is there anything else, Mr Write?"

"As a matter of fact, there is. Tell him also, that my friend and I will be waiting here in the lobby. And be sure to let him know that we do have all day," Mad-C said.

He told Debo that they might have a wait on their hands. Mad-C knew that Johnson was in his office, and if he mentioned Raymond and Yin, then Johnson would soon mysteriously appear.

Gregory Johnson was debating whether to go downstairs. But, he remembered that they had sent a police sergeant over to the fishing and boat club; at least that's what Carlyle told Robert Cruse and Cruse told Johnson.

And someone is giving information to the police…, Information about him. The only people that can do that are people that have access to that information. The only people with access are Robert Cruse and Randy Carlyle. Obviously, Carlyle is no longer a problem. But how in the hell did they find out that Raymond Anderson was his brother? And, Write also mentioned Yin. Johnson thought maybe he'd better go ahead and listen to what they have to say. The phone rang again, and Mad-C answered it.

"Mister Write?"

"Yes, Mister Johnson?"

"I'm sending my secretary down to show you up."

"Thank you, Mister Johnson."

Dorothy Mills came walking through the lobby looking stunning. She was as gorgeous a blonde as Debo or Mad-C had ever seen.

She looked more stunning than the first time they had seen her.; wearing a short navy captain's uniform, with long beautiful legs, her long silky blonde hair bounced at her shoulders, and she had the most beautiful and perfect tan you've ever seen. She smelled as sweet as cotton candy as she walked up to Debo and Mad-C and said,

"Gentlemen, please follow me."

They all went to the elevator and Dorothy pressed the button that summoned the large motorized box. They all entered the elevator and she pressed the button displaying the number (13) and was on their way to the thirteenth floor. They arrived at Gregory Johnson's office and Dorothy led the way to the outer office which was hers and said,

"Just a minute, gentlemen." She walked through a floor-to-ceiling door and closed it behind her.

"This is a nice office," Mad-C complimented.

"Yeah, and she's a nice-looking girl," Debo commanded. "Hey watch that…, you're a married man."

"Well, it doesn't hurt to look."

"It could, because your eyes may see some shit your ass don't need. So, don't look too hard."

"You looked!!"

"Debo, I'm not married, remember."

"Oh yeah…, right."

Dorothy returned as they were just finishing their conversation; unaware that she was the main topic of the conversation.

"Gentlemen, you may go in now," Dorothy said. "She's very polite also," Mad-C noticed.

Johnson looked like he was sweating balls; great big cannon-balls. He looked like a man that has been plagued by his billions.

"Mister Johnson… good to see you again," Mad-C said. "Gregory, how are you?" Debo greeted.

"I don't have a lot of time, what is it you want?"

"You know, that's the same thing I was wondering. You see, I was minding my own business, going about my life, and now somehow you and your shit-for-brains brother are screwing around in it. So, what the hell do you want, Gregory?" Mad-C asked.

"I have no idea what you're talking about. I barely know who you are."

"Cut the bullshit, Johnson. You know just who I am and you've known for years. Now, the question I am going to ask you again is what the fuck do you want with me, Johnson?"

"Mister Jackson, Mister Write… has anyone ever told the two of you about me? Do you know who you're fucking with? I mean do you know the hole you're digging for yourselves? You are digging your own graves, gentlemen. You are barking up the wrong fucking tree fellas."

"Look, Johnson, we know more than you think we know about you and who you are. We know all about the yacht you have; the 'Yacht Reyal.' We know where you dock it; dock seventeen, slip nine, San Diego, California. We know all about the private jet you own at an airfield, also in San Diego, California. We know all about the ranch at 11001 Oak-pine Lane in San Gabriel, California. And do you know what? Fifteen hundred acres is a lot of land for five horses," Mad-C finished.

"Yeah, and I love horses and that cozy little club you own over on Gage in Los Angeles… South Los Angeles at that. You know the one where your brother's people almost killed my little sister trying to rob her," Debo added.

"You do know you are committing suicide?" Johnson asked them.

"I'm not committing shit. You and your brother started this shit and it's only a matter of time before I blow his fucking brains out. How many men have you lost in the past month? Your brother and some of his gang-banging ass friends robbed me ten years ago. I went back to get my money and my shit back. One of your brother's friends pulled a sawed-off shotgun on me, and I don't take kindly to looking down the barrel of a sawed-off shotgun. And the bastard that was aiming it at my head had his finger on the fuckin trigger. I had no choice but to blow his ass away.

This is baby shit for you, Johnson. Your brother wants revenge for his brother-in-law. You asked me if I knew you…, hell yeah, I know you well enough to know that this is not you; It's not your style, even if Rodgers was your brother-in-law. Now, I'm going to ask you one more time, Johnson. What the fuck do you want with me?" Mad-C was getting extremely angry and impatient.

"Mr Write, the shipping dock you bought from politician, Donald Warwick; do you know why he sold it and left the country?"

"Yes, he was up for retirement and he wanted out of politics."

"Do you remember the scandal?"

"No, not clearly… Something about some money came up missing from a fundraising or charity event… some shit like that. What does that have to do with me?"

"Everything!"

"Look, Johnson, I've owned that shipping dock for over fifteen years now," Mad-C said.

"I'm aware of that, Mister Write, and I'm also a politician. Mister Warwick was my political colleague. This yacht club is just one of my many hobbies. I'm chairman of the board and CEO here because I've been a member for many, many years. Do you remember a man by the name of Joe Sacks, Mister Write?"

"I'm not sure, who is he?"

"Mister Sacks is my business manager and my personal financial advisor," Johnson explained.

"Wait a minute; Short, gray-haired man about 5'4" and 160-165 pounds!! He's Hawaiian, I believe," Mad-C said.

"That's the one."

"He was the man that bid against me for the dock: That was you?" Mad-C asked.

"Yes that was me, I couldn't bid any higher because there would have been the question of taxes. And even a well-to-do politician like myself, my income bracket was way too low for that kind of purchase, so I had to allow you to overbid me."

"So, all of this is about a loading dock?" Mad-C asked.

"Warwick and I owned the dock, but he sold it from under me and I couldn't claim it on my taxes."

"But, you had the money to buy it. That makes you the crook I told you that you were then, right? And now you want me to give or sell it back to you."

"Now you're getting the point."

"Point my ass, Gregory.., that dock belongs to me and I'm not selling it, giving it away, throwing it away, or tossing it out to you or anybody else."

"Mister Write, I need that shipping dock; name your price!"

"There is no price, Johnson."

"How does $100M sound, Mister Write?"

"You know something, Mr Johnson; forget about the loading dock and tell your brother to stay his ass away from me and my friends, and I won't say it again…, Is that clear?"

"You're making a big mistake, Mr Write. I can assure you of that."

"Look, Johnson, I'm tired and I'm going home, I can assure you of that. Since I'm making such a big mistake, I'll watch all helicopters flying over my head. Oh… I'm sorry, I forgot your people shot yours down. You know something…, It's very bad business killing a Sheriff's Sergeant… very bad business. Let's go," Mad-C told Debo.

"Forget about the dock, Johnson," Debo said on his way out.

"You'll be hearing from me, Charles!!!" Gregory Johnson yelled as Mad-C, and Debo were going out the door.

"Bye, pretty lady: Hey, did anyone ever tell you that you have the most beautiful legs?" Mad-C asked Dorothy Mills.

"Alright.., you know I'll tell Pauline," Debo said, so Dorothy could hear.

Dorothy blushed and went into Gregory Johnson's office. "Next time we come, remind me to bring roses," Mad-C said.

"Well, what do you think? Should we keep looking for Robert or what?" Debo asked Mad-C.

"We won't have to after today he'll come looking for us. I wonder why Johnson wants that dock so bad."

"I don't know, but I don't think he wants it for shipping," Debo said. Joy was downstairs checking things out in the lobby and out front.

She was looking for anyone or anything that didn't look right or didn't fit into the norm.

12:00 PM

Shelly woke up and knew right away where Joy was. Had she gone somewhere, she would have left a note. She decided to eat something, she had picked up Debo's habit of eating when she got hungry. She had a taste for some eggs, ham, grits, and toast. They already had fruit juices and some more refreshments stacked in the fridge; compliments of the hotel. She picked up the phone and placed her order with the kitchen downstairs when Joy walked in.

"Hey, sis…, I'm ordering something to eat; hungry?"

"Hungry isn't the word, hell I'm starved."

"I'm having breakfast food, how does that sound?"

"They still serve breakfast food this late, It's 12-noon?" Joy asked. "Girl, they have to accommodate us, with all that money we're paying for us staying here."

"Well, I'm with you, I don't want to be an oddball; breakfast food it is, only I want wheat toast," Joy said.

"After we eat, let's go to a movie or to the beach or something; get out of here for a day, we'll be fine. I have my own security," Joy said, and pulled out the Glock nine-millimeter she keeps close by her at all times.

She doesn't mind Shelly seeing it or knowing she has it. Shelly already knows why she's there. She was a little uncomfortable at first because their relationship started out as bodyguard-client, so Shelly knew she had the weapon, but they had become a lot closer. Shelly had let it slip her mind, but when she saw the gun it brought back the reason that she and Joy were there and the danger they both could be in.

"Are you sure it's alright?" Shelly asked.

"If it'll make you feel better or more comfortable, I'll call D-Angelo to see what he says."

"I know what he's going to say: He's going to say, 'go ahead on, you girls have some fun, Joy can handle things, that's why I have her there.' How much you wanna bet?" Shelly asked.

"Well, let me call and check, it won't take but a minute. I want to go somewhere and do something myself."

Joy called Debo., "Hey, Sis… what's up?"

"Hey, Big Bro, Shelly and I want to know if you think it would be a good idea to go out to the beach or a movie someplace."

"Go ahead on, you girls have yourselves a ball, Sis, you can handle things. That's why I picked you to watch, Shell for me, be careful."

"Okay, bra, thanks.., I'll let you know where we decide to go."

"Okay, Sis.., have fun."

"Hey Mad-C… guess what?"

"What's that?"

"Do you want to go to Griffith park?"

"You know something… it's a nice day for having fun. It's one of California's warm winter days. Well, actually it's autumn but it feels like winter at night anyway. The weekend might be rainy and cold. Sure… why not?"

"I have a plan.., I'll call Pauline and Freddy and we'll surprise the girls. We'll have a sort of 'get together' at the park," Debo suggested.

He called Freddy and told him to suggest to Joy that they all go to Griffith Park. Freddy called Joy and did as Debo instructed him. Joy and Shelly agreed to a picnic for the three of them at Griffith Park. Debo called Pauline and invited her. She said, 'she wasn't doing anything.' Besides, when she heard that Mad-C was going to be there, nothing short of a heart attack was going to stop her from going. She was to meet Debo and Mad-C at the Beverly Hills office. The three of them would go from there. Joy, Shelly, and Freddy went in Freddy's Mercedes SUV and arrived shortly after Debo, Mad-C, and Pauline, the way it was planned. Freddy had already been told where to set up camp. Actually, it was a very good day for a day at the park, even though it was unusually warm and the wind was blowing off and on at about 15-miles per hour. Mad-C had suggested a barbecue rather than a picnic with sandwiches and chips. A barbecue is more fun and you get full. Joy, Freddy and Shelly began to unload the SUV; lawn chairs, blankets, games, and a rather large radio that plays CDs. They were all set-up when Freddy said,

"Hey, who brought the food?"

"Oh my, God!" Joy said.

"Well, I'm sure glad I ate something before we left," Shelly said. "Hey, there are some people barbecuing over there," Freddy said as he pointed about thirty feet from where they were set up.

"I'm going over there and ask them if we can join them."

Joy and Shelly looked over to where Freddy had pointed and saw three people sitting in lawn chairs with their backs to them. All three of them wore big straw hats and sunglasses.

"Look at those big straw hats… those could be Mexicans, Freddy," Joy warned.

They couldn't see the people's faces. This was all planned by Debo and Mad-C. Pauline had her head in Mad-C's lap while he held her hand as they pretended to engage in a conversation. It appeared that they were really enjoying each other. Freddy started walking toward Mad-C, Debo,,and Pauline.

"Freddy!!!" Shelly screamed.

Freddy kept walking faster getting closer. "Freddy, come back here!!!" Joy yelled. Freddy stopped where the three were sitting.

"What are they doing, Freddy?" Debo asked.

Shelly and Joy had jumped up and ran to catch Freddy before he got to the other people, but they were too late.

"They're running over here," Freddy answered.

They were both out of breath and looked extremely embarrassed. "We're so sorry, our friend took it upon himself to ask… "

Shelly couldn't finish talking, before Debo took off his hat, turned around, and said, "It's quite alright ma'am."

Shelly saw Debo and started jumping up and down screaming and yelling,

"My baby!!!… Joy it's… !!! Oh my God, it's my… "

She grabbed Debo around his neck, and with tears of happiness in her eyes she said, "I'm going to kill you, D-Angelo Jackson." She let go of Debo, then turned to Joy, and said,

"AND, YOU!!!"

"Hold on, sis, I didn't know anything about this," Joy tried to explain, and they both went after Freddy but he was too fast for them as he was running and laughing at the same time.

Shelly was out of breath as she walked back to where Debo was, after running Freddy around the park.

She threw herself at Debo and said,

"God, I missed you baby, I'll be so glad when this is behind us."

"Me too, sweetheart, but you know what they say, 'absence makes the heart grow fonder,'" Debo told her.

"Well, I'm tired of you being absent," Shelly told Debo.

"Hey, Freddy check them out," Joy told Freddy, referring to Mad-C and Pauline.

"Okay, it's over. You two can stop pretending now," Freddy said.

"I don't think they're pretending," Joy told Freddy. "Well, it looks like we're elected to cook for us and the love birds." Shelly and Debo were in a dreamland of their own. Mad-C and Pauline didn't know whether they were dreaming or not.

"You know something… they make a really good couple," Joy told Freddy.

"You mean you knew about them all this time?" Freddy asked. "Well.., it came up. Pauline called me and confided in me to help her make the decision and the rest was up to them," Joy said, and looked at Freddy.

He glanced over at her, then turned his head toward the barbecue pit and began to blush. Joy noticed him blushing.

"Stop it Fat-Head, maybe if you can find it in yourself to take the nose-ring out of your nose… maybe!!"

Freddy imagined the ring in his nose and resisted the temptation to touch it.

"Is that what the problem has been all these years?" Freddy asked Joy. "Calm down, fat-head…, I said, 'maybe!'"

Joy always did like the kind of man Freddy is, and she loves what she sees in him. He respected her enough not to try to come on to her. Because of her prior relationship, she didn't want to start another one so fast. But it's been a while, in fact it's been close to ten years. Freddy has known Joy long enough to know that he wouldn't mind spending the rest of his life with her. Joy is a beautiful woman: She's self-sufficient, self-supportive, smart, and a hell of a lot of fun to be with. They looked at the two couples and heard Major Harris singing, "Love Won't Let Me Wait," on the CD player. The six of them had a lovely time. They didn't want the day to end. "Hey, Debo, do you still have that camera in the Navigator?" Mad-C asked Debo. "Yeah."

"Is it on?"

"It comes on when the engine comes on, or if I turn it on without the engine being on. But it isn't on now, why.., are you thinking what I'm thinking?" Debo asked.

While the ladies were watching the food and setting the table, the three men found time to discuss a few things.

"Do you think he'll try anything out here?" Freddy asked.

"No..,, too many people. Chances are, if they're out here they'll most likely follow us leaving, and wait for a better opportunity to make a move."

"But who do you think they'll follow, us or the girls? Debo asked.

"Good question," Mad-C answered.

"They should know we have heat," Freddy pointed out.

"Yeah, but they'll figure the girls don't and follow them. Besides, if they follow the girls they'll have some damn good hostages," Debo enlightened.

"Do you see anything that stands out?" Mad-C asked the two men. "No, but I feel something: Slowly take a look to your right, there's a car parked on the other side of that road over there," Freddy said.

He was looking where there were two big trees and a building that looked like it could be a park maintenance building. A car was sitting there with someone inside. They couldn't tell who was in it from that distance.

"I have to use the men's room," Debo said. He walked over to where the toilets were.

It's a small concrete structure with four sides and an opening where a door should have been, only there was no door. He stood on the side where no one could see him. He wanted to get a better look at who was inside the car so he peered around the corner of the small public men's watering shack and saw that the car was still there and its occupants were still in it. He ducked inside to check the Glock-45 to make sure it was ready to do its job, then he walked around the building and down a slope. When he got to the bottom of the slope he was at ground level. He walked all the way around making sure the men in the car didn't see him. He walked about a hundred feet and came up from behind one of the trees that were next to the parked car. He pulled the Glock-45 automatic out and came from around the tree so fast that if the guy in the car had seen him through his rear or side-view mirrors it would have been too late for him to react.

Debo leveled *Crazy* at the drivers' side window, which was rolled all the way down, and said,

"Don't breathe…, I need to see some hands… or I can see your brains splattered all over your friend sitting next to you."

"We are friends of Sergeant Billings," the one with the barrel of Debo's Glock-45 at his temple said.

At that time, Debo saw Freddy come up from behind the other tree with his 357-magnum aimed at the passenger.

"What the hell do you mean you're friends of Sergeant Billing?"

"Can I show you my badge?" the man at the wheel asked.

"I don't have to remind you of what this thing will do to your head at point-blank range, do I?" Debo asked the driver.

The officer reached inside his shirt and pulled out a badge attached to a small chain.

"What the hell are you doing here?" Freddy asked them. "My job!"

"Which is?" Freddy asked.

The officer reached on the seat and picked up a cell phone and and dialed Sergeant Billings and handed it to Debo. Debo put the phone to his ear and heard a voice say,

"Jackson, what the hell are you doing at Griffith Park in the middle of the day?"

"I'm having a barbecue and enjoying some time with my family and friends. How did you know I was here?"

"If you had your cell phone on, you would know. I heard about the conversation you had with Gregory Johnson. He's making some pretty powerful phone calls. The word on the street is 'that there's a price on your head… You and Write.'"

"So, what am I supposed to do…, hide?"

"No, I know you're not going to do that. That's why I put those two guys on you. Jackson, let me tell you one thing. Gregory Johnson is no small-time push-over."

"Yeah, I know, he's a big-time political prick."

"That he is, and he has big-time political power."

"To hell with him and his power… I'm not a pushover either."

"Yeah, I know that also, that's why I'm watching your back."

"Thanks, Bob, I knew I could count on you."

"Count on my ass, hurry up and finish this shit so I can retire!!"

"I'm working on it as we speak, Bob."

"You've got a lot of balls, Jackson… a whole lot of balls. Give me the detective at the wheel," Billings said.

Debo gave the phone to the driver, thanked them, and apologized, then he and Freddy walked back over to where Mad-C, Joy, Pauline, and Shelly were. Joy was ready for action in case something went down, or someone came upon them while the men were at that car, and Mad-C was right there by her side.

"Is everything okay, Bra?"

"Yeah, it is now," Debo assured them.

Shelly relaxed but was still a little nervous. Debo saw that she was and put his arms around her waist and said,

"Look around you, you have your own army right here. Everything is fine baby, and I'm not going to let nothing and no one ruin our day. So, cheer up little lady and let's have a ball." He looked over at the car with the two men in it and said,

"Those guys are on our team."

"Hey, everybody, let's play some volleyball; the women against the men!!!" Pauline yelled.

They all relaxed and went back to having a beautiful day. Freddy helped Joy, while Mad-C and Pauline tied a volleyball net to two trees. When they finished, Joy handed Shelly the volleyball and said, "Here girl… you serve!"

8:30 PM

Mad-C and Pauline, Debo and Shelly, and Freddy and Joy had the time of their lives.

"I'll talk you to sleep tonight, Baby..,, okay?" Debo told Shelly. "Okay, that was a lovely surprise, thank you baby," Shelly said. "My pleasure, beautiful: The best for the best," Debo said.

Mad-C and Pauline agreed to talk more at the office when they got back.

Freddy, Joy, and Shelly got in the Mercedes Benz SUV and were headed back to the hotel. Mad-C and Debo took Pauline back to the office to get her car. However, she didn't leave right away, she wanted to spend some time with Mad-C. They went into his office and Debo went into his office to get ready for his shower. He proceeded to the workout room and from there, on to his shower. After his shower, he dressed in something to lounge around in and laid on his bed and caught the rest of NFL Today on the all-sports network.

"I had a wonderful time," Pauline said.

"Yeah, I did too, for the first time in years I was able to go out with a woman and actually enjoy myself. You were really great company, Pauline, and the very best hostess."

"Thank you…, hay, did you get a look at Freddy, and Joy? Seemed to me like they were made for each other," Pauline mentioned.

"Yeah… like us, huh," Mad-C whispered in her ear.

"Yeah…, like us."

Pauline was wondering if it was love she was feeling, or was she just lonely and needed to be with somebody. If it was going to be then she wanted it to last for a long time. Not just some temporary fling or a date. She wanted and needed a man she could call her own, a man that would want to call her his own. She wanted Charles Write and he wanted her. Robert Cruse called his brother, Gregory Johnson to respond to a message that Gregory left on his phone.

"What's going on, Robert?"

"I'm returning your call," Cruse said.

"Why didn't you tell me that Charles Write killed, Mack?"

"I didn't want to bother you with my problems."

"Misty is my sister too, Raymond, don't forget it. What's taking so long to get rid of Write, and Jackson? Or, should I do that myself too?"

"Those guys are small potatoes."

"If you feel they are so damn small, why haven't you been able to kill them yet?"

"I didn't do the job myself, I put Randy and Jonny on them."

"Yeah, and what does the fact that they're dead instead tell you? It should tell you that Write is no pushover. He's killed two of your guys and I don't know how many of mine: What is it, five… six? And he said, 'that if you don't lay off he's going to blow your fuckin brains out.' You know, the one you don't have. He's going to have them coming out of the back of your fuckin head."

"Fuck him, when did you talk to him?" Cruse asked.

"He was at the yacht club today, drilling me about you and the Yin murder. He won't sell me back my dock."

"What do you want me to do?"

"There's nothing you're qualified to do. You're not at his level. He'll smell you coming and pick you off like a duck. I've called in some people and made it worthwhile for whoever kills Charles Write and D-Angelo Jackson. Where are you now?"

"I'm almost at the hotel I just left Mama Morris' place over on Brooks. I'm five-minutes from downtown Los Angeles."

"OK, give me a call tomorrow," Johnson instructed Cruse.

Joy, Freddy, and Shelly were just arriving at the hotel. Freddy let the valet park the Mercedes and gave him a tip, and the three of them turned to go inside the hotel. They were almost inside when the black Mercedes driven by Robert Cruse pulled in behind Freddy's Mercedes SUV. A valet walked up to his car and told him that he would take care of it for him.

"Thank you, sir, that's a beautiful SUV that just pulled in," Cruse told the valet.

"Yeah, it's a 2014, damn near new," the man wearing the green and black valet parking uniform said.

"Yeah…, too rich for my blood," Cruse said, not knowing how close he had come to meeting the lovely wife of D-Angelo Jackson.

Joy wanted to set the reminder in her cell phone to wake her up early for duty. She gets up at 6:30 every morning to make sure she's up in case something happens. She patted her back pockets and the only thing she felt was sore from landing on her butt during the volleyball game, as well as the horseback ride at the park.

She went in her room and looked in her purse; no cell phone. She wondered if Freddy was awake: Jeffery wasn't there anymore. Debo found a friend of his to help him detox and kick the drugs Carlyle had shot into his veins.

10:00 PM

Joy used the hotel phone to call Freddy.

"Hello.., room 2200," she told the operator. "Just a second please," she responded.

Freddy came to the phone. "Hello?"

"Hey, Freddy."

"How did you know I took the nose ring out before I went to bed? I'll be right up."

"Freddy…, stop it now. I left my cell phone in the Mercedes. Can you check and see for me please?"

"Do you have to have it tonight?"

Which was a pretty stupid question. Because, for one thing, if she could wait until morning, she would have called him in the morning, and another thing, he knew that Debo told all of them to always keep their phone with them and keep them on at all times.

"Sure you do," Freddy said, after he gave it a second thought. "Can you go check for me, sweetheart… please?"

"Well, since you put it like that, I'll go look and call your room, or I'll just bring it up to you… Okay?"

"Okay…, thanks, Freddy."

"oh, now it's Freddy. I liked sweetheart better."

"Hurry up, crazy man."

Freddy hung up, sat the piece of barbecue he was munching on back on the plate, and got up to go check on Joy's cell phone for her.

"Black 2014 Mercedes SUV," Freddy told the valet. "Hold on a sec while I check the board."

The short chubby man turned and walked over to a box that was attached to the wall beside the two sliding doors Freddy had just come out from.

"Here we are, Mister Moss, sorry for the delay. You are parked on the third level, sixteenth stall."

"Thank you, I'm sure I'll find it," Freddy said and walked toward the outside elevators located under the parking structure.

He got to the floor his SUV was parked on and walked over to stall sixteen. He had to squeeze between his car and the car parked beside his in order to get in his car.

"What asshole parked this thing so close to me?"

Maybe it was the same guy that just handed him his keys. But, Freddy remembered the guy that parked his car. He was much taller, not as fat, and had a darker complexion.

Joy had left her phone in the front passenger seat. She wanted to sit next to Freddy on the way back from the park. Freddy reached across the driver's seat and got the phone. He squeezed his way back out of the SUV and bumped his door against the side of the car parked next to his. "I need to find out who parked my car so close to this damn thing. This paint job cost me too much money," he said, in protest.

He checked to see if there was any damage done to the car parked next to his, even though it was only a bump. They make them so cheap and yet charge a fortune.

But there was no major damage. Freddy checked his door to see if it was closed all the way, set the alarm, and walked back between the two cars. He couldn't help but notice that the car parked beside his had a Mercedes symbol on the trunk.

"Hey, this is a wonderful car," he said to himself, realizing that someone else had good tastes in cars.

Then he saw the license plate, P-L-A-Y-E-R-5 and remembered Joy and Debo mentioning the PLAYER plates. He knew the doors were locked and the alarm had to be on, so he used Joy's phone to call Debo.

"Yeah, Sis.., what is it?"

"This is Freddy, boss. Guess what I just stumbled across parked in the parking structure next to my car at the hotel?"

"Okay, Freddy, I give up What did you stumble across?"

"A black Mercedes Benz, license plates P-L-A-Y-E-R-5. Joy left her cell phone in my car when we got back and she asked me to come down and check to see if it was here," Freddy explained.

"Well, that certainly explains why you are in the parking structure and why you called me on Joy's phone. Okay, move your car where you can sit in it without being seen by Cruse if he comes down and keep an eye on it until I get there. Do you have a weapon on you?"

"Every time I walk out the door."

"Okay, I'll call Joy and explain to her what's going on. I'm on my way, where is your phone?"

"I was so excited, I forgot to charge it. It's on the charger," Freddy explained.

"Excited about what?"

"I'll fill you in later, Debo."

"Yeah, you do that..., I'll call Shell's phone, I don't want you to talk business over the hotel phone," Debo said and hung up.

He dialed Shelly's phone. She knew to keep her phone on at all times in case of an emergency like this one.

"Hey, Baby, I see you feel like talking. I thought that you'd be dead tired after today. Okay, let me wake up."

"No.., go ahead to sleep, put Joy on for me. I'll call you tomorrow, sweetheart, okay?"

"Okay, honey, I love you."

"Love you too, goodnight."

Shelly pressed a button on her bedside table, sending a beep to the intercom in Joy's room.

"Sis, you okay in there?"

"Yeah, I'm fine, D-Angelo wants to speak to you on my phone." Joy entered her room quietly as if Shelly was asleep. She walked up to her bed and Shelly handed her the phone.

"Thanks, Sis I'll put it back on your table when I'm done." Joy put the phone to her ear and said,

"What's up, Bra?"

"Joy, Freddy was in the parking structure when he went to get your cell phone, and ran into Robert Cruse's car. I told him to sit on it. Grab your piece and stand by with Shell. I'm on my way, don't leave her alone for any reason whatsoever…, I mean, 'NO' reason."

"Bra?"

"Yeah?"

"Is he here?"

"Apparently so, sweetheart. We shot up his house so I guess he had to have somewhere to stay. Mister Write and I are almost there."

After they finished talking, Joy kept Shelly's phone in case Debo or Freddy called her. Shelly opened Joy's door and asked if everything was alright.

"Yeah, he wanted to check on something. He might call me back, can I hold on to your phone for a minute?"

"Sure, keep it as long as you need it."

Joy knew that Shelly wanted to know what was going on, but Joy couldn't tell her and Shelly didn't ask. Debo figured it was best. It kept Shelly from being afraid and worrying about Debo.

"Okay I'll get back to bed, just hold on to the phone for as long as you need it," Shelly said, wondering why Joy couldn't use her own phone, or why Debo couldn't call her on the hotel phone.

"Everybody's trying to spare my feelings and keeping me from worrying. But, all this keeping things away from me, only makes me worry more," Shelly thought to herself.

"Thanks, Sis, I left mine in Freddy's car and he went down to get it for me," Joy explained.

"Oh, I see."

She understood now that Joy seemed to have read her mind and answered her unasked question.

"I think it's time to move Shelly, Joy, and Pauline out to my cabin. This looks like it's about to get real messy and I want all of the girls out of the way. Joy is good with a gun and all, but she could have been killed a couple of times. She'll do us more good out at the cabin with Shelly and Pauline." Mad-C explained to Debo.

"Yeah, I guess you're right; get it, 'I guess you're Write."

"Yeah I get it, and why is everybody doing that? Stop making fun of my name, 'Jack'... get it... Jack. Now how does it feel? Pauline just did that to me yesterday," Mad-C cried.

"Well, boss, when you got it, you got it."

"Yes sir, you sure do, Jack."

"Here we are, I'll let you out here."

"Okay, go on up..., I'll walk up. You said, 'third-level sixteenth-stall?'"

"Yep, that's the one," Debo assured him.

"OK, I'm on my way," Mad-C said.

Debo wouldn't let the valet have the Navigator. He just informed the valet that he was going to the third level to meet a guest... and to call Shelly's room to verify that he is indeed meeting her. Joy would answer instead of Shelly for verification. Joy verified who he was and Debo was waved up. When he got to the third level, Freddy saw the Navigator and blew his horn to let Debo know that he saw him come up. Debo found an empty parking stall and parked. He got out of the Navigator and went over to Freddy's car and got in.

"Where is it?" Debo asked.

"Over there," Freddy said, pointing to the black Mercedes Benz that was parked five cars down and across the aisle.

"What do we do, boss?" Freddy asked.

"You can go back up and help Joy keep an eye out. Mister Write and I can handle things down here."

Debo handed Freddy his keys and told him to move the Navigator where Cruse wouldn't spot it.

"Go on to your room, but keep your eyes and ears open. You can take Joy her phone, but call her and let her know you're bringing it so you don't wake, Shell. Call her on Shell's cell phone."

"Okay, got it, boss," Freddy said, and went to the Navigator, got in, and was on his way down the ramp. On his way down, he saw Mad-C coming up.

"Mr Write, my boss isn't in stall sixteen, he's in stall twenty-two sitting in my car. It's the black Mercedes SUV. He'll see you, just go on up. Freddy pulled off and Mad-C went to where Freddy directed him. He walked up to Freddy's black Mercedes SUV and got in on the passenger's side. "Where is it?" Mad-C asked Debo

"Over there, the fifth car down on the other side."

"Okay, now what?"

"Now we wait," Debo said.

"Okay, Debo…, I'll get some shut-eye while you take the first watch, then I'll take second watch. Wake me in a few hours."

"Got it…, it's late, he might go to the club over on Gage. It doesn't shut down until 3:00 or 4:00 am, according to Freddy.

After two they just eat and dance, no liquor. California state law prohibits the sale and consumption of alcoholic beverages after 2:00 am," Debo said. "Alright, Debo, I'm gonna get me some shut-eye. Shake me up if something jumps, or when you get sleepy."

"Will do," Debo said.

Mad-C laid his head against the window and went to sleep. Freddy took Joy her phone.

"Just in time, I was getting worried. Nobody called me and I didn't know whether to call you: How's it going?"

"It's going okay, the boss and Mr Write has it all under control. He sent me up here to give you your phone. It's funny how Cruse wound come here."

"Yeah, and it's scary as hell too," Joy said. "I'll help you keep an eye out."

Although they had a busy day, Joy invited Freddy inside and they sat and talked for a while.

"How do you think Pauline and Mr Write are going to turn out?" Freddy asked.

"I see something there; I see a nice future for both of them. A future with someone that won't hurt each other. Mr Write is much too intelligent, wise, and smart not to know he has a good thing. He sure knows one when he sees one, so does, Pauline. I believe they will be just fine," Joy told him. "Yeah, I guess love just has to happen, you can't make it happen. Love is not a sexual attraction it's something that builds up inside you, it's everlasting depending on the relationship. That's how you can tell when it's love," Freddy said.

"You seem to know a lot about love, why are you single, Freddy? Is it because love hurt you and you're afraid of being hurt by love again?"

"Well, Joy…, I have been so busy trying to build something for myself; something to be able to offer the woman of my dreams, the woman that's going to be in my life until the day it ends. That's the main reason I've been single for as long as I have been. I don't want anybody that's going to be here today and gone tomorrow. I want someone that's going to be permanent. No, I've never been hurt by love because I can't see myself giving a woman the satisfaction of ever hurting me or breaking my heart. I guess they call it 'waiting for the right woman,' and I strongly believe in that concept."

"When do you feel the right woman will come, Freddy?"

"Joy, you never really know, it just happens. I think she'll come when I lose the nose ring. Who knows, she might be already here. I don't believe in being hurt by a woman, so I would never hurt my woman."

"Do you feel you've built up enough of what you were building?"

"Yeah, but for some reason, I just can't bring myself to leave the boss. I mean, I have enough money. It's just that he has done so much for me and I feel I'll always owe him."

"My brother is very good people, and I don't think he would want you to feel you owe him anything. In fact, it would disappoint him. When he does something from his heart, he doesn't expect anything in return. He does what he does for people so that they can and will have a rewarding life to return to. He would not want you to go on thinking you owe him. He would want you to live your life, that's why he gives us the opportunity. Look at, Jeffery …, do you think he would have tossed him back out there in those streets when he was drugged up and of no use to him? No, he found help for Jeffery. Robert Cruse didn't get my brother's money or the drugs he had that belonged to Mr Write. Jeffery told him that, and do you know what he did? He gave him the money and whatever was left of the twelve and a half keys. Do you think he wants that back from him? All I'm saying, Freddy is that, if you do offer to pay him back for giving to you from his heart, don't expect him to accept or appreciate it. You might just find that to be insulting to him; kinda like throwing it back in his face. Now, you wouldn't want to insult a man that has given you damn near the world, would you, Freddy?"

"Thanks, Joyvette…, I see why you are his little sister, you truly understand him, don't you?"

"Yeah, and I truly love him too," Joy said.

"Now, that's the kind of love I was talking about. That's the kind of love I need."

"And, Freddy…, that's the kind of love you deserve."

"Hey, I did this little thing using the word love,.. wanna hear it?" Freddy asked her.

"Sure, why not, I might like it," Joy said.

"Okay here goes; Long, Ongoing, Vibrations of Emotions."

"That's nice I like it, did you read it somewhere, or is it yours?"

"It's mine; it's not corny is it?"

"No, sweetheart, I like it…, I really like it,' Joy said.

The room grew quiet and Freddy used that time to think about what Joy had said, and to let it sink in. Shelly couldn't go back to sleep after Debo called to speak to Joy earlier. She had been awake all that time standing by her room door listening to everything that Joy and Freddy said: The way Joy stands up for Debo is amazingly beautiful. Shelly remembered what Joy said to her a while back when Debo first told her what he did for a living. Joy said to her…

'You've got a damn good man, just don't stop loving him.' And that brought tears to Shelly's eyes. And now, to stand behind that door and listen to her tell Freddy her fillings for Debo brought more tears to her eyes.

CHAPTER 18

FRIDAY, NOVEMBER 23RD, 2:00 A.M.

Debo was tired from the day's get-together at the park. He couldn't help but let his eyelids fall and nod off. He and Mad-C were sitting there with their eyes closed snoring loud enough to wake a bull. Until a loud car horn snatched them both awake. It was the sound of a car alarm. It was almost closing time and Robert Cruse decided to go to the club and help close.

"Well, looks like your plan worked, I'll follow him," Debo offered. "Okay.., but give him enough leeway so he won't know that we're on his ass," Mad-C suggested.

Robert took the freeway, it was easier and faster than the streets; easier because Debo and Mad-C could be any motorist on the freeway. Cruse took the I-10 San Bernardino Freeway north, to the I-10 Harbor Freeway south, and exited at Crenshaw Blvd.

"Where is he going?" Debo asked Mad-C.

"I don't know, I guess to the club. You can get to it off Crenshaw, it's easier and faster than going all the way out the Harbor Freeway."

"Yeah, I guess you're right."

They both looked at each other with a confused look in their eyes. "Yeah, maybe you're right," Debo said again and looked at Mad-C after he said it.

Mad-C looked back at him with warning eyes "Don't you dare," he told Debo.

He wasn't in the mood for name jokes. Debo got the message and decided he would be much better off leaving well enough alone.

"Where the hell is he going?" Debo wondered aloud.

"He's turning on Slauson, slow down right here it looks like he's pulling into that parking lot."

Robert Cruse had pulled into an L-shaped shopping center parking lot. "Pull over right here so he won't know we're on his ass."

Debo pulled the Mercedes SUV over and parked. "Well, what do you know; Look at this shit."

Debo saw Robert Cruse get out of his car and get into another car. "What the… what is he up to?" Debo asked again, not really expecting Mad-C to answer his question.

They saw Robert get out of the other car and go back over to his car and he pushed a button on his key chain to open the trunk. He reached in and pulled out a roll of cash and went back over to the other car and got back in. After what seemed like fifteen to twenty-minutes, Robert got out of the car empty-handed.

"Now I've seen it all; a fuckin drug deal just went down," Debo said. "I've got an idea, follow the other car when it leaves. Robert just paid for the shit. It looks like they're delivering it to Johnson.

Robert is no doubt going to the club, we can always get him, either there or at the hotel," Mad-C said.

Debo pulled out of the shopping center parking lot behind the car that Robert Cruse had just got out of and followed the car until it got to Crenshaw and Vernon where it made a right to seventh avenue.

"Where the hell are they going," Debo asked. They saw the driver get out and go into a house and stayed for about three-minute, he came out carrying a large briefcase and Debo said, "Follow his ass."

Debo saw Mad-C check the 44-Magnum to make sure it was ready for business. After a mile or so the man pulled into another driveway.

"He's pulling into that driveway over there. Don't let him; turn in front of him," Mad-C told Debo.

Debo went around the car and turned into it forcing it to stop. Mad-C got out of the Mercedes SUV and went up to the passenger's door, while Debo got out and went over to the driver's door with CRAZY at the ready.

"Hey... what is this?" the man asked with surprise in his voice and eyes. "Shut the fuck up and give me the briefcase, and I'm not gonna repeat myself," Mad-C told the guy on the passenger side. Debo saw the passenger's hand slowly move down between his seat.

"How many kids you got?" Debo asked the man. "What?"

"You heard what the fuck I said ... How many kids do you have?"

"Two, why?"

"Because if you want anymore, you'll leave that mothafucka on the floor where it is," Debo said while aiming the Glock-45 at his penis.

"It's in the back seat," the driver told Debo.

"Mad-C open the passenger's door and get whatever it is on the side of it. If he moves, I'll blow both of these mothafuckas to to hell and back."

Mad-C opened the passenger's door and discovered a thirty-eight revolver lying beside the seat. He picked it up, and said, "I got it."

"Turn around and unlock the back door; Wait!!. If you do anything but unlock that back door, then say goodbye to the rest of your life."

The passenger reached back and unlocked the door behind him. "Okay get the briefcase," Debo told Mad-C. Mad-C slid the briefcase off the back seat and close the door. "Where's your heat?" Debo asked the man at the wheel. He was too afraid to move so he nodded down toward the front of his pants and said,

"There, in my waistband."

Debo had already pulled the slide back on CRAZY. A weapon of that caliber could do a lot of damage at point-blank range. He pushed the barrel into the man's ear, and with his free hand, he reached down inside the car and removed the nine-millimeter automatic handgun from the the guy's waistband.

"Now, I want the both of you to get out of the car and stand over there on the sidewalk," Debo ordered.

Mad-C moved back to let the passenger out and walked toward the SUV. He got in and started the engine while Debo held the forty-five on the two men, making his way to the SUV. Mad-C drove around the front of the car and headed down the sidewalk where the men were standing. They saw the SUV headed toward them and dove for cover on a nearby lawn to avoid being run over which gave Mad-C a chance to get down the street before either of the two men could get to their feet and start shooting if they had backup weapons on them.

They had just taken $250,000 worth of heroin from Robert Cruse's men, Gregory Johnson's men, or both.

"This should make up for what they took from my man, Jeffery," Debo said while patting the briefcase full of dope.

"Yeah.., and I'm sure that there's much more to come," Mad-C added. "Yeah…, I'm sure there's a helluva lot more," Debo agreed.

"Where the hell is my fucking smack, you stupid mother-fucker!!!" Gregory Johnson screamed at Robert Cruise.

"I gave them the money at 2:30 this morning like you said and they were suppose to go get it and deliver it to you," Robert cried.

"The people you were supposed to have given the money to said, 'they didn't get it.' As a matter of fact, they said you never showed. Now, where is my shit or my money, Anderson?" Johnson repeated.

Robert Cruse reached into the pocket of a now sweaty shirt and pulled out a cell phone and attempted to call the two men he met at the shopping center parking lot on Crenshaw this morning.

"The number you've dialed is no longer…" He hung up the phone before the recording could finish.

"Those son-of-a-fucks ripped us off," Robert cried.

"No.., they ripped yo ass off. I want my shit, Raymond, and I want it now. You are really beginning to become a major pain in my ass and I don't need a major pain in my ass, little brother. That means get me my shit or my money and I don't want to go through any more of your bullshit. I don't want to have to get rid of yo ass, and I don't want to see yo ass until you've got my shit or my fucking money.

Do I make myself clear, Robert!!!" Johnson screamed. "Perfectly," Cruse said.

"Now get the fuck out of my face."

Gregory Johnson had no problem using the "F" word.

Everything that came out of his mouth was "F" this and "F" that. Cruse's face tightened as he balled his hands into big sweaty fists and stormed out of Johnson's office.

"There's a call for you on line two, Mr Cruse," Dorothy informed Robert as he was walking through her office.

"A what!!!" he screamed.

"Someone is on the phone for you, sir," she repeated.

"Robert Cruse accepted the receiver Dorothy was handing him and put it to his ear and said,"

"Yeah, this is me..., who is this?"

"Charles Write."

"What the hell do you want!!!" Cruse screamed.

"Do you know it's a bitch trying to find you? I still can't believe I'm talking to you. What happened to my money you took from Jeffery Smith?"

"What the fuck is a Jeffery Smith?"

"The man you had locked in that basement over on Ocean Park Way."

"You kiss my ass."

"Oh, I forgot to ask you: Did you lose something this morning?"

"You black bastard, you took my shit!!!" Cruse yelled.

"Well, look at it this way, I got my shit back. As a matter of fact, I'm looking at it as we speak, sweetheart. How's Dorothy? She sure is a beautiful woman. Who's fucking her... you, your brother, or both? Hey, dickhead, look out the window."

Robert did as Mad-C said, and what he saw outraged him.

"Shit," he cursed, as he looked down thirteen stories and didn't see anything but parked cars.

"Okay, I'm looking... now what?"

"Now this, mothafucka," Mad-C said, and as soon as he said it, Robert saw one of the biggest explosions he had ever seen. He saw the black Mercedes Benz he parked in the yacht club parking lot, go up in pieces of fiberglass, fire, smoke, and twisted metal.

"Oh my God!!!" Dorothy screamed when she heard the explosion. Gregory ran out of his office and almost ran into Dorothy. She was on her way into his office to tell him to look out the window. "What the fuck was that?" Gregory asked.

Cruse had no choice but to tell him, because Mad-C would have told him anyway on his next visit. And one way or the other, there will be a next visit.

"That was your car," Gregory heard Robert's frightened voice say.

It wasn't Mad-C he was afraid of, it was Gregory Johnson.

Gregory Johnson's veins literally popped out of his neck as he screamed "My what!!!" He dropped down in Dorothy's chair and folded his arms on her desk and laid his head in his folded arms and didn't say a word.

"Are you still there, Cruse? Now I know everybody got a real blast out of that one. Put this thing on intercom, Robert."

Robert Cruse had Dorothy put the phone on the intercom where they all could hear and be heard.

"Don't worry about what was inside the trunk.., it's perfectly safe, see mothafucka!!"

Robert, Gregory, and Dorothy looked down on the parking lot to see Mad-C holding in the air the briefcase he took off Johnson's men.

"Robert, I'm gonna tell you what I told your brother to tell you. Stay your ass away from me and my friends, or I'll blow your fucking brains out. I gotta go, gentlemen," Mad-C said, hung-up and was gone.

"That was Charles Write and D-Angelo Jackson. They blew up your car and robbed the guys for the heroin this morning," Robert told Gregory.

"But, they said you weren't there this morning," Gregory said. "Write told me before he had me put the phone on intercom. The guys probably lied because they figured we wouldn't believe the truth.

So, they made like I never showed up," Robert assumed.

"They're following you... they followed you to the exchange spot this morning, and they followed you here."

"I don't even know how they found me," Cruse cried.

"I don't either, but they are starting to piss me off. Where are the assholes I had to come out here to deal with them? Get out of my office, Raymond, I've got to make a phone call," Gregory Johnson told Cruse.

"How did you get Johnson's direct phone line?" Debo asked.

"When I leaned over Dorothy's desk to tell her how beautiful she was, I looked at the memo pad she had on her desk… and there was the number: The oldest trick in the world. You're getting clumsy in your old age, Debo. I have my eyes on Pauline, and you know once I set my sights on a woman, I'm hers and I don't mess around."

"Okay…, okay, big cat… my bad."

"Alright then, get yo shit straight, and don't let me catch you doing it again either."

Not that he would tell Shelly, but he does have a certain amount of respect for Shelly and Debo. And he won't stand for Debo cheating on Shelly to his face. He never have and hopefully, he never will.

"Now, you know I love Shell, and no one can even come close to my Shell. Let's get Freddy his car back."

"Yeah, and besides, Cruse should be going back to the hotel. We've got to keep an eye on things so we'll know where he goes, when he goes, who he sees, and why he sees them," Mad-C said. Debo called Freddy to let him know that he and Mad-C were on their way back with his car.

11:30 AM

"Hey, Freddy, we're on our way back, and don't worry your car is still operational. We stopped and had a little breakfast after we finished talking to Cruse."

"Did I miss a lot?"

"No, not a whole helluva lot. Just don't figure on seeing the black Mercedes anymore. Cruse knows we're following him, so I'll have to put you back at the club on Gage. They won't try anything until they get me or Mad-C. At least that's what I figure."

"I wish they would try some shit; they don't know I'm itching for some. Let them come on with it so I can get to scratchin," Freddy said. "I know Shell was up worried all night, is she okay?"

"She's holding out pretty well. I stayed up here last night in case I was needed I wanted to be closer than just a floor away."

"Yeah, okay... 'floor away'... I saw you and Joy at the Pitt yesterday; I don't miss too much. I'll be there in about forty-five minutes to an hour; Put, Joy on for me."

"OK, hold on a sec."

Freddy called Joy to the phone. She stopped what she was doing in the large kitchen and came to see what Debo wanted.

"Hey, Big Bra," Joy greeted. "Hey, are you okay?"

"Yeah... I was worried."

"Sorry kid, we were trying to tie up some loose ends. How are you and Shell fixed for cash? You girls are probably low. I'll send you some by Freddy when I give him his car."

"I'm not too sure about how much Shelly has, but I'm okay bra. If she needs any, I got her."

"Okay, Sis.., tell her I'm fine, and tell her that I said for her to relax. Hey, Joy.., tell me something."

"If I can."

"Is everybody paring up on me or what?"

"It certainly looks that way to me. At least we're keeping it in the family. We all love and know each other and we are about as close to a family as anyone can get... wouldn't you say so?"

"Yeah, I guess you're right."

That's exactly what they are, a family with a bond so strong a team of wild bulls wouldn't be able to tear them apart. There is a lot of love, blood, sweat, tears, trust, and laughter all wrapped up in those six people... well, seven with Jeffery Smith.

"Mad-C, Johnson hit the office building Saturday while we were at the park."

"I know, I'm here now," Mad-C said. "You don't plan to stay there do you?"

"I don't see why not, I won't run from no man, D-Angelo."

"Yeah, but look at it this way. You once told me 'to never give up on anything. To give up would be hiding the person you really are, the person you could truly be. The things you set out to accomplish will all be a waste if you don't see it through.' You also said, 'utilize your resources and stop at nothing to achieve your goals.' And for you to stay there knowing these guys are waiting for you to come there to fall into their trap so they can kill you. Why do you think they didn't take out the whole office? Because they knew you would go back there hoping they would return. I'm all the way with you. Whatever you decide, I'm on your team. We are the team, and I'm not gonna back out on you or leave you alone for them to pick you off. But there is a way we can win this thing and make it out alive. And going back there waiting to be killed is not the way. If Johnson's men don't sneak up on us, Beverly Hills Police will. They won't take kindly to us packing heat and shooting and blowing up their town. Those guys play rough, and we don't have them on our payroll."

Debo has Mad-C's car, he had dropped him off at Freddy's place. Mad-C wanted to go and rent a room, but Freddy had talked him into kick-in-it with him at his house until Debo returns from talking to Sergeant Billings downtown.

"I can stay out here, I don't mind the drive back and forth," Mad-C told Debo.

"I have a better idea. Why don't you give me some muscle and let me handle everything on the LA end. Me, Freddy, and about four of your guys will be enough."

"Have you lost your mind, son?"

"No…, because by doing it this way you can keep a check on the business. This is taking way longer than I thought it would. I'll keep you posted on everything, and when the big shit hits the fan, you can step in. This is my job, it's what I do. I get paid enough so that you wouldn't have to dirty your hands, and so does all the guys and ladies that works for us."

"Okay, Debo…, but you're running everything, you are the boss, you call all the shots.. If you have any problems out of my men, I want you to let me know. I'm only doing this because, for one thing, I like the way you work, I like the way you think. And what you just said made damn good sense and you know how to handle Cruse. I saw the way you handled Randy Carlyle at the hospital. You are definitely the man for the job. I'll be fine at home, and I'll keep you caught up on what's going on out at the cabin. My men will report to me every day, and if anything goes down, I'll hear about it before it does. So, don't worry about the girls. I can't recall ever having to ever worry about any of your decisions. I have faith in your ability to make good decisions. I know you can handle this, D-Angelo," Mad-C awarded.

4:30 PM

South Los Angeles, California is not one of Debo's favorite places to go and visit, especially after the "Rodney King Riots: The riots that devastated a whole community. Freddy lives right in the heart of where it all got a lot of notoriety; Florence and Normandie Avenues.

Freddy's house is just a typical two-story, stucco, five-bedroom, two-bath house with black wrought-iron bars covering the windows, and a black rot wrought-iron door on the front and back of the house to keep unwanted intruders out. The backyard is spacious but not big enough for a pool. He added a patio, a barbecue and a portable Jacuzzi instead. He paid $180,000 for it years ago. It's tripled in value since then. Now it's worth over half a million dollars.

Debo got there close to 5:00 pm. Mad-C and Freddy were already in the backyard sitting on the patio discussing their new found loves. Debo knocked on the front door but no one answered. He was going to blow the horn in Freddy's car but the windows were rolled up, so he decided to go around back, and that's where he found them.

"I heard my name… anything I should know about?"

"Nah… we were just sitting here saying how thankful we are for the two wonderfully beautiful ladies you brought into our lives and trying to figure out what we did to deserve such blessings," Freddy enlightened.

"You both are beautiful brothers and you both deserve beautiful things, that's it, that's all. Now come on,d let's stop talking so much about the women before I start missing Shell. It's a chill out here, what are you guys sippin on?" Debo asked.

"Oh, just some Martel," Mad-C answered.

"One of my favorites, Freddy, where can I find a glass?"

Debo knew where the glasses were, he just wanted Freddy to get it for him but Freddy wouldn't bite.

"Boss, have you forgotten where the kitchen is? You're at home, go in the kitchen and get yourself a glass," Freddy said.

He was too tipsy to move anyway. He and Mad-C had been at it since about 2:30 pm. Martel is a smooth drink, but when it kicks, it kicks.

"Mister Write told me about the office," Freddy told Debo when he returned from the kitchen .

"Yeah, Freddy… we have a big mess on our hands," Debo shared. "Hey, Mister Write… did the Boss ever tell you about the time he went horseback riding at Griffith Park?"

"No, I don't believe he did, Freddy. Why don"t you tell me."

"We were out having the time of our lives one day at Griffith Park. It was just me, Shelly, and the boss; anyway, we were riding on a horse trail and a wounded skunk was lying in the middle of the trail. My horse bucked and stopped; nearly throwing me off its back. Those Things can't stand skunks; anyway, the boss' horse did the same thing, only he was thrown off his horse and landed on the skunk. Shelly and I laughed until our sides hurt. It took us nearly an hour to clean him up before he could get in his own car.

It took us months to stop calling him, 'Big Stinky'. He wouldn't go anywhere with me or Shelly for two month. We got a good laugh out of it."

"Tell the truth, Freddy: The truth is… the skunk had already sprayed his spray on the ground and I fell in it. I didn't fall on the dog-gone thing. Those things are like rats, aren't they?" Debo asked.

"I guess they are, because I smelled a big-ass rat that day," Freddy jokingly teased.

"I'll never take you horseback riding again," Debo cried.

"That's okay, joy said, 'she can out-ride you anytime and without a saddle.' "What do you say to that?" Freddy bragged.

"I say I'm gonna call, Joy and…, hold on a sec, Mister Moss," Debo said and dialed Joy's cell phone.

"Are you serious?" Mad-C asked Debo. "As a heart attack," Debo said. Joy answered her cell phone and was surprised to learn it was Debo. "Hey, Big Bra, this place is the best, I'm loving it, what's up?"

"Did you tell Freddy you could out-ride me on a horse?"

"I sure did, I told you the same thing, remember? Oh, and I heard about your horseback riding incident: Smelly was it, or was it Stinky? 'Big Stinky,' yeah, that's it," Joy teased.

He heard Shelly laughing in the background. "Give me the phone Sis," she told Joy.

"Are they teasing my baby?"

He heard Pauline laughing uncontrollably and started laughing himself. "What are you guys doing baby?" Shelly asked.

"Just sitting around reminiscing; hold on a sec." He heard his call waiting alert signal and switched over to accept the call. "How can anybody call you and you're on the phone? I had that taken care of for you. Guess what they…,"

"Hold on a minute, let me tell Shell that I'll call her back." Before Billings could respond, Debo had switched back to Shelly.

"That's Sergeant Billings baby, call me back later, it's an important call."

"Okay, Sweetheart, go ahead and talk to him, I'll talk to you later," Shelly said, and Debo switched back over to Sgt Billings.

"Okay, Sarge you were saying… "

"I was saying, do you know what they put under your car?"

"No…, what, Bob?"

"They blessed you with two pounds of C-4 plastic explosives. That's enough to blow you, Write, and half this block to hell and back. My boys were scared to touch it but we took it off for you. We're still out here finishing up. I wasn't surprised at what it was, I know how Johnson and his boys work."

"Did they leave a detonator?"

"Jackson, what are you thinking? No, never mind… don't tell me," Billings said before Debo could answer him.

He was thinking he could get one of his war buddies to help him plant the explosives inside Johnson's Jet hanger.

"No, they didn't leave one, you didn't give them time to. If they had left it, we wouldn't be having this conversation."

"Did they find one on the body?"

"I'm not sure, all I got was the report and it didn't mention one."

"So, you knew about this then?"

"I knew about the two men that were killed behind your office, and the two that were killed across the street from your office. But, no… I didn't know about any bomb being put under your car. You want the bomb, right?"

"Yeah, no one knows about it do they?"

"No, no one knows about it: You want it right?"

"Yeah, you can leave it in the car for me and I'll get it."

"How am I supposed to do that and the car is locked?"

"There is a combination pad under the door handle."

"Okay, Jackson I'm going home to my daughter and my wife and forget about you, your bomb, your Navigator, and some my problems."

"Thanks, Sarge, I owe you one."

"Jackson, you owe me plenty my man," Billings said, ending their conversation. "I have an idea, why don't we rent a trailer-hitch so I can pull the Dodge to San Diego and you can ride with me? I'm sure the Navigator will pull it with no problem; we'll be on straight open road. We can leave late and miss a lot of traffic and get there faster," Debo suggested.

"Sounds like a good idea to me I'd better take a nap, the Martel has me kinda woozy," Mad-C said.

"Yeah, I don't think either one of us should be driving anytime soon. We all had better sleep it off a couple hours; you and I should anyway," Debo said.

"Do you guys need me to ride out there with you?" Freddy asked. "You're sure welcome to, and on that note, I told my baby to call me back," Debo said.

"Yeah, that's a good idea," Freddy said. "I'm all for that," Mad-C added.

"Boss, I wanna thank you from the bottom of my heart," Freddy told Debo.

"Thank me for what?"

"Allowing me to be in Joy's life. I know you could have prevented it if you didn't feel I was good enough for her. The only thing I can do is thank you and give her the love and respect she deserves. I'm saying thank you because I'll never be able to repay you for any of the many blessings you have given me."

"Well, Freddy you just did; repay me by taking care of her, loving her, and don't hurt her or break her heart. She's been through enough of that. It's time for her to be happy and content with the man in her life," Debo said.

"Let's toast to the girls," Freddy purposed. "To the girls," they all said in unison, and raised their half-filled glasses to initiate the toast. Freddy told everyone to fall out wherever they wanted to or they could have their own room until morning.

"Sounds good to me," Mad-C said.

"How does 4:30 or 5:00 in the morning sound? No, we'll run into all that rush hour traffic. How about… let's see… it's seven now, how about 2:30 or 3:00?" Mad-C suggested.

"Okay… 2:30 or 3:00 it is," Debo confirmed.

Debo didn't get much sleep, he was up late last night on the phone with Shelly. He didn't mind as long as she knew that he was alright. When he did nod off, it seemed like only seconds before Mad-C was shaking him awake.

"Let's get ready to hit the road, sleepy head!"

"Okay, but you'll have to drive, I'm still sleepy. I was on the phone with Shell all night" Debo said and yawned.

"No problem," Mad-C said.

"Hey, boss, you don't mind riding with a bomb in the car, do you?"

"A what!!!" Mad-C yelled.

"A-bomb, some C-4."

"Where in the hell did you get a bomb, and what are you going to do with it?"

"The one Johnson's boys left us."

"Debo, you're getting scarier by the second."

"I wanna get Johnson's ass big time."

"Okay, sounds like a plan."

"He blew up the office, damn near blew up my car, and tried like hell to kill us. So, I figure we can go by the club at about 8:00 pm: and handle some business and be back in San Diego by about 11:30 pm. How does that sound? I mean I was really thinking of blowing up his Jet hanger in San Diego."

"Debo.., you might have something there; sounds like a hell-of-a plan."

"Yeah, I figured it would."

Debo called a demolition expert that he served with in the military and had him meet them at the club on Gage.

8:40 PM

Freddy went there after his conversation with Debo and Mad-C. He arrived at a little past 8:00 pm. He had been there waiting for what seemed to be hours, then went in and asked for Misty. The bartender, the kitchen help, and the DJ all said they hadn't seen her. He went outside and sat in his car, hoping to see her when she got there. Hours went by and still no sign of Misty. It was almost 11:30 pm on a Friday evening and Freddy was hungry. He checked the 357-Magnum and put it back in the glove compartment of his car. He couldn't take it in with him, because after what happened there with Joy, Mad-C and Debo, the police and Gregory Johnson had required they have metal detectors installed so that no one enters carrying a weapon but security. Freddy went in to get something to eat in the dining section of the Club. He ordered spinach greens, smothered pork chops, corn-on-the-cob, yams, and a large coke.

"Are you going to eat all of that yourself, handsome?" he heard a voice from behind him ask. Misty had been standing there for only a minute. She slid into the seat next to him at the counter.

"Well, hello stranger, how have you been?" Freddy greeted. "I've been fine, are you buying dinner?"

"Well, the last time I bought you a drink, you disappeared on me," Freddy answered.

"Marty, bring his order over there for me, will you?"

She pointed to a table in back where they would be out of the way. She took Freddy's hand and led him to a both, then she slid in and he slid in across from her.

"So, where have you been?" Freddy asked, to start a conversation. "First of all, let me get something out of the way. I know who you are and I know why you're here...,"

"But, I...," Freddy started to say something but she cut him off.

"Please listen, don't talk or you might miss something. Now, as I was saying, I know who you are and I know why you're here. Ten years ago a friend of yours shot and killed my husband. My brother has been after him ever since.

"I don't know that much about any of that, but I do know that Mack Rodgers; my late husband was living a lifestyle that kept him in constant danger. He was destined to be killed at the hands of another man; it was just a matter of time. I'm not saying that I'm okay with it because seriously I'm not. I'm only saying that I was prepared for it. My husband and my brother were very close friends. Closer than he was with me and I was his wife. My stepbrother, I'm sure you've heard of him; Gregory Johnson wanted me to meet you here and try to get information from you, and I'm sure you were told to do the same. Gregory Johnson; my stepbrother, and Raymond Anderson; my blood sibling, don't give a rat's ass about me. All they've done since I can remember was use me. I work here for free but they make sure I have a place to sleep, food to eat, not to mention the best clothes to wear, and all the friends I can have in this lifetime. But I can't do anything but work my ass off here day-in and day-out. And now they want me to help them set your people up. I'm not like my brothers, I wanted my own life but they wouldn't let me have it so they kept me depending on them. They keep me needing what they have to give me. But, no one, and I mean, 'NO ONE' messes with me or they will be found someplace and that's only if they're lucky enough to be made an example of. If not, they won't be found at all. I don't mind doing what I do here at the club; for one thing, this place will soon be mine anyway, Gregory is giving it to me. I'm not telling you anything you don't already know by telling you that Gregory owns this place. You and your people already know that. I've been around, I'm not a damn fool. I said that to say that I'm not going to assist you in killing my brother. And at the same time, I'm not going to help them kill you or your people. So, you guys handle your own shit, because I'm not in it. I told Gregory the same thing when he asked me to come here and meet with you. Here comes your meal.

You seem like a very sweet person, I hope you don't go out the way my husband did. If you ever see me again in this lifetime, please do me and yourself a favor and keep walking. Enjoy your meal," she said.

"But I… "

She stopped Freddy again before he could finish his sentence. "Please, Freddy, whatever it is you're about to say, please don't," Misty told him, then turned around and walked away; leaving him stuck and baffled to finish his meal.

TUESDAY, NOVEMBER 27TH, 2:45 AM

The Club was still closed when they arrived. There were close to fifty remaining customers scattered about the place.

Debo, Mad-C, Freddy, and Debo's friend were waiting patiently for everyone to leave. Chocolate was there and Freddy recalled what she said about not wanting to set up Mad-C or his friends. He also remembered her saying that the club would soon belong to her and how hard she works there, and how long she's been there. She also shared that the club was all she knows how to do. He thought about the fact that she could have saved their lives. Now, Debo is going to take the only thing she lives for; take her life away, which is the club. Maybe there was something that Freddy could do about it.

All the lights outside and inside the club were turned off. The only light left on was the neon light in the window, advertising the different brands of beer and malt liquors. The last light to go off was the one to the entry. The person locking up for the day backed out, pulling the doors shut and locking them. When she finished she turned around to leave. Freddy saw that it was Misty, aka Chocolate, the future sole owner of the "Happy Hours Nightclub, Bar and Grill".

"Is that Cruse's sister, Freddy?" Debo asked. "Yeah that's her, can I say something?"

"What is it, Freddy?"

"Gregory Johnson is leaving that place to her. She said she wants no part of her brother's mess. They wanted her to set us up and she told Johnson and Cruse no."

Freddy told them about the whole conversation between him and Chocolate.

"Think about it boss, please," Freddy said, with sympathy and an open heart.

And he did, he thought about it, and so did Mad-C. In fact, they thought about it for a long time. Freddy sounded like the Club was already Misty's, and that it was already in her name.

"Well, Freddy…, Robert Cruse will never see it again, and Johnson knows it's going to create problems with selling drugs and prostitution. I'll tell you what, Freddy.., I killed this woman's husband; not that I had a choice, but still and all I did. I can't take her husband's life and hers. And, if this place is her only means of living, then it's her life." Mad-C said, then turned around and looked at Debo.

Debo honked his horn, and Misty Rodgers turned around and saw a huge SUV Lincoln Navigator sitting on the other side of the street.

"Go over there and tell her to come over here, Freddy," Mad-C said. Freddy walked over to Chocolate and said,

"Hi, Chocolate, how are you?"

She turned around and started walking faster, getting closer to her car. Freddy broke into a fast trot, trying to catch up to her. She put the key in the car door and opened it. But before she could get in, he put his hand on her shoulders, and without facing him she said,

"We're closed, and I asked you not to bother me anymore. You must want to become that example I was telling you about."

"It's very important that you listen to me," Freddy told her. "Look, I told you…"

"Freddy cut her off before she could finish what she was about to say. "Listen, this is not about your brother, it's about you. Those are the men that I spoke to you about sitting in that Navigator across the street."

"I don't care, I… "

Freddy stopped her again

"Please don't cut me off again, Chocolate. Let me finish and you will never hear from me again. I have to be going, but first I need you to walk over to that Navigator with me."

"For what, so your friends can kill me like they did my husband?"

"Misty, please.., just trust me."

"I guess if you all wanted me dead or kidnap me you would have done it by now. Okay, Freddy, but one minute only." She closed the car door and walked across the street behind Freddy.

They got to Debo's window and it was rolled down.

"Hello, Miss Rodgers, my name is D'Angelo Jackson, and this gentleman is Mister Write. I'm sure you've heard of us."

"Yes, vaguely; one of you killed my husband."

"Yes, but I had no choice. You see, he pulled a sawed-off shotgun on me and was about to blow my head off. And now your brother or stepbrother tried to blow up my friend's car. We got to them before they could complete the first attempt. Then they came back and did a great deal of damage, so I came over here to blow his club up."

"Oh my God!!!" Misty cried.

"Now…, if you can stop the sales of drugs and prostitution in this place and run a legit club from now on, I'll forget about blowing up the club. Freddy told us it's all you have and a lot more of what you told him," Mad-C said.

Misty looked at Freddy confused and said, "So you stopped him from blowing up my club?"

"I talked to them and got them to understand it would do no good to make you suffer for what your brothers did. You are going to keep them from blowing it up by shutting down all drug transactions and prostitution."

"Mister Write.., is it?"

"Yes..., Charles Write."

"Mr Write, can I ask you something?"

"Sure you may," Mad-C said while looking at Freddy in time to see that he had drawn the 357-magnum he kept tucked away on his side in case Misty wanted revenge and pulled a gun on Mad-C and Debo.

"Mister Write, do you have a wife, sir?"

"No, I'm a widower, Mad-C told her."

"So, you must know how I felt when you killed my Mack."

"Yes, I do."

"Do you still feel the pain of losing your wife?"

"Every day I breathe, and yes I know what you are going through."

"Do you Mr Write?"

"Yes."

"Good, then since you went through the same suffering, the same pain, the same loneliness, the same hell I went through, then I forgive you. I'm a Christian woman, Mr Write, the old me died years ago. I was just like my brothers but I couldn't see myself being that way; being that kind of human being. The only reason I'm at the club is because my brother needed me there. Is he dead too, Mr Write?"

"No he isn't, but he is in the hospital. He went to this gentleman's house and tried to kill us," Mad-C said, referring to *the Shell-Debo.*"

"I understand, I know my brother and my stepbrother. Thank you for not killing Raymond, and thank you for having a heart. I know if you didn't have to kill, Mack, if you could have avoided it you would have. And I heard he had robbed you. He and my brother bragged about it to everyone after they did it. That's probably how you found out it was him and Mack. Everyone and anyone could have told you who it was and where they were. And, I'm sure whoever told you was rewarded very handsomely."

"Do you have any children, Misty?"

"No, why?"

"Well, I just figured that if... "

"No, I'm fine, you've done enough just letting me have my club."

"So, you agree that if we leave the club alone, you'll stop drugs and prostitution trafficking?" The reason I ask is because my friend's little sister was almost killed here at your club. She was a victim of a drug deal gone bad."

"Yes, I heard about that. You must be Mr Jackson?" she said. Misty has never met Debo, she only heard about him through her brothers and Randy Carlyle.

"Yes, Chocolate, I am.., and it was a pleasure meeting and talking with you," Debo-C said.

"Please, call me Misty… Misty Rodgers is my name."

"I wish we could have met under different circumstances."

"So do I, Mister Jackson, you both seem to be really good people," Misty said.

She turned to Freddy who had put the gun away long ago, and said, "It was nice meeting you too. If we hadn't met, I wouldn't have my Club. Thanks, Freddy."

"You're more than welcome, Chocolate, Uh… Misty."

"And, Mister Write, be careful Gregory is a very sneaky person and you have something he wants."

"Yeah, what's so important about the dock out in Long Beach?" Mad-C asked Misty.

"Mr Write, I'm sorry but I'm not answering any questions. I tried to make that as clear to Freddy as I could. Didn't he tell you?"

"Yes, he did, you take care," Mad-C told her. "You do the same, you too Mister Jackson." She walked up to Freddy and said,

"You take care also, and thanks again."

She walked back across the street to her car, got in, and left.

"You're getting soft in your old age, huh big fella?" Debo jokingly asked Mad-C.

"Yeah, okay.., 'Big Stinky', leave me alone and drive."

"Hold on a sec.," Debo said and got out of the car and walked over to the car that his friend the demolition expert was waiting in and said, "we're not doing the job here, but there is another location I want to hit in San Diego. I'll call you with all the details this afternoon," Debo said, and handed his friend an envelope containing fifty $100 bills.

"I'll double that after the next job is finished," Debo said, and got in the Navigator and left.

Freddy, Debo, and Mad-C were headed to San Diego. Mad-C took the wheel so Debo could get some sleep. He was in the passenger's seat laid back. He reclined the seat, and with closed eyes he said,

"Mad-C?"

"Yeah," Mad-C responded, with his eyes still on the road ahead of him.

"I was just wondering if you were okay."

"What do you mean, 'am I okay'?"

"Well, the question Misty asked you about Cassy, I thought…"

"No, Debo…, I'm not okay, I remember it like it was yesterday that I lost Cassy and my little, Tina. No, I'm not alright at all right now, and realizing her loss was the only thing that changed my mind about the club. I thought about the pain she must have gone through as a grieving widow. And then for her to ask me that question, I felt it all over again," Mad-C confessed, then turned to face Freddy who was sitting in the back seat, and said,

"Thanks, Freddy, I didn't realize what a mistake I almost made."

"Do you want me to take the wheel?" Debo asked.

"No…, I got it, keeping my mind on the road will take it off of that tragic evening in my life."

"Yeah you're right about one thing, it's not everyone's fault so why punish everyone for someone else's wrongdoings?" Debo asked.

5:00 AM

When they arrived in San Diego, everyone went over to Mad-C's estate. They all took an early nap before leaving Los Angeles, so they weren't too tired. Debo caught up on some sleep during the ride down, even though it's early in the morning, he thought it would be a good idea for Mad-C to have a small shot of brandy to clear his thinking, or to remove the thoughts he was having, and it did. Soon he let it go to the back of his head to rest and to once again become dormant.

Freddy broke the ice by holding his glass up and saying,

"A toast to two great and considerate men, Mister Write and Mister Jackson."

They acknowledged and initiated the toast.

"Freddy, I want to thank you again," Mad-C said, then raised his glass in the air again and said, "To Freddy" And they all followed suit.

2:00 PM

Mad-C went to the Chula Vista Police Department in San Diego to get the information and location of Gregory Johnson's private jet hanger. The officer he spoke with gave him the name of an airplane captain; James Wentworth: Wentworth is the one who provided Mad-C with the airfield location and the hanger that the jet is housed in. The rest was up to them.

"Well, I'm sure a professional demolitions expert could get in to do the job for $10,000, 00.," Mad-C said.

"Yeah, and that includes the $5,000 he got for the job at the club which we didn't do," Debo said. He called his military friend to set up the job for 2:30 Wednesday morning.

"Mad-C," Debo said after he hung up the phone. "Yeah, Debo?"

"There was nothing you could have done once you made the decision to go over there. Cruse, Rodgers, Morris, Jones, or Carlyle would not have given you what you went over there after. That woman's husband put himself in harm's way when he robbed you at that liquor store that night ten years ago. Let me ask you this; If you had it to do over again, how would you handle it differently? What would you do differently than what you did?"

"I don't know, Debo."

"I know…, You wouldn't have done anything differently. Do you know how I know? Because anyone being in the same frame of mind you were in and not thinking clearly would have done the exact same thing you did, over and over again. That's how our minds work when we're angry and not thinking. Your wife and daughter's deaths were an accident. Mack

Rodgers and Jones' deaths weren't. Someone else would have done it if you hadn't. That's why I think Misty forgave you, so you can go ahead and put it behind you. You understand that you did what you had to do."

"Debo, I've killed a great many men in my day and I'm still doing it today. But, it was something about that particular killing, that's all. Thanks, Debo…, I'm okay the brandy is getting to me, I guess. I'll just take a nap," Mad-C said, and went to his room to lay down.

It's Tuesday and the week is just starting, but it doesn't appear to make much difference. Everyday is a very busy day, weekends are no different, except there's more traffic on the highways and freeways, people doing weekend things… whatever that may be. For some it's catching up on things, little things, business things, things that you had forgotten to do or wish you could forget to do, important things, and things that are not so important anymore but still needs to be done. So, everybody's running around doing… "things".

Debo wondered how people ran around all day doing things, and at the end of their day they say, 'I haven't gotten a thing done all day.'

The world is crazy… or it's the people in it… or the people who runs it, or the people in it who want to run it but can't… or don't know how, or that's not allowed to. Whatever; Debo loved the world for its many benefits and the luxuries of life it has to offer. For the beauty of having someone to live a happy life with. He just wanted to get on with that wonderful life of his and Shelly's. He wanted to put all this mess behind him but he knew he had one thing to do and it has to be done now.

"Hey, boss, Just say we keep blowing up things; very expensive things that belong to Johnson. What happens when and if he decides to blow up the dock and just say to hell with it all? 'If he can't have it, no one can.'"

"That's a good question, Freddy, but the way I see it is if he's willing to pay millions of dollars to get it, there must be something of very significant value there; Something that if he should blow it up, it would be destroyed. He doesn't want it destroyed or he would have done that long ago. That would have been his first option rather than the office."

"Okay, why not Mister Write's estate? I'm sure he knows where he lives."

"What makes you so sure Freddy?" Mad-C said when he came into the room.

He woke up from his nap feeling fresh and convinced it did him some good.

"Oh, you're back among us?"

"You don't think those people are following us?"

"Yes, I'm sure they are, Freddy. Come here let me show you something," Mad-C said.

He led Freddy into his home office and pointed to one of two chairs sitting on either side of a coffee table in the middle of the room and told him to have a seat.

Mad-C walked over to his desk and took out a remote control from one of its drawers. He walked over and sat in a chair opposite Freddy and pressed a button on the remote and a panel on the wall across from them slid back to reveal a dozen closed-circuit television monitors. He pressed another button and all the screens came to life.

"Okay, what am I looking at?" Freddy asked Mad-C.

"Security cameras are installed around every inch of this property."

"Who are all of..., never mind I see."

Freddy was looking at heavily armed security personnel. Each monitor showed a guarded parameter: There were three men with A-K-47 assault rifles guarding the front gate, three men armed with 30-30 assault rifles guarding another part of the property appeared on another monitor. Mad-C pressed another button and Freddy saw four more men on another screen with automatic weapons and Kevlar vests strapped to them as they guarded the property.

"And that's not all... this property is guarded by motion sensors for areas that don't have security personnel. So, you see... it would be very difficult for anyone to get in here and make it out alive. That's one of the reasons I haven't suggested going to Johnson's ranch.

He could very well, and I'm almost sure he does have shit loads of security. If he were to send his boys out here it would have to be a sneak attack. The same goes for his place, but I think the jet should be easy," Mad-C explained.

"Well, you are heavily guarded, Mister Write," Freddy said.

"Let's go see what my man is up to in there," Mad-C said and got up; leaving the monitors on and the panels slid back.

Debo heard them come into the room and ended the conversation he was having with Shelly.

"Boy, I haven't been here in a while," Mad-C said when they got to *the Shell-Debo.*

"Make yourself at home," Debo said, looking through a pile of mail. He had a gardener bill, the bill from the vet for Rex, a lot of junk mail; bank statements, checks he had written, and a bill from the car leasing agency for the tire for the Explorer that he forgot to get. The scratches were paid for by the agency's insurance company.

"Everybody wants money," Debo said, as he looked through the mail. Debo and Mad-C took off their weapons and got comfortable.

"I sure miss home, even worse I miss my dog," Debo said.

"I'm beat, I think I'll go get some shuteye myself, it's a nice tiring ride back," Mad-C said.

"Okay, you know where to find everything. You can shit, shave, shower, or whatever makes you happy. I'm going to finish checking this mail and go to sleep myself!!!" Debo yelled from the living room.

Mad-C was already in the bathroom. "Where is the shampoo!!!"

"What!!!" Debo didn't understand him because the bathroom door was closed.

3:30 AM

"What's up this early in the morning, Freddy?"

"I followed Cruse to the club and waited to see if he was closing, and he did," Freddy excitedly said.

"Okay, so...?"

"So, I'm still following him on the 108 Freeway headed for the 109."

"You mean Cruse is on his way here?"

"Yes, him and three more of his little girlfriends."

"Okay, let me know when he gets off the freeway."

"We'll be off in about five minutes."

"Yeah I know, just call me when he gets off," Debo repeated.

He yelled toward the back of the house for Mad-C, where he was still in the restroom. He didn't know if he heard him or not because he couldn't hear Mad-C, so he walked down the hall and knocked on the bathroom door, in an attempt to get his attention.

"What's going on, is something wrong!!!" Mad-C yelled through the door. "We have company coming in about ten to fifteen-minutes."

"Who is it?"

"It's Cruse and about three of his little bitches. Freddy just called and told me he's following them. I told him to call me back when they get off the freeway."

As soon as Debo finished talking, Mad-C turned the shower off, put on one of the guest robes, and came out of the bathroom.

"Put something on, they should be here soon."

As Debo was finishing his statement, his cellphone rang and It was Freddy calling again.

"Boss, we're outside your house."

"What are they doing?"

Debo had turned off the lights in the house so no one would know anyone was there.

"No one is inside the house, the lights are off," one of the men said. "Yeah, I don't see his car, and those assholes didn't blow it up like they were supposed to. They got themselves killed instead, and they're supposed to be professionals," Cruse said.

"They're just sitting there," Freddy said. "Exactly where are they parked?"

"About two houses down to my left. If you were standing in front of the door inside the house, it would be to your right, opposite the mailbox," Freddy described.

"We're coming out from both sides. When you start shooting, be careful not to shoot us," Debo told Freddy.

Debo was on his phone and Freddy was using Bluetooth because he was driving.

"Okay, talk to me, Freddy; where are they?"

"They're coming up the sidewalk."

Mad-C stood on one corner of the house, and Debo stood on the other. Freddy let the men get far enough up the sidewalk and walked crouched down on the outside of the other parked cars.

"I see them," Debo said.

Mad-C spotted four men coming toward the house aiming their weapons at the front of the house, about to open fire.

At the same time, Debo, Mad-C, and Freddy let loose on them. Lead was flying, and smoke filled the air. Mad-C took down the man closest to him with one shot to the man's head. Debo hit two of them with automatic fire, taking them both to the ground.

Freddy nailed Cruse with the 357-Magnum but he didn't kill him. Debo wanted Cruse alive so he could question him. He wanted to know when and where the hit-men would strike next.

Mad-C knows a police lieutenant down at the Chula Vista police department in San Diego where he had Cruse put on ice. No phone calls, no visits, not even an attorney visit. He was guilty of the Yin murder and didn't really want too many people to know where he was. But, he had to somehow get to his brother to let him know he had been shot. Mad-C had men he could depend on not to let Johnson's men near him. No one but Debo and Mad-C could get in to see Cruse. He was admitted into a hospital that only accepts anonymous patients. They knew; however, that they couldn't keep him from an attorney for very long.

"Well, it doesn't look like we'll be staying at my place tonight," Debo announced.

None of the men were killed on Debo's property. They all died outside of his property line. It could have been a drive-by, and as late as it was nobody saw anything, it all happened too fast.

"We can go over to my place," Mad-C told Debo and Freddy. Debo agreed and they both got in the Dodge Ram and went to Mad-C's estate in San Diego, California. They sat up and drank and talked a little.

"You know, Johnson shouldn't be too upset with us for getting Cruse out of his way. I mean, he was getting all of his men killed, and I know that had to be a pain in Johnson's ass. Cruse needed to thank us for making him sit his ass down somewhere," Debo said.

Freddy and Debo later decided to stay the night at *the Shell-Debo*. Debo was glad to be home at the shell Debo. He thought about staying there permanently, but he didn't know if he wanted all this to go on at his home. What would the neighbors think? Maybe something in Los Angeles would be the best thing to do. He doesn't want Shelly's home destroyed.

"Freddy, I need you to go to Burbank or Hollywood and see if you can find me something, somewhere to kick-it until this mess blows over. I don't want it going on here at my house anymore: Nothing spectacular, just an apartment or a condo; something out of the way."

"Debo, I told you that you're welcome to stay at my place until this is over."

"Yeah, and I appreciate it, Freddy…, believe me, I do. But, I don't want to take it to your home either," Debo told him.

"Okay, boss…, I'll go look in the morning and see if I can find something for you."

"I know where there are some pretty nice condos that they are building in Hollywood somewhere off Vine. I'll get the address and phone number for you this evening and you can check on it in the morning."

"As long as it's done by Friday or the weekend If it's a condo, I might keep it and give it to one of my nieces or both of them when they move out of yours and Joy's place," Debo said.

"I think it's time to move the girls out to the cabin, this mess is getting too crazy," Freddy suggested.

Debo told Mad-C the same thing and he agreed.

"I've already made preparations. The cabin's ready whenever you are," Mas-C told them.

"Do you think I should put one of the guys out there with them?" Debo asked.

"I can come up with someone that will keep an eye on them and make sure they're safe," Mad-C assured him.

(Meanwhile)

"What did you say!!!" Gregory Johnson yelled over the phone.

"I said, I'm calling to inform you that your jet was destroyed in an explosion early this morning," Captain James Wentworth repeated to Gregory Johnson.

"What the fuck did you just say? That son-of-a-bitch!!!" Gregory yelled loud enough to be heard by the Captain over the phone.

"I beg your pardon, sir?"

"No, not you. What time did this happen?"

"A little after 1:00 this morning."

"Okay, thanks," Johnson said and hung up.

He yelled at the top of his lungs for Dorothy to get Chicago on the phone. She heard him through the thick doors that separated the two offices. She knew who he wanted in Chicago and immediately dialed the number. She knew the number by heart because she had dialed it for him so many times. She opened the office door and announced that she had Chicago on line two, then she closed the door and went back to her desk.

"What the fuck am I paying you assholes for? Charles Write has got to be dealt with!!!" Johnson screamed, with anger.

"But, Mr Johnson, you told us 'to hold off until you found out what happened to your brother'."

"Yeah, you're right, I did. To hell with him, he's gotten me in enough shit. Whatever happens to him let it happen. Just get Write and Jackson; whatever it takes, whatever you have to do. I don't give a damn how you do it... just do it, NOW!!!"

Gregory demanded.

At that point, he didn't care about Robert Cruse or anything else. The only thing on his mind was getting Charles Write and D-Angelo Jackson. He hung up and made another call.

"Where the fuck is Write and Jackson!!!" Johnson screamed.

"I don't know, he's not at his office, you had it blown up. So, I guess they're staying someplace else. I don't have a location on their whereabouts other than their homes, and they both have their homes very heavily guarded by round-the-clock security."

"Since when?" Johnson asked.

"Since all this shit started," DEA agent Dick Patch said.

"$150,000 a month and you can't find those mothafuckas. Find them or somebody will find your ass," Johnson demanded.

"I'll do what I can, Mister Johnson," Dick Patch said.

"Fuck what you can do, you'll do better than what the fuck you can and do it now; RIGHT NOW!!!" Johnson yelled and slammed the phone down. Gregory Johnson's blood pressure soared to the ceiling; he was devastated. "Here we are, where is the Navigator parked?"

Freddy told Debo where he had parked the Navigator. Debo saw that he wasn't the only one that found the Lincoln SUV. The birds also found it and decided to decorate it for him.

"I guess he was hiding this big-ass truck under this tree!"

"Well, look at it his way, the birds bombed your car and it's still here. But on the other hand, we bombed Cruse's player mobile and that mothafucka is history."

"Yeah, I'll bet that knocked the hell out of Johnson didn't it?"

"Yeah, he's pissed," Mad-C said, then pulled the 44-Magnum out and laid it in his lap. It was a four-inch barrel, chrome-Plated pistol, with sky-blue-pearl pistol grips.

(Four days ago)

"Hey, Freddy I need you to see if you could find Chocolate at the club. But let me tell you, Johnson is probably going to send her out looking for you and that's what I'm counting on. She'll probably think you want some ass and that's what we want her to think. In fact, ask her out on a date, get to know her. She might not tell you too much of anything but you can keep an eye on her that way."

"Boss, I'm interested in your sister for Christ's sake, what if this woman gets serious?"

"Yeah well you just keep your brain in your head, and that thing in your pants and everything will be just fine. I wanna know where Cruse is every step of the way. He's pretty pissed at us and there's no telling what he might do."

Freddy had a duty to perform; Joy or no Joy he has a job to do.

11:00 PM

Chocolate left the Club after her talk with Freddy and went back to Gregory Johnson's house. Freddy called Debo because he didn't know whether to wait for Cruse or follow Chocolate.

"Hey, Boss, I know it's late, you want me to follow Chocolate or what? She just left here, or do you want me to wait for Cruse to show up?" Freddy told Debo everything that Chocolate told him. Debo wasn't surprised at all to hear that she said all she did. If she's a sister of Cruse or Johnson, then she's already been schooled.

"Okay, wait for Cruse to show up, see what he's up to and where he goes. The girl will more than likely go see Johnson, we know where Robert Cruse lives. I'm gonna go back to sleep, call me when you get something," Debo said, and went back to sleep.

Gregory Johnson met with the men he had called in to kill Mad-C and Debo. He sent them to the office on Robertson Blvd in Beverly Hills. There was a three-story telecommunications building that sat behind a dry cleaners across the street from the office building that Mad-C and Debo were in. Two of the men were stationed on top of the telecommunications building across the street with high-powered rifles ready to execute the two men they were hired to kill. The other two men were behind Mad-C's office where he and Debo parked their vehicles.

Debo hadn't quite managed to get back to sleep, he kept hearing a beep, beep, beep sound coming from his desk where his keys were laying. Debo's Navigator was equipped with an alarm that, when you go inside a building you can set the car alarm not to sound the alarm from under the hood. Rather it sends a beeping signal to Debo's key ring, which makes the beeping sound he was hearing. Debo got out of bed and took 'CRAZY', his (Glock 45-automatic handgun) off the bedside table and walked to the outer office and looked out the back window. He moved the curtain back just enough to be able to see two men; one was standing by the Navigator, and the other one was under Debo's SUV with his legs and feet sticking out. Debo pulled the magazine from the bottom of the Glock 45, checked to see if it was loaded, then pushed it back into the butt of the pistol until he felt it snap back in place. He pulled the slide back and then let it go, loading a shell into the chamber. He went in Mad-C's room to wake him up and saw that he was already sitting on the side of his bed checking his weapon also.

"I heard the alarm. We'll go out the side, but be careful there might be a couple more out front," Mad-C said.

"I'm sure there are," Debo told him.

They went out the side door and around to the back of the building with Debo in the lead. Debo got down behind one of the other cars parked in their prospective parking spaces, and Mad-C stood over the hood of the car. Then Mad-C dropped his right arm to his side and balled his hand into a fist. Debo recognized it as a military maneuver .Mad-C unballed one finger, then two fingers, and after the third finger was unballed, Mad-C let off two rounds with his 44-magnum. One went crashing into the armor-plated driver's side door, and the other one found its target... splattering bone, flesh, and brains all over the ground and the outside window of the Navigator, dropping the man where he stood. At the same time, Debo stuck the Glock 45 under the car that he was crouched down beside and fired four rapid rounds at the man lying under the Navigator. He saw the man jerk with every round that went in his body. The two men on the roof across the street out front were waiting for their companions to emerge from around the back of the office building but their plan had failed, and Debo and Mad-C got the drop on the two men out back and got into the Navigator.

Debo backed out of the parking space that the Navigator once occupied; running the man he had just killed under it over and drove down the alley with Mad-C in the passenger's seat. Once he got to Robertson and Olympic boulevards he drove about a block east of Olympic boulevard and made a right, putting him and Mad-C at the back of the telecommunications building across the street where the other men were on top waiting for them or their men to emerge from the back.

"How the hell did they get up there?" Debo asked.

"How the hell did you know they were up there?" Mad-C asked.

"I heard the one standing on the side of my truck tell his partner 'that their guys on the building across the street weren't going to wait all night.' Then he told him 'to hurry up and finish.'"

"He said, 'Hurry up and finish'? What the hell was he finishing?" Mad-C was extremely nervous and concerned.

"D-Angelo Jackson, what was that guy doing under your car?"

"I don't know, but are you thinking what I'm thinking?" They both looked at each other and said,

"A BOMB!!"

"Oh shit… let's get the hell out of this thing," Mad-C said. "I'm with you," Debo replied.

They both opened their doors very slowly and jumped out of the Navigator. Debo spotted a fire escape at the back of the building, and they both climbed up to the roof and came up from behind the two gunmen who were up there waiting to kill them. One of them was lighting a cigarette and just happened to see Mad-C. Mad-C put his index finger to his lips, motioning the man not to speak. His mouth dropped open and the cigarette fell to the ground. Mad-C fired one shot at the man, hitting him in the chest, and throwing him over the top of the building. He was dead before he hit the ground. Debo saw the man's partner turn and reach inside his jacket and put three rounds in his head and chest, dropping him to the floor of the roof.

They got back to the Navigator and Mad-C asked what happened?"

"What do you mean, 'What happened'? What happened to what?"

"The car…, It didn't blow up."

"Check and see if the bomb is still there."

"Hell no, you check, it's your car, Debo."

"Okay…, here's what we're gonna do, you check that side, and I'll check this side, how's that?"

D-Angelo, what makes you think I love you enough to wanna be blown to hell with you?"

"Well, hell.., you get shot at with me."

"That's different."

"You know what I think; I think we interrupted him and he didn't get a chance to finish the job."

"Well, there are two ways to find out; One… we can get in and go, or two… you can check to see if there's a bomb under your car, D-Angelo."

"Hell.. I'll check, Beverly Hills PD will be here in a minute. You forgot about all that noise we just made."

"Yeah, and if that bomb goes off we'll be part of the next noise," Mad-C said.

"I'm gonna look," Debo decided.

Actually, if the guy had finished he wouldn't have still been under the car. Debo checked and there were explosives under the Navigator, but they stopped the guy before he could arm them.

"I'll call Patch so he can get someone to take this thing off my car." Debo had decided that once the explosives were disconnected he would keep them.

"Okay, they're acting nervous and they're moving. Well, the office isn't safe anymore," Debo said.

"Well, we'd better get our asses over there and get the girls moved before Johnson's men find out where they are and that won't be good at all," Mad-C said.

"Yeah, that hotel can be a death trap for them now, they may not be as lucky as we were," Debo told him.

"That wasn't luck.., if you hadn't had that key-chain alarm we would be dead asses by now. I'm giving you your props for that."

"You wanna shake on it?"

"I'm already shaking my ass off as it is, because we're still sitting on a fuckin bomb," Mad-C reminded him.

"Oh yeah, I forgot about that," Debo told him.

"I don't see how you can forget about possibly having your ass blown to kingdom come," Mad-C said.

They rode in silence for the next few blocks and Debo broke the silence by saying,

"What's on your mind?" Debo asked. "Thinking about Pauline."

"Pauline!! At a time like this? Yeah.., you know that's a good idea, call Pauline."

"She's probably asleep."

"Pauline never sleeps," Debo told him.

Mad-C thought better of it and decided not to call her at this hour. "I thought you knew how to shoot."

"I can out-shoot you."

"Well, why is there a big-ass dent in my door where you missed your target?" Debo asked.

"Yeah, well look at how many rounds you had to fire before you killed that guy that was under the car, and he was lying on the ground like a big fat-ass duck."

"Yeah, but every round went in his ass, I was just having fun. I like watching him jump every time a round went in his ass."

"He jumped because he was afraid you were going to hit him. You ran once the poor guy stopped jumping, so I wouldn't know you missed all those rounds," Mad-C said, and they both started laughing.

Debo and Mad-C happens to be excellent marksmen. They have target practice at Mad-C's estate every week. But, because of the business at hand, they've been at the range only when the opportunity presented itself.

"Hey Debo, I hit that door with a forty-four round and only put a dent in it. When you told my man you wanted a tank, he gave you. one," Mad-C bragged.

Debo used Mad-C's connections for what needs to be done. Especially the armored product's engineering company. Mad-C knows some very powerful and important people also. After all the police and fire officials leave the crime scene, Mad-C and Debo would go back and get whatever they needed from the offices and lock the place up until Mad-C either rents it out or sells it.

"What time will they be finished with your car?"

"Sometime this evening Whenever Billings' boys get started so they can hurry up and finish."

"I thought you said, Patch and his guys were doing it."

"I thought the same thing, but he said something about having to pull in some feds. And we both know I don't need that. So, I called Billings and asked him to do it. He's supposed to call me and let me know everything when he gets off tonight."

"Well, go ahead and keep mine, I'll go back over to Freddy's until you get there. I want you to ride out to San Diego with me."

"Okay, Anything else?" Debo asked Mad-C.

"Naw, I'm good, I'll meet you guys at Freddy's. Billings won't be off until about seven or eight tonight."

12:10 AM, SATURDAY, NOVEMBER 24ᵀᴴ

Debo called Freddy and told him to get the girls ready for travel by 4:00 tomorrow afternoon.

"What happened? I mean, why all of a sudden?" Freddy asked. He was half asleep and he thought he was dreaming.

"Okay, so this is not a dream, right?"

"Right, Freddy…, this is very real; Johnson had some of his guys try to hit me and Mr Write at the office. We figured it won't be too long before they find out where you guys are and try something stupid. Johnson wants that dock, and if he's willing to pay millions to get it, then it must be worth a hell of a lot to him. I mean, he's willing to kill or be killed to get his hands on it."

"Okay, I'll have everyone ready to roll by 4:00 pm tomorrow."

"Alright, Freddy, I'll call you when I'm ready to move."

Those people have their ways of finding people, that's what they do.

Debo and Mad-C went back to San Diego to spend some time at home. They were unable to get inside the office building.

"Hey, Mad-C," Debo said while he drove Mad-C's 2014 Dodge Ram convertible down the highway on the way.

"Yeah… what is it?" Mad-C asked.

"The only reason I want to go to the house is because Cruse knows I stay there and he might go out there when he finds out we killed their four men in Beverly Hills. We need to move him out of the way. The club closes at about three or four in the morning. It's the weekend and he's pretty hot at us for taking his drugs, the $100,000,00, and for making him look like an ass in front of his brother again."

"I see what you're getting at, Debo. We can be right there waiting for him."

"Yeah, or them."

"Now, that sounds like a plan; pullover… I'll drive, you go ahead and get yourself some sleep."

"Are you sure?"

"Of course I'm sure, go ahead and pull the car over."

Debo pulled the car over to the shoulder and exchanged seats with Mad-C.

"Thanks, I'm tired as hell."

"Yeah, I know.., go ahead and get you some shuteye," Mad-C said. 'Mad-C was relaxing to the smooth tunes of Bony James. He looked over in the seat next to him where one of the most valuable assets and the most loved person in his life sat sleeping. This was a man that has put his life and the lives of those he loves and cares for, people he would give his life for so they may live in comfort. And Mad-C was most definitely one of those people. The man at his right sitting in that seat asleep trusts the fact that these people; his people and friends, his loved ones are the very best at what they do. Therefore, he takes it for granted that nothing will or can happen to either of them. He trusts their ability to make split-second decisions, life-threatening decisions, and come out unscarred, unharmed, and alive and kicking. D-Angelo L. Jackson employs these precious loved ones of his to protect and serve Mister Charles Write!!!

"I don't know what it was that made me choose you ten years ago in that seven eleven parking lot. Whatever it was, I most definitely would choose you over and over again," Mad-C thought to himself.

He pulled the car over to the shoulder and sat there looking at Debo, and with a slight tear in the corner of his left eye, he held his head up to the sky and said, "Thank you," then pulled the car back out into traffic and headed back down the highway.

"That bump always fucks with me," Debo said when Mad-C hit a pothole, waking him up getting off the 109 Freeway in San Diego.

"I think they put that thing there or left it there so it can wake up sleepy drivers. That's what I thought it was when someone shot my tire out that night coming home."

Debo had left the Navigator in Beverly Hills and decided to call sergeant Billings either first thing in the morning or when he got to Beverly Hills. He didn't want them fooling around with his car if he wasn't there.

(Present day)

"Hey you guys, the girls said, 'hello.' Boss we need to pay Cruse a visit. My man called and asked me if I had a layout of some kind of the jet hangar at the airfield. He said, 'he doesn't want to go in there blind. Any mistakes, and it's a federal rap for him, and the more he knows about security and getting into and out of the hangar, the faster he can do his job and get out of there'," Debo explained.

"Okay, Cruse it is… let's go."

4:30 PM

"I don't have time to waste," Mad-C told Robert Cruse.

Mad-C, Debo, and Freddy arrived at the hospital at half past four. Freddy waited in the car in case Johnson or some of his boys showed up, and Debo watched the lobby for the same reason.

"How do I get into Johnson's jet hanger, Cruse? Wait, I want you to think before you open your mouth. You know what happened to Carlyle; he never made it out, and if you warn your brother, you won't either. You'll do some time for the Yin murder, but that's all, at least you'll live unless your brother gets to you first.

There are people that I know who can put you up where Johnson won't be able to get to you, but there's no other way out for you."

"There's no place he won't find me. He'll find me wherever I go."

"Look, Cruse, Anderson,… whatever your name is… you are going to county jail where you can get protection. On the other hand, like you said, 'he will find you.' But, if you help us put him away you'll be protected during and after his trial, so what'll it be, Cruse?"

"You can get the fuck out of my room and go straight to hell," Cruse demanded. "Okay, I expected this. Let me tell you something, you, your brother-in-law, and your friend robbed me ten-years ago. I was minding my own business. Personally, I understand the loss of a friend or family member. But, you assholes brought this shit upon yourselves, so stop blaming me. Your sister knows that Mack Rodgers brought his death upon himself. You put a gun to my head the night you robbed me, and Rodgers pulled a sawed-off shotgun on me. I had to take him out, it was me or him. I gave you a chance to live then, and I'm giving you one now. I can just as well tell Johnson where you are. I can also tell him that you implicated him in the Yin murder and you told me he ordered the hit on me and D-Angelo Jackson, which ended the lives of two more of your friends. That's two more murders he's responsible for.., not to mention Randy Carlyle's failed escape attempt. A sheriff's sergeant was killed in that helicopter crash. Do you know what they'll do to him? And if I told him that you told me all this, do you know what he'll do to you? Oh yea, and we can pull you out of here so it'll be easier for him to get to you, and also take away all the police that are guarding your door. Then we'll see who gets to hell first," Mad-C said.

Robert Cruse laid there thinking. Mad-C gave him three-minute to think; time to let what he had just told him sink in.

"I can find out what I want to know, Cruse. I just want you to save me some time and save your own ass at the same time. I just don't want my man to get caught going in there or coming out. I want that jet out of the way because as soon as all hell breaks loose the airports, train stations, boatyards, and any possible way to leave the state or the country will be blocked. So, I'm giving you a chance and you need to take it. The only way out for you is the way I'm giving you, Cruse."

"The guards take their break at 12:00 in the morning. The front gate is guarded by only two guards and they are at least fifty feet apart. There are two guards in the back of the hangars guarding the airfields and runways. He makes his rounds every fifteen-minutes.

The two guards take an hour and a half lunch. That puts them back there at 1:30 am. That will give your man enough time to get onto the grounds. Gregory keeps a spare key to the side door on the side of the hanger, buried under the window."

"Which side?"

"The left side, the key only works on the side door. He chose that door because if someone got in through that door they wouldn't be able to taxi or push the jet onto the runway."

"That's pretty smart. Okay, so the only way to get the jet out is to dismantle it or blow it up. And, just for the record..., it was Mack and Johnny who planned the robbery ten-years ago. They were watching you in Beverly Hills and followed you to all your drop-off spots. I didn't even know who you were," Cruse added.

"Where is the money you took from my man, Jeffery Smith? And who ordered his kidnapping and torture?"

"My brother and I split the money. He ordered the kidnapping and torture of your friend," Cruse lied.

"What's Gregory's cell number?"

"If I tell you, he'll know I've been talking. Him, Dorothy, and myself are the only ones that have one of his cell phone numbers. No one but business associates has the other ones," Cruse said.

"Okay, I'll let you off the hook on that one. Sorry about Rodgers, but you guys did this to yourselves. What were you thinking? Didn't you know I'd come looking for my shit? Well, maybe one day you'll open your eyes and stop blaming me for his death. Who are you going to blame for your imprisonment for over half the rest of your life? Just like you brought this on yourself, he brought his death upon himself. Face it... live with it," Mad-C finished.

"I might make it to prison, but even I know that I won't make it out alive."

"Take it easy, Cruse," Mad-C said, and turned to leave. Robert Cruse stopped him before he got out the door.

"Write?"

"Yeah, Cruse... what is it?"

"If there's any way you can, don't mention my sister."

"I'll do the best I can, she seems like a pretty nice lady. I spoke with her and she has a head on her shoulders. Like I said, I'll see what I can do," Mad-C repeated, then left the room.

Debo was still waiting downstairs when he got there.

"Well, Debo..., the big bad wolf is as soft as hell . He told me everything..., let's go," Mad-C said, and he and Debo walked out to the parking lot, got in the car, and left.

"Johnson's after your dock," Debo told Mad-C.

"Yeah, Johnson's mind is on something way bigger than what his brother's mind is on," Mad-C said.

WEDNESDAY, NOVEMBER 28TH, 12:01 AM.

Debo called the guy that was to blow up Johnson's jet and told him to meet him at a nearby seven-eleven parking lot. They arrived at 12:01 am, Wednesday morning. Debo gave him the instructions on where to go, where to find the key, what time the guards take their break, and the whole layout. The demolitions expert agreed to have the job done within the hour.

"It's going to be all over the news," he promised.

"Okay, there's a thick envelope waiting for you in the end and I see it on the news."

"No problem, it'll be on the morning news," the man assured Debo. "Okay, handle it," Debo said and called Mad-C to let him know that the meeting had gone well, and that the guy assured him that he should be hearing about the explosion on the 6:00 morning news.

"One of the worst explosions in the history of San Diego occurred this morning at approximately 1:15 am. A privately owned jet hangar was purposely blown up. Fortunately, no one was killed or injured, and a full investigation is now ongoing. All we can tell you is that a small private jet belonging to Yacht Club Pioneer and CEO Gregory Johnson was inside the hangar at the time of the explosion. A highly explosive device caused the explosion that destroyed the jet and the hangar. Damages are said to be in the hundreds of millions of dollars. We will have more on this story as it unfolds; and now in other news."

Debo turned the television set off and called Mad-C. "Job well done, let's get ready for all hell to break loose."

"Debo, when this started, I told you that this was my war."

You have a wife, a life, and something to look forward to. What the hell is wrong with you, man?"

"Charles Write?"

Debo hardly ever called Mad-C by his full name unless he was dead serious... or very sorry.

"Don't make me disrespect you, okay. let me put it like this, you are involved with a very dear friend of mine and I don't mind, but what I do mind is if something were to happen to you; especially now, that would hurt her so very badly. I was with you on this from the start because you are my friend and I don't turn my back on a friend. And now, I'm even more on your side because you are involved with a person that is close to me. So, what does that tell you?"

"Uh..., you don't want to see me lonely?"

"I don't want to see you hurt or killed, you can be lonely all you want. I just don't want to see a good man with a good heart go unappreciated. Two perfectly good hearts have been put together. I would go to the limit with you, Mad-C. You saved my life years ago and the only way I can show you my appreciation is to show and give you my love. That's why this is, our war. You saved my life, and now you could very well be saving a dear friend of mine's life; Pauline's. You've taken her away from loneliness and given her a reason to push forward. There's a very good man in her life now, and I don't intend to let anything happen to him."

"Well, Debo.., since you put it that way...,"

"Well, that's the way it is," Debo informed him. "Does that mean we're a family?"

"We've always been a family; we'd better be.., and I mean that," Debo said. They both got some sleep. Freddy had gone hours ago because they had less than twelve hours to be in Los Angeles to pick up the girls.

8:30 AM

Joy got up early and went downstairs and looked around. She is so bullheaded, but she's strong and doesn't mind getting in the middle of it all. Debo didn't want anything to happen to his sister. Freddy didn't mind keeping an eye on her and Shelly, at least he's with Joy.

Debo had Mad-C set the alarm for 11:00. He told him why and they went back to sleep.

Freddy had stepped out for a while, and when he got back Joy and Shelly were already awake. He called Joy's cell phone and explained to her what Debo told him about going to the cabin, and what time. He told her he was checking out of his room and coming up to their room until they were ready to leave for the cabin this afternoon.

"Something really bad is about to happen, has already happened, or my brother is out of his mind, is he alright?" Joy asked Freddy.

"Yeah, they have Robert Cruse in a hospital out in San Diego. I followed him from the Club on Gage this morning at about 3:30 or 4:00. He jumped on the freeway and was on his way out to the boss' house. So, when we got there..."

"We..., who's we?" Joy interrupted.

"I rode out there behind Robert Cruse's car. He didn't know I was following him though," Freddy explained.

"Okay... what happened next?" Joy excitedly asked.

Freddy told her the rest and asked if she had anything to drink. "I don't drink, but I think there is a bar here someplace."

"I don't drink this early either. But sweetheart, I've been through a lot. I don't want to get drunk, just something to get the blood flowing again."

"You're not turning into an alcoholic on me, are you?"

"No... hell no!!"

"Yeah, I know this job can be stressful, can't it?"

"Yes, it can," Freddy agreed.

Joy is the most beautiful woman Freddy had ever laid his eyes on. Their eyes met and locked onto each other's. Freddy moved closer to Joy, then held her by the hand and gently kissed her sweet, soft lips.

"Well, don't let me disturb you two, I know it's part of the job, right?" Shelly said and smiled.

"Well, as a matter of fact, the job has nothing to do with the way I feel about, Joy," Freddy confessed.

"Well, I certainly don't see anything wrong with that. In fact, I think you two make a lovely couple. Why are we going to the cabin so soon?" Shelly asked Freddy.

"Something's come up and you know I can't go into details with you about it or the boss will have my tail." Freddy tried not to use foul language around the ladies, he likes to show respect for them. He has his own motto; "Beauty deserves respect, and women are the most beautiful creatures in creation… and yet, the least respected by man. We use them, curse them out, beat them up, exploit them, then ask them to have our children. If it weren't for beauty there would be no ugly, and there are a lot of ugly people in this world with even more ugly intentions, ugly motives, and a disrespectful outlook on life and the benefits of living."

Joy brought Freddy his drink and said, "Here… this should take the edge off."

Freddy accepted the glass with about two tablespoons of brandy in it. As a gratuity of the hotel they always keep the penthouse suites stocked with everything from soap to liquor.

Mad-C loves Big Bear Mountains, he owns an exclusive cabin with windows all around it; located right in the middle of a gigantic nine-hundred acres of California land. You can see the surrounding mountains and a lake that runs right in the back about 100 yards from the cabin. There are trees that range from 100 to 150 feet tall and narrowed to only 20-feet tall in a perfect row on each side of the cabin. It's equipped with central heating and air. All of the bathrooms have marble floors, the hallways and walk-in closets have pearl-blue, plush, shag carpet. The game room was decked out with a bowling alley, ping-pong table, a pool table, and a wet bar that seats up to twenty people. In another building off to the side was a mini-casino that was equipped with dice tables, blackjack tables, poker tables, one-armed bandit slot machines, a tennis court, a basketball court, and a baseball field. There were also two smaller cabins outback; a

Game-room and a movie theater. Across the yard was a pistol range and bow and arrow target boards.

To the left of the bow and arrow target boards was a gymnasium, equipped with a steam room, shower, and massage tables.

"The girls are gonna love the cabin," Mad-C told Debo.

"I know I did when I first went there. I beat you playing basketball and pool. Oh yeah…, and on the shooting range. I told you that you can't shoot," Debo joked.

"I just let you win. I had to, you were my guest."

"I distinctly remember you saying, 'you're no guest in my home… my home is your home… make yourself at home, Jackson.' Now didn't you?"

"Yeah…, well, I still let you win."

"Okay, we'll see," Debo said.

Debo called Pauline to let her know that he didn't want to chance her being out in Los Angeles. Johnson is on one and he'll do just about anything to prove he means business. He just lost seven more men for a total of twelve men since this thing started. And among the twelve were the two sharpshooters at the office that were waiting to kill Debo and Mad-C. Johnson wanted Randy Carlyle, no matter what the cost, no matter what it took… and he got him. And now he wants Mad-C and Debo under the same circumstances. But it won't be easy, Johnson would have to deal with them from a whole new perspective, a whole different level of combat.

He needed to call in someone that wouldn't only kill them but plan their disposal carefully. No matter who goes down with them, they must go down, they must be assassinated.

Pauline had no problem going out to the cabin, it would be like the vacation she never got to take.

"I would love to go; Charles told me about his cabin. He said, 'it was huge with lots of goodies, including a tennis court.'"

"Yeah, it's packed," Debo told her. "When are we were leaving?"

"Between 4:00 and 5:00 this evening. Bring anything you want, we're going to ship everyone's things up there, and rent cars for everyone when we get there. Everyone will have one, I'm driving my car out there to get you girls situated, and Mad-C and I will head back here to the city."

"Okay, I'll be ready; I've never been to Big Bear."

"Well, I'm sure you'll love it," Debo said.

They hung up, and Pauline began getting ready for the trip.

Debo called the hospital Robert Cruse is in, to check on his recovery. He figured Johnson would want to try to get him once he finds out where he is. But, Debo doubted that he would kill his own stepbrother. Then too, the only way Robert Cruse would break is if he knew he would be facing a lot of prison time... and he is. Johnson and Cruse could be also if Cruse talks. Johnson can't let his brother talk, so what choice does he have but to kill him? If he could get to Cruse before the Feds does, then great, but if not then Robert Cruse is in deep shit.

The nurse at the hospital in San Diego assured Debo that Cruse was doing fine and is heavily guarded.

"A couple of detectives have been here to see him They said, 'that a Mister Write... Charles Write sent them to question him.'"

Detective Marvin Hallburger is a close friend of Charles Write. They served together in the military and he's the one keeping Robert Cruse on ice. He's supposed to make sure no one gets to him. Anyone requesting entry into Cruse's room must know a password specified by Mister Charles Write and detective Marvin Hallburger.

CHAPTER
19

SATURDAY, NOVEMBER 24TH, 7:30 P.M.

They made it to Mad-C's cabin in Big Bear, and it's just as Mad-C described. "This is breathtaking, I can really get used to this. I have got to get me one of these," Joy said.

"Yes, we do, don't we?" Freddy added.

Mad-C had Debo play one of his old-school CDs, The OJs; "For the Love of Money." It was just ending, as they drove up to the front of the cabin. Debo was in the passenger's seat by then. The drive from the road to the cabin's front door was half a mile drive. The bus went around back to unload. Debo and Mad-C were just coming around back where Freddy, Pauline, Joy, and Shelly were just getting off the bus. Mad-C had chartered a tour bus to get them there. They all left from the rear entrance of the hotel so that no one would follow them. Mad-C and Debo were also careful not to be followed. Freddy rode along on the bus for security reasons in case the bus was interfered with along the way, but everything went as planned. The things they couldn't ship; Joy's arsenal of weapons and some of Debo's weapons were taken in the car with Debo and Mad-C.

The men had decided to spend the night and head on back in the morning to finish dealing with Gregory Johnson, and try to pump some information out of Robert Cruse. Debo wanted to spend the night because he wanted to be with his wife. It's been a long time since they were together, except for their little outing at the park. The others were glad to be able to spend some time together as well. No one knew for sure what would become of the men, but they all hoped and prayed that they made it back alive.

Debo kept Shelly focused on the fact that he will be coming back to her alive and well. She knew that her husband had to do what he was doing; not because of an obligation to Mad-C, but as an obligation to himself; to be who he is…, there is no other way.

They were assigned their own rooms, each room had twin showers, a study, and a balcony. They were sitting around a natural gas heater that supplied heat for the comfort of outdoor gatherings; talking and holding or cuddling their better half. Debo was holding Shelly, Freddy, and Joy were holding hands, and Mad-C was lying down with his head in Pauline's lap. "I would like to propose a toast to our little family here," Mad-C announced.

He held his glass up and the others followed. Their glasses met and they sipped from the glasses they were holding. The girls didn't drink liquor, they had ginger-ale while the guys drank brandy. Mad-C turned on the outdoor surround sound stereo system and played some CDs while they absorbed this glorious moment. The snow was beautiful; the mountains, the ground, the trees, and the cabin's tops were covered with snow. It looked like it was daylight at 9:00 pm. It was a bit chilly for some, but they all wore winter gear: heavy coats, and thick gloves. Freddy knew to bring his big heavy coat and thick black gloves. They sat outside and roasted marshmallows and enjoyed all the luxuries of the great outdoors in California's Big Bear Mountains. They had become so comfortable that they stayed outside until 11:00 that evening. They lost all track of time but no one cared, it's a memorable moment for everyone.

"One more toast before we turn in for the night; to prosperity, success, and long-lasting relationships," Pauline said.

They all agreed that was a suitable toast and repeated the custom of toasting as before and went in the house.

The women went to the kitchen to put the glasses away and clean up while the men sat in the living room and talked.

"Well, are you guys ready for this? I've heard a lot about Gregory Johnson. He's said to be a very serious man, and he will stop at nothing to get what he thinks belongs to him…, and he has the money," Mad-C said. "I'll call Billings and let him know what's about to go down when we get there tomorrow morning," Debo said. Freddy sat up in his chair and said, "I'm as ready as I'll ever be."

"Let's do it then," Debo said.

"Enough of that, let's enjoy this moment with our women," Mad-C suggested, and enjoyed it, they did.

When Debo woke up, he called Shelly.

"Hey, Baby.., how's things out there so far, having any fun yet?" Debo asked.

"I just have to get used to the snow, otherwise it's lovely. Mister Write owns a little town here, doesn't he? Are you sure this is not a surprise vacation, that's what it looks like to me?"

Shelly sounded joyful and gleaming, like she was having the time of her life.

"I'll tell you what, you can treat it as if it's a vacation and have yourself a ball; go skiing, play some tennis, that'll warm you up."

"Pauline wants to but Joy and I are thinking of taking lessons ."

"I'll ask Mad-C if he knows a ski instructor who'll give you girls some lessons. I'm riding out to Diego with him tonight. Do you want anything from the house?"

"Uh.., no just check on the mail for me, and see if I have anything important. Not that I'm expecting anything important, but you never know."

"Okay, Baby.., I'll check, you girls go on and have some fun. You were stuck-up in that hotel without any fun long enough."

"Okay, honey, I'll talk to you later.., love you," Shelly said. "I love you too, Sweetheart," Debo said, and hung up.

MONDAY, NOVEMBER 26TH, 9:00 A.M.

Sgt Billings was feeling good today, he had won on the green. He finally won the golf tournament he'd been trying to win for years, and was in an extremely good mood. Nothing anyone could have said or done would have messed up his day, it just wasn't going to happen. Richard Buringham was at the front desk at the Parker Center Police Station as he was every day for the past twenty some odd years.

"These people are going to tell me they don't need a pass to get on these elevators. I don't care if they are officers from other precincts, I've been here for many years of my life, I should know!!!" Richard yelled at whoever was in earshot.

The officer already had his pass and was on the elevator.

"Calm down, calm down, Rich, it's gonna be alright, it'll be just fine. Just let them know that it's your way or the highway. They're not going to get their asses chewed out, you will and they'll just have to understand and except that.

Don't let them give you a heart aneurysm. May *have a* pass so I can go up and visit with Sergeant Billings, please? I'm going to go get my ass chewed out now."

Debo was talking as calmly as he could because he didn't want the poor man to go into convulsions.

"Yeah, let me check to see if he's in, or if he wants to see anyone."

"Oh, he'll wanna see me," Debo stressed.

Richard pressed several buttons on the phone in front of him, and then spoke into the receiver, hung up, and said,

"Go on up, Mister Jackson here's your pass."

Debo accepted the pass, thanked Richard, and went toward the bank of elevators. He pushed the button with the arrow pointing up and waited for the doors to open. Minutes later the twin door parted and he got on and was on his way upstairs to go catch hell.

"D-Angelo L Jackson... I'm not going to ball your ass out this time, and do you know why? Well, for one thing, I saw this coming for a long time, and for another thing, I won yesterday. I won the "Year-Round Golf Tournament."

"Well, congratulations, Sarge."

"Jackson, it seems like every weekend you go on your rampages. The only thing I want to know is did you know your office was blown up Saturday evening?"

"Yeah, I know that son-of-a-bitch blew up my shit!!!" Debo yelled.

You could see veins popping out of his neck and rage in his eyes. "It's not a total loss, they were only able to take the front and back doors off, and some damage to the courtyard outside. It wasn't enough explosives used to do any real damage to the second and third floors. All this was on my desk this morning when I got in; courtesy of a friend of mine at Beverly Hills Police Department. I told you, Jackson, Gregory Johnson is a tough piece of shit when he feels he's been crossed. And I heard about the explosion at the yacht club, a black Mercedes was blown up. Now you know when the local gangsters and drug dealers get hold of military weapons, the whole country is gone to hell. Patch told me to let you know that in order for him to help you with your problem. He didn't say what your problem was, but he said, 'that he would have to pull some federal boys in on it and he didn't want to trust them with that kind of job off the record.' He also said, 'that you can help him, Sergeant.' Those were his exact words. Now what is it you need help with, I'm in a helping mood today?"

"Well, I was gonna get him to take a bomb off my car but,..." Sgt Billings wasn't about to hear the entire story.

"I know what you wanted him for but I wouldn't trust him doing it. I'll go out there and see if I can get it done for you, Jackson."

"Thanks, Sarge, how are your wife and daughter?"

"They're doing very well, Jackson; better than I am right now. I must put up with the bad guys... and yes, you're one of them. You're not one of the headache ones yet, but you're getting there. Thanks for asking about my family. Now, let me know if you need anything else, Jackson."

"Okay, I will, Sarge."

"Talk to you later.., now out, I've got work to do; Mondays are my busiest days."

"Okay, I'm gone, call me later," Debo said, and was out the door. He dialed Mad-C's number and waited for him to answer. "Yeah my man, what's up?" Mad-C growled into the phone.

"So, is Billings going to take the bomb off your car?"

"Yeah, it's all just one big piece of shit after another," Debo said. "Yeah, tell me about it."

CHAPTER 20

WEDNESDAY, NOVEMBER 28TH, 9:30 A.M.

"Dorothy, get me Chicago on the phone again will you please." Johnson had calmed down a bit and was thinking clearly again.

Dorothy pressed a few buttons on her intercom, and when Gregory Johnson responded she announced she had Chicago on the phone.

"Hello.., yeah, I need some guys on standby over where my yacht is docked, in case these bastards decide to blow it up too." After he finished his call to Chicago, he called Agent Patch back.

"Patch here," he said, when he answered his phone. "Do you know where my stupid-ass brother is?"

"You didn't hear?"

"Hear what?" Johnson asked.

"Your brother and a couple more men, I don't know if they were your men or his... but they went over to Jackson's house out in San Diego and tried to kill him. Write and Jackson killed the three guys that were with him and wounded him. He's in the hospital jail ward under close guard. They're not allowing him any visits; an attorney, friends, or family members. No one is allowed to see him or talk to him," Patch reported.

"I told that stupid mothafucka to go underground, not try to get his ass put underground. He knows he's no match for Write or Jackson. Oh well, he's gone and so are three more of my fucking men, let them keep his ass," Johnson said.

"Is that all, Mister Johnson?"

"Yeah.., that's it for now. I want you to keep trying to locate Write and Jackson. I'll throw in a little something extra for you. How's your partner... what's his name?"

"Rayass," Patch answered.

"Yea.., Rayass, tell him to get off his ass and help find, Write and Jackson," Johnson ordered.

"I know where they are, I talk to them every day," Patch assured Gregory. "Yeah, but it might be a bit difficult for you to set them up. I want them and their families."

Debo and Mad-C were proud of the job his friend had done. It was well worth the $10,000 they paid him. Debo knew it would probably take a few days for Freddy to get the place he wanted. So, he planned to be at the house an extra few days. It was a fairly nice day out at *the Shell-Debo*. He took out a couple of the cars and the bikes so he could start them and let them idle and put oil and water in the engines, then wash the Navigator. The dent in the door wouldn't be a problem, he could get Mad-C's friend to repair it. But for now, he'll just wash it, check the oil, tires, brakes, and brake fluid. It shouldn't need any antifreeze. He misses Rex being there to help him. Even if Rex did just keep him company while Shelly was either gone someplace, busy, or sleeping. She wasn't too much for doing maintenance on cars. "It's a man thing," she would always say. But, Debo and Rex enjoyed it because it was relaxing. He said 'it's therapeutic and sedates the mind; that and the smooth jazz he listens to while working.' But, he knew that at that particular time in his life things weren't normal. But he had gotten so into what he's doing, that everything seemed to be normal. It's like being in prison waiting to get out. You can't live your life to its fullest until the imprisonment is over. This long ongoing war with Gregory Johnson is sort of an imprisonment, a confinement which makes life abnormal. But, he managed to relax in the front seat of the Navigator and folded his arms across the top of his head and began to think.

"This will be over soon and I can really relax and enjoy all of this again." But, for now, he just wanted to be alone, he had some hard thinking to do. He had to sort out a lot of things and try to come out of all this alive.

8:30 PM

He looked in the fridge to see what he had to eat. He knew he hadn't been home in quite a while and there wouldn't be much of anything… no one had been shopping. If there was something to eat, it was either frozen or canned goods. He took a steak out of the freezer, peeled some potatoes, and diced them. After he did the preparations for his meal, he put the food on and went to turn the TV on to watch some sports, a news broadcast, or maybe just a movie.

He sat down on the sofa and felt something moving and realized it was his cell phone vibrating. He removed it from its case, turned it on, and saw that it was Dick Patch.

"Yeah, Patch what's up?"

"Where are you, Jackson?"

"I'm around… what gives?"

"I need to speak with you, where have you been these days?" Patch asked that question, thinking Debo wouldn't suspect him of trying to set him up since he always asks Debo where he is or what he's doing.

"What's up? I'm in the middle of dinner," Debo said, only now there was a hint of irritation in his voice.

"Did you hear about the jet hangar explosion out in San Diego a couple days ago? Johnson's jet was inside; someone blew it up."

"Yeah, I heard, so!"

"I need to see you Jackson, something has come up. When can I meet with you?"

"I don't know, Patch…, how about tomorrow? I'm tired, can it wait until then?"

"It sure will, tomorrow is perfect. How about say 4:30 tomorrow afternoon?"

"Okay, see you then," Debo said and ended the call.

"I wonder what he wants now," Debo thought to himself.

He didn't really trust Patch, for one thing, he was always there, for another, Rayass was too quiet… like his partner was doing something that wasn't good or healthy for either one of them, besides being as crooked as hell. Maybe Debo should have someone look into his background and do some checking on him. Debo has known Los Angeles Police Sgt Robert Billings for years. He knows he can trust Billings, but he only met Patch and Rayass right around the time all this mess got started. You can't fully trust people you just meet, especially the kind of trust where everything and everybody are at stake, and with so much to lose. If they are legit and as crooked as hell, they can't be trusted anyway.

"Now Gregory Johnson's jet and Mercedes have been blown to hell and Patch wants to know where he can find me. When my office was blown up, there was no Patch, when they tried to blow my car up, there was no Patch, When they tried several times to kill me and Mad-C, there was no Patch. Now, all of a sudden Johnson's shit is fucked with and Patch wants to know where he can find me. If Dick Patch knew about me, Mad-C, the workers, Billings, and my favorite outing places, then Johnson should most certainly know. Money does some crazy shit and it can go a long way doing it," Debo thought to himself.

He decided to call Mad-C to let him know what he was thinking. Then give Billings a call to see if he can get more information on Drug Enforcement Administration Agents Dick Patch and Monty Rayass.

"Speak, Jackson," Sgt Billings said when he answered Debo's call.

"Sergeant, I need to ask you something.

"Okay, ask."

How well do you know agents, Patch and Rayass?"

"Almost as long as you have. They came to me about the same time they did you, only it was two weeks before they came to you. So, I really don't know too much about them, why?"

"Something doesn't smell right, they're too convenient and too easy to get. I'm sure you've heard about; Johnson's private jet being blown up."

"Yeah…, I heard about it on the news."

"Okay, now when my office was blown up…" Debo told Billings about everything he was just thinking.

"Well, Jackson, I can count the people I trust on one hand, and you're one of them. Now, on the other hand, there's Patch and Rayass, which are on the handful of people I don't trust. My whole career is in your hands. You could turn me over to my superiors right now or you could have a long time ago but you didn't. I looked for more dirt on Patch and Rayass, but I couldn't find any. And do you know why?"

"No, Sarge, why?"

"They don't exist, there is no Dick Patch or Monty Rayass working for DEA. At least they're not in their active files: Meaning they are not active agents anymore, or never were. I've checked all there is to check until there's nothing else to check. I've checked all the files in Washington and nothing. I've checked all the databases… nothing. Either they've changed their names and full identity, or they were never DEA agents. Anyone can acquire the required credentials and pose as agents or even police officers, for that matter."

"Why haven't you told me this?"

"Because I wasn't sure, and I wasn't finished checking. I'm still waiting on faxes to come back. I didn't want to mislead you."

"So, you mean it's possible that Dick Patch or whatever his name is, has been feeding information about us to, Johnson?"

"Tell me something: Were there times when things just seemed odd or looked out of place with them?"

"That incident in Beverly Hills when he wounded Carlyle instead of killing him. And one night at, 'Bens'… a soul food restaurant also in Beverly Hills. He was there and he made up some story about him watching out for me and Write.

He just happened to spot Carlyle's gray Tahoe; the same Tahoe that was there the day Joy had my Navigator. Why did he wait so long to respond knowing who the Tahoe belonged to? And it had been sitting there all the while he was watching it. Why didn't he call to let me know? If he was out there, he saw us go into the office building. He also saw Joy come out that afternoon driving my car."

Debo stopped and took a deep breath when he finished talking. Not because he was winded, but because it was all unfolding in his head.

"I didn't know all that," Billings said.

"Okay, he wants me to meet with him, what do I do?"

"Go ahead and meet with him, see what he has to say."

"Okay, I'll let you know how it goes."

"You know where to reach me," Billings told him.

"I might not have to... you'll probably hear about it on the news," Debo said.

THURSDAY, NOVEMBER 29TH, 2:30 PM

Debo called Mad-C and told him that he was in LA for a meeting with Dick Patch.

"Debo, whatever you do, keep me posted, do you hear me? Keep me posted," Mad-C repeated.

"I'm about to exit the freeway, I'm in Los Angeles."

"Okay, let me know what happens."

Debo got there with time to spare and went and ate a late lunch or an early dinner. He called and talked to Shelly and Joy for a while to kill some time. He just said hello to Joy and asked her how she was doing. They didn't talk long because she was on the phone with Freddy. Debo relaxed after the long drive to Los Angeles. He was listening to some smooth jazz on his CD player and nodded off. When he awakened it was almost 4:00 pm but he wasn't too far from his destination to meet with Patch. He drove east on Pico Blvd until he got to LaCienega and made a left to Olympic Blvd, then another left. He parked on a street called Corning, got out of the car, walked across the street to La Cienega Park, and waited for agent Dick Patch to arrive. After a few minutes, he went to the seven eleven across the street and got a small sandwich with a cup of coffee. He walked out of the store and saw Dick Patch standing in the park across the street and walked back over and asked Patch where he was parked. Dick Patch pointed to a white GMC truck parked in the park's parking lot.

"There she is, I got tired of that Maverick; not bad, huh?"

"You're doing big things these days, really big things Debo said. "Oh, I've seen better days, still making money."

"Don't I know it, what's on your mind?"

"Well, Jackson, word has it you blew up Johnson's jet hangar and private jet yesterday morning."

"Whose word, Johnson's?"

"Jackson, you pay me to keep you informed of what's going on and to serve you any way I can, and anyway you see fit for me to. Let's walk," Patch said, and he and Debo started walking slowly down the sidewalk and onto the park's grassy area.

"Jackson you are being watched by some heavyweights. They don't screw up like Cruse or Carlyle did. I'm here to tell you that the man has his arms around all the neighborhoods reaching for you and Write. He's throwing big bucks and some pretty stern orders around to bring you and Write down... whatever the cost. Now, I can help you by making sure that doesn't happen. I can move you, Write, and your workers someplace where you won't be fucked with. And how are your workers, by the way?"

"They're fine," Patch."

"And, Joy... how is Shelly holding out?"

Wherever the conversation's going, Debo didn't like it. He wanted to tell Dick Patch where he could go and help him get there but he had to play along with Patch's little game in order to expose his hand.

"Yeah.., Shelly, Joy, everybody is doing fine."

"Yeah, but they may not be for long. Where are they if I may ask?"

"They're safe!"

"I think you should consider moving them. And I would tell Mister Write to do the same if I were you."

"This guy is up to his ass in bullshit," Debo thought. "Mister Write and myself have our own security... as you should already know."

"Okay, I'm sure you know that Gregory will go after your workers, you, and your wife. He's desperate and he thinks you have done a tremendous amount of damage to his property and his ego. And he's afraid you will continue to do damage until you get to him. That's why he wants you and Write stopped."

"How the hell do you know what he wants, Patch?"

"I mean, wouldn't you?"

"Yeah, Patch, sure I would. He has a thing for my boss' shipping dock, what is it?"

"Do you know the history of that dock, Jackson?"

"No, and personally I don't wanna know."

"He has a lot of money invested in that dock."

"Like I said, I don't want to know."

"Okay, suit yourself, I'm just here to help, just doing my job."

"Help who… me, you, or Johnson?" Debo thought to himself.

"Well, Patch I can't blame you at all for doing your job and you're doing a damn good one. But, I'm fine, Write's fine, everybody's fine. Pasadena is a very nice place to be this time of the season. Everyone is out there safe in a six-bedroom condominium on Eucalyptus & Sunset. So, don't worry about them, they're just great."

"Okay, Jackson.., I guess my job is done. Be careful and call me if you need anything," Patch said, and got up to go to his truck.

"Later, Patch.., and thanks for the information," Debo said. "No problem… anytime!"

Debo went to his car, got in, and sat there for a moment thinking that if Patch was trying to set him and his workers up, then he would probably say that his job is done. Now it's Johnson's move, he doesn't know that the condo Debo told Patch about is really part of some that were just completed a week ago and are not yet ready for leasing. Debo was going to suggest that Freddy look at one of them for him but he didn't know whether or not he wanted one in Pasadena. He called and told Mad-C everything he and Patch had just talked about.

"That was a good idea, now I'll have to get ready to ride out."

"Oh, no you don't!! Our agreement was that you stay right where you are and let me handle this," Debo scolded.

"Okay, Debo…, I'll have four men meet you in Los Angeles within the hour, where are you?"

"I'm on my way to Pasadena. I know once Johnson gets the news, and he will get the news. I'm sure he'll want to act fast because time is running out on him. I'll be at Eucalyptus and Sunset where there's an Arby's Roast Beef place across the street from the condos, I'll be inside. Freddy is going to be there also, so there'll be six of us. I'm sure we can handle it."

"Oh, I have no doubt about that, you're a pretty good bunch of guys," Mad-C awarded.

"Okay, thanks…, I'll talk to you later."

"Yeah.., you'd damn well better," Mad-C told him. Debo called Freddy and told him to meet him at the Arby's Restaurant in Pasadena, and be ready for action.

"I'm always ready for action, I'll be there in about forty-minutes," Freddy assured him.

5:15 PM

Debo arrived at Arby's restaurant in Pasadena ahead of everyone and ordered a sandwich and a cup of coffee. That way he would have a reason for sitting there while he waited for the others to arrive. He was still hungry, the sandwich he had at the seven eleven didn't do the job. He sat there watching the people going about their day, totally unaware of what was about to take place across the street. He looked over there and saw there were women and children. Hopefully Johnson wouldn't move until after 6:00 pm. That'll give innocent bystanders time to be out of the way and out of the line of fire. He didn't like when innocent people got hurt or killed in the crossfire. Cassy and Tina were killed as victims of crossfire and Mad-C suffered dearly for it. Two black SUVs pulled into the Arby's parking lot. Debo had been there only five minutes and was surprised that Mad-C's men got there so fast. He got up and walked over to where the four guys had parked.

"Mister Jackson, I presume," one of the men said.

He seemed to be the one the other three answers to, but they all answer to Debo now.

"Yes, I'm D-Angelo Jackson, I'm sure Mister Write filled you in."

"No, Sir.., he said to meet you here and you would fill us in," the tallest of the four men said.

"Yeah.., just like Mad-C! Well, he did say I was in charge and that means I am running things," Debo thought to himself.

"Okay, those condos across the street is where everything is going down. First of all, let me tell you guys something. We are up against some pretty heavy boys here," Debo enlightened.

"Yes.., I'm sure they are, Mister Jackson. That's why Mister Write sent us, because we are pretty heavy boys ourselves. You don't have any worries with us."

"Well, that's certainly encouraging."

"Okay, what do we do?" the one that seemed to be the one Mad-C will crush if anything happens to Debo, said.

"We blend in with those cars parked across the street in front of the condos. Two of you grab a spot in two of those parking spaces, and I want the other two, to pretend to be inspectors of some kind and stick close to the entrance of the building. My man and I will be backing up your boys." And just as Debo was finishing what he was saying, Freddy pulled up and parked his car next to Debo's in the parking lot, got out, and walked over to where the five men were seated. They all took their positions and waited. Debo took the precaution of supplying a communications device for each of them so they would know where everybody was, or if anyone went down. He also took the liberty of bringing two hand grenades. "Well, Patch came through like a true trader," Debo said as he looked across the street and saw two black sedans: each carrying four men pull up to the condos.

"One of Patch's men looked up and saw two of Debo's positioned in front of the building.

"They're just pulling up Mister Jackson."

"Thanks, I see them, we're getting into position now."

Three men in the sedan surrounded the condominium complex and came out with their weapons drawn. Debo's two men in front of the building posing as inspectors turned around and saw the three men coming toward them firing semi-automatic Uzis. Freddy took down two of them. One of Debo's other men pulled the trigger of a Glock 45-automatic handgun and hit the other man in the head, putting him to sleep instantly and ending his life. Another one of Debo's guys parked on the street in the SUV, came up from behind the other four men getting out of the second sedan and fired a shot, slamming a round into the windshield of a parked van. The man from the sedan ducked behind the van to avoid any more gunfire. He turned around and fired at Debo's man with a nine-millimeter handgun, sending several rounds crashing into the SUV, punching quarter-size holes in the door, and shattering the driver's side window.

He tried his luck at looking around the van to see if the coast was clear and he met face-to-face with a piece of hot lead from Freddy's 357-magnum to the side of his head, putting him to sleep on impact. One of the guys posing as an inspector saw another one of Patch's boys coming from around the side of the building, and fired two shots at him, missing his target and hitting a brick wall. When the man looked to see where the shot had come from, he saw that it was one of Debo's men, and fired three consecutive rounds at him, pulling huge patches of stucco from the building. Debo's man fired back and looked around the building to see that he had landed a round in the man's midsection, sending him to the ground.

Debo saw two men from Johnson's team coming from around the back running and firing. One of them let off three automatic rounds toward him and Debo returned his fire and missed his target. He jumped between the building and a brick wall and fired another two rounds, missing his target once again. Johnson's man returned Debo's fire and hit him, taking a piece of flesh from Debo's shoulder.

"I'm hit!!!" he screamed into the communication device he had. When Freddy heard that, he went to the back of the building to Debo's aid, only to see that he was pinned down by two of Patch's men and was bleeding from his shoulder. Debo saw Freddy and pointed once to where Johnson's men were. Freddy shook his head to let him know that he was aware of their position. He threw Freddy one of the hand grenades and he caught it with one hand and pulled the pin and tossed it across the yard toward where the two men were positioned. Seconds later a huge explosion came from across the yard. Freddy and Debo saw brick, dirt, fire, smoke, and Patch's two guys being blown across the yard, and about twelve feet into the air. When they came down it was all over for them. The only man left was the one that stayed inside the sedan. He got on his phone and was making a call. He tried to drive off when one of Debo guys saw him and jumped in one of the SUVs and went after him. The man in the black sedan was almost to the end of the street when the last thing he felt was pressure and a sharp pain in the back of his head. Debo's man had fired four rounds through the back window of the sedan, hitting the driver in the back of his head, sending the sedan speeding out of control and into the intersection at speeds of up to forty-five miles per hour; slamming into a car that was trying to pass.

"Is everybody alive!!!" Debo yelled into the device. Everybody came back on the blue-tooth and said that they were okay.

"I'm okay boss, how are you holding out?" Freddy asked.

"It hurts like hell, but I'll live," Debo said, with pain in his voice and a painful look on his face.

"Gather everybody up and let's get the hell out of here before the laws get here!!!" Freddy yelled.

"They're already here!!!" one of their men yelled back. They could all hear sirens in the not too far distance.

Freddy managed to get Debo to the SUV that Mad-C's man was driving and got him out of there. Freddy took Debo's Navigator, and one of the other guys drove his Mercedes to the rendezvous point.

Debo had one of the men in the SUV he was riding in look out the window to see if anyone had died in the car crash.

"It looks as though the only one dead is the one I shot trying to get away, sir," the one named Tommy reported.

"Well that's good news," Debo told him. "Sir, don't you think you need attention?"

"I think we've attracted enough attention," Debo jokingly said, trying to find a reason to laugh.

"No, Sir.., I meant medical attention," Tommy said. "It's that bad, huh?"

"Yes.., I can patch it up for you until we can get someone to look at it."

"What's your name again?" Debo asked

"Tommy Rush."

"Thanks, Tommy Rush, you did a wonderful job. How long do I have you guys for?"

"For as long as you need us."

Freddy heard a buzz in his ear, then he heard Debo's voice. "Yes, Boss?"

"Can you hear me, Freddy?"

"Yeah."

"You did a damn good job out there. I like the way you caught that grenade."

"Yeah, I didn't get rid of it because you gave it to me. I got rid of it because you gave it to 'ME'. I've never handled one of those things; never made it to the military."

"Yeah, but you did a good job," Debo awarded.

Cosmo drove the SUV that Debo and Tommy were in. Tommy has special skills; he could get into Fort Knocks without anyone knowing.

"Okay, that'll stop the bleeding, but someone needs to look at it. It's only a flesh wound, but we don't know what he put on the tip of that round and needs to be looked after," Tommy said.

"Okay, thanks, Tommy"

Debo decided to let the guys stay in the guest quarters where security stayed when he was in Los Angeles for long periods of time. After everyone rests-up and eats something, they'll all head to San Diego to *the Shell-Debo*. Freddy was driving the Navigator when Tommy suggested they put Debo in there with Freddy. They pulled over to make the shift and Tommy got in with Debo so he could monitor his bleeding. Freddy pulled over at a Rite-Aid Drug store and got some Advil with ibuprofen for the pain. Debo wanted Scotch to ease the pain but Freddy didn't want to mix the medication with the alcohol. Freddy had convinced Debo that it could be worse than the gunshot wound itself. Freddy won and Advil it was, if Debo wanted a drink, he'd have to talk to Mad-C when they got there.

"Where is he? Get his ass here!!!" Mad-C yelled when he heard that Debo had been shot.

Mad-C thought Debo had been killed in the shootout. "Talk to me, Moss, where is Debo?" Mad-C repeated. Freddy was surprised that Mad-C knew his last name.

"Here, take this before he pisses his pants," Freddy told Debo, and handed him the phone.

"Hey fella... what gives?"

"'Hey fella what gives' my ass, what happened out there? How the hell did they let you get shot? Tell them I'm kicking some ass when they get back here; that's some scary ass shit. Hell, I thought you were gone."

"Calm down, big fella, I was just hit in the shoulder. It's just a scratch. Tommy said, 'it needs some stitches'... that's all."

"Okay, I'll have someone waiting here when you get here."

Mad-C pretty much told them to go to his estate without actually saying it in those words.

"Okay, we'll see you when we get there."

"Is everybody else okay?" Mad-C asked.

He was much calmer after he found out Debo was going to be okay. "Yes, everyone is healthy, alive, and accounted for; we'll be there shortly," Debo assured him, and ended the call.

He was starting to feel his wound and getting dizzy from loss of blood. "Freddy, this medication is starting to wear off."

He felt a weight; a sort of heaviness in his shoulder and back, and when he turned to talk to Freddy, he frowned.

"Yeah, I see.., I'll give you a few more, but we don't want to OD you. Besides, we only have a few more miles left to go."

Freddy called Mad-C back to see if the doctor would be there when they arrived.

"Yes, he's here now, tell Debo I said to hold on and don't give him any more pain medication, the doctor is going to give him a sedative. He'll be fine until you get here. How far from here are you now?"

"About twenty-minutes."

"Okay, he'll feel like hell for the next twenty minutes but he'll be okay. Did the bullet go in?"

"We don't know yet, the wound is too deep. Tommy stopped the bleeding but he's weak. I think he's about to go into shock."

"Okay, I'll tell the doctor," Mad-C said.

Debo was getting weaker and the pressure was worsening. "Five more minutes," Freddy said as he exited the freeway.

"Watch that..." and before Debo could finish speaking, Freddy had already run over the bump that everyone tends to forget about.

"Ouch, Shit!!!" Debo screamed.

Freddy looked at Debo's shoulder and saw that it was bleeding more.

"Okay, we're here," Freddy told Debo and Tommy.

He didn't have to say a word to security, Mad-C had already informed the guards at the front gate that the Navigator and the other three SUVs were on the way and should be arriving at any minute. They got to the front door and Mad-C was standing in it with Doctor Hall standing beside him.

"Hurry up… get his ass in here, and be careful," Mad-C ordered.

"I'm okay, just a little weak, but I'll live," Debo said.

"Yeah, well it doesn't look or sound like it. Get yo ass in here, doc fix him up," Mad-C ordered. He went in his office and got a bottle of scotch from his private and most expensive collection.

"I pumped him full of pain medication Mr Write. I don't think you should…," Mad-C stopped him from finishing his sentence.

"This is not for him; I need a shot, man you scared the living shit out of me. Doc put him under something so I can calm the fuck down," Mad-C cursed.

The doctor gave him a stiff shot of Demerol and patched him up. "I want you to sit tight, I'll be back soon."

"Where are you going?" Debo asked.

"I'm taking Freddy, Tommy, and Cosmo with me to check on the dock. I'm leaving Peter and the doctor here with you. I haven't been there in a while and I need to check on Chris, my foreman and see how things are going out there," Mad-C said.

"This is one hell of a shipping yard, my God," Freddy said. "Yeah, it's a beauty," Mad-C said.

"I see why Johnson wants it."

"I don't think he wants it for the way it looks. There's much more to why Johnson wants it. You are looking at one hundred yards of shipping dock That's equivalent to a football field," Mad-C bragged.

Freddy couldn't count all the cargo trailers lined-up in rows of fifty. There were close to 2,000 if not more.

"Mister Write, what do you ship if you don't mind my asking?"

"No, Freddy…, I don't mind; I ship telecommunication equipment all over the world," Mad-C told him. "And all of this belongs to you?"

"Yes, Freddy…, I have a staff of 250 employees."

"My goodness," Freddy excitedly said. "How much did it hit you for?"

"I paid $5 million for it fifteen years ago and now it's worth five times that much, and that's just the property alone," Mad-C explained.

After the tour was over and Mad-C had taken care of his business, they left. Mad-C had a funny feeling about his foreman. He met Christopher Berman when he was eighteen years old and gave him his first real job. Now he wonders if Gregory Johnson had grabbed hold of him. Something bothered Mad-C; something very uncomfortable, and it could be dangerous. He didn't know for sure what it was, it just kept gnawing at him. He"s had this feeling for about a year now. At first he thought Chris was taking money from him, which he probably was. But, it was something else, something deeper than that. Even after the ten keys came up missing when Chris let Jonny Morris take the place of the man who had become ill. Mad-C became even more suspicious. Now, he feels that Johnson is behind that as well. If Cruse is, then Johnson is also. Well, he knew he would get to the bottom of it sooner or later.

Debo couldn't go see Sergeant Billings so he called him to let him know that everything was going alright in Pasadena.

"Hey, Bob.., guess what, Dick Patch and his partner are moving against us. I threw his ass a bone and his he fetched it. He tried to…," Billings cut him off in mid-sentence to say,

"I keep telling you, I don't want to hear anything, is that hard for you to understand? As long as you are okay, I'm okay."

"Alright, Sarge.., sorry, I'll keep that in mind from now on."

"I don't doubt that Patch and Monty Rayass are crafty, Jackson. It's just that they know about me also. That's one more reason why I don't wanna hear details. Something has to be done about those two now. All I can say is handle your business. Oh yeah… I nearly forgot the rest of the C-four; somebody somehow let Patch find out why you needed it. They're saying, 'you used it to blow up Johnson's jet hanger and private jet.' So, if you have any more of it left, get rid of it as soon as possible."

"Yeah, I shouldn't have even told him about the explosives being under my car. I'm the one that let him know I had it, thanks, Sarge."

"No problem, keep me posted, Jackson."

"Okay, big guy I will," Debo said.

8:45 PM

Mad-C, Freddy, Cosmo, Tommy, Peter, and Mark made it back a little over an hour ago. Debo was ready to go home and lay down in his own bed, but Mad-C had talked him into staying the night.

"Mad-C, Joy and Shell wanted me to ask you if you had a ski instructor out there, or if you knew anyone that could teach them to ski," Debo informed him.

"I have my own personal ski instructor. A ski lodge without one is of hardly any use. I'll call him for you and set up an appointment for him to go see the girls. He stays right here in Diego."

"What good is a ski instructor living in the city?"

"He's not there year-round, he enjoys the city-life sometimes also," Mad-C explained to Debo.

"Okay, so what are we going to do about Patch and Rayass, they're too dangerous to us now?"

"Well, Debo.., you know we can't let them live. Peter…

Mark, I want you guys to do something for me." Mad-C ran down what he wanted done and how and when he wanted it done.

"Johnson might send them to us," Mad-C continued.

"To hell with that, I got shot because of Patch's ass, I'll get him," Debo said, and took out his cell phone.

"Hold up, Debo, think a minute. You just killed eight of Gregory Johnson's men, thanks to Dick Patch. He knows you are on to him and as a result, he and Johnson are really pissed. Maybe Rayass and Patch will show up at the yacht club. I'm sure Gregory will want to see him in person. And that's where Mark and Peter comes in. They'll be waiting for them. If Rayass is not with Patch then we'll wait until he is. We can't hit just one, because the other one will run and have our asses locked up or killed. So, if they're not together at the yacht club, then Patch gets a pass. If they are then send them both home to rest," Mad-C said.

"Yeah, that sounds good to me. If we move too fast or jump the gun we could make a mistake; one that might cost one of us our lives, or all of us. So, we'll hold on and see what happens," Debo agreed.

"I'm starved, what is there to chew on?" Tommy asked. "Look in the freezer… everything is frozen," Mad-C said.

"I'll order out," Cosmo said and picked up his cell phone off the coffee table.

"I vote Chinese," Freddy said.

"I'll go with fried chicken," Mad-C told them.

"Well, some good ole ribs sound good to me," Debo chimed in. "It all sounds good to me," Mark said.

"Yeah, I'm good with whatever," Tommy added.

"Maybe I can call one of those little Chinese places where they have it all; barbecue, fried chicken, and Chinese," Cosmo offered.

"Good idea," everyone agreed.

11:00 PM

Everyone ate until they were full, had a stiff drink, and went to bed.

"I would have thought that you of all people had sense enough to handle a simple setup and not get set up. Jackson tricked your ass with his bullshit. You are one dumb motherfucker, Dick Patch. I have lost over fifteen men fucking with you and my stupid ass brother. I just called those men out here and already you wind up getting them killed. Now, Jackson knows for sure you're working for me. He'll be out to move you and your partner out of the picture because that's all you are now… in the picture, no use to no one, just in the fucking picture. I'm going to give you $150,000 and you go somewhere and hide. I doubt Write or Jackson will come to my office, but I do know I'll be hearing from them. I'll take care of that myself. I should have taken care of it myself in the first fucking place. Not one man you sent to Pasadena came back alive. Meet me at the yacht club tomorrow, I'll bring the money and two one-way tickets away from here someplace for you and your partner on the first fucking thing smoking!!!" Gregory yelled.

"Okay, see you in the morning," Patch agreed.

"Be careful, Patch," Johnson said before they hung up.

FRIDAY, NOVEMBER 30TH, 8:00 AM

Debo and Shelly was just finishing up a conversation on the phone. Okay, baby, I'll call you back tonight."

"Whatever happened with the ski instructor?" Shelly asked.

"Oh yeah… Mister Write said he would have his instructor get in touch with you girls. I really enjoyed our conversation."

"I did too honey, I'll talk to you later."

"Okay, Shell later.., Oh, Shell, are you still there?"

"Still here."

"I need you to do me a favor. Will you check the database and see if you can find out as much information as you can on DEA agents Dick Patch and Monty Rayass?"

"Yeah, sure..,why, are they bad news?"

"Pretty much, see what you can find out for me, okay baby?"

"Okay."

"Thanks, sweetheart."

"You're welcome, now what am I looking for?"

"Anything that says whether or not they are indeed DEA agents, what other names, if any, do they go by or have used in the past. I just wanna know if they are real DEA agents."

"Okay, I'll do what I can," Shelly told him and they both hung up. Shelly loves the snow and the mountains. It reminds her of when she was a kid growing up in Ohio. It was always something special for her to see the daylight that the snow provides at night. It was like it never got dark on snowy nights. And you can see the different shapes of Ice cycles hanging from everything and everywhere. She used to love to eat them, and to pretend she was wearing ice skates while skating on the ice that was left after the snow melted. A lot of it turned into ice cold mud, but it was fun while the ice lasted and before the snow melted. She and her friends would make little angels in the snow by spreading their arms and legs and closing them while lying in the snow. She loved waking up to a real Christmas tree, the real fire in the fireplace, real smoke coming from the chimney, the smell of different kinds of fruit and Christmas candies. It was so wonderful for her growing up in Ohio. Debo could relate since he's from Saint Louis, Missouri.

"Honey, how about we get one of these cabins and have our own little resort… our own vacation spot in the mountains."

"Does that mean no trip to Maui?"

"Of course we're going to Maui, don't you try it," Shelly said, with stern authority.

"Okay, baby, I'll tell you what. While you're up there do some looking around and let me know what you find. I'll see what the boss can do about helping us get one. I'm sure Mister Write has a broker of some kind. How does that sound?"

"An estate out there in San Diego and a Cabin in Big Bear. That's so wonderful, thank you darlin. I'll tell Joy and Pauline they'll help me shop for one. I won't forget about Patch and Rayass."

"Thanks, sweetheart," Debo said.

"No, thank you, Mister Jackson," Shelly softly said, and they hung up.

* * *

Peter Rains and Mark Redding arrived at 909 Pacific Coast Highway in Malibu, CA at 8:45 Friday morning. They passed by the yacht club parking lot and pulled into the parking lot of an eighteen-story office building across the street. Peter managed to get into one of the offices on the 13th floor and setup a high-powered rifle and trained it directly at Gregory Johnson's office window. Debo had provided the two men with photographs of Dick Patch and Monty Rayass. Mark stayed downstairs in the lobby to make sure no one went to that office unexpectedly. Everything was prearranged by Debo. He knew that no one would be occupying that particular office, it cost him a pretty penny to make sure that it was available.

Peter looked through the high-powered scope of his sniper rifle and could see clearly into Gregory Johnson's office across the street. He could see Gregory Johnson on the phone talking for what seemed to be hours. He also saw Dorothy come in and say something to Gregory Johnson; taking peter by surprise.

"She is one beautiful lady; boy what I could do with miss thang in my life," he thought to himself.

Peter was not a peeping-tom or a pervert. It's just that on some of his jobs it's require that he look through some windows. It has certain advantages and benefits such as the opportunity of watching beautiful women without their knowing. If he had to hit her he would hit whoever put the hit on her.

"My goodness, she is lovely," this time he said it aloud.

Peter and Mark used the same communication device they used in Pasadena to let one another know what's going on. Peter heard Mark say that a green 2013 Toyota truck had just pulled into the Glory Days Yacht Club parking lot.

"We have a situation here, Peter."

"What's that?"

"It's supposed to be a GMC pickup… and there are two guys in the truck, but only one is getting out," Mark told Peter.

"Okay, maybe they're driving his partner's truck, and apparently one of them decided to stay behind."

"I have him in my scope. He's Patch…, I'm going to take him out as soon as he gets upstairs and I see him in Johnson's office. You can handle Rayass however you see fit, as long as you handle him."

- 405 -

"Okay, got it," Mark responded.

"A delivery truck just pulled into my view, what's going on down there?"

"Patch just went into the building and Rayass is still in the truck, he seems to be eating something."

"Okay, I'll tell you when to go," Peter told Mark.

Mark looked inside the building that Peter was in and saw a short gray-haired woman at the desk. He walked over to where the lady was standing so he could hear what she was saying to the desk clerk. He heard her ask the man standing behind the desk not to let anyone disturb her. Peter is in room 1354; the lady is going to 1356.

"Peter there's a woman coming up, she's going to the office next to the one you're in, be careful," Mark warned.

"Okay, thanks," Peter replied, and reached inside his pocket and pulled out a silencer.

The one he'd put on there would only absorb enough noise so you couldn't hear it from far away. The one he just attached to the rifle absorbs much more noise but also slows down the round. It'll have to do for now. He heard the woman's keys outside the door, then he heard the office door to 1356 open with a squeak and slammed shut. He heard the window open, five-minutes later he heard music, not loud music, just loud enough to drown out the sound of the shot.

"That's perfect, now she won't be able to hear the shot and I can do this and get out of here."

Peter's eyes fell away from Dorothy, who had just minutes before opened the office door to announce Agent Patch's arrival to Gregory Johnson. He focused his attention on agent Dick Patch, who had just entered Gregory's office. Dorothy closed the door and went back to her office.

"Patch my man, have a seat," Johnson greeted the agent.

Dick Patch sat in the chair he sits in directly across from Gregory Johnson's desk.

"Where is Rayass?"

"He's out in the car finishing his breakfast."

"Okay, here give this to him, this one's for you," Johnson said and handed Patch two manila envelopes, each containing $150,000 and a plane ticket to the Bahamas.

"You and Rayass get lost, and thank you for your services I put a little something extra in there for each of you."

"Thank you, Mister Johnson. Do you know that Write and Jackson are an interesting duo? Those assholes thought I gave a damn about them and their petty-ass problems. They bored the shit out of me trying to get information about you; crying like little bitches. And when I didn't give it to them, they bugged me to damn death."

"What did you give them when you did give them something? I know you had to give them something if only to make them think they're getting their money's worth."

"The same shit they already had."

"Yeah, well they sat your ass up pretty good; cost me eight more of my men. Chicago is not gonna wanna give me anymore men, I'll have to recruit some guys. I need some military boys; someone that knows what the fuck they're doing. Write and Jackson were ex-military men. I was told they used hand grenades at the fishing and boat club and again at Robert's place. Do you think you could get someone that I can depend on with military training? Patch did you hear what I just said? Patch… Patch, I'm talking to you."

Johnson didn't know that Peter had hit his target from across the street. He didn't hear or see the bullet that pierced a hole in the plate glass window and entered the back of Dick Patch's head. Gregory Johnson walked over to where Patch was still sitting and shook him. His eyes were still open and Gregory Johnson didn't know what to think until he saw the blood pouring from the back of Dick Patch's head in a thin stream, running down the back of his neck and down his back. Then he knew that Patch had been shot; but how? He looked at the window behind Patch, and there it was. The hole where the bullet entered the office and Dick Patch's head. Jonson considered picking up the remote that controlled the picture that slid across the window where the bullet had come through, and pressing the button on the remote sliding the picture back over the window. He called Dorothy into his office and had her call the authorities. He knew who it was, and he also knew it wasn't him that they wanted to kill; not yet anyway.

"These bastards just killed a man right here in my fucking office. This shit has gone too far."

Peter radioed Mark that the hit on Patch was executed and it's a go on Rayass. Mark walked across the street to where Rayass was sitting in the truck, pulled the Glock nine-millimeter handgun out of its holster and aimed it at the back window on the passenger's side of the truck, and fired three rounds into the back of Monty Rayass' head, killing him instantly.

"I want that window moved; did you call the police?"

"Yes, Sir, Mister Johnson, I did. They should be here any minute."

"Get in touch with my lawyer too."

"Yes Sir, Mister Johnson; oh…, Mister Johnson."

"What is it?"

"I think you should see this, Sir," Dorothy said, and led Gregory Johnson into her office and told him to look out the window at what was unfolding in the parking lot.

He saw several police cruisers, an ambulance, and a coroner's van scrambling to gain control of the situation and cordon off a parameter for a homicide investigation. Johnson saw the coroner wheel Rayass to the coroner's van, and went back to his office and took the two manila envelopes off of Dick Patch's dead body. He put them along with the two plane tickets in his safe and heard a knock at his office door; it was Dorothy.

"Yes, Dorothy?"

She opened the office door and Johnson saw four uniformed police officers and two detectives standing behind her.

"These gentlemen are here to see you, Sir," she announced.

"Show them in," Johnson said.

"You called the police?" one of the detectives asked Johnson. "Yes, I did, and my name is Gregory Johnson."

"I'm Malibu Homicide; Detective; Lewis Forbes."

"The body's over here," Johnson said, leading them over to where Patch was still sitting in the chair dead.

The four officers, detective Forbes, and his partner walked over to where Patch's dead body was. Forbes examined the body, and when he touched Patch's body it fell over. Forbes saw the stream of blood running down Patch's neck and back. He looked back and saw the hole in the wall which confused him. He looked at Gregory' and said,"This man was shot from behind. He looked on Johnson's desk and saw the remote and kept quiet about it until the trial.

"Do you know anything about what happened in the parking lot?" Detective Forbes asked Johnson.

"I don't even know what just happened in my office. Apparently someone was out to get these guys," Johnson said.

"Yeah, or you…, anyone you know who would want you dead, Mr Johnson?"

"I think that if they wanted me dead, I would be dead."

Johnson didn't want these guys to know about Charles Write and D-Angelo Jackson; not yet anyway. It could open a whole new can of worms.

"What was the nature of Mr Martinez's visit, Mr Johnson?"

"Mister Who!!!" Johnson asked… surprised.

He never knew Dick Patch's real name, nor did Rayass for that matter. "I've said too much already, detective. I'll wait for my attorney, he's on his way."

Gregory Johnson couldn't explain what a man that had just been assassinated in his office was doing there. And he couldn't understand why the detective didn't find a badge or firearm on Patch. Maybe he couldn't search him or something. He probably had to wait, or maybe Patch didn't have a weapon or a badge on him when he came there. Johnson went to the door and asked Dorothy if she would see what was taking his lawyer so long to get there.

She went over to her desk and turned right back around and said, "He's here now, sir."

Gregory looked up and his attorney was coming through the door of his office.

"Forbes, meet my attorney, Mr Lakeman. Mister Lakeman, this is Malibu Homicide Detective Lewis Forbes."

7:45 PM.

"Hey baby, how is it going out there?" Shelly asked Debo, over the phone. He had called to see if she found out anything on Agent Dick Patch and Monty Rayass.

"Well, sweetheart, tell me something good"

"Okay, I'll have to check further because I couldn't find anything on either of them showing whether they are, or ever have been drug enforcement agents. The names Dick Patch or Monty Rayass didn't come up on the LAPD database. They either don't exist, or they are very top secret. And, if they are top secret, we won't find anything on them anyway, not from the LAPD computers."

"Well, one thing that's not a secret, and that is who he has been giving all the information about me and Mad-C to. The same person he got the DEA credentials and badge from: Not to mention the fake police car. They even had a red and blue light installed in the front grill. Gregory Johnson planted them on us and Sgt Billings and made a small fortune doing it. That means they knew about Billings. I have to warn the sergeant."

"D-Angelo..., hello, D-Angelo... are you still there?"

"Yeah Baby, I'm sorry.., I was thinking, what did you say?"

"I said do you want me to keep checking or what?" Shelly asked, when she finally got his attention.

"No, sweetheart..., thank you, you did plenty. Call this number, it's to the ski instructor; The guy's name is Shane Robins. Mad-C is supposed to have him call you, but in case he forgets you can call him. Give him about a day or so, he stays out here so he might not get in touch with you until he goes out there. You have the number, so If Mister Write doesn't get around to it, then you call him. Tell him that Charles Write referred you to him, and that he wants him to bill him for you, Joy, and Pauline's ski lessons."

"Okay, baby, is that all you want, or do you want to talk a while?" Shelly asked.

"No, I have to make a few calls, I'll call you later."

"How's Rex doing?"

"I have to go over there, I haven't been over there in a while, but he's doing okay. The last time I went over there to see him, he tore up Gail's screen door. I'll go over there; I've just been busy trying to deal with this mess. I know you miss him and I'm sure he misses you also," Debo said. "Yeah, I'm sure he does; he misses my garden, I know that much. Okay, baby go on and make your calls and I'll talk to you later."

"Okay, Sweetheart.., and thank you for checking on that for me..., I love you!!"

"I love you too, bye," Shelly said, and hung up the phone.

8:00 PM

"Two men were shot and killed here in Malibu today; Our Diane Green has the story."

"Yes..., early this morning, two men were shot and killed here in Malibu. At about 9:00 this morning police responded to a called at this Malibu Yacht Club, where an apparent execution-style homicide was committed. Once again, multi-billionaire Gregory Johnson is in the news. Just two days ago a private jet hangar was blown up with Mister Johnson's private jet inside. And today a man was shot and killed while sitting in Mister Johnson's office located on the thirteenth floor of this building behind me. 'The fatal shot was apparently fired from that building across the street,' crime scene investigators said.

The cameraman panned over to the building from where Peter fired the fatal shot.

"A second man was shot through the back of the head at point blank range about two-minutes later in the yacht club's parking lot. We don't know if the two homicides are related. Gregory Johnson is CEO and chairman of the board of operations at the Glory Days Yacht Club. An investigation into the two murders is ongoing. The deceased are Emanuel Martinez, fifty-one years of age from Los Angeles, and Dustin Pollard forty-eight, also of Los Angeles. There is no one in custody, and the motives for the murders has not yet been established. We'll return with more news after these messages." And the network went to commercial.

Debo picked up his cell phone and called Sgt Billings.

"Hey, Sarge, I hate to bother you at this hour. I know you're on the green tomorrow and you won't be available."

"Jackson, I'm not on the green tomorrow, I already won the match I was competing in. Now what can I do for you?" Billings aske, sounding tired.

"You sound beat for one thing, are you, at work?"

"Yes, I'm working late, us sergeants can't go home with the rest of the guys, sometimes we have to work late."

"Have you heard the news today?"

"No, but I am a police sergeant, and I do have access to certain information, like what happened at the yacht club, and something about Gregory Johnson. He keeps his foot in somebody's backyard doesn't he, Jackson?"

"Sarge, do you know who the guys were that were killed?"

"No, I can't say that I do, do you know them?"

"Emanuel Martinez was agent Monty Rayass and Dustin Pollard was DEA agent, Dick Patch. Martinez and Pollard were Patch and Rayass, and they were on Johnson's payroll. I don't think they had evidence on either one of us. It was all a sham by, Johnson to get information from us; Information like where we went, what we did, when we did it, who we saw, all kinds of shit. That's why we could never catch up with Carlyle or Cruse. Now, the only thing that bothers me is how much Johnson knows about you."

"Well, I'll be damned, the two guys at the yacht club were fake-ass, Patch and Rayass. I told you Gregory Johnson is a slick motha. I'm sure he knows about what I'm doing. If he didn't he wouldn't have put Patch and Rayass (or whatever their names are) on me. And if he did in fact put them on me as well as you and Write, then he's known about me for a long, long time. He was probably using me to get information about you and Write. That's the only thing I can see for them even coming here. But, I must admit, they did have me fooled."

"So, what do you think he'll do with the information, Bob? I mean the information he has on you."

"Well, Jackson, I can go ahead and retire now, or I can stay here and hope for the best."

"And the best being? You know that once they find out about you, you won't be able to collect your pension."

"Well, like I was about to say… I can stay here and hope for the best; and the best being, that either Johnson doesn't open his mouth to my superiors, or something unfortunate comes his way."

Something that would alter his capacity to communicate.

"You mean like what happened to Patch and Rayass."

"Something like that."

CHAPTER 21

"Okay Jackass, You and Write killed a lot of my men, now I'm coming for you myself," Johnson warned.

"Well, let's put it this way, those were your boys, so why not hit them right where they live; with you, Johnson."

"I've got something I want you to hear, Jackson," Johnson said, then left the line for a second.

He came back on the line and said, "Listen to this."

"D-Angelo, D-Angelo, don't..!" Johnson snatched the phone.

"Does that sound familiar, Jackass?" Johnson asked in a gruesome tone. All Debo could think of, all he felt, all that ran through his veins was rage, hate, pain, and confusion. He balled his hands into fists and bit his lower lip.

How could he have gotten hold of someone as important to him as she is. She's now in the hands of a man that would stop at nothing, go to no ends to get what he wanted, what he believes to be his, and would do whatever his sick mind tells him is necessary in order to win.

"I want that dock, Jackson: That's all I want and you can have her back. I'm sure I don't have to tell you how long you have before I kill her, do I, Jackson? I don't think so, because you are going to do everything within your power to get sweet little Mrs. Jackass back; Meaning, give me my shipping dock."

"I know I don't have to tell you that if you lay one hand on her, I'll…,"

"Yeah, Jackson.., I know, but I don't wanna hear all that bullshit. You know what I wanna hear, Jackson? I want to hear you say, 'Here, Mister Johnson, here's the deed to the shipping dock.' Tell Charles Write I want it…, NOW!!!"

"Look, don't fuck with me, Johnson…, Johnson!!! "

After Gregory Johnson had hung up the phone, Debo immediately called the cabin. He knows Shelly's voice when he hears it, and that wasn't Shelly's voice on the phone. Johnson has Joy, and as long as he thinks he has Shelly, then Joy should be safe. He wouldn't hurt her, thinking she's Debo's wife which would give him bargaining power. Pauline answered the phone when Debo called.

"Somebody hurry the fuck up and tell me what happened; how in the hell did Johnson get my sister?"

"How did what!!! She went to see Sheila and Tammy, but no one knew she was going. She left a note on the frig saying she would be back," Pauline explained. "What did the note say exactly?" Debo was on fire.

"It says, 'Sis, I'm going into Los Angeles for a few hours to see my daughters. Don't tell my brother or he'll have a fit. I'll be back before morning; Joy'."

"They think she's, Shelly."

"They think, Joy is, Shelly?"

"Yes, and as long as they think that, she's safe. Stay by the phone, I have to make a phone call," Debo said and hung up.

At least they don't know about the cabin and Joy won't tell them regardless of what they do to her. But he didn't want his little sister to have to suffer, and Johnson will make her suffer if it takes too long for him to get her to talk. He called Pauline back and asked if there were any body guards there.

"Well, there are a couple of guys standing around outside."

"Okay, I'll keep you guys aware of what's going on so you won't have to worry about Joy, how is, Shell?"

"She's sleeping."

"Okay, don't say anything about Johnson having Joy."

"Alright, I won't."

"You and Shelly stay put, and that's an order, Pauline!"

He never gave any of his workers direct orders in that capacity before. "Okay, Handsome, no one will move, and I won't say a word to Shelly," Pauline assured him, shaking like a leaf. "Pauline, are you okay?"

"Yes, I'm fine: Shelly is awake, do you want to speak to her? I think she heard me talking."

Debo decided to go ahead and let her know what was happening because he promised her that he wouldn't keep anything from her any more.

"Yeah, put her on."

Pauline was so upset and worried about Joy, she almost dropped the phone, handing it to Shelly.

"Hi, honey, sounds like someone is in trouble. Don't worry, she'll be okay," Shelly assured him.

"Shell, Johnson has her. Do you remember the night you guys went to the hotel?"

"Yeah."

"There was a car following me and Joy, they think she's you."

"Me!!! You mean they wanted ME?"

"Yeah baby, these guys play rough. That's the reason you three are out there."

"That was the plan, to make them think she was me?"

"Yeah, and the plan worked, it worked too well."

"Does Freddy know?"

"No, I'll tell him after I talk to Mister Write."

"Yeah, and he's gonna trip."

"Freddy knows what Joy's job consists of. The only thing we can do now is to get her back," Debo said.

"I pray that you do: D-Angelo?"

"Yes baby?"

"D-Angelo, don't let anything happen to my sister. She's the only one I've ever had…, please baby," Shelly begged.

"I won't, sweetheart, I'll get her back. She's smart and she's strong, don't worry, baby."

"Just hurry and get her back," Shelly pleaded again.

"I will.., now I'm going to get off this phone so I can make some calls."

"Okay, Baby.., be careful," Shelly told Debo, and their call ended. Before Debo could dial Mad-C's number, his cell phone rang.

"I've been trying to get in touch with Joy and she's not answering her phone. Have you talked to her today?" Freddy asked.

"Freddy, Johnson has her, he must have picked her up at her mom's place."

"Her mom's place, what was she doing at her mom's place?"

"She went to see Tammy and Sheila, Johnson must have been watching her house.. She probably stopped there to pick somethin up at her house first. They think they have, Shelly. Joy should be safe as long as they think that," Debo explained.

"They want the dock boss."

"Yeah..., I know."

"What do you think Mister Write will do, does he know?"

"No, Freddy, I was about to call him when you called. I'll call him and get back with you after I've had a chance to get his reaction and see what our next move is."

"Call me, or I'll call you."

"Yeah, Freddy, I know you will; believe me... I know you will," Debo said and hung up the phone.

He didn't know how Mad-C would react to Gregory Johnson trying to intimidate him. Now they have another hostage, and this time it's Debo's sister. He dialed Mad-C's number and he picked up. "Mad-C... how's things going?"

"As well as can be expected, how about your end?"

"Johnson has my sister."

"WHO HAS WHAT!!!" Mad-C yelled. "Gregory Johnson has my little sister."

"How the hell did that happen!!! My men were supposed to let me know the minute anyone left that cabin. I'll fire the asshole that knew about her leaving and didn't call me, then I'll blow his fuckin brains out. They want that damned shipping dock," Mad-C said in anger.

"Yeah, I know, so what's our next move?" Debo asked.

"Our next move is to give it to him. It's already caused a shit load of problems," Mad-C said.

"No.., Don't do anything yet, I have to make a phone call," Debo said.

"When does he expect to hear from you, and why is he kidnapping your sister, you don't have anything to do with the dock?"

"He needs bargaining power, and what better collateral than Shelly, or who he thinks is, Shelly."

"Okay, I'm going to call cabin security and see how this got past me. Are the men enough, or do you need me on this one?"

"I'll let you know later, I'm gonna play a hunch, just stay by the phone," Debo instructed.

He sent Tommy, Peter, Cosmo, Mark and Freddy out to the Glory Days Yacht Club at 909 Pacific Coast Highway in Malibu, California; Slip seventeen, Dock four. He told them they would be looking for the "Yacht Reyal", and to get aboard the yacht anyway they had to… but get aboard. He wanted them to check to see if Joy was there. He told them not to do anything, just check and report back to him. Cosmo can get aboard with no problem. The other four could watch his back from either side of the yacht.

11:00 PM

The guys went to the yacht club in Malibu as instructed.

Cosmo got aboard the Yacht Reyal, thanks to the diversion caused by the other four. Cosmo heard talking coming from down a long hall where he stood at one end. It seemed to be coming from what could have been a living room where the men were having a conversation. Cosmo eased his way down the hall and heard a television playing in one of the bedrooms, and peeped around the corner to see if anyone was in the room watching TV, but he didn't see anyone. He decided to wait and see if anyone would come out of the bathroom located in the middle of the hall, but no one did. He thought he heard water running; maybe the sink was running over.

He looked under the bathroom door to see if a light was on, and there was no light. He looked in each one of the four bedrooms, and when he got to Johnson's master bedroom he paid special attention and did a thorough search. He had wished one of the men had come in with him to watch his back inside. But, he has his Uzi, and if anything went down, or if any of the guys outside heard gunfire they would come running ; hopefully not too late.

He continued his search of Johnson's master bedroom until he got to the walk-in closet and looked around. The man notably had pretty good taste in clothes and very expensive shoes, silk ties, cashmere hats, and a pure silk and satin golf hat. Cosmo finished his search and was on his way out of the closet when he felt something under his feet close to the entry. Whatever it was, it was hollow; like the floor had a door in it. He bent over and pulled up a corner of the deep plush carpet. He pulled more and more, and the more he pulled, the more he could see there was a trap door built into the floor. He lifted the carpet all the way back and opened the trap door. Darkness flooded the room beneath him. It felt and looked like he was looking down a hole or a cave. There were small steps that were about three feet wide that ran down into the dark dungeon. He slowly walked down the steep steps; almost losing his balance and falling. Once he got down the steps and was on level ground, he was alright. He lit his cigarette lighter and saw a single light bulb hanging from the ceiling by a short metal stem. Hanging next to it was a long, four-foot chain. He pulled the chain, and the small dungeon lit-up.

"Joyvette are you down here? Joyvette… are you down here? I'm with Mister Jackson, I'm here to help you… are you down here?" He couldn't yell any louder because the men upstairs might hear him. And speaking of the men upstairs… he figured it would be in his best interest if he hurried and got off that yacht.

He looked around the room with only a forty-five-watt light bulb to see by. He heard the sound of water dripping in a far corner of the room and smelled a stench that smelled very familiar to him. It was the smell of wet wood and dirt. He felt himself walking in water and was thinking how lucky he was he didn't get shocked to death when he pulled the chain to turn the light on. The water he heard must have been coming from the bathroom upstairs; probably the water he heard running up there. He didn't see or hear any sign of Joy, but there was one thing he did see. He saw a door off to the side in a place where there was no light. The light from the small bulb cast a bright gleam off the doorknob. He walked over to the door and pulled out the Glock nine millimeter pistol he carries as a backup weapon and tried the door knob but it wouldn't turn because the door was locked. He walked back to where the stairs were and climbed back up to check to see if anybody was coming, or if he still heard the TV playing. There was no sign of anyone around so he closed the trap door. That way no one could hear him if he decided to break the door open. He went back to the door to see if he could get in. He tried the knob again and felt a small metallic latch. He moved the latch up and nothing, the door still wouldn't open. He moved it down and got the same result. He pushed the latch inwards and heard a click. He then turned the knob and the door opened revealing a small room. The room was dark, except for a little light coming from a small porthole.

"Joyvette," Cosmo softly whispered.

"What... I'm still not telling you anything, so you might as well do what you're going to do to me or leave me the hell alone," Joy said, without even a hint of nervousness in her voice. And, if Cosmo could see her eyes, he would have seen pure rage, hate and anger.

"I'm not here to kill you or hurt you, Joyvette."

"The men that have me captive keep calling me, Misses Jackson. This guy must be on my side because he keeps calling me Joyvette," she thought to herself.

She realized the man in the room with her was on her side.

"I'm working for Mr Jackson and Mr Write, I'm here to help you."

"Oh, thank God... are you here to get me out of here?"

"It's not going to be as easy as that, Mr Jackson only told me to see if you were here and to let him know. However; I have to leave you here."

"Leave me here for what? Well at least my brother knows I'm here, but how did he know?"

"Quick thinking and good judgment I suppose. Mr Johnson is not a very bright man."

"Okay, so what do we do now?"

"We do nothing, Miss Hernandez. I'm going to sneak back out of here and off this yacht and report to Mr Jackson that you are here and how to get to you. Here… this will keep you secure until we come for you.

Put it away where they won't find it," Cosmo told her, handing her a Glock nine-millimeter pistol and an extra magazine.

"Use it only if you have to, but don't try to free yourself, we'll do that. Put it away someplace until you need it. I've been down here too long; I have to go."

"Well, don't worry, I'm sure as hell not going anywhere. How long will this rescue take?"

"I'm not sure, maybe a couple of hours, days, a week; here you ask him," Cosmo said, handing her a cell phone.

"Hello?"

"Have you lost your mind young lady?" Debo said trying not to sound too upset.

He had to control his anger at that point, because he didn't want to say anything that would disrespect her or hurt her feelings.

"I'm so very sorry, Big Bra!"

"Joyvette, what on earth were you thinking?"

"I just thought that if I…," Debo cut her off to say… "Cosmo can't stay long, are you alright?"

"Yes…, I'm okay."

"Good, Shell is worried sick about you. I'll send some men in there to pull you out. It's a little dangerous right now.. I wanna get you out without getting you hurt or killed."

"Why can't they just take me with them now?"

"Because, as long as they think they have, Shelly, I have time to come up with a plan. They want Mr Write's shipping dock, and if I move you now they'll go after Sheila and Tammy. Did they follow you to your mom's?"

"Yes, that's where they kidnapped me. I went outside to get my purse out of the car."

"I'm sure you had your piece on you; we'll talk about that later. Okay, let me get your mom and daughters out of the way, then I'll come for you. We don't want children involved… especially my nieces. It's bad enough they have you."

"I'm sorry, Bra!!"

"Okay, what's done is done, Just stay put and do what they say. I don't want them hurting you, do you understand?"

"Yes, I understand, I am so very sorry."

"We'll talk about that once you're here. I'm going to hang up now, Cosmo has to leave. Don't worry, nothing is going to happen to you. I know someone comes to check on you, don't they?"

"Yeah… there's a guy that comes every once in a while to feed me, and then just to check on me every so often."

"Okay, give the phone back to Cosmo."

"Hello… yeah… I'm out of here now. I left her a weapon, sir."

"Okay, leave her the phone too and tell her to keep it on silent."

"Okay, I'll do that now. I'm out of here, bye," Cosmo said, and left.

They all got back to San Diego around 1:30 Saturday morning. Freddy wanted to go aboard that yacht and kick some ass; knowing. Joy was indeed held captive there, but he was powerless to do so.

"How did you know Joy would be on that yacht, boss?"

"Just a hunch, Freddy: Knowing that Johnson would want to protect his image, and the only logical place for him to hold a hostage other than where he lives or actually works; where his friends and security wouldn't become suspicious… is his yacht. Johnson has been in the news twice, and both times he was the center of attention, and that put him up against the gun. Anymore illegal activity on his part would bring more unwanted suspicion upon him, and right now he doesn't want that. By having her on that yacht, he can take her out and dump her body and no one will ever be the wiser. Anyplace else he would have to transport a dead body should he decide to kill her. In which case, someone would notice," Debo explained.

"Not bad, not bad at all, Debo. You know, I like the way you think, Debo," Mad-C awarded.

"Okay, now let's figure out what strategy we're going to use. We still have some C-four left we can use," Debo reminded Mad-C and Freddy.

"Okay..., I'll call Johnson in the morning and get the ball rolling, then see which way it rolls. If it rolls our way, then it's in our court. If not, then we're assed-out and so is Joy," Mad-C said.

SATURDAY, DECEMBER 1ST, 9:00 AM

"I see you've finally come to your senses, Charles. But then again I don't count you for stupid either. So, when do I get my shipping dock? You know this shit is getting way too old. Why Can't we just go ahead and get it over with?" Johnson said.

"Does the offer of $150 Million still stand?"

"You know something, Charles? You tickle the fuck out of me, do you want the bitch or not? I'm just about out of patience with you and your bullshit. Now don't waste anymore of my time."

"How did you know where to find Jackson's wife?"

"I know where to find, Jackson, you, and that fucking mutt of his; right where his brother, Omar and Gail his sister-in-law are. South Los Angeles is a very bad neighborhood and very bad things happen there; drive-byes, walk-ups, car accidents, houses catch fire... all sorts of bad shit, you get my drift? You should have stayed a loner while you had the chance, it would have only been you and I. Now you've gone and adopted all these new friends and loved ones. So, now their lives are in your hands... even the dog's," Johnson said.

"It's a good thing Debo did leave Joy there, it gave us a chance to see what else Johnson has and he has a lot," Mad-C thought to himself.

"Are you listening to me, Charles?"

"I was thinking, what did you say?"

"You'd better be thinking about getting me my dock. I said that if you want to play games with me, I can make a phone call and have Jackson's lovely little wife dealt with. Then, if you don't get the message, we'll do his brother, then his nieces, then that fuckin mutt of his and every fuckin body he knows until I get my shipping dock: even his mama. Do you understand me, Wright!!!"

Johnson screamed.

"Yeah, I understand you perfectly. I'll get my attorneys to draw up the necessary papers and get back to you," Mad-C told him.

Mad-C had no other choice, he couldn't endanger the lives of his friends because of his pride.

"Yeah, you do that, Charles..., you just do that," Johnson said and hung up.

Mad-C called Debo and told him everything Johnson had just said over the phone.

"My brother!!! That bitch mentioned my brother? We'll have to kill him, that's all there is to it. He still goes to that yacht club, I'll handle this mothafucka myself.., I'll call you later."

Debo was out of control and Mad-C never wanted him to be alone when he was like this.

"Don't hang up, have you lost your mind? I just verbally rewarded you for the way you think, and now you're going to make me regret it? If you're standing, sit down, if you're sitting down, stay seated. You walk out of that house and I'll kick your ass myself. You'll lose Joy for sure and everyone else you care about; Where are the guys?"

"Out back," Debo answered.

"I'm gonna call Tommy and Cosmo and have them come up front and keep an eye on you, and when they get there let them in... is that clear?"

Debo didn't say anything, he was engulfed in deep thought. "Don't make me come over there, Debo, do you hear me?"

"Yeah.., yeah, I hear you."

"Okay, now here's what we're going to do; I told him I would get my attorneys to draw up some papers to turn the dock over to him."

"You did what!!!"

"Don't shit your pants, it was just to buy us some time. So, pull yourself together, and keep in mind that if push comes to shove, I will give him that dock. Now, I need you thinking clearly on this one."

"Okay, thanks, I'll take a shower and be there in about an hour."

"Are you sure?"

"Yeah, I'm on my way."

"Do I need to have a couple of guys come with you, or should I come there and that way we can all talk?

"No, I'll be there, we can fill them in later."

"Okay, I'm depending on you not doing anything stupid: Don't get Joyvette killed!!"

"I won't, I'm on my way to you now," Debo said, ending their call. (Meanwhile)

"Who's gonna feed the lady downstairs?" one of the men holding Joy captive asked the other men he was playing cards with.

"I'll do it, you guys'll disrespect the lady," the one called Solomon said.

"Okay then, you just take your little ass down there and feed her; with your bitch-sympathizing ass. Go ahead, there's some Alpo, give her that," Steve remarked.

Steve is the one that makes sure everything gets done. Solomon used to see his mother and sisters being mistreated and abused by his father when he was growing up, and he couldn't stand to see a woman; no matter who she was being disrespected or disgraced in any form.

"There should be some Chinese food left. I don't think anyone has been out to get anything else," Solomon said.

"Why not, Solomon, it's your job?" Ray-Ray asked. "I just haven't gotten around to it, Ray-Ray."

"Yeah…, well go ahead and feed her, maybe you'll get lucky and get you some," Ray-Ray remarked.

Ray-Ray is the one they called, 'the crazy one, or just crazy.'

No one argues with or smart mouths *Crazy* Ray-Ray. Solomon went into the kitchen and got what was left of the Chinese food. There was some rice, Kung-pao chicken, and two egg rolls he took to Joy, along with a coke. "Hi, Mrs Jackson, here's something for you to eat. I didn't get to go shopping today, so leftovers are all there is."

"Thank you, Solomon…, you are so nice to me and the others are assholes. What happened, Solomon? I mean how did you get mixed-up in all this; what led you down this road?"

"Well, it's a long story."

"Solomon, apparently I have time to hear it."

"Okay, Misses Jackson; can I call you by your first name?"

"No, Solomon, I think Misses Jackson is fine. I call you Solomon because I don't know your last name."

"It's okay, I came from a family where my father physically and verbally abused my mother. He used to beat her almost every day for the smallest things. Sometimes for no reason at all; just because he could. He would cheat on her and feel guilty then try to accuse her of doing it, which always resulted in her getting beat up. He just totally disrespected her and other women also, and sometimes my sisters. I couldn't take it anymore, so I left home when I was fourteen and had no friends, no one else to turn to. So, I hooked up with these guys and I've been with them ever since. And now, they're doing the same things; Calling you dogs and bitches… all kinds of cruel names. They were going to feed you dog food, and I know, *Crazy*… he'll do it. You know, once you're in with these kinds of guys they don't let you out because you know too much and that sort of thing. I really screwed my life up.

"You can get out, Solomon, just make the right choices, and you can start by letting me go."

"They'll kill me for sure, God knows I wish I could. I heard them say, 'that if you got away, Mister Johnson would just go after more of your husband's friends and family members.' I feel so bad about you being here, but there's nothing I can do to help you or to stop Gregory from killing you if he wants to."

"Thanks, Solomon, I believe that if you could help me, then you would, and I appreciate that. What kind of work do you do or did you do?"

"Well, I used to work for a carpet company, well actually a sub-contractor.

He had his own business; I was doing that for a few years, a friend of mine turned me on to the job. Then I started using drugs and one night I was on my way to get me some crack to smoke and thought I could make it across the street before the cars got close to me, but it didn't happen. I was knocked into the air by the car before I made it across the street. And that ended my carpet installation career. I used that as an excuse not to work. They gave me SSI but it wasn't enough to live on."

"I see."

"Well, I'd better be getting on back up there or Ray-Ray will come down here and disrespect the both of us. It was good talking with you, Misses Jackson."

"Same here, Solomon, everything will be alright, just keep being who you really are and I have a feeling this mess will soon be over for you. I've seen many guys in the same boat you're in get killed or go to prison for the rest of their lives."

"Yeah… well thanks again, Mrs. Jackson. I'll try to get some shopping done; It's fast food but it beats dog food anytime.

"Thanks, Solomon."

"You're very welcome, Mrs. Jackson," Solomon said and went back upstairs. I've got a twenty says he doesn't even wash his ass," Ray-Ray said when Solomon came into the room.

Solomon looked at how pitiful the men looked and sounded.

"Oh stop it, Ray-Ray, That was some good stuff, wasn't it Sol?" Bobby said, and everyone but Solomon started laughing.

"Yeah it was the bomb, who are you guys screwing… each other?" Solomon remarked.

"We're gonna to screw your ass if you don't watch your fuckin mouth," Ray-Ray threatened.

"Ray-Ray, why do people call you *Crazy*? Is it because you really are crazy, or as stupid as fuck?" Solomon asked.

"That's it…, I'm finna beat the living shit out of you."

And before Ray-Ray had the chance to act on his threat, his cell phone rang. He answered it and it was Gregory Johnson.

"Yeah, Mister Johnson?"

"How is she doing?"

"She's doing much better now."

"What is that supposed to mean, Ray?"

"Well, Sol just came back up from feeding her, ask him."

"Put him on the phone," Johnson demanded.

Solomon got on the phone and immediately started to explain that nothing happened, and that Ray-Ray was over-exaggerating.

"You tell those assholes I said that whoever touches her is going to have to answer to me... and that means sexually or otherwise, and I mean it."

Solomon took the phone from his ear and repeated to the other men what Gregory Johnson had just said.

"I want all of you to sit tight. When the time comes, all of you can have the bitch, but for now, DO NOT TOUCH HER!!!"

Johnson screamed in a way they all understood.

Joy didn't have to worry about being humiliated and left smelling like piss, her own vomit, hungry, in pain, or being strapped to a bed and shot-up with dope. She didn't have to worry about any of the things Jeffery Smith endured. Randy Carlyle is not in charge, Gregory Johnson himself is running the show. He made it clear he didn't want her touched until he gets what he wanted. The woman is being held hostage in a room down in the belly of that huge house on water and is worth a hell-of-a-lot of money to Gregory Johnson. And if he doesn't get what he's after, someone is going to die a slow, painful, death. Mad-C has only two days to complete the transaction... or goodbye Joyvette Hernandez. Gregory Johnson finished talking to Solomon and hung up. Solomon gave the cell phone back to Ray-Ray.

"So, you didn't get any, did you Sol?" Steve asked.

"I'll be back, I'm going shopping for something to eat," Solomon said. "Get fried chicken and mashed potatoes this time... and some buttermilk biscuits," Ray-Ray demanded.

Mad-C had a plan, but Debo was right; Gregory Johnson did have to die because if and when they get Joy back, Johnson's going to know he's not going to get the shipping dock, and it just doesn't seem like he's going to live without it.

1:00 PM

They all met at Mad-C's estate at just past 1:00 in the afternoon. They decided to go with Debo after all; for security purposes and they were right. It was for everyone's security, especially Debo's. Johnson is desperate, so Mad-C ordered them to stay with Debo.

"How does it look from the outside?" Mad-C asked Cosmo.

"I only saw a few men from where I was standing. I was trying to concentrate on getting aboard. Once I was aboard the yacht, I heard about four or five voices that seemed to be coming from the living room or the guest quarters," Cosmo told him.

"I noticed about a dozen men guarding the outer perimeter from all four sides. There were three men on each side of the yacht and all of them were on deck," Tommy said.

"That means that we have a total of maybe seventeen men in all guarding Johnson's yacht, and four or five of them are on the inside guarding, Joy I want her off that boat," Debo demanded.

"Freddy, Tommy, Cosmo, Peter, and Mark; Go get Joyvette off that boat," Debo ordered.

He didn't have to tell Freddy twice.

"My pleasure," Freddy said, with a big wide grin on his face. "Hold up, Freddy…, I have someone I want you guys to meet there; my demolitions expert," Debo said, and went to the Navigator and got the remainder of the C-four explosives and four hand grenades and handed them to Freddy.

"Boss, is this what I think it is?" Freddy asked Deb, shaking like a leaf. "Yes, Freddy, it is."

"Okay, then here Cosmo take this," Freddy said, handing him the bag of articles.

"Give him this also," Debo said, and handed Cosmo an envelope. He didn't have to tell Cosmo what was inside the envelope. Debo's friend already knew. Mad-C and Debo didn't have to go with them. They knew that the guys knew what to do and would get it done with no problem. The demolitions expert already had his orders and what he needed to know. Cosmo is to go in first, because once the shooting starts he may not be able to get aboard the yacht.

3:30 PM

"You have something for me?" The demolition expert asked Freddy. "No, I do," Cosmo said handing him the bag and the envelope. "I believe these are for you," the man said, and handed Cosmo back the hand grenades he took out of the bag. The man knew that the most important part of his job was to wait until Joy and all of Mad-C's men were off the yacht before he destroys it.

Cosmo went aboard the yacht, while the others and Debo's friend remained on the dock. Freddy, Tommy, Mark, and Peter surrounded the yacht. They each had three men to deal with. Cosmo went to the walk-in closet and pulled the carpet back to reveal the trap door. He raised the door up and went down the stairs, lowering the trap door on the way down. He reached the door to the small room where Joy was being held and pushed the tiny latch inward and turned the door knob and the door opened freely; Joy was asleep.

"Joyvette… Joyvette, are you in here?" Cosmo whispered.

"Yes I'm here, I thought you were Solomon until I heard you use my name. Solomon is the guy that feeds me, he's a pretty nice person. What are you doing back here so soon?"

"We came to get you out of here."

Solomon wondered who was feeding Joy, because when he got to the walk-in closet the rug was pulled back. He opened the trap door and slowly walked down the steps leading him into the darkness of the small room and felt around for the chain that was hanging from the ceiling next to the small light bulb and pulled the chain. The room was once again lit up by the tiny light bulb. Cosmo had closed the door behind himself, but he didn't lock it. Solomon turned the knob and the door opened and he stepped inside the room. All he saw was a silhouette of Joy sitting on the bed. He went further into the room and Cosmo came up from behind him and put the short barrel of the Uzi to the back of his head and Solomon froze on the spot. Cosmo reached inside Solomon's waistband and pulled out his weapon, not knowing he had another one.

"You won't be needing this. Joy, do you have the weapon I gave you?"

"Yes."

"Okay, get it, and I want you to stay here on the bed as if nothing happened. If any of Johnson's men come down here, take them out. It's about to get real nasty upstairs. If one of our boys comes down here, he'll call you by your name. That way you'll know who it is… got it?"

"Got it," Joy said.

Cosmo knew that the men upstairs were head security personnel, that's why they were stationed inside. The guys outside were only secondary security personnel but just as lethal as the four inside.

"Joy hold him down here until someone gets here, it won't be long. If he gives you any problems, kill him."

"Okay, but I don't think that'll be necessary."

"Just watch him, okay?" Cosmo said and went to the upper-deck where he heard shooting.

Freddy, Tommy, Peter and Mark had already started in on the men on deck. He fired couple rounds from his Uzi semi-automatic.

Peter fired half a dozen rounds at his targets, but only managed to hit one of the three men he was trying to extinguish. The other two men returned Peter's fire and Peter saw dirt flying into the air; caused by the bullets that dug holes in the ground next to his head. He fired a couple more rounds and this time one of the 45-caliber shells drilled a hole through the chest of one of the men he was shooting at. The third man shot back and caught Peter in his back; piercing a hole in his left lung.

Tommy saw that Peter had been hit and fired back at the man who had just shot Peter. He knocked him to the deck with a 45 round to the man's head. Freddy didn't have any pity on the three men he saturated with lead from his 357-magnum. When all the shooting stopped, Mark looked around and the three men he had in his view had scattered all around the deck of the yacht and were shooting wildly at Freddy and Tommy with no success at hitting either of them. Ray-Ray, Steve, and Bobby had all come running out of the cabin and joined in the activity that was unfolding outside on-deck. But Cosmo had come out behind them without them knowing and opened fire with the Uzi, taking down all three men instantly. Freddy, Tommy, and Mark ended the lives of the three men that had scattered around the deck. Cosmo told Freddy where Joy was being held and how to get to her.

Once Freddy and Joy were safely off the yacht. The demolitions expert had the go ahead to do his job and make sure that yacht never sails again. Solomon was sure his men would win the war upstairs, so he decided to test Joy. He somehow managed to reach into his ankle holster and retrieve a 25-automatic handgun.

Joy noticed what he was doing and told him to hand her the gun.

"Solomon you've been doing alright so far, please don't mess it up for yourself by doing this. Now, hand me the gun, Solomon."

"Yes, Solomon, hand her the gun or I'll blow your brains all over this room," Freddy said when he came into the room.

Solomon slowly raised his weapon to his head and put the barrel to his right temple, in an attempt to commit suicide.

"No, Solomon, you don't want to do that," Joy told him.

"But, if I don't do it, then Mr Johnson will. He said, 'that, 'if you got away, he'll kill every one of us left standing,' and I know for a fact he will do it. He'll kill me before I can blink. So why give him the satisfaction? My life was over way before I came here. I told you that Misses Jackson," Solomon said.

He had fear in his eyes and pain in his voice. The same fear and pain that Joy saw when he was telling her about his father beating his mother and disrespecting her and his sisters. His hands were shaking so bad that the one he held the gun in kept pulling away from his head and back to his temple. Joy and Freddy just stood there waiting for the gun to go off, and hoping it didn't.

"Joy, what do you want to do with him?"

"Let him go, Freddy, he's no threat to anyone…, not by himself anyway. He was respectful and very considerate toward me. I believe that if he could have, he would have let me go," Joy explained.

"I'll tell you what, Solomon; If you can make it off this yacht before it's blown to hell then you're a free man," Freddy told him and grabbed Joy by her arm and led her up the stairs and off the yacht.

They made it outside and Freddy gave the demolition expert the go ahead to blow the yacht. Solomon made it off the yacht before it blew. When it did, the explosion took almost half of the dock with it.

6:00 PM

"Good evening, I'm Jane Lavender, and this just in at 6:00 on your local evening news… Just a little less than half of the Glory Days Yacht Club's yacht and boating dock were blown up. Diane Green has the story live from Malibu."

"Yes, Jane…, we are here live at the Los Angeles County Sheriff's Department's Detention Center covering what seems to be an ongoing war between Yacht Club member and billionaire Gregory Johnson and unknown suspects. And, once again Gregory Johnson has suffered the loss of yet another prize possession, his $32,000,000.00 private yacht: The Yacht Reyal was intentionally blown up. Apparently the same C-four plastic explosive was used that was previously used to blow up a private jet and its hangar, also belonging to Mr Johnson. Gregory Johnson is being held here at this Los Angeles County Sheriff's Department Detention Center in Malibu for questioning. Now, if you would recall, two men were recently shot and killed at the yacht club. One of the victims suffered a gunshot wound to the back of his head when a bullet was fired through the window of Mr. Johnson's office where the victim was in a meeting with Mr Johnson. Only minutes later a man was shot and killed in the parking lot of the world famous yacht club. Mister Johnson is believed to be a political colleague and business associate of multi-billionaire and politician, Donald Warwick. It had been alleged that; Warwick fled the country after a scandal involving him in the disappearance of over one hundred and fifty million dollars in political campaign contributions.

An investigation has been launched into the possible involvement by Gregory Johnson which could prove to be the cause of the sudden rash of explosions in the past week. We'll have more on this story as it unfolds:

Reporting to you live from outside the Los Angeles County Sheriff's Detention Center here in Malibu..., I'm Diane Green."

"My goodness, those guys are the best, aren't they, Mad-C?" Debo asked.

"Yeah, they do know how to handle the job," Mad-C agreed. "And, as for you miss lady," Debo said, as he turned his attention toward Joy.

"The next time you want to see Tammy and Sheila, you let me or Mr Write know. Don't go off on your own thinking no one would find out. Because as you can very well see, anything can happen. This man is devastated with us all and he will stop short of nothing to get what he believe is his. It's just a good thing he thought you were Shelly. Had he known who you really were, he would have probably made an example out of you, young lady. You had Shelly, Freddy, Me, Mr Write, and Pauline scared to death; and poor, Pauline!! We can protect you from yourself as well as protect you from Johnson... don't make me do it... Understand? Just one more stunt like that, and I'll make you think you were in prison until this is over, got it?"

"Got it, Bra!"

"And why didn't you have your weapon on you when they grabbed you, young lady?"

"It was in my purse; they didn't give me a chance to blink."

"Pull another stunt like that and I'll make sure..., oh never-mind. What happened to Peter, Freddy?"

"He was hit by one of Johnson's men; a round went through his back and took out one of his lungs, he died instantly."

Did you get him to our people? I mean his body."

"Yes, Sir.., we took him to the undertaker."

"Okay, good then he's well taken care of," Debo said.

Moray Bennett works for Mad-C. He's been with him since they met when he was at war with other competition that stumbled onto his path. Bennett owns a mortuary in San Diego, California, and three funeral homes in surrounding cities. Anytime a man is killed Mad-C gets the undertaker. And when a man is injured, Mad-C calls Dr Brian Russell, a retired medical surgeon.

"Hello, is Mister Johnson in?"

"No, he isn't, who's calling?"

"This is Charles Write," Mad-C told Dorothy.

"Oh, Mr Write.., Mr Johnson is not available at the moment. May I take a message?"

"No, I'll call him back, thanks, Dorothy," Mad-C said and hung up. "Boss, Johnson got arrested today, or did you forget?"

"No, I thought he bailed out. I thought they were just holding him for questioning."

"Yeah, well they have some pretty serious questions to ask him. They don't let you go if they suspect you of being involved in blowing up half of Malibu. He might have to sit for a while. He can make himself hard to get in touch with, and they know it. But whatever the case, he's going down hard, whether he goes to prison for the rest of his natural life or have his hat brought to him by us," Debo said.

Johnson was in jail being held in the investigation into all the crimes that have been committed around him and especially those that were committed against him. The law feels that somewhere there's a link between the sudden rash of crimes and Gregory Johnson. Even other chair persons at the yacht club are starting to have doubts about whether Johnson's involvement in all this is in fact a true assumption, and whether or not he's an asset or a liability to the club. When he gets back he will no longer be a board member. Mad-C knew that; that's why he called to talk to him, to see if he's on the run or if he's still on the warpath. Either way, the threat that Gregory once posed to Debo and Mad-C, is no longer a threat.

MONDAY, DECEMBER 3RD, 8:30 AM

The interrogation room was stuffy, and smokey from the cigarettes that sheriff's deputy lieutenant Jay Orwell was smoking back-to-back.

"Mr Johnson, I get paid for overtime, which gives me all day and all night to play games with you. On the other hand, cooperate with us and everybody goes home early."

DENNIS CHARLES JOHNSON

"I'll wait for my attorney, thank you," Johnson told the lieutenant. "Lieutenant, Mister Johnson's attorney is here," one of the deputy Sheriff stepped into the room to announce.

"Well, let him wait," the lieutenant said.

"But, Sir.., he's been waiting and screaming bloody murder."

"Okay, let him in.

The deputy left the room for about two minutes and returned with a short middle-aged man with gray streaks running through his neatly combed black hair. He wore his eye glasses on the tip of his nose and spoke very proper English.

"Good morning, sir, my name is Durant; Rudy Durant, and yours, detective?"

"I'm Jay Orwell… Lieutenant Jay Orwell," the lieutenant said as he accepted Mister Durant's right hand which was extended for him to shake. "May I ask the nature of my client's detainment?"

"Your client is being held for questioning for his involvement in the murders and explosions that have been going on around him."

"I see…, has my client been charged or arrested for any crime or crimes in which he may have committed, Lieutenant?"

"No, he hasn't, he's only here for questioning at this time, then…"

"Then what, Lieutenant? Then he's free to go? I certainly hope that was what you were about to say, sir,"

"Yes, Mr Durant, that is what I was about to say."

"Then, you have concluded your line of questioning, Lieutenant?"

"Yes, as a matter of fact I have."

"In that case, Mr Johnson, you can come with me. Lieutenant, just for the record I would advise against questioning my client without my presents or permission in the future. Let's go, Mister Johnson."

"Not just yet, he'll have to be processed out before he is permitted to leave."

"But, you just told me yourself, Lieutenant that Mr Johnson has not been charged for any crime or crimes."

"That's correct, Mr Durant, but the procedures for letting him go only require a couple of minutes. All we need is a fingerprint and photograph and Mr Johnson is free to go. And, Mr. Durant, I would advise your client not to go too far. I'm sure we'll be wanting to see him again," Lieutenant Orwell said.

"Yes, I'm sure you will, Lieutenant.., I'm sure you will."

"What happened?" Durant asked Johnson when they got to his car. "These assholes are blowing up my shit and killing my damn men."

"Did you say anything at all to the lieutenant?"

"No, I waited for you."

"He said, 'they questioned you.' What kind of questions did they ask you?"

"A bunch of stupid-ass questions that I didn't answer any of, and I don't want to repeat them. I just want to take my black ass home and think about this shit."

"What will make this go away, Gregory?"

"That's what I need to think about, Rudy. It'll all go away once that son-of-a-bitch is dead," Gregory Johnson said.

"Well, there's been a lot of that going on and it hasn't ended yet. What else would you suggest?"

"I'm not backing off, Rudy, if that's what you mean. I want that shipping dock and I intend to get it, whatever the cost."

"Even if it cost you your freedom or your life, Mr Johnson?"

"Look, I'll take care of this, you just do what I pay you to do and that's all I need you to worry about."

"And that's what I'm doing.. It's not too good for you to constantly stay in the news and having all this negative publicity, that's all I'm saying. What is going on, Gregory? Do you want to tell me about it? You'll have to sooner or later, you know."

"Yeah, I know and I will, but not now. I just want to go home, take me home, Rudy… please."

"Okay, but stay put or next time it won't be so easy getting you out of there."

"Yeah, I know, I'm not going anyplace, at least until I get what I want."

"Well, whatever it is you're after won't do you any good if you're locked up or dead. Just remember that," Durant told him.

10:05 AM

Desk sergeant Richard Buringham was looking well. He noticed Debo walking through the doors of the Parker Center Police Station in downtown Los Angeles and didn't realize he was smiling.

"Hey, Rich…, I'm happy to see you too, if that's what that big grin on your ace is for. How have you been, my man?" Debo asked.

"Oh, just about as good as can be expected. I'm still here trying to figure out why I'm not gone yet."

"You're not going anywhere, Richard. This job is your life, it's in your blood… you and Sergeant Billings. How is he old guy coming along?"

"Good, but don't let him hear you call him that, or he'll have you writing parking tickets."

"Richard, I don't do parking tickets."

"What is it exactly you do, Mister Jackson?"

"Richard, I told you a million times, I'm a businessman."

Every time Richard asked Debo that question, he became irritated.

"Oh, my, bad," Richard said.

"Yeah Rich…, whatever; is Bob upstairs?"

"Hold on, I'll let him know you're here. You're looking good, Mister Jackson," Richard commented.

"Thanks, Rich"

Debo was wearing a silk alabaster suit with his gold quartz watch, and a gold and diamond pendant. Engraved in the pendant was, 'I'll love you forever,' and You are my heart was engraved in the back of the watch. He was also wearing several gold rings, including his gold wedding band with four five-karat diamonds mounted in it, and the cologne that Ed had given him for Christmas.

"What's the occasion, Jackson?" Sergeant Billings asked.

"No occasion, I just came to come to see my good friend?"

"Oh, hell…, I know a con when I hear one, and I hear one. What is it, Jackson?"

"You mean you're not mad at me?"

"Mad at you for what? As long as you're not killing and blowing up my precinct. You seem to forget, I already know what's going on, just keep it away from downtown LA… thank you."

"Yeah, Sarge, you told me that Johnson would be a big one. So, what do you think?"

"I think you should hurry up and get this over with. It's bigger than I thought it would be."

"Yeah, you know, I heard that they moved Robert Cruse down here someplace."

"Yeah… they're holding him in protective custody in maximum security at Men's Central Jail. His upcoming court date is Friday for the Yin murder, then he goes back in two weeks for that thing out at your place. He refuses to implicate Johnson as the mastermind behind the murder and the attack on you at your estate."

"Yeah, I don't think Johnson sent him to my house, that was something different. I don't think Cruse will make it to court, he's going to roll over on Johnson… just wait until the DA gets finished with him. He won't leave the county jail alive, or if he does make it to prison, he won't make it out of there for sure."

"Yeah.., and I know how Johnson works," Billings said. "How's the family doing these days?" Debo asked.

"Oh, they're hanging in there, Yolonda is almost ready for college. That's when I retire, as soon as she hits the classroom or the dormitory. That's why I chose a rewarding career, so she can go to college and also have a rewarding career. She'll have a nice comfortable life when her mom and I are gone, not to mention part of my pension and my will."

"You have a will?"

"Thanks to you, Jackson, I do."

"Yeah,well, I guess she will be very well off, and whatever I can do for her."

"You've already been a big help with everything, and I appreciate it, and everything that you have done and the trust that you have displayed. Which is more important than anything else you could ever do. You've given me what a lot of people would find very difficult to possess. It's very rare these days and for days to come."

"Yeah, Sarge,..and when I find a good friend, I keep that friend."

"Well, you have certainly proven that, Jackson. And like you said, 'I don't think we'll be hearing from Raymond Anderson (aka) Robert Cruse anymore.' He'll either be locked away or put away," Billings said.

"Keep up the good work, Bob!"

"Oh, I'll try…, catch you later," Billings told Debo as he walked out the door.

"Dorothy, I won't be in the office today; will you cancel all my appointments and forward all my calls to my voicemail. I'll be at home if you need me, only if you need me," Johnson said over the phone.

"Mister Johnson, Mister Write called earlier, but he didn't leave a message, sir."

"Well, if anyone else calls, just do like I asked you to do!!"

"Okay, Sir…, will that be all?"

"Yes, that'll be all for now, thanks, Dorothy."

"You're welcome, sir."

1:30 PM

Gregory Johnson made it home to his ranch in San Gabriel. He picked up the newspaper and saw his picture posted on the front page.

MULTI-BILLIONAIRE GREGORY JOHNSON BACK IN THE NEWS

Ex-politician and multi-billionaire; Gregory Johnson was released from jail today, where he was being held for questioning. During questioning by Sheriff Lieutenant Jay Orwell, Mr Johnson's attorney, Rudy Durant asked that the lieutenant refrain from questioning his client; Mister Johnson, and release him immediately, and Lieutenant Orwell complied with Mister Johnson's counsel and released him."

He dropped the paper on the dining room table and walked over to the cordless phone sitting on a table next to his suede sofa and love-seat. He pressed a button on the phone's base and the answering machine came on. "You have four new calls!!"

He pressed another button and heard a beep, followed by another recording.

"You have a collect call from an inmate at Men's Central jail. If you wish to accept this call, press one, if you wish to decline the call, hang up or press zero."

After that, he heard a dial tone. Robert Cruse was trying to contact him. He tried to call him earlier today because he read about his yacht having been blown up over the weekend, and that he was released from jail. He pressed the button to listen to the next message. After he heard all of the messages, he went to his bedroom and threw himself across the bed which offered comfort and relaxation. He closed his eyes and tried to will all the events of the past month or so away, wondering how he could have let things get so out of hand. He tried to weigh his options and came to the conclusion that Mr Durant was right. But he couldn't just let $300 Million dollars go just like that. It's costing him money and causing him more problems than he cares to deal with. He was thinking 'that maybe he'll just tell Write about the money and offer him half of it.' $150 million dollars is a lot of money.

The only thing greed is doing is getting him deeper and deeper in trouble. But then too, $300 Million dollars is also a lot of money. The only thing standing in the way of him getting it is one man, one lousy ass man. Johnson had an idea; one that could solve his problems and keep him out of trouble and out of the news. This plan has to work because he can't kidnap any more of Debo's friends or family. Now they are all on alert and they're ready for something to happen. He decided to play their game and called one of his friends in Chicago and ordered a half-pound of C-four plastic explosives. Then he hired a demolition expert of his own and told him to meet with him at his ranch in San Gabriel to discuss some business that would raise his net-worth by $100,000 after the job was done. All he had to do was blow up enough of the shipping dock to be able to get to the money. He didn't want to destroy the whole dock, and heaven knows he had enough C-four. He just wanted to blow a hole in the floor and about five-feet deep. He wanted a hole dug under it because that's where the money is buried. Johnson expected the job to go just about as smooth as the thought of planning it.

2:15 PM

Joy was shocked when Mad-C's security staff showed up at the cabin with her daughters; Tammy and Sheila. As soon as they dropped the girls off with Joy, her cell phone rang.

"Big Bra… you are the very best, I love you so much. But, what about school?"

"They have a couple of weeks off, something about being on track. We don't want them out there for that long, just long enough to see you and spend a couple of days with you. Joyvette, all you have to do is let me know and I can have the world brought to you."

"Big Bra you already did, thank you so much," Joy thankfully said. She was still shocked from the surprise.

"You're very welcome, and you can also thank Mr. Write. I didn't really want to put the girls in harm's way, but he convinced me that they would be safer there than where they were, especially after what happened. You gave him quite a scare, he really thinks a lot of you."

"Do you think it could be because I'm your sister?"

"If you weren't my sister, he wouldn't even know who you were."

"Yeah, you have a point there," Joy said. There was a short silence, then he heard Tammy in the background say,

"Mommy is that my Uncle Debo, can I talk to him?"

"Hold on, Bra.., your niece wants to say something."

"Hey, Tammy."

"Hi, Uncle Debo, this is great, thank you so much."

"You girls are more than welcome," he told Tammy, then he heard Sheila in the background say…

"Thank you, Uncle Debo, I love you."

"Tell Sheila I said she's welcome and you girls have fun with your mom. Tammy put your mom on the phone for a minute."

"Bra, they are loving it, thanks. They have never been in the snow, hell they've never even seen real snow."

"Well, you've earned it, put Tammy on for me please."

"Yes, Uncle Debo?"

"Tammy, you know that I love, you, your sister, and your mom very, very much with all my heart. And I'll never let anything happen to any of you, okay?"

"Okay, but how come you're not here with us?" Tammy asked. It really touched his, and Joy's hearts.

"Because I have to work so I can buy you and Sheila a big Christmas present. Don't you want a big Christmas present?"

"Yes, but it would be a better Christmas if you were under the tree for me," Tammy said.

"Well..., we'll see, sweetheart, I'll try my best to be under there for you, okay"

"Okay, Uncle Debo, I can't wait."

"I can't either, sweetheart, let me speak to your mom."

"Yeah, Bra?"

You could tell she was crying, but he knew it was because she was having a very special moment. After all, she risked her life to go see her twelve and fourteen-year olds. She's been through a lot and Debo knew how much they miss each other.

"You deserve it kiddo, have a ball," Debo said, then hung-up.

Debo nor Mad-C were taking any chances, they doubled security at the cabin. Joy called Freddy and told him about the surprise.

"That was thoughtful of them, you must be everybody's favorite, Joy. And that makes you special in a lot of people's lives. It must be a wonderful feeling," Freddy said.

"Well, you're my favorite person, so I guess that would make you a very special person. So, tell me..., is it a wonderful feeling?"

"You are everybody in the world to me, Joy. So, I guess that makes me everybody's favorite, and it is a beautiful feeling. I won't take up your time, this is the girls' moment, I'll have mine. And when I do, no one will be able to interrupt our special moment. I'll talk to you later baby, enjoy the girls," Freddy said, and their call ended.

Debo's cell phone rang and he picked up on the first ring. He knew it was Shelly because he had changed the special ringtone; It's Our Anniversary so it played only when she called. It used to play when anybody called, but she convinced him that since it was a dedication to their wedding anniversary, that certain tone should be hers alone, and her request was granted.

"Yeah, sweetheart?" Debo said. "Hi, honey, how's things going?"

"Oh, fair.., and to what do I owe the pleasure of this unexpected call?"

"I just called to tell you I love you, and to tell you how proud I am of you for what you did for, Joy. She is so happy. D-Angelo Jackson you are the very best," Shelly awarded.

"Thanks, baby, I guess I am, huh?" Debo proudly said.

"You are not only the best person in others' world, but you are exceptionally the very best in mine; Just please stay in mine."

"Okay, baby, I will. You couldn't put me out of your life with an atomic bomb."

"I love you, mister. I called to let you know that the ski instructor called, and we'll be taking ski lessons starting next week or maybe this weekend. I meant to thank Mister Write and you. I'm sorry, I guess he thinks I'm unappreciative, doesn't he?"

"No, sweetheart, I thanked him for you."

"How have you been coming along, are you okay?"

"Yeah, I'm doing fine. I just want my baby with me and my life to be normal again, that's all," Shelly said.

"I'm about to wrap this mess up; Hold on just a bit longer, okay?"

"Okay, Baby.., stay sweet." she told him.

"Okay, I love you."

"I love and miss you too," he said.

3:30 PM

Gregory Johnson's phone rang, and he let the machine pick up. It was the same operator he heard earlier; the one that announced the call from Men's Central Jail. He pressed one, and the call was put through.

"Hello, Raymond.., what's going on in there with you?" Gregory Johnson asked, when he answered the phone. He felt a nagging and a throbbing in his stomach.

"Greg, they have me in here on some bullshit no-bail arrest warrant in connection with the murder of, Sue-Lang-Yin, and possession of a loaded firearm."

"Okay, what is it you want me to do?" Johnson asked him.

He had a pretty good idea where this was leading: Cruse wanted him to somehow get him off the hook, and Johnson knew exactly how he wanted him to do it. Johnson would have to take the rap for the Yin murder.

"They're offering me eighteen-years and that's a plea-bargain, but they want me to rat on you, otherwise I'm looking at twenty-five years to life."

"Take it, you'll be out in twenty years. Let me just say this, take what they give you and I'll do all I can to get you through it. If you don't, I won't be able to help you if you know what I mean," Johnson said, with stern authority.

"Gregory, I'm your brother, for Goodness sake, I have a life to live. You did something and got caught for it. If I had done something and got caught, I would take my own heat."

"Raymond take the deal, If you try to fight it, you'll lose."

"You would do this to me?"

"Do what to you? You want me to do sit there in prison for you?" Gregory asked.

"No, I want you to sit in here for your fucking self," Cruse angrily said. Robert Cruse knew what Johnson meant by what he said, and he also knew he wasn't talking about losing in court. Gregory Johnson meant that if he opened his mouth to anyone, someone in the jail or prison where they put him would kill him.

Gregory Johnson is ruthless enough to have his own brother killed to save his own ass and his reputation. "This conversation is over, Raymond. I have some business to take care of. If you need anything, let me know; money, packages, someone to write, whatever, I'll get it for you, just let me know, okay?" Gregory said.

"Yeah, okay," Cruse said.

He felt like Johnson had already killed him, he might as well have done just that. He's leaving him in there to rot, and he knows he won't make it past the reception center before his so-called brother has him hit. Gregory Johnson did indeed have business to take care of. He has one week to put his plan into action; to blow up the shipping dock and get the money.

CHAPTER
22

MONDAY, DECEMBER 3RD, 3:30 P.M.

Gregory Johnson made a call to Christopher Burman; Mad-C's foreman at the shipping dock in Long Beach.

"Ralph, put that on the forklift and load it on number fourteen, it's going out on the Oklahoma shipment. John, get me an invoice on the Collins Manufacturing order and tape it to the board, Harvey, move that rig to dock two and hold it for inspection!!!" Christopher yelled.

"Mr Burman… you have a call on line one in your office, sir," a short sweaty man with coveralls on and a fat cigar protruding from his thin lips announced.

The mandatory hard hat he wore barely fit his too-big head, his shoes squeaked when he walked, and one side of each heel was worn down.

"Tell whoever it is I said to call back," Chris told the man as he wiped perspiration from his chin, forehead, and nose.

"It's Mister Johnson calling, sir, he says it's important."

"Yeah, it's always important when somebody calls, but what I do every day is not important enough to give me a raise. Okay, tell him I'm coming and put him on hold."

He told his lead dockworker to take over while he answers the call. He walked through the warehouse which was unusually neat for a warehouse.

Everything was organized and you could actually find your way around with your eyes closed. The floors were waxed so well, you'd think you were walking on glass or ice. Everything was neatly put away or stocked on their shelves. The fresh smell of pine accented the entire building. Christopfer's office was state-of-the-art. He has a flat screen plasma television, surround sound stereo, a nice little living room setting with two matching suede sofas, a glass coffee table that sat between the sofas, and a minibar.

His desk is a thick black fiberglass with a white and gold high-backed office chair. He sat behind his desk and pressed the button on the phone, and Gregory Johnson came on the line.

"What took you so long?" Johnson impatiently asked.

"I'm at work, what is it you need?"

"I need a favor."

"It depends on the nature of the favor and if it's worth my time."

"Do you know who the fuck you're talking to?"

"Yeah, Greg, I know exactly who I'm talking to. And every time I talk to you, you need a damn favor, what is it now?" Chris asked.

"Just shut the fuck up and listen," Johnson harshly said. "Look, don't call my office with your head in your ass. My boss is pissed as hell at you as it is."

"Don't test me, Christopher, just pay attention."

"What do you want, Gregory, I'm busy. Hold on a minute," Chris said. He had to answer a call that had come in on another line.

"Hello..., yeah, boss, everything is going great. That order was scratched, I put it over on dock two for inspection. Yes, the Collins Manufacturing order. Alright boss, I will..., Okay... Okay, Bye."

Chris switched back over to line one where Gregory Johnson was awaiting his return.

"Okay, that was my boss, what's up, I have to go?"

"Listen to me, I have some money buried under that dock, I need you to help me get it and it's not up for negotiation!!!"

"Hold on, let me get this straight: You mean to tell me that you think you can order me to help you screw my boss and expect me to do it."

"You helped with the ten keys."

"I was hungry and didn't know any better."

"Bullshit.., you knew what the fuck you were doing. like I said, it's not up for negotiation."

"Yeah, well I'll think about it."

"I'll tell you what… you can make yourself a million dollars, or you can be a memory…, what'll it be?"

"Like I said… I'll think about it."

"Okay, Christopher, you have one week to make up your mind. One million dollars is my only offer, take it or leave it."

Christopher Burman was sick and tired of being pushed around by people. He knew that if he didn't help Johnson, he would tell Mad-C about the ten keys. And not only would Chris lose his job, but he'll also lose Mad-C's trust. But, on the other hand, one million dollars sounded damn good. If he did do it; with the million dollars plus what he has saved, he could buy his own dock.

Mad-C doesn't take kindly to being double crossed, and Gregory Johnson just might decide to kill Chris once he gets what he wants whether he goes along with it or not. If he doesn't, he's sure to tell Mad-C about Gregory's plan. Chris decided to go ahead and help Johnson. After all, a million dollars is a lot of paid bills and a chance to go out on his own and start his own business.

"Los Angeles Sheriffs Department!!. Everybody down!!!, get on the floor now!!! Show me some hands…, show me your hands!!! Put them out at your side… MOVE!!!" were the orders Lieutenant Jay Orwell yelled when he and a team of a dozen sheriff's deputies broke down Gregory Johnson's front door at 11001 Oak Pine Lane in San Gabriel, California. He had given his security personnel the evening off, so he was the only one there. He had said he needed to think and wanted to be left alone, which made it easy for the Sheriff's deputies to get as close as they did to his front door.

"What's the meaning of this, Lieutenant?" Gregory asked.

"I have a warrant for your arrest for the murder of, Sue-Lang-Yin."

"The murder of what? I don't believe this shit. Who the fuck told you I killed somebody?"

"Put your feet under you, I'm going to help you up.

Don't struggle, or the cuffs will cut into your wrists," the lieutenant advised. "That damned, Anderson gave me up. Does he know who the fuck I am? I'll have his ass hit before he wakes up in the morning. That stupid motherfucker," he thought to himself.

The lieutenant got Gregory Johnson to the sheriff's cruiser and put him in.

"Watch your head," he told him, as he put him into the cruiser. And now, Gregory Johnson is once again subjected to the stale leather and sweaty smell of the back seat of the sheriff's cruiser. And, once again Gregory Johnson experienced that familiar, uncomfortable, irritating feeling of imprisonment.

"I kind of figured something would break soon, Johnson. You're becoming a regular celebrity. You wanna tell me about what's been going on? Oh, that's right, you want your lawyer.

Well, you're gonna need him, Greg…, you're certainly going to need him."

Lieutenant Orwell doesn't know that Gregory Johnson has political ties which includes judges and district attorneys.

Orwell led him inside the San Gabriel County Sheriff's Station, where he was cuffed to a long bench out in the hall and was to wait until he was searched, fingerprinted, and booked into the jail.

"What are you in here for?" a man sitting next to him on the bench asked.

Gregory looked at the man and figured he must have traveled miles by foot and had surely seen much better days. He was missing three upper teeth, smelled like urine, tobacco, liquor, must, and was filthy.

"You smell like shit, shut the fuck up talking to me, and mind your own business. Hey, Orwell get me the hell away from this shitbag!!!" Johnson yelled.

"You girls play nicely!!!" Orwell yelled . " Call my attorney!!!"

"You'll have a chance to do that in a minute, Johnson, just hold tight!!!"

He sat there for an hour and a half before Lieutenant Orwell came and got him for booking. After he was fingerprinted and booked, he looked at his booking slip and saw the words, "NO BAIL!!"

He made a collect phone call to Rudy Durant, his criminal attorney. "Hey, Rudy, these assholes got me back in this bitch on a murder charge," Johnson told Mr Durant.

"Have you said anything… anything at all?" Durant asked. "No, I'm not an idiot."

"I guess if you weren't an idiot, you wouldn't have put yourself in the position to be sitting where you are; charged with murder," Durant thought to himself.

"Okay, hold tight, I'll be there."

8:00 PM.

"Hey, are you watching the news?" Mad-C asked Debo when he called him. "No, what happened?"

"They have your boy Johnson on a 'no-bail' arrest warrant for the Yin murder."

"What.., is it on now?"

"Yeah, turn on the 8:00 news."

Debo was at home watching the Monday night football game and wondering why Mad-C wasn't doing the same; anyway, Johnson's arrest is more important. Mad-C turned it on just in time to hear the news anchorman say…

"The top story tonight evolves once again around, Mister Gregory Johnson. As we all know, Mr Johnson was being held just a few days ago for the investigation into the bombing of his $23,000,000.00 private yacht, and for questioning in numerous other illegal criminal activities, which includes the shooting of two victims at his yacht club, or the yacht club where he was employed as CEO on the board of directors. He was also questioned about the bombing of his private jet and the hangar in which it was housed.

Now he's being held at county jail for murder. Gregory Johnson, the multi-billionaire, and former chairman of the board of directors at the Malibu yacht club has been implicated in the murder of fishing boat captain Sue-Lang-Yin six years ago. All our sources told us was that Mr Johnson had Yin killed to gain possession of a large shipment of illegal drugs. The case was never solved, and until now was put on the shelf of cold cases; (cases that are unsolved). A new investigation into the mysterious Yin murder has been launched. It was first believed that Mister Yin had drowned when his body washed up on Sierra Aveda's Lake Davis near Porto-la and they ruled it an accidental drowning. We will keep you informed of more breaking developments as we get them…, and now in other news."

"Well, big fella are you thinking what I'm thinking?" Debo asked Mad-C.

"I'm thinking Robert Cruse is the source of that information."

"Yeah he rolled over on Johnson just like we figured he would." Christopher heard the same news broadcast and he decided to wait until Gregory Johnson bailed out of jail because with Johnson's clout, resources, and his reputation as a former politician, he would have no problem getting the judge to grant him bail or an OR. But, Christ might have to wait a while, and a Million dollars is well worth the wait.

MONDAY, DECEMBER 10TH, 6:00 PM… ONE WEEK LATER

Johnson had to somehow let the demolitions expert that he met with know he's in jail. Maybe he already knows, the broadcast aired nationwide, how could he not know? But still, he had to make sure he knew by 2:00 Tuesday morning. He'll call Christopher at home and somehow let him know to call the guy for him. But, he'll have to watch how he talks on the phone because they monitor all the inmates' calls and mail. He went ahead and called Chris' home phone and he accepted the call.

"Chris… thank goodness you are there. I need you to call someone for me."

Johnson told Chris what he wanted him to do, not really knowing whether he was going to help him or not.

"I've decided to go ahead and help you, Greg; I can use the money, and I want…"

Gregory stopped Chris from finishing his statement to remind him that their call was being monitored, and to say, "There's a friend of mine that's going to be going to your job at about 2:00 tomorrow morning. If he doesn't know I'm here, let him know. Tell him that I said I'll give him a call when I get out. Can you do that for me?"

"Sure, Greg, I can do that for you," Chris said, smiling as if he had something up his sleeve… which he did.

He decided to cross Mad-C and Gregory Johnson. The guy that was supposed to blow up the dock wasn't told what was there or why he was blowing it up; just what part of it to blow up. Chris met him at the dock in Long Beach at exactly 2:00 Tuesday morning.

TUESDAY, DECEMBER 11TH, 2:00 A.M.

"Where is Mister Johnson?" the man asked Chris.

"He's not here he sent me instead. Mister Johnson chose not to be here personally, just in case something went wrong, you know?" Chris lied.

"Nothing ever goes wrong when I do a job. You have the money?" the man asked.

"Yes, right here," Chris said and handed the man a duffel bag with the money for the job in it.

"Okay, you can go get yourself some breakfast. You don't wanna be standing around when she blows."

"Okay, I'll see you later."

"I don't think so," the man told him. Chris got in his car and turned on some music. It was unusually cold for Long Beach, but at least he had a heater in the car. He didn't know how long the wait would be, so he rolled the window down a little to let some of the morning air in while he waited. He read about people dying from carbon monoxide poisoning due to failure to let air into the car while it was running. He knew that once the job was done, he would have to wait until the police, news, and the large crowd of spectators that would gather had left. Mad-C would probably be there also. After all, it's his shipping dock and someone will have to call him. Speaking of which, he thought it possibly should be him that made that call.

"Mister Write, I'm sorry to bother you at this hour. I just got a phone call from…"

"I know, Chris…, I know, they called me too. I'm on my way out there now. It's going to take me a while to get there from here. So, can you go out there and get all the information you can for me?"

"Yes, Sir Mister Write, I'll be here when you get here," Chris said.

Mad-C called Debo to let him know what had happened. Debo offered to ride with him. Freddy still hadn't found the condo for Debo. He had gotten comfortable being back at home anyway and didn't press the issue. He had all the security he needed. He knew it would only take him at most about ten minutes to get to Mad-C's estate. Since at 2:30 in the morning there is no traffic, or very little if any. He walked out of the house and found it to be freezing cold; in fact it was colder than usual outside. His head and ears were cold but his body was warm from the warm clothes and heavy coat he wore. He also wore his thick gloves so that his hands were warm as well. He got in the Navigator and it was even colder. He asked himself if he was in a car or a freezer, hoping it'll warm up shortly.

Christopher got out of the car but not for at least half an hour. He had to let them know what to do about whatever wasn't destroyed.

So, in a minute he would go over there as if he had just arrived on the scene.

Debo drove to Long Beach since Mad-C wasn't in the right frame of mind to drive. He pulled the Navigator next to where all the fire engines and police cars were, and where Chris pulled his car and was now parked. Mad-C and Debo walked over to where Chris was standing and asked how much information he had about his dock being blown damned near to hell. "The arson investigators said, 'that the dock was intentionally blown up; some sort of heavy explosives were used.' That's all they were able to tell me at this stage," Chris said.

"How much damage do you think they did?" Debo asked Mad-C. "They didn't do this shit, Johnson did," Mad-C said.

He did everything he could to keep from exploding himself. He was petrified and as hot as the heat from the explosion itself. He was so hot, that if you put a thermometer in his mouth the mercury would shoot out the other end. He was pissed because he got there too late to check anything for himself; as far as what the investigators said. He would have to call the detectives that were in charge at the scene; the ones that will be investigating. If he wanted to get onto the crime scene, he would be able to do that in a few hours or days. But for now all he could do was just stand there on the side of the crime-scene tape where onlookers and spectators were allowed to stand. He looked at his life's work blown to rocks, wood, and mangled metal. Chris said, 'the fire chief advised it wasn't safe to go in at that point.'

"Okay, Johnson you son-of-a-bitch, you'll pay dearly for this," Mad-C said aloud.

"But, Johnson is in jail, how could he have done it?" Debo asked. "Just like I did his yacht and his jet I didn't have to be there either. He had someone do it for him," Mad-C answered, with flagrant anger. Debo stayed outside the Navigator and questioned Chris for more details. Mad-C walked over to a grassy area that was located at the foot of the dock where the warehouse is. The crime scene tape kept him from going any further. He couldn't believe what he saw. He just stood there motionless, The bright street lights glared in his eyes; revealing a tear that had not yet rolled down his cheek. He felt his flesh tingling from the biting cold and decided to go sit down in the Navigator. He leaned his head back on the seat's headrest and put his palms on his knees and shut his eyes tight. That's when the tear found its way down his cheek. And with his head tilted back on the headrest, he opened his eyes and reality had hit him head-on, and pain brought his hands to his face. He shook his head and wished none of this had ever happened. But he knew there was a chance and a possibility that Gregory Johnson would do something like this. He had accepted the possibility without forethought.

And the person that angered him so had now frightened him. Debo walked up to the Navigator, opened the driver's door, and got in. "I'm not going to ask if you're okay because I know you're not and I know I'm not," Debo told him, with consideration and true heartfelt love that only brothers shared between each other.

"I knew the possibility was there and I expected it. I can re-build, but a lot has been destroyed, irreplaceable things. The explosion took out my entire office and a lot more," Mad-C cried.

"Someone else is behind this, I'm willing to bet my life," Debo told Mad- C.

"The investigators told Chris 'that the place was blown from the inside.' Someone had to give the final order and Gregory wouldn't chance doing that on a jail phone. Someone had to let whoever did this, inside the building. A professional wouldn't have acted without the orders. Someone gave him the order, and it wasn't Johnson. Do you remember when we went to blow up the club on Gage,… my man was there? He knew where the job was but he didn't go out there on his own to do it. He waited for me to arrive because shit happens like Misty Rodgers, who stopped us from blowing up her club. Well…, Johnson's going to jail should have stopped his guy, unless someone else gave the orders to blow the dock. And, as I said, someone had to let the guy in. There were very few people that had a key; you, Chris, and maybe one or two other people."

Before Debo walked away from Chris' car and went over to the Navigator, he told Chris to sit tight in case Mad-C wanted to ask him more questions before he left. Chris was sitting in his car thinking about how he just stood there and betrayed the man that trusted him with a multi-billion-dollar business. He felt like pure shit knowing that what was done, was done.

Debo kept looking over at Chris' car and then back at the dock. Something wasn't adding up. Something was way out of place but what was it? It was something as simple as hell and it was right on the tip of his tongue, but he just couldn't put his finger on it.

"I have the number of the investigator if you want to call and talk with him."

"Yeah, I can call him later, Debo. Right now I'm too upset to talk to anyone."

"Okay, I'll take you home."

Debo blew the horn and Chris got out of his car shivering from the cold. He walked over to the Navigator and Mad-C rolled his window down and said,

"Is that all you have for me?"

Chris hesitated for a second, then said, "Yes, Sir.., that's all the detectives and the fire chief said. They did tell me there were no witnesses probably because it was so early in the morning.

There wasn't a motive established yet, but they determined that some kind of high explosives were used… maybe C-four."

"Okay go on home and I'll call you if I need you again, and I'll mail you your severance pay. You should get it in a few days. I don't know when she'll be up and running, but I'll sure keep you in mind. Thanks, Chris," Mad-C said.

Christopher walked back over to his car, got in, and drove off. All he could think of was how he betrayed Mad-C; a man he had grown close to and a man that would have probably helped get the dock he wanted or maybe made him a partner in his business once he got it up and running again. But there was one thing he never gave Christopher Burman; a reason to stab him in the back. He stood there and watched Mad-C go through the pain, the heartache, the loss of what he worked so long and hard to build. It wouldn't have been any worse if he had driven a knife through his heart, or if he had taken a gun and blew his brains out.

"Money is a bitch, and will make you do the damndness things to people you love, people you like, or even people you just care about. This had better be worth it," Chris thought to himself.

And then there's Gregory Johnson… what about him? He offered him a million dollars just to let the man in. Is that enough money to start a new life somewhere… somewhere out of the country maybe? It damned well better be since he just made a very dangerous move if it isn't. He just simply screwed Mad-C, Gregory Johnson, and who knows… maybe even himself.

The television in the day room for the inmates at Men's Central Jail in downtown Los Angeles was mounted and bolted to a small platform just big enough to accommodate the twenty-seven inch color TV set. It and the benches in front of it were in an area where the urinals, showers, and the dirty clothes bins were located. If you wanted to watch TV, you had to put up with the stench of stale urine, molded clothes, and sweaty bodies. The inmate with the most seniority wanted to watch a syndicated program that they always watch around that particular time, which is just after count at 6:00 pm. Gregory, not understanding the jailhouse rules and the politics of the day-room, got up to turn the TV to a different station.

"What the hell do you think you're doing, brother?" one of the biggest and meanest inmates asked him.

"I'm putting this thing on the news," Gregory answered in a simular tone of voice the inmate that asked him had used.

"Well, in here.., inmate we have rules and everybody obeys and respects all those rules."

"I just want to see something," Johnson said and continued turning the channel. "You just fucked-up, homeboy," the inmate said as all 280 pounds of him got up off the bench.

"Hey wait, that looks like him on TV!!!" one of the other inmates yelled.

"Well, I'll be damned, it sure the hell is homeboy. Are you famous or something?" the big man asked Johnson.

"Something like that... Can you be quiet so I can hear it?" Johnson asked without flinching.

"Well whoever you are, you sure as hell got a lot of balls."

"Sit yo big ass down, Moose, we can't hear the damned thing," the smallest inmate in the day-room said.

They broadcast all the earliest news concerning Gregory Johnson and the inmates wondered why he wasn't in the high-power unit where they put high-profile inmates; a one-man cell in protective custody; better known as the (PC UNIT).

> **"And now, in today's news; a Long Beach shipping dock was blown up this morning at about 2:30 am. The twenty-five-year-old shipping dock belonging to telecommunication Empire: Charles Write, was nearly destroyed. The reason for this crime is not yet known,**

and there were no witnesses or suspects. Apparently, the same explosives used to blow up billionaire Gregory Johnson's private jet was used to also blow up the dock. Investigators are looking into the possibility that these bombings are all somehow related, including the recent explosions in Long Beach, California."

"Shit!! Who the fuck told him to…," Gregory stopped himself from saying anything further. He didn't want everyone to know any more of his business than they already know: After all, he's in jail.

"Thanks, and sorry about the disrespect," Johnson said. He was confused and angry.

"No problem Mister VIP, no problem at all," the big man said. One of the other inmates walked up to Gregory Johnson and pulled him to the side and said,

"You'd better see about getting moved from this module. You don't belong in here with us. It's for your own safety; Do it soon… real soon," the inmate warned.

Johnson had his lawyer make some phone calls to the courthouse where he was due to appear Thursday morning at 8:30 am. He knew he would be getting out and Christopher Burman is going to pay dearly if he doesn't get his money. That would give Chris less than three days to make his next move and go for the money. Meanwhile, Mad-C had Tommy, Cosmo, Mark, Jeffery, and Freddy guarding the dock; not to mention a little surveillance from the Long Beach Police Department. Some of the dock workers had family and friends who worked on the dock, or in the warehouse. It was said to be the largest shipping dock in Long Beach, California.

"The LBC," Johnson heard one of the inmates say while mimicking gang signs with his fingers. It brought him out of his thoughts and back to the smelly day-room. The module he's housed in holds 206 inmates. A little less than half of them went to the day-room that evening to watch TV. That's a lot of pissing, showering, and dirty clothes. The clothes bins were from the entire module and were left sitting there by the trustees and apparently forgotten about.

"Hey, deputy, can we get somebody to clean this shit up in here? It's bad enough we're locked up, we don't have to smell all the ass, sweat, piss, shit, and funk from these clothes," one of the inmates yelled, through the day-room door.

Gregory Johnson found himself a corner and sat in it and thought about who was messing with his money. Now all anybody needs is a jackhammer, a truck, and the location and the money's gone for good; all Three-Hundred-Million-Dollars.

Johnson is in the right place to get to his brother; Raymond Anderson (aka) Robert Cruse. He knew Cruse fingered him in the Yin murder. Now all he needs to figure out is how he's going to get to him. He walked back over to the inmate that warned him against being in that module and said,

"If I wanted to get to another inmate, how do I go about doing it?"

"Well, Mister VIP.., I can see that you are into some really heavy shit, which means that you must have some heavy money. You know it costs to get what you want done in here."

"How much?"

"Oh… say five thousand dollars. How long will you be here?"

"What does that have to do with anything?"

"Well, inmate, if I give you this information how do I know that I'm going to get my five thousand dollars, and the people that does him are gonna wanna get paid too? And if you leave here without… "

"I'm not going anywhere until I go to court. I'm in here on a no-bail warrant."

"Let me see your booking slip."

Johnson took out the pink booking receipt and showed it to the man. "Yeah, okay.., here's how it works; you have somebody on the outs give the money to my lady to put in a bank account on the streets But, first I'll give you what you need, and If by chance my money is not in that account when I call my lady. Then you, Sir…, will not be going to court, or anywhere else."

"The money is not a problem, you'll get it," Johnson promised. The inmate looked around the room and wiped the corners of his mouth with his thumb and index finger, then said,

"The phones are on the wall over there." He pointed to a row of about a dozen telephones on a wall on the other side of the room.

"You can start making the call; What's the guy's name?"

"He should be here under, Raymond Anderson or Robert Cruse."

"How long has he been here?"

"About a week or so."

"Okay, then he might be out at wayside by now, or he could have a PC hold. But don't worry he can still be touched, he won't make it home. They call me Angel…, I've been down for three years fighting my case. I blew up some mothafuckas too, but I didn't use dynamite. I used my desert eagle.., and for the record,… don't make the mistake I just did. I mean, in here you don't tell anybody that you did what they say you did, they set us up all the time in here. You won't hear about your friend on the news, but you'll be notified before you go to court Thursday."

"Thanks, Angel."

"Don't thank me, In fact.., we never had this conversation. Now go on and make the call, day-room is almost over."

Chris had some money saved… a lot of money. So, the truck and the men he needed wouldn't be a problem. But getting past Tommy, Cosmo, Mark, Freddy, and Jeffery might be.

If Johnson was going to blow the dock, he would most likely do it close to where the money is buried so he can get to it without any problems. Chris just needs to go in where the dock was blown, get the money, and get the hell out of there, which was his plan.

WEDNESDAY, DECEMBER 19TH, 8:30 A.M.—ONE WEEK LATER

Gregory Johnson was still awaiting the judge's decision. He was still locked up at Men's Central Jail, but he should be out any day; via $2 million dollars for the judge and $2 million for the district attorney. Four-million dollars just bought them both. And that's just peanuts for Gregory Johnson.

9:15 AM

Some inspectors and construction workers came to start moving away the concrete, wood, and twisted metal left by the explosion. They showed Freddy and Tommy the necessary paperwork to clean the debris. Freddy called Debo to let him know what was going on.

"Boss, tell Mr Write that some people are here to start cleaning up."

"Hold on," Debo said and gave Mad-C the phone.

He had stayed at Mad-C's house that night to go over some things. "Yes, Freddy?"

"Mister Wright, there's a cleaning crew here. They said they have your permission to start cleaning up the place."

"Yes, Freddy, they called me yesterday. I met with the supervisor and checked all their papers. The investigators should be finished because I need my dock opened. It's been a week since the explosion and I have shipments coming in within a couple of days and they can't be sent back."

"I'm on it as we speak."

"Thanks, Freddy, I appreciate that."

"Just doing my job, sir..., just doing my job," Freddy said.

The construction crew worked into the night and early Thursday morning.

THURSDAY, DECEMBER 20TH, 7:45 A.M.

They finished cleaning up and moving the debris. All that was left was an empty hole where the other half of the dock and warehouse was. Chris had pulled it off; the dump trucks left there with all the wood, concrete, and twisted metal along with something else... thirty body bags containing $10 million each that was buried under the dock. Christopher Burman had pulled off the biggest job in the history of Long Beach, CA... maybe even the world.

> **Robert (BIG BOY) Cruse's body was found in the showers at 11:30 this morning. That's the time the**

County Sheriff's deputies take their afternoon count. He was stabbed to death by several inmates at Pitches Detention Center in Santa Clarita, CA: Better known as "Wayside Honor Rancho."

Gregory Johnson's attorney, Rudy Durant pulled some strings; not to mention the $4 million that the judge and district attorney got. Johnson was released on $25 million bail forthwith.

Mad-C's phone rang, and Edward answered it. "Write's Residence, who may I say is calling?"

"Hello, I'm Ralph Showman, and I'm with the Showman Insurance Company."

"Hold on a second, Mr Showman."

"Yeah, Write here."

"Hello, Mister Write, my name is…"

"Yeah, I know, what can I do for you, Mr Showman?"

"Well, Mister Write, I was told by your insurance company to clean up the dock you have in Long Beach that was blown up about a week ago."

"You were told what, by whom?"

"Mister Write, Showman have a contract with In-Sure Insurance Company. We do all the construction and cleanup work for their insurance company and their clients."

"So why are you calling me, the sight has already been done."

"Can you tell me what company did it, sir?"

"A company by the name of 'Dcaje Construction' did the work," Mad-C explained. He was becoming very confused and agitated.

"Mister Write, I don't mean to sound out of place, but I have been in the construction business for many, many years, and I have never heard of 'Dcaje Construction', they don't work for Showman anyway."

"Let me straighten it out and I'll get back to you."

"Okay, Sir.., thank you, and I apologize for the mix-up," Showman said. He hung up and let out a sigh, along with a deep breath that he had drawn when he realized he wasn't going to get the contract.

Mad-C called Debo and told him about the call. Debo promised to come right over.

11:30 AM

Debo arrived at Mad-C's estate at 11:30 am.

"Okay, Mad-C, what is it that has you in such an uproar?" Debo asked as he took off the thick black gloves he was wearing and laid them on the table next to him. He had already given his coat to Edward when he came in. "I got a call from a construction company asking if I was ready to have the dock cleaned up from the explosion."

"But, that's been done already, hasn't it?"

"Yeah.., do me a favor and call your man at LAPD… the Sergeant, and see if you can find out how the Dcaje Construction Company got a permit, or a contract to work on the Charles Write Properties in Long Beach, California."

"Okay, and you know what…, they did get finished pretty quick."

"Yeah, it only took them a little under two days. They weren't finished, they just didn't come back. They left the place a mess, but at least they did board up what was left of the warehouse," Mad-C said.

"Okay, I'll hit, Billings up."

"And I'll see if I can get in touch with Chris. Something is pretty fishy, and I think Chris is involved," Mad-C assumed.

"Yeah, I had a bad feeling about him when we were there after the explosion," Debo said.

Mad-C wasted no time dialing Christopher's number.

"I'm sorry: The number you are trying to reach is not in service, please hang-up and try your call again," a voice on the phone said.

"I don't think he's using that number anymore; I'll try his home number." He dialed Chris' home phone and was agitated when no one answered. "I don't like what's going on here," Mad-C said.

"Didn't Johnson keep saying 'that he wanted what belongs to him'? He was referring to the dock, but the dock doesn't belong to him."

"Yeah, and he was pretty pissed off about not being able to get it. And all he did was blow up part of the dock. If he wanted to destroy it, why blow up part of it?" Mad-C asked.

"Unless whatever it was he wanted was exactly where he wanted it blown-up. Nothing was found of any enormous value."

"Yeah, and the fake construction company just waltzed right in," Mad-C added.

"Yeah, and a lot of money had to be spent to get the trucks and equipment they used to haul whatever it was away, but what was it that called for all that?" Debo wondered.

"To get whatever it was that Gregory Johnson was after. The dock was blown from the inside; the investigator said, 'that a jackhammer was used to dig a hole in the floor of the building where the C-4 was placed and put into the ground under the floor.' That's why it only took out a certain part of the dock. He didn't want to blow up the entire dock or the whole warehouse. The C-four just dug a hole under the floor, that's all."

"Yeah, and the fake construction people drove right out of there with whatever it was Gregory Johnson wanted," Debo concluded.

"Get hold of the guys and have them check out all the bus stations, train stations, and the loading and shipping docks. Chris is good with boats… and check all the airports. I want all the roads, water, sky; anything and anyway to get out of here covered. Chris had a direct deposit account at Wells Fargo Bank."

"I'll see if I can get something on that from Shell or Billings. Patch and Rayass might have had a hand in this, but we've done all the checking on them we could," Debo said.

"Okay, you guys get moving, who knows how far he's gotten by now," Mad-C told Debo.

Debo picked up his gloves, called Ed to give him his coat, then put on his coat and left. Mad-C pulled at his chin and felt a tightness in his jaw. The thought he had been so uncomfortable with was finally confirmed. Christopher Burman his lead dock worker and warehouse foreman had stabbed him dead in the back. Whatever they took and whoever it is, his shipping dock, warehouse, and his business were destroyed getting to it. Somebody must pay and pay dearly. Either Christopher Burman, Gregory Johnson, or all of the above.

Shelly's heart jumped when her cell phone rang and it was Debo calling. "Hey, honey?" Shelly answered.

"Hi, baby, how's everything going up there?"

"What did Mister Write do? Security is tighter than a vice up here now; we can hardly move."

"Yeah, Mr Write thought it would be best, so do I. Besides, Tammy and Sheila are out there."

"Oh yeah, that makes a ton of sense. What's on your mind, getting lonely?" Shelly asked.

"Yeah, very, that and I need you to check something for me on your computer."

Shelly put down the shopping list she was making for when she went shopping for groceries and went over to the computer.

"Anything for the love of my life, Mr Jackson. What do you need, honey?"

"I need anything you can find on Christopher Burman. All Mr Write has from his employment application is that he was born in Kansas City, Missouri, on May 2, 1955. He's 52 years old, 5-ft. 7-in. tall, and weighs 180 pounds, male, black, Social Security number 555-44-1100 Address at the time of employment was 14001 South Western Avenue. That's close to the Pike in Gardena, California. He loves boats, fishing, and dock work. See what you can come up with on a relative and possibly where he hangs out. Whatever you can find and give me a call."

"Okay, Sweetheart, is that all?"

"No, one more thing."

"What's that?"

"I love you, and thanks baby," Debo said.

Shelly took a long breath, then exhaled slowly and said, "I love you too, honey."

"Thanks, Shell. Tell sis I'll holler at her next time I talk to you. I have to go see someone downtown at LAPD," Debo said.

"Okay, I will…, bye," Shelly said and hung up without waiting for Debo to say goodbye.

3:10 PM

Debo was headed to downtown Los Angeles to Sergeant Billings'. He was thinking about everything that's happened since that day back in October when Dick Patch called his home phone number and left that message with Shelly. His cell phone rang and brought him out of his train of thought.

"Yeah," he said when he answered the phone.

"Hey, Debo…, I just found out what was bothering me earlier."

"Yeah, what's that?"

"When I talked to Chris on the phone the day of the explosion at the dock, he said, 'the detective called him and told him the dock had just been blown up.'"

"Okay.., and!!"

"And he said the detective had just called him."

"Okay, where are you going with this? I'm almost at Sgt. Billings office," Debo impatiently said.

"Debo, hold your ass, I'm getting to it. The son-of-a-bitch said, 'I'll be here when you get here.' That meant he was already there. They didn't call him, he knew they would call me so he did. He knew that in a case like that, they call the owner and he didn't want me to know that his ass was there when they got there."

"Yeah, or before they got there," Debo said.

"I knew he was mixed up in some shady shit. He probably stood there and watched my property and all my merchandise get blown to hell."

"Yeah, I knew there was something going on with him when I looked at him sitting in his car that morning like he was in a hurry to leave. He didn't tell us what the investigators said happened, he told us what he saw happen."

"Or what his ass made happen. "An inside job," Debo whispered. "It looks like Chris back-stabbed me."

"Hold on a sec," Debo said.

His cell phone had just beeped to let him know someone else was trying to call him. He pressed a button to switch the line over to the second caller. "Hello… yeah… uh-huh… he's what? When… okay… okay, thanks," he said and switched back over to Mad-C.

"Hey… you still there?"

"Yeah, what's up?"

"Johnson's out, that's what's up."

"I thought he didn't have a bail?"

"Well, you have to realize who we're dealing with."

"Yeah; Gregory Johnson."

"I'm going to go on up to see Billings before he leaves. I'll be out there as soon as I'm finished out here," Debo told Mad-C and ended the call.

3:50 PM

It was just about 4:00 pm, Debo was glad he didn't have to worry about the meter maid giving him a ticket. He put 50¢ in the meter anyway. It was a bit chilly so he closed his jacket and fastened it, put on his gloves, set the car alarm, and walked to the police station, which was crowded for it to be almost 4:00. He walked into Billings' office and was greeted by Gloria. "Good afternoon, Mister Jackson," Gloria greeted, looking like she was about ready to end a long day.

"Wow, Glo…, you look like the big guy put you through the wringer."

"Do I look that bad? I thought it was only the way I felt; I feel beat to death."

"You don't look bad at all, sweetheart. Just a bit tired and ready to go home. Can you let Bob know I'm here, please?"

"Okay, hold on."

When Debo went into Billings office he stood there looking at Debo with one eyebrow arched; a look that could put fear in a bull.

"Did God hear me when I said, 'Please, God don't let anyone come into my day and mess it up'?"

"I love you too, Sarge," Debo replied.

"Why on earth would you wait till I'm almost ready to leave to wander in here wanting something? And I know you want something."

"We'll, Sarge actually I do, and in return, I'll have something for you in about a week."

"Well in that case have a seat Mister Jackson, I'm all ears and I'm full of favors, what's on your mind?"

"Johnson just had Mr Write's dock blown up."

"Are you sure it was, Johnson? He's been in jail for the last week or so."

"Sarge, you know as well as I do, that he doesn't have to be there to have the job done. We think his foreman, Christopher actually blew it up or had it done."

"What is it he wants from, Write?"

"I don't know, but whatever it is, it had to have been hidden there," Debo assumed.

"Okay, Jackson.., humor me. I don't know what he could possibly have hidden there, and apparently, Mr Write can't figure it out either. Unless…"

"Unless what, Sarge?"

"Jackson, do you know how write came about that dock?"

"Yeah, he bought it at an auction; his bid was the winning bid."

"Okay, do you know who owned it; the man that put the dock up for auction? Donald Warwick, left the country because he was about to be indicted for defrauding political funds.

There was said to be, or to have been a lot of money… millions of dollars missing from Warwick's campaign contributions fund. Before anyone could prove anything illegal on his part, he sold the dock, some stocks, and left the country. No one knows where he is, and no one knows whether or not he's alive or dead, he just disappeared."

"So, you mean to sit here and tell me that this has to do with millions of dollars?"

"That's the only thing I can see. It's the only thing I can think of that would tie Johnson's ass to all this. Johnson and Warwick were political colleagues."

"WOW!!! Well, Mister Write and I think his foreman ripped off the money when they cleaned up. They had a fake construction crew out there. I don't know if he did it all himself or if someone else was in on it with him."

"Of course not, Johnson had to tell him where it was, and how to get to it. Johnson was in jail when the dock was blown. And if Mister Write's foreman was in on it with or without Johnson, Johnson will be looking for the foreman. You need to try and find Johnson's foreman before Johnson does," Billings told him.

"Yeah, because somebody is gonna pay for Mr Write's dock being blown up."

"Yeah, and pay big-time. Now can you get out of here, Jackson so I can get finished and get out of here myself?"

"Thanks, Sgt., you've been a big help."

"Yeah, just don't forget about whatever it is you have for me in a week."

"Don't worry, I won't," Debo said and got up to leave.

"Oh..., Jackson!"

"Yeah?"

"Be careful out there, there's a lot of money involved, and a lot of people have been killed already."

"Okay, Sarge, I will; see you later," Debo said and was out the door.

"Bye, Glo, and get some rest," he said as he passed Gloria's desk.

"Thanks, Mr Jackson, I will!!!" Gloria yelled back.

He took the stairs after he left Sergeant Billing's office. He tried to take the stairs as often as he could to keep in shape. He reached the bottom flight of stairs, and as he was about to open the door and walk out, his cell phone rang. "Yeah, what's up?"

"I need you to get out here now. Are you finished with whatever it was you had to do?" Mad-C asked Debo.

"Yeah, I'm on my way to you now."

Alright, come straight to me when you get here," Mad-C ordered. Debo arrived in San Diego at 8:30 pm. Mad-C had let Edward go early and was in the house alone. Debo pulled up to the gate and security let him in. Even though he and Mad-C were close, he still had to have clearance to enter the grounds. He knocked on the door to avoid ringing the doorbell. Mad-C opened it with a look of surprise and confusion on his face. He wiped at his forehead with the back of his hand, as the nervousness had caused him to perspire.

"You look like you've seen a ghost, what's up?" Debo asked, with a look of concern in his eyes.

"Come in and sit down, I gave Edward the evening off. If you want a drink, help yourself."

"Yeah,… I think I'd better. You don't look so good," Debo said, and got up to go fix his drink.

He poured a third of a glass of brandy and the rest ice and walked back over to where Mad-C was sitting and said,

"Okay spill it."

"Debo, I got up this morning… not because I was ready to get up, but because security got me up. And guess why they got me up."

"Why?" Debo asked.

Mad-C got up and walked to his office in another part of the house and came back carrying a small box.

"This is why they woke me up," Mad-C said, and handed the box to Debo.

"Go ahead… open it!"

Debo opened the box, and in it was a laboratory test-tube bottle about the size of a finger. In fact, that's exactly what was in it. Debo's heart skipped a beat, and all the blood seemed to have drained from his head. He felt faint; not because of the contents of the box, but because it was delivered to Mad-C's estate.

He took the tube out of the box along with a slip of paper. He read the header and it was from a forensics laboratory. On the form was a box, and in the box was a printout of a fingerprint. The fingerprint was a match to the finger that was inside the test tube.

Debo read that the finger once belonged to Christopher Burman; Mad-C's former foreman. The note attached to the form read…

"I want my money!"

"Do you think Johnson did this?" Debo asked Mad-C.

"Who else has the balls to send some shit like this to my house?"

"Okay, this has gone far enough, and Johnson won't stop until he gets that money. But if they have Chris, and Chris has the money… " Debo stopped in the middle of what he was saying.

"I was thinking the same thing; Maybe he stashed it somewhere or he sent it somewhere."

"Yeah, like wherever he was going. Johnson must have figured that Chris and I were in on this shit together, and now he thinks I have the money," Mad-C said.

"That means nobody has it then."

"Well, one thing is for sure, I damn sho don't," Mad-C said. "Yeah, but where is it and who has it?"

"I don't know, I'm going back to the dock. Christopher's office wasn't touched by the explosion, only mine. His office was on the other side of the building. Maybe there's something there that can tell us something."

"Okay, I'll go along with you," Debo offered.

The drive back to Long Beach was about two hours long: Not too bad for 8:00 in the evening, and the week is nearing its end. They were both tired, but Debo got to relax while Mad-C drove. Mad-C had taken a late nap so he was good to go. The road was smooth and Mad-C put on his favorite Kenny Gee compact disk. Debo reclined his seat and felt the cushion of the shocks and the comfort of the tires rolling against the paved road. He laid back and thought about what it would be like in Maui. He wondered if a cruise ship ride would feel as comfortable as the car does right then. He was in a world of his own, but he was brought back to the real world when his phone rang. It was Shelly calling to tell him that she couldn't find anything other than what Debo had already told her about Christopher Burman.

"The man doesn't even have a police record or a present address."

"Well, nothing on Chris!!"

"Yeah, it sounds like he was squeaky clean. Okay, we'll see what we can dig up out at the dock," Mad-C said.

10:15 PM

They arrived at the dock at a little after ten. Mad-C had let Tommy, Mark, Cosmo, and Freddy go home after he found out the money was taken. No use having that much muscle out there. The dock was of no more importance to anyone but Mad-C. They arrived at the front gate and the yellow crime scene tape was gone. This meant the crime scene was no longer being kept closed by law enforcement or investigators. They walked into the building, and the first thing that hit them was the scent of burnt and melted metal, wet cardboard, machine oil, and chemicals. They noticed the huge hole in the spot where the other half of the building used to be, with boards nailed up where walls and windows once were. There were still boxes of merchandise on the shelves and destroyed merchandise scattered on the floor and shelves. They took their time trying not to trip over anything because rubble was still all over the place and everything was still wet or damp from the firemen's hoses and retardant.

"It's a mess in here," Mad-C said, frowning from the smell and the tingle from the fire retardant that was irritating his nose.

"Which way is Chris' office?"

"This way," Mad-C said and led the way to the other side of the building where the explosion had not wreaked its havoc or destroyed.

"About how much did they estimate the damage to be?"

"Roughly four to five million. That's machinery, merchandise, equipment, the building, the dock…"

"Not bad compared to what he lost," Debo said.

They got to Chris' office and the door was locked. Mad-C used the key on his key-ring with the other hundreds of keys. He unlocked the door handle and pushed it down and the door came open.

"Man, he had it made up in here, didn't he?" Debo said when he entered Christopher's office.

"I always make sure my employees have the best of everything. I try to keep them comfortable; they work hard enough."

Mad-C went to Chris' desk and looked through a pile of papers and found nothing but business transactions, memos, phone messages, orders, and invoices. He opened the middle drawer of the desk and saw pretty much the same thing; business papers, blank memo pads, ink-pens, paperclips, gum, and some condoms.

But there was nothing that could give them a clue, not a trace of information that would tell them anything. Mad-C opened the top drawer and saw a stack of papers. He lifted the papers out of the drawer and there was a tiny hole in the back corner. You had to pull the drawer all the way out and then move whatever it was that covered the hole, the same way Mad-C did. He couldn't get his finger in the hole, he needed something small and pointed. He put the tip of an ink-pen in the small hole and lifted up. When he did, it revealed a small book that was about ten pages long. He opened the book and inside it read…

Christopher,
I love you and I will always keep you in my prayers. S.R.

Mad-C read further, and in the back of the book was written:

Tuesday morning 2:30
And under it in smaller writing, it read Sally Ryan 15016 Eucalyptus Lane Pasadena, CA

Mad-C figured the girl had to be a lover or a girlfriend of Christopher's, or someone that no one was supposed to know about.

It also read;

I'll be home Tuesday evening.

"Well, that explains the condoms. Chris didn't go straight home, he left the dock at about 3:00, right before we did," Mad-C enlightened.
"Yeah, I wonder where he stopped off at."
"I don't know, Debo…, but I'm willing to bet this is where the money is," Mad-C said, pointing to the address in the book.
Debo noticed a door to his left that was ajar and he couldn't resist the temptation to go check it out. He walked over to the door and tried to open it further.
"Mad-C, give me a hand over here, will you?"

Mad-C put the book in his pocket and walked over to where Debo was to see if he could move whatever it was keeping the door from opening They both pushed as hard as they could against the door and it gave way just enough for one of them to squeeze through. The light was off and Debo couldn't see in there.

"What is this room?"

"A restroom," Mad-C answered.

Debo managed to get the door open a little more, and Mad-C heard him say under his breath, "Oh my, GOD!"

"What is it…, Debo, what is it!!"

"It's Gregory Johnson!!!" Debo yelled back to Mad-C. "WHOA, no shit," Mad-C softly said.

"I'll move him so we can get the door open," Debo told Mad-C. He only moved Johnson's legs enough to allow the door to open. Johnson was laid out on the floor between the door and the toilet.

"Who the hell did this?" Mad-C asked, in a surprised tone of voice. "I don't know, Christopher is dead… or is he?"

"Three-to-one will get you somebody else is in on this little caper. How much money did the Sergeant say was missing?"

"$150 million; he just said, 'millions of dollars.' I did some checking and it turned out it was $150 million, if not more. You have to realize they were both into drugs and prostitution, and maybe gun sales."

"Damn, with that kind of money, who's not in on it? Let's get the hell out of here, this is a dead body and we don't wanna be caught bent over it," Mad-C suggested.

They left the building and went back to the car. Debo got in on the driver's side and Mad-C rode on the passenger's side.

"What do you think?" Debo asked.

"I don't know, I'm still thinking. We need to find out whether or not Christopher is dead. Johnson just got out of jail so he damned sure wasn't in that bathroom during the time it was blown up."

"No, he wasn't, this just happened. Whoever did this just could be watching us right now."

"You could be right, Debo, let's head back to my place."

"I'll head on home, by the time we get back to Diego, it'll be one or two in the morning and there's nothing we can do at that hour."

"Yeah, you got a point there. In the morning I'll check to see if I can get the name of the medical examiner who did the forensics on the finger and see if Mr Burman is in fact dead."

"And if he is?" Debo asked.

Mad-C looked in the rear-view mirror, then the side-view mirror, then he looked straight ahead as a safety precaution. After a moment he said, "If he is, then we have our work cut out for us."

"Yeah, and we can start with that address in Pasadena, maybe we'll get lucky. No one else should know about it, Chris kept it hidden away," Debo assumed.

Mad-C took a long hard look at the small book he had gotten from Chris' drawer and looked at Debo, and said, "$150 million. My, God..., what was he doing with that kind of money?"

"I think there was more... a lot more than that. That was only from his campaign funds, he had a lot more from other sources."

"Yeah, like you said earlier, 'you got your organized crime, drugs, prostitution, mafia ties, and a whole list of illegal shit.' That's probably why Warwick left it there. He couldn't account for it all if the IRS ever got hold of it," Mad-C said.

FRIDAY, DECEMBER 21ST, 9:00 A.M.

Debo kept hearing a ringing sound. No matter what he did, the ringing wouldn't stop. He checked the phone, then the door to see if anyone was there and no one was... but that annoying ringing would not subside. He pressed every button on the phone. He even turned off the power and unplugged the house phone, and the ringing still persisted. He checked the timer on the kitchen stove and still no relief from that nagging ringing. Then his eyes opened; on the table next to him, his cell phone was ringing. He had been sleeping and heard the cell phone ringing in his sleep.

"Yeah?" he said in a sleepy tone.

"Wake up, I'll be there in a little while to pick you up. We have a date in Pasadena, or did you forget?" Mad-C asked him.

"No, I didn't forget; I'll be ready in a couple of hours. I have to get up, shower, eat, and I'll be ready to roll. How long have you been up?"

"Since seven. I talked to the ME that did the work on, Chris."

"Well, if the medical examiner did work on him, then he's most likely dead..," Debo stopped Mad-C to say.

"Yeah, Johnson could have done it."

Debo rubbed his eyes, yawned, and told Mad-C he was getting out of bed now.

"Okay, get a move on sleepy…, time is money… my money!!"

CHAPTER 23

FRIDAY, DECEMBER 21ST, 11:45 A.M.

Mad-C and Debo arrived at 15016 Eucalyptus Lane in Pasadena. The house was the usual peach-colored stucco with three bedrooms and two and a half baths. The bathroom was decorated for the lady of the house, giving it a personified feminine look. It had pink shower curtains, pink paint on the walls, pink toilet seat covers and bathmats, and pink toothbrush holders with a matching cup for gargling The other bathroom was just a shower and a toilet with a sink and a small medicine cabinet. It was there to accommodate either the man of the house or a house guest.

Mad-C rang the doorbell and waited for someone to answer, but no one answered. After all, it was almost 12:00 on a Friday afternoon. Whoever lived there, or whoever Sally Ryan is was most likely at work or school. Debo took it upon himself to look around a little. It was kind of chilly outside so he put his hands inside his coat pockets and closed the light jacket he was wearing. He didn't button it up since it was warm in the car on the way over. There was not much he could see; the backyard was closed-off by a 7-ft tall cedar wood privacy fence. The garage had no windows, there was only a door that was raised and lowered by remote control or a switch on the wall inside. He couldn't get into the garage unless he had the remote to the garage door. The curtains inside were drawn; making it virtually impossible to see inside the house. Mad-C knocked on the door again and no answer.

"Okay, Debo…, let's move the car down the street, I don't wanna sit outside on the street in front of the house: The neighbors might get suspicious and call the cops."

He parked the car further down the street where they could watch the house and sat there talking and trying to make sense of all that had been going on for the past couple of months.

"Debo, what on earth would you do with that much money?"

"Wow…, you got me, that's a lot of money. I would probably help the poor, sick, mentally ill, some of those poor animals that people leave outside starving and freezing when they move."

"Yeah, you always have been a do-gooder," Mad-C teased.

"I couldn't spend that much money in one lifetime, not at my age. I'd buy myself an island and just stay there and live forever… Me, Pauline, and have about five children, and invest my money and watch it grow," Mad-C said.

"An island doesn't sound too bad. I wouldn't mind having one myself. Hey, what if the money is here or on the way here? Man, all that money, no wonder so many people were killed."

"Yeah… not to mention us almost being killed. Well, we'll see what happens; we could get lucky," Mad-C said.

"Tell me something!"

"What?"

"Why would he leave the money buried under the shipping dock for fifteen years?" Debo asked.

"Well, I've had it for that long, and I guess by me not knowing it was there, it gave him a chance to let the heat blow over. When I got the dock, he couldn't just go in there and start tearing up shit. So, Johnson tried the only thing he knew to try, and that was to either buy it from me or move me out of the way and take it from me. Now Warwick figures that everybody has forgotten about it."

"And everybody being who?"

"Everybody being; the IRS, the authorities, all the politicians he stole money from, not to mention the mafia, his supporters."

"Yeah, he did deceive a lot of people. The city where he ran for office was devastated that he had turned crook. I guess it didn't really matter how long the money was hidden because the people in that county, city, and the whole community; hell, the entire world is not going to forget what he did. Plus he was filthy ass dirty, tied up in so much bullshit with Johnson. That's probably why he left and never came back," Debo assumed.

They sat there in silence for a moment thinking over what they had just been talking about,when Debo's eyes got as wide as bow dollars. "Mad-C?"

"Yeah, Debo?"

"Do you see what I see?"

"No, what do you see?"

"Look down the street."

"Well, I'll be a monkey's uncle," Mad-C said.

The thought of finally having all that money was becoming a reality and was getting more real by the second. Mad-C turned around and looked up the street and saw a Q-Haul truck.

"Get down there before we lose it."

"Okay, but I want you to drive."

"Okay, let's get down there and get it," Debo excitedly said. One of the men in the truck got out and walked toward the house. He had a cell phone to his ear and a pistol in his hand. Debo took the Glock-45 from the shoulder holster he was wearing and walked on the other side of the street. He found a pick-up truck that was parked in front of one of the houses and crouched down beside it. Meanwhile, Mad-C walked up to the man getting out of the truck on his way to the front door of the house where the money was to be delivered.

"Uh... excuse me, I believe that's for me," Mad-C said.

The man didn't know who Mad-C was or what was in the truck. All he knew was that he was paid $10,000 to deliver it and was told to guard it with his life. He reached in his pocket and pulled out a piece of paper and read something from it, then looked up at Mad-C with the pistol still in his hand and said,

"Good afternoon, Sir.., are you Mister Burman?"

At that time, Mad-C heard gunfire. Debo had just slammed a round from the 45-automatic into the head of the man that stayed in the truck. When the man that was standing there talking to Mad-C heard the shot, out of reflex he turned to see what was going on; giving Mad-C a chance to put the 44-magnum to the man's head and sending a round of hot led tearing through the back of his skull, ending his life. Mad-C picked up the cell phone that the man had dropped when he went down and put it in his pocket.

Debo got in the truck and started it, then waited until Mad-C pulled up behind him and drove off with Mad-C following him.

Mad-C calls Debo's cell phone.

"Do you think anyone got my license plate number?" Mad-C asked. "Don't worry, I switched them when I had your car, in case something went down. I forgot to tell you," Debo confessed. "You what!!!"

"Sorry, things were moving so fast."

"Who's plates are they?" Mad-C asked. "The ones I took off, Joy's car."

"You mean the car she used at the club on Gage?"

"Uh, yeah… that's the one."

"Are you crazy, that car was used in a crime, man!!? Mad-C told Debo. "So was this one," Debo said.

"Man if… "

"Hey, guess what, Mad-C."

"What is it, Debo?"

"We did it!!!" Debo screamed loud enough to be heard outside the car with the windows rolled up.

"Yeah… how does it feel to be driving a truck with millions in it?" Mad-C asked Debo.

"Wonderful; heavy but wonderful."

"Okay, head on out to the house, I've got your back. Don't stop for anything but traffic and old ladies," Mad-C said.

"Okay… gotcha."

They were headed to San Diego with over three hundred million dollars in cash. Mad-C called his security team and told them that he and Debo were on their way with special cargo.

6:15 PM

They got to San Diego and took the truck full of cash to the back and parked it. Debo got out of the truck, raised the back door, and saw that there were boxes stacked as high as room would allow; front to back. Mad-C started thinking that possibly the truck was a decoy, but Chris wasn't a professional at what he had just done. He just wanted to get the money moved. He couldn't use the truck that he used to get the money from the dock because it's known by Mad-C, and maybe even the law by now. That's why he used the Q-Haul truck. And, if Mad-C and Debo had not gone into his office, his plan would have worked because no one knew about the house in Pasadena. He knew it was safe to move it there and he and Sally Ryan would be very rich right now.

Debo opened one of the boxes and removed a plastic covering and saw stacks of $100 bills encased in Styrofoam. Chris had the money taken out of the body bags and put into boxes. That made it less conspicuous and easier to transport.

"Okay, unload the truck, I want all these boxes underground in less than a minute," Mad-C ordered.

He looked over at Debo who was still wide-eyed, and said, "Come on… this calls for a drink."

"Yeah, I'm with you…, I could use one right about now."

Edward brought a bottle of Mad-C's best brandy and left the bottle. "Mad-C?"

"Yeah?"

"Something's wrong."

"We just got all this fuckin money and you say, 'something's wrong.' What is it, Debo?"

"I just have a feeling."

"Well feel like celebrating with me because that's what I'm doing."

"Yeah, maybe all that money just 'got me on one'," Debo said, and lifted his glass of brandy and ice.

Mad-C followed suit and Debo said, "To us!!"

Their glasses met and they both sipped their beverage. "You want to call the girls and give them the good news?" Debo asked. "I don't see why not."

It's our anniversary, played on Debo's phone just as he was about to call Shelly.

8:00 PM

"Hey baby, I was just about to call you. I have some terrific news for all of you. Mr Write and I just… "

Shelly cut him off before he could finish. "D-Angelo… "

"Yes, Shell… Shell?"

"Well, hello, D-Angelo. How's things with you these days?"

"Who the hell is this?" Debo asked, confused and upset.

Mad-C looked at him and saw a look of surprise, hatred, and anger on his face. He sat his glass on the table and studied Debo's facial expressions and body language.

"Put Charles on the phone," the voice on the other end of Debo's phone said.

"Here, it's for you."

"Yeah.., who is this?"

"You have twenty-four hours to get my money to me, or all these ladies will die; even the two little girls. You have $300 million that belongs to me, and I want it."

Mad-C dropped the phone and his mouth dropped open with it. He was sitting there with his mouth wide open, looking like he was in shock. "Mad-C… Mad-C… hey,… who was it?"

Debo had brought him out of a temporary shock.

"That was Donald Warwick," Mad-C finally uttered. "But he… I don't understand."

"He wants the money within twenty-four hours or, 'Shelly, Joy, Pauline, and Joy's daughters are going to be killed,'" Mad-C quoted.

He felt a lump in his throat and his head got light, and it wasn't from the brandy.

"But, how can it be him? You mean he waited fifteen years, and then all of a sudden he shows up here for the money?"

"Debo, I think he's always been here. I don't think he left the country. I think he was just waiting around for someone to dig it up and hand it to him," Mad-C assumed.

"You mean he waited all that time?" Debo wondered.

"Yes, and by the way… it's $300 million, and yes I would say it's worth the wait" Mad-C told him.

"So, he just sat back and watched everyone's every move from day one. He even knew about where the girls were."

"Debo, the man wasn't a dummy, he made himself invisible by pretending to be out of the country. That way nobody would suspect him or even think about him. All the time we were watching Gregory Johnson, Robert Cruse, and Randy Carlyle, no one's mind was on Donald Warwick. And, I'm willing to bet he's the one that killed Christopher Burman and Gregory Johnson. Johnson probably went to the dock looking for the same thing we went there looking for and got it just like Christopher did. He probably took Christopher somewhere else and killed him, cut his finger off, had someone he knew at forensics do the lab and paperwork on the finger and sent it to my house. He knew Gregory didn't have the money, he probably just stumbled upon him, killed him, and left him in the bathroom on the floor. He knew Johnson was after the money and was getting close to getting it, but his untimely incarceration threw a wrench in the whole thing. And here we come to do it all for him. If he would have shown up trying to get the money, he would have been caught a long time ago," Mad-C explained.

"Okay, so what do we do now, he has the girls?"

"We put our heads together and do what we always do."

"What's that?"

"We win, man…, we win!!"

Mad-C decided it was time to get Mark, Tommy, Cosmo, Jeffery, and Freddy back over there ASAP.

"We're going to need all the guys, Debo, and we're going to need them now. Call your boy, Billings, and let him know it's about to be some more shit," Mad-C said and got on his cell phone.

"He already know about it, he's just waiting his turn to move in and take over," Debo said.

"Yeah, Billings here, what can I do for you, Jackson?" the Sergeant said.

"Hey, Bob, I know you're off work and probably on your way home, but I need…,"

"No, I'm not off yet, I'm putting in some overtime, what is it you need?"

"You said, 'there were millions of dollars missing from Donald Warwick's campaign contribution fund'?"

"Yes, why?"

"Exactly how much money, Sarge?"

"Hold on, Jackson, let me look it up," Billings said, and left the phone. Debo could hear him punching keys on the computer, and after a short period of time the sergeant came back on the phone. "Okay, Jackson…, Jackson are you still there?"

"Yeah, Bob…, I'm here."

"Okay, it was $100 million; No, $150 million."

"Okay, Sarge, stay by your phone; the office phone .You're about to get an anonymous phone call. The caller is going to tell you where to pick up Donald Warwick and the missing money."

"I thought that's what you were talking about when you said, 'you had something for me by the end of the week.'"

"That's it, Bob."

"Well, I'll be damned; when you do shit, you do it don't you?"

"Pretty much, Bob…, that should put you up to Chief or Captain, or Mayor, or wherever you go when you do a better job than you have been doing."

"Jackson, you just be careful."

"Okay, Bob…, wait for the call."

"Jackson?"

"Yeah, Bob."

"Warwick's back, right?"

"Yeah, Bob, wait for the call, Bob."

"I'll be waiting, and stop calling me, Bob!!"

"Yes, Bob."

"Oh…, Jackson, how long do you think it'll take; the call I mean?"

"Warwick is supposed to call me when he's ready for me to deliver the money. He'll let us know where and when. I don't know exactly, just stay by the phone," Debo said and ended the call.

10:00 PM

"We're all set," Freddy said.

"Okay, let's do it," Mad-C said.

Donald Warwick is supposed to call Mad-C's cell phone when he's ready to tell them where they are supposed to bring the money. Mad-C wrote on a piece of paper the word, 'now' and told Debo that when Warwick calls, he would give Debo the paper and it means for him to call Billings and let him know it was a go. Mad-C's cell phone rang and he picked-up on the third ring.

"Yeah?"

"Meet me at the dock in thirty minutes," Warwick said.

Mad-C wrote on another piece of paper, 'the dock', and handed it to Debo and he immediately made the call to Sergeant Billings.

"Look, Write I don't want to have to kill these people, and I won't if things go right," Warwick said.

"How can I trust that, and you can't even be trusted with your own fuckin money. Or should I say the money you stole from all those people who trusted you. If one of my people have so much as a nose bleed, don't worry about tomorrow because you won't see it.'"

"You'll just have to trust me… now you're wasting my time."

Debo had Cosmo put a trace on the call the minute Debo's phone rings. Somehow Cosmo had connected it to a GPS tracking device.

Cosmo: the genius of the crew turned around and said,

"Got it, boss, he's at a warehouse in Long Beach near the docks."

"Got an address?"

"Sure do."

"Okay, Freddy, let's move, I'm sure they took Joy's hardware; take a toy for her…, here take her this."

Debo had given him the gold nine-millimeter that the guy at the club on Gage had taken from her; the one he had given her that goes to a set. After he shot the guy that took it from her at the club, he picked it up. Freddy put the weapon in his back pocket and they all headed for the warehouse.

"I didn't know you knew how to fly one of these. I didn't even know you had one of these," Debo said, as he held on for dear life.

Mad-C had taken his personal custom-made 2014 Bell-H private helicopter. There was no way they would make it to Long Beach in time without it. Mad-C called and had it brought to his estate Debo called Sergeant Billings and had him have a small truck waiting at the warehouse as soon as the call came from Warwick, and to leave the keys in the ignition.

Upon their arrival in Long Beach, California. Mad-C dropped Freddy, Cosmo, Mark, Jeffery, and Tommy off at the warehouse where Shelly, Joy, Pauline, and the girls were being held captive. He and Debo got to the dock and saw the truck waiting. They unloaded the money from the helicopter onto the truck.

"Here… right here," Cosmo pointed to a one-story building.

There were lights on inside the building, and Freddy saw some movement inside. Four of Debo's men men surrounded the building. Each one was armed with their prospective weapons. Freddy stuck close to the front with Cosmo in case he was able to get inside the building. Cosmo tried the front door and it was locked. Then he tried a window next to it, and it was also locked.

"I have an idea," he said.

When he traced the call, he also got the phone number to the phone Warwick used at the warehouse. He called the phone number and a man's voice answered.

"Yeah, what is it?" the man said. "'Good-n-Hot Pizza', sir!!"

"I didn't order no damn pizza!!!"

"Well somebody at this address did."

"Hey, who ordered pizza!!!" he yelled to whoever was listening. "I don't know, but whoever did I'm starved. I hope it's combination," a guy called Bear said.

"Yeah, well it's outside waiting. Don't let nobody in here, go with him, Stone."

Bear walked over to the door and opened it with Stone in tow. When he opened the door he couldn't move because he was looking down the barrel of Freddy's 357-Magnum. Freddy pulled the hammer back with his thumb and signaled with the gun by waving it from side-to-side for the guy called Bear to move aside, which gave Cosmo a clear aim at the guy behind him called Stone.

"Okay, I want both of you to walk or be carried out of there right fuckin now."

They both followed Freddy's orders and Mark and Tommy tied them up with zip-ties and escorted them away from the building and stayed there to watch them while Cosmo, Jeffery, and Freddy entered the warehouse and smelled a thick order of cigarette smoke and beer in the air. These guys with the weird monikers; Bear and Stone are two big 300 and 275 pound ex wrestlers.

"What's taking all day long with the pizza, Stone!!!" the man that answered the phone; Willy yelled.

At that point, Freddy came from around the corner with the 357 aimed straight ahead. Willy got up and went for his weapon, but it was too late Freddy had drilled a hole in the man's forehead with a single shot, while two more men came running up the hall; Cosmo slammed several rounds into one of them, dropping him to the floor, and the other one caught a single round to his head, spewing blood and skull from his head onto the wall behind him.

- 488 -

The four men that were guarding the ladies heard all the shooting upstairs and came running, but Freddy heard them from the top of the steps. The first one caught a round in his chest and fell back, knocking the other three backward. Cosmo ran down the steps before any of the other three could catch their balance and kicked one of them in the face, sending him falling further down the steps. Two of the men ran away from the action and disappeared around a corner. Freddy and Cosmo walked slowly in the direction that the men went in, with their guns ready.

One of the men came from around the corner holding Tammy by her waist, as her feet dangled above the floor. He was using her as a human shield.

"Slowly drop your hardware, or I'll put a hole in her head and take one of you out before you can get off a shot."

He looked at Freddy, then Cosmo and neither of them responded. "I said put the guns down… NOW!!!"

Freddy and Cosmo did as the man ordered. Freddy looked to one side of the man and the other two were standing next to him also pointing guns at them. The one that Cosmo kicked in the face had blood running down the front of his shirt and neck.

"Okay, let's go," the man holding Tammy demanded.

He put her down, once Cosmo and Freddy did as he ordered while the other men collected their weapons. He pushed her toward the man with the bloody face. Freddy looked at Tammy and saw that during the excitement Tammy had peed herself. The men took Freddy, Tammy, and Cosmo to the room where the women were being held.

"Freddy!!!" Joy yelled, in excitement when they entered the room.

"Sit down," the man ordered Freddy, Cosmo, and Tammy. Freddy sat on one side of Joy, and Tammy sat on the other side. Shelly, Pauline, and Sheila were sitting on the other side of Tammy. Cosmo sat on the other side of Freddy while Freddy got as close to Joy as he could without actually sitting on her or in her lap. She knew why when she felt the Glock 9-millimeter pistol in Freddy's back pocket. The man had zip-tied Freddy's and Cosmos's hands in front of them. The one that took charge, which was the one that was holding Tammy as a human shield earlier, took out a cell phone and was about to call Donald Warwick, when a large hole was drilled into his head by a single shot which came from a window behind him. The other men had long before put their weapons away, leaving the one in charge to cover everyone. He went down, and before the other men could get to their weapons Joy pulled the Glock 9-millimeter automatic weapon from Freddy's back pocket, laid back across the bed and fired one shot at the man that was standing over her; sending a round of hot lead into the bottom of his chin and out through the top of his head.

Mark put the last man out of his misery with a bullet to his neck and jaw. Everyone saw him go down, but no one was for sure whether or not he was dead or even hit. His face was already bloody, so Joy put three rounds in his head just to be sure.

"Thanks, guys!!!" Freddy yelled out the window to Tommy and Mark. "Don't mention it!!!" Mark yelled back.

"Come on guys.., let's get out of here," Freddy said. "I'm for that," Pauline cheered.

"Uh…, excuse me, can somebody get these things off of us?" Freddy asked, with his head coxed to one side and his eyes wide open. He was referring to the zip-ties the men used to tie their wrists.

"UH, how do we get them off," Pauline teased. "I don't wanna break my nails, sorry fellas," Joy teased.

"Oh, come on girls…, help us out here, huh?" Cosmo begged.

"There's a knife in my back pocket, use it and cut them off,"
Freddy said.

"What don't you have in your back pocket? And speaking of which, where did you get this?" Joy asked.

"From the boss, he said, it was yours."

"Yeah, he gave it to me, it goes to a set."

"We have to get out of here before the laws gets here," Freddy suggested and picked up Tammy, and Cosmo picked up Sheila and they were gone. Shelly just sat and observed everything.

(Meanwhile)

Debo and Mad-C waited in the truck for Donald Warwick, who was already there watching them as they unload the helicopter and loaded the boxes onto the truck. Debo's cell phone rang.

"We're all clear here, everybody is safe and sound. We're on our way to you now, Freddy reported."

"Okay, Freddy, someone's on the other line, let me get it," Debo said, and switched over to the other line. Donald Warwick was trying to call him. "Speak to me," Warwick said.

"We're here, where are my people?" Debo asked. "Shut up and put Write on."

Debo clenched his fists and gritted his teeth, then handed Mad-C the phone.

"Yeah, I'm here," Mad-C said.

But, if Donald Warwick could see his face, he'd know he had death written all over It, along with anger, and rage. But for now he had to keep his cool.

"Get out and walk over toward the building," Donald ordered. "What building? It got blown up because of this stupid ass money."

"Look, Write don't play games with me, it's almost over. Now get out of the truck… both of you… and start walking."

Mad-C looked at Debo, and Debo looked back at him. After Mad-C hung up he asked Debo,

"The phone call you got earlier, are they safe?"

"Yeah, the boys got them out."

"Okay, let's go."

They both opened their door and got out of the truck: leaving the keys in the ignition and the money in the truck. They started walking toward the building and Debo's phone rang once again and Mad-C answered it.

"Okay, you're doing good," Donald said.

"Do you see what I see?" Mad-C asked Debo. "Yeah, I see them."

Mad-C had his hand on the butt of his 44-magnum, and Debo had CRAZY already out and down at his side ready for action. When they got to where the two men were standing they heard a cell phone ring, but it wasn't Debo's. The ringing was coming from the direction of the

- 491 -

two men. One of the men answered the phone and said something that neither Mad-C nor Debo could hear. He hung up, and before he could get whatever it was he wanted from his waistband, a piece of hot led entered his skull through the front and took a massive chunk of skull, flesh, and blood out the back of his head, dropping him where he stood. At that time, CRAZY; Debo's Glock 45-automatic screamed at the other man, knocking him back with two rounds to his upper torso. He was dead before he hit the ground but Debo still let go of another round, catching the man next to his heart and spinning him around and to the ground. Debo heard sirens wailing and screaming, and they looked back to see that Sergeant Billings had come through and was putting Donald Warwick and the $150 million into a police mobile transport unit.

Mad-C stood back while Debo walked over to where Billings was and said,

"Well, Bob, this should make you popular at the station."

"Yeah, Jackson, it sure will."

"Who are those guys?" Debo was referring to Long Beach PD.

"That's Long Beach, it's their jurisdiction. They had to be on the scene, but it's still my collar," Billings assured Debo.

"Okay, just as long as they don't beat you out of your glory."

"Oh they won't, Jackson, trust me. Hey, Jackson?"

"Yeah, what's up, Bob?"

"Thanks…, I mean it… thanks a lot," Billings said, smiling. "That's the first time since this whole thing started that I've seen you smile, except for when you won the golf finals," Debo said.

"Yeah… you just don't know how happy I am that this shit is over. And where in the hell did you find Warwick?" Billings asked.

"We didn't, he found us." Debo looked past Billings and saw four police SUVs bringing Joy, Shelly, Pauline, and the girls along with Freddy, Cosmo, Tommy, Jeffery, and Mark: Courtesy of the Los Angeles Police Department and Sergeant Billings. They all rushed over to their prospective better halves and the hugs, kisses, and tears started.

MONDAY, DECEMBER 24TH, 11:58 P.M.—CHRISTMAS EVE

Everyone went back to Big Bear to finish their vacation. The next morning Mad-C went to everybody's room door and woke them up

"HO!!!.., HO!!!.., HO!!! Get up everyone, it's Christmas. Merry Christmas!!!"

Mad-C got everyone together and continued..,

"I want to truly and from the bottom of my heart, thank each and every one of you. Debo, I knew I wasn't making a mistake ten years ago when I put my heart and my belief in you. I have never once had any regrets about meeting you. You brought a lot of wonderful people into my life, and I'd like to thank you all. So, this year I'm playing Santa," Mad-C told them and handed everyone an envelope.

"I want you all to open your envelope before you do anything else this morning.

Debo opened his and there was a check for $5 million for him and Shelly, made out to Mr and Mrs D-Angelo L Jackson.

Freddy opened his and there was a check made out to Fredrick C Moss in the amount of $5 million dollars.

Joy opened hers, and there was a check made out to Joyvette L Hernandez in the amount of $5 million.

Pauline wasn't handed an envelope. She was given a small box made of solid gold; In it was the most beautiful wedding ring in the world... a $3,500,000.00 Emerald and diamond wedding ring. Mad-C got on his right knee and said, "Pauline, I am on my knee before an angel, because when God called mine home, he replaced her with a wonderful new one; one that I will cherish, love, honor, and admire. And with you came the hope, love, contentment, and the happiness that will seal our fate forever. I would love to have the pleasure of being your husband. Pauline..., will you marry me?"

And with tears of joy in her eyes, she looked down at him, then got down on her left knee, kissed him lightly on the forehead, and said, "Mister Write, I would love for you to be my husband. Of course I'll marry you."

Joy couldn't hold it in any longer, she burst out in tears. Freddy held her hand, leaned over, and whispered,

"You're next."

She stopped cold in her tracks, wiped the tears from her eyes, and just stared into Freddy's eyes, then whispered,

"Are you serious? You really want to marry me, Freddy?"

Her heart was pounding harder and her head lit-up with happiness. She felt like she was floating on clouds. Freddy's eyes never left hers as he gently kissed her lips and said,

"With everything in me, I truly do want to marry you, Joyvette."

Tammy and Sheila ran over to where Freddy and Joy were sitting and gave the both of them the biggest hug they had ever received from two children, and they both said in unison,

"Welcome to our family, daddy."

Christmas was finally here, and everyone had a lovely time. Joy, Shelly, and Pauline went on their last skiing escapade. Sheila and Tammy tried their hand at the sport, with very little success but they had a ball anyway. Shane Robins did a wonderful job teaching Joy, Pauline, and Shelly to ski. Jeffery opened his mailbox, and found a check from Debo for $1,000,000,00 and a card that read, 'Thanks for being part of the team. We all love you and will miss you, take care.'" It was signed D-Angelo L Jackson, Michelle Jackson, Freddy Moss, Joyvette Hernandez, Charles Write, and Pauline Frazier. Jeffery had recovered wonderfully from the heroin that Robert Cruse and Randy Carlyle had been shooting him up with, and is back with Molly. Debo and Shelly went on their cruise to Maui. Debo got the Havana cigar that Mad-C was holding for him. When he and Shelly returned home from Maui, Debo went over to Omar's house and got Rex and gave Omar and Gail $100,000.00 more for Christmas .

Mad-C and Pauline kept the other $100 million dollars that was left from the money he got from Warwick. He sold the rest of the shipping dock and got out of the drug business.

Debo kept his promise to Shelly and to himself, and retired. They were back at the Shell Debo. Shelly decided to put on some coffee while Debo checked the mail. He got through all the junk mail; bills, letters, advertisements and he found a letter that caught his attention. It was addressed to D-Angelo L Jackson: No return address, no post date, no post mark, not even a stamp. He looked at it and was about to put it in the trash can, but he gave it a second thought. He went into his home office while Shelly was making a cup of coffee for the both of them, and slowly opened the envelope. He finally got it open and a newspaper clipping fell out. He picked it up and saw a picture of Sergeant Robert Billings, pictured standing among his colleagues, shaking hands with the chief of police and the mayor of Los Angeles. And the article read:

"Sergeant Robert Billings of the Los Angeles Police Department's Parker Center Division, made news this morning when he apprehended former longtime politician and multi-millionaire, Donald Warwick. As we all know, Warwick was said to have embezzled $150 million from his own political fund-raising campaign contribution fund. Warwick, 57, top left, disappeared some fifteen years ago; around the time he was to be indicted on charges of fraud, embezzlement, and grand theft.

At approximately 11:15 last night, Sergeant Billings received an anonymous phone call that led him to a shipping dock. The same shipping dock that Donald Warwick owned and put up for auction fifteen years ago. During several criminal investigations that were launched against him, including the shipping dock in Long Beach. Warwick is also facing charges for the murder of billionaire, CEO and chairman of the board of directors at the Glory Days Yacht Club; Gregory Johnson who's body was found inside one of the offices in the warehouse where the dock was located. It is believed that Warwick somehow hid the money beneath the warehouse which is believed to be the reason for that particular explosion.

Sergeant Billings was offered a promotion to lieutenant at Parker Center by the Chief of Police, but declined; saying, 'that 'it was time for him to retire.' He further said, 'that he appreciates the promotion but he promised his wife and daughter he would hang up his badge and spend the rest of his days at home with them.' Sgt. Billings later added that his family has been very supportive of him during his long career in law enforcement, and that his crime-fighting days are over. There was also a $250,000 reward leading to the arrest and conviction of Donald Warwick, but, no one has claim the reward money."

Debo put the newspaper clipping back inside the envelope and put it inside a manila folder and put the folder in a filing cabnet and called Billings on his cell phone.

"Stop calling me, I'm retired," Billings said, and laughed. "Bob, you made it, have you checked your mail?"

"No, but I see you have."

"Go check your mail, I'll hold."

Bob Billings got out of his favorite recliner and walked into the living room and picked the mail up off the floor that had fallen through a builtin mail slot by the front door. He preferred that kind of mailbox, rather than one that was attached to the fence, or a pillar on the front porch. That way the mail comes into the house and he doesn't have to bother going outside in the cold or rain or opening the door to get it; no one else can bother it either. He sifted through the mail until he came up on an envelope that stood out. It read: "URGENT PLEASE READ!!!" It had Debo's return address on it.

He opened the envelope and removed two pieces of paper. One was a note which read,

"Thanks for everything. You have the biggest little guy I know, and I wish you and your family the best of happiness and comfort in your retirement. This is for you, Bob!"

He looked at the other piece of paper, which was a check made out to him in the amount of $1 million. Billings was not a man for crying, and he would very seldom be seen doing so if you saw him crying at all. He got back on the phone and said,

"Thanks, so much for being my friend. I thought I would have to choke you a million times. But, Mister Jackson, you are the best crook I've ever had the pleasure of meeting."

Debo thanked the sergeant, and although he couldn't see the tears in Billings' eyes, he knew they were rolling down his cheek. He knew he had touched Sergeant Billings' heart like he had so many others.

D-Angelo L Jackson has touched the hearts of a lot of people, and they all love him dearly....

Milton Keynes UK
Ingram Content Group UK Ltd.
UKHW031123261124
451618UK00005B/46